Praise for *The Bloodprint*

"*The Bloodprint* is extraordinary. The book is wonderfully written; its poetic prose and mix of history, faith, and adventure reminiscent of a postapocalyptic *Odyssey* . . . this time with a pair of women warriors at the helm."

—S. A. Chakraborty, author of *The City of Brass*

"Khan's latest is a tale that will grip readers from the start. With beautiful, vibrant storytelling . . . Khan's first installment in her new fantasy series is truly remarkable."

—RT Book Reviews

"For fans of complex fantasy series with a girl-power theme."

—*Booklist*

"One of the year's finest fantasy debuts."

—B&N Sci-Fi & Fantasy Blog

The Black Khan

BY AUSMA ZEHANAT KHAN

The Khorasan Archives
The Bloodprint
The Black Khan

The Esa Khattak/Rachel Getty Mystery Series
The Unquiet Dead
The Language of Secrets
A Death in Sarajevo (a novella)
Among the Ruins
A Dangerous Crossing

The Black Khan

Book Two of the Khorasan Archives

AUSMA ZEHANAT KHAN

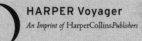

HARPER Voyager

An Imprint of HarperCollins Publishers

THE BLACK KHAN. Copyright © 2018 by Ausma Zehanat Khan. All rights reserved. Printed in the United States of America. No part of this book may be used or reproduced in any manner whatsoever without written permission except in the case of brief quotations embodied in critical articles and reviews. For information, address HarperCollins Publishers, 195 Broadway, New York, NY 10007.

HarperCollins books may be purchased for educational, business, or sales promotional use. For information, please email the Special Markets Department at SPsales@harpercollins.com.

Harper Voyager and design are trademarks of HarperCollins Publishers LLC.

FIRST EDITION

Maps created by Ashley P. Halsey, inspired by Ayesha Shaikh
Map backgrounds by caesart/Shutterstock, Inc.
Half title, frontispiece, and chapter opener art and star art by Gala Matorina/Shutterstock, Inc.

Library of Congress Cataloging-in-Publication Data has been applied for.

ISBN 978-0-06-245920-6

18 19 20 21 22   LSC   10 9 8 7 6 5 4 3 2 1

For Hema,

whose friendship, love, and decency

have saved me all these years

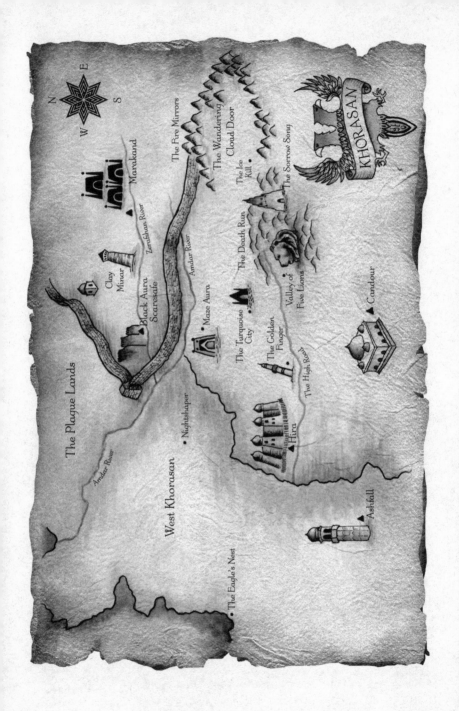

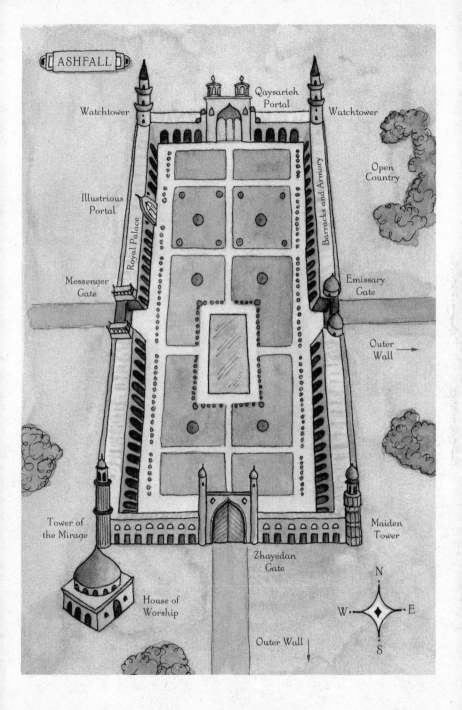

The Black Khan

IN THE DESERTED COURTYARD OF THE CLAY MINAR, THE BODIES OF BAS-machi fighters were gathered in a pile beneath a stunted tree in the shelter of a square stone base. White ribbons streamed down from the tree's slender limbs, tied to its branches and twigs. The ribbons were bare of script: the people of Black Aura could not write. The ribbons were meant as a reminder of their sacred traditions; they were desperate, desolate prayers. The bodies piled beneath the tree formed the Authoritan's answer to those prayers.

No wind stirred the ribbons or the dying branches. Sunlight blunted the edges of Arian's vision, and she found her way around the tree more by instinct than anything else. She knew she was about to be taken inside the house of worship, just as she knew the Authoritan expected a demonstration of her power, a compulsion she had resisted with all the force and determination she was capable of as a Companion of Hira.

There were only three people in the courtyard: Arian, the Authoritan, and his consort, Lania, Arian's older sister. Each night since she'd been captured in Black Aura attempting to retrieve the Bloodprint, Lania and the Authoritan had brought Arian to this place. They showed her the stunted tree and the bodies moldering beneath it, then coerced her into entering the blue-domed house of worship to test her abilities with the Claim.

Situated on the eastern side of the square, the dome was the pinnacle of a massive structure. Four arcades met at its doubled entrance, each lined with portals decorated with mosaics and glazed bronze brick. At the entrance to the main portal, a sand-colored octahedron with open arches could be reached by a set of stairs. Here great recitations of the Claim had once been addressed to the people of Black Aura, the Bloodless sharing the teachings of the Bloodprint, an ancient and powerful manuscript long believed to be lost. The manuscript that was the oldest, most venerable record of the Claim—the powerful, mysterious magic seeded throughout the history of all the lands of Khorasan, but lost to a people now condemned to a final Age of Ignorance.

Skirting the pulpit, Arian was taken through to the indoor galleries covered by dozens of smaller domes perched on a peristyle. Though well lit, the interior space was cold, and as quiet and deserted as the courtyard.

They stopped at a niche in the wall where multicolored mosaics were arranged in a magnificent declamation. Lania read the words first, verses commonly known to the Companions of Hira, though Lania's inflection was different, the words gathered up in hubris and flung out, outlining the niche in a darkly radiant fire while the Authoritan nodded his approval.

Prodded by her sister, Arian repeated the same words, her strong voice giving them distinctions of grace that coaxed out their inner meaning.

The Authoritan looked down on Arian from the top of a flight of wooden stairs positioned beside the niche. He stood tall and thin, enclosed in his white robes, his ghastly crimson eyes flickering out from a bloodless white face, a nimbus of silver hair floating above the harshly etched bones of his skull. He seemed too frail to do her any damage, yet his hands and voice transmitted his inescapable power.

"Now the rest."

His reedy voice was like a needle in Arian's ear.

"That's all there is," she said.

"You know the conclusion of these verses from your training at the Citadel of Hira. Recite them for us now."

The cold command in his voice whipped at Arian's nerves. It was a compulsion to do as he asked or suffer intolerable pain. Yet she'd learned that though he could otherwise affect her, he could not compel the Claim to issue from her lips. It was a tiny point of victory that Arian held to herself, infusing her with a strength of self-reliance that was no reproof against the pain.

He raised a bony finger in the air and aimed it at the top of her skull. "Recite."

The word stabbed at Arian's temples, a sharp, probing injury. She reached for Lania's hand, insisting that her sister acknowledge the injury being done to her. But Lania stepped back, her painted face impassive, the bonds of sisterhood sundered by the tortures she was forced to endure.

"Recite!"

Now the word thundered through Arian's skull. The muscles of her throat seized up; Arian began to shiver. The Authoritan could visit pain upon her—this he had shown her night after night, cruel and imaginative in his punishments. Yet her training at Hira resisted him. Of greater significance, the Claim resisted him, refusing to issue from her throat, a pitiless battle of magic against magic that caused her palpable injury. It was no different this day: she was forced to her knees by the Authoritan's power, pressure building in her skull. Teardrops of blood leaked from her eyes, a sickening residue on her skin. She choked on the scent of it, tainted and dark, and tasted it in her mouth.

She had exerted this power over men—the power of the Claim—but it had never been used against her—a battle of the occult against the uncorrupted. It was a setback, nothing more. She wouldn't let the Authoritan twist the beauty and power of her magic. She fought to raise her head. She held on to her circlets, the two gold armbands that signified her status as a Companion of Hira, one of a group of women entrusted with the care of the sacred scriptorium at the Citadel. The Citadel was the stronghold of the Companions of Hira, a place where they sought to protect the written word from the devouring onslaught of the Talisman, men—and it was always men—who waged war upon all forms of knowledge, under the flag of the One-Eyed Preacher, a tyrant whose will Arian had spent a decade trying to subvert.

As a Companion, Arian had been charged with a mission to rescue the women of Khorasan from the Talisman's efforts at enslavement. But then the leader of her order, the High Companion Ilea, had assigned her to seek out the Bloodprint as a means of unseating the Talisman. Arian had been chosen for this Audacy because of her exceptional gifts. She was Hira's most accomplished linguist, fluent in the Claim and armed with the power of its magic. She was First Oralist of Hira.

And because of that—and despite the tortures the Authoritan inflicted—she *should* be able to resist.

Gasping at the effort, she tried to draw power from the inscriptions on her circlets. Her fledgling attempt failed, just as it had before. She was brought to a posture of submission once more, her arms stretched out before her, her forehead pressed to the floor in a perversion of the prayers of their people.

"Lania—" Her sister's name came out as a croak, weakly demanding an apology.

"It's a pity to watch you suffer." Yet there was no trace of pity in Lania's voice; a cool impassivity ruled her as she ignored Arian's entreaty. Lania took her place at the Authoritan's side, gliding gracefully up the stairs, her long robe trailing behind her.

The Authoritan brought her hand to his bloodless lips and kissed it. "She tires me," he said. "If she will not share what she knows of the Claim, perhaps the Silver Mage can be put to better use than his trials with the whip."

"No!" Arian's courage flared to life again.

Lania ignored her. The crimson tips of her fingers ran along the surface of the niche, tracing the outer layer of white script in a gesture that was a caress. "My sister is less powerful than I imagined. The opposite may be true of the Silver Mage."

"Why would you think that, Khanum?" Diverted, the Authoritan relaxed his grip on Arian, his blood-tinged eyes caressing her face, inflamed by her helpless submission. She crawled into the hollowed-out space of the niche, resting her hot face against the glazed tiles, grateful for the respite.

"You've seen his eyes. He is strongly marked by the birthright of the Mages. Who knows how his magic burns? Or what tricks he might attempt to secure my sister's freedom."

The Authoritan dismissed this with a contemptuous wave, the gesture as languid as a heron's extension of its wings into flight. His movements suggested a weightlessness, as if he were a creature animated more by sorcery than by his physical form. His power resided in his voice.

"The Silver Mage can do very little on his own. I burned the Candour with a word; he did nothing to defend it."

"He loves her," Lania objected. "It may awaken depths within him."

The Authoritan curled his fingers, the gesture enough to pull Arian from the cover of the hollow. She opened her mouth to venture the Claim in her defense. A viselike grip closed about her throat, swallowing the sound. She choked for breath on her hands and knees, struggling to protect herself against the Authoritan's aggression.

The Authoritan and Lania stood breast to breast on the narrow landing. The rubies in Lania's headdress glittered against the Authoritan's white robes, striking sparks off the scepter in his hand. He decorously kissed the mask at her cheek, careful not to disturb it.

"For the Silver Mage to develop his skills, he would need to attend the Conference of the Mages. The Mages strengthen one another, not unlike your sisters at Hira. Without their congress, he remains unschooled. His is a rudimentary magic, perhaps because of his tenure in Candour."

"It was his choice," Arian gritted through her teeth. "He *chose* to serve his city."

"So?"

"So do not belittle him for it."

The Authoritan clenched his hand in a fist and brought it down. Pain seared through Arian's skull. She couldn't withstand it. Lania witnessed her pain without protest.

"Then we have nothing to fear from either of them," she observed finally. "Perhaps these little experiments serve no purpose after all."

"Not quite." The Authoritan helped Lania down the stairs, seeming to glide within the careful arrangement of his robes. He paused beside Arian, extending a hand to touch her sweat-slicked skin. Her face was pale, her body drenched in perspiration. She recoiled from the skeletal finger he dipped in a teardrop of her blood. He brought it to his lips and tasted it, his tongue flicking his skin.

"Invigorating." His red eyes rested on her face and drifted down her body, an assessment that stripped her to the bone. Arian shuddered in response.

"Lovelier than you," he said to Lania, missing her grimace. "What a pretty prize she would make for Nevus, as he cannot have you."

A smile played on Lania's lips. "There's no hurry, Khagan. I've yet to plumb the depths of my sister's talents. I would know the secret to her fame. Why was *she* selected as First Oralist? Thus far, the showing is not as impressive as I'd hoped."

"No," the Authoritan agreed. "Keep your pet until you tire of her. But make certain she expands your knowledge of the Claim. You are useless to me without your gifts."

"It shall be my first concern, Khagan, I assure you."

The painted mask of her face echoed the Authoritan's contempt for Arian's abilities. "There is nothing to be gained by bringing her to this mihrab. I will find another way to unlock her voice."

"You fail to understand, Khanum. I bring her to this place for reasons of my own."

Lania shot him a glance, her pale green eyes long and narrow. "And they are?"

He raised both hands above Arian's head, his fingers poised to strike. "Do you mark how close we are to the underground cells?" He turned his gaze to Arian, his rictus smile stretching the corners of his lips. "Sing for your beloved, First Oralist. He is eager to hear your voice."

It took her a moment to understand. Daniyar was *here*—near

to her, yet kept from her—and the Authoritan wanted him to experience the agonies of her torture, to suffer them with her . . . She closed her eyes in helpless protest. She could bear his cruelties herself, but she couldn't access the magic that would shield Daniyar from this. And though she longed for him with a fervent desire, she wished him away from her now. She knew what her pain would cost him—what his love for her had already demanded of his strength. She had served him nothing but anguish, and now he would be broken again.

Heart of my heart, he had called her. When he shouldn't have loved her at all.

"Please, no," she whispered to Lania. "Do anything you wish to me, but I beg you—do not do this to him."

The Authoritan laughed, his voice high and wild with triumph. Then the savage power of his magic blasted her from all sides.

Her screams went on and on, rising to the skies . . . penetrating the depths of the cells. The grace of Hira was ripped from her spirit and her thoughts. She couldn't stand aloof and apart when she was writhing in blood at the Authoritan's whim. The answer came to her too late.

She needed to summon new weapons against an enemy like this.

ELENA WAITED IN THE NEAR DUSK THAT ENVELOPED THE HAZING. A member of the Usul Jade had left a message for her at the house across from the crumbling blue dome, telling her Larisa needed her. She wasn't used to ignoring her sister's commands or to being away from Larisa's side. But she'd returned to the Gur-e-Mir to see what had become of Ruslan's body. She'd found her entrance at the pishtaq to the tomb. Ruslan's head was on a spike, his body dismembered, his limbs littering the courtyard. The Ahdath had forced his jade green bracelets into his mouth, which gaped open in a perfect round.

The sight of him was like a blade cutting deep into the bone, exposing the marrow of her grief, yet Elena didn't cry. She *couldn't* cry, no matter how deep the wound. She had learned to guard herself through practiced dissociation, but now her emotions raged wildly. Would everything she loved be taken from her with such brutal and cold finality? She removed the bracelets from Ruslan's mouth and slipped them onto her wrists. Then she kissed both his cheeks with a tenderness she had never expressed before.

I should have buried you, spared you from this. I should have chosen you above any emissary of the Black Khan's, any Companion of Hira. As Larisa should have also.

What didn't you do for us, Ruslan?

She wanted to ignore Larisa's summons—her rage, her grief were still too new. But if Ruslan was lost to her, Larisa was all she had left.

She would return and bury her beloved, but time was against her now. It was foolish of Larisa to have summoned her to the Hazing. The streets around the Gur-e-Mir were swarming with Ahdath. After the First Oralist's sundering of the Registan, the Ahdath had doubled their patrols. They hunted the Usul Jade with a singular determination. She hadn't forgiven Larisa, but she needed to get her sister out of the necropolis of the Hazing. She had already sent orders to the Basmachi to retreat, knowing Marakand was lost. She'd told them to regroup at the ruins of the Summer Palace. Its rugged surroundings would shelter them until Larisa returned. Then they would be able to get word to the warriors of the Cloud Door in the mountains. The time to strike at the Wall was almost upon them now. She knew Zerafshan's men were ready, just as she knew that without Larisa's support, she could not prod them into action.

It was time for Larisa to remember that she led the Usul Jade—her duty was to the women behind the Wall and to the people who still upheld the teachings of their father. As the daughters of Mudjadid Salikh, they bore a responsibility unlike any other: resist until the battle was won or until their resistance atrophied into dust.

As leaders of the Basmachi, she and Larisa were not tools to be used by the First Oralist, no matter the nature of the bargain Larisa had struck with the Black Khan. The First Oralist may have dismantled the Registan, but she'd also delivered Ruslan to his fate at the gates of the Gur-e-Mir. Ruslan, her dearest companion, the one who'd rescued her from Jaslyk, risking agonies greater than hers. She closed his eyes with her fingers, his bracelets softly striking hers. Then she spat out her rage on the ground.

She was on the hunt for the First Oralist.

And she would take her measure of blood.

3

SEVEN DAYS. SINNIA HAD BEEN IN JASLYK SEVEN DAYS, EACH DAY BRING-
ing forth new torments, new reasons to pray for rescue. Not that
she'd been idle—her first course of action had been to attempt to
rescue herself. The wardens of Jaslyk seemed to have no memory
or knowledge of the Claim, and she had been able to use it with
some success, escaping a room, a ward, a building . . . only to run
into Jaslyk's guards or its impenetrable defenses. The watchtowers
were like the eyes of a dragon-horse. Red and fiery and unblinking. No matter which route she took to steal from her cell, the
watchtowers picked her out along the perimeter, setting off a col-
lision of horns. Then the guards of Jaslyk would come, dressed
in black, wearing blind-eyed masks, four crimson slashes marking
their chests and spreading across their ribs.

They looked like they'd been clawed by demons.

She'd never seen their faces or heard their voices. She'd simply
felt the grip of implacable hands covered with leather gloves whose
palms were studded with tiny spikes. Her arms were marked with
dozens of pinpricks that healed over, then formed again with each

12

new attempt to escape. The pinpricks burned, but they were only a reminder of her failure.

And they were nothing compared to the mask.

On the third day, Sinnia had learned about the mask. Two of the guards had chained her to a bed in a locked room at the far end of a dismal corridor. At once she'd missed the cruel teasing of the Ahdath. When they'd turned her over to Jaslyk, she'd met an incarnation of their regiment more to be feared than the soldiers who guarded the Wall. They were called the Crimson Watch, a name given to the Ahdath elite. The crudely jovial soldiers of the Ahdath who'd handed her over to their care had fallen silent during the transfer. One had flashed her a look of regret, muttering to his partner. The other man shook his head. They spoke with surprising deference to the soldiers of the Crimson Watch. The masked men didn't speak. They waved the Ahdath away.

When they'd chained Sinnia to the bed, her body had tensed in dread. The Claim coiled up in her throat. The scent of blood was fresh in the room. It oozed from every door in the ward, a patina that formed a pattern on the floor. Fear ripened in her mouth.

"Please," she said, "don't do this."

A third guard entered the room, pushing a steel-framed cart before him. It bore a tray of instruments. *Torture,* she thought. *They've come to torture me.* For a moment, it seemed like a reprieve.

But the largest of the three guards lifted a bizarre contraption from the cart: a thick leather mask with sightless glass eyes that protruded like eyeballs distended from a skull. A long black hose at the back of the mask was attached to a dark green canister on the cart. It appeared to breathe on its own. At the base of the mask were six round nozzles, three to either side.

The guard wheeled the cart closer to the bed where Sinnia lay chained.

She wanted to scream, but the sound died in her throat. She wrestled with the chains they had fiendishly attached to the circlets on her upper arms. One of the guards held her down. The other raised her head so the third could fit the mask over her head.

Her body bucked on the bed. The inside of the mask smelled of horror and fear. It suffocated her. Her breathing constricted, she mumbled the Claim to herself. There would be words, there *had* to be words, to stop this.

In the name of the One—

In the name of the One, the Merciful, the Compassionate—

Ah, by the powers of the One, where were Arian and Daniyar? Surely they would save her from this . . . unless somehow they had fallen or been taken at the Ark. She wished she could think of them, pray for them . . . but in this moment of extremis, she could think only of herself.

She could see through the bulbous eyes of the mask. The guard at the cart flicked a switch on the canister. A terrible gurgling sound came from the hose at the back of Sinnia's neck. She breathed in sharply, her mouth filling with the acrid taste of smoke. With her first inhaled breath, the nozzles at the base of the mask fastened to her neck. She felt a searing pain.

Inside the mask, she cried out. Her mouth and throat filled with gas. The three men loomed above her.

Burning tears scalded her eyes. When they misted over her skin, the tears seemed to catch fire. Sinnia screamed again. The men didn't touch her, didn't tear at her clothes. One of them produced a small bundle wrapped in a leather cover. He watched Sinnia with careful attention. Then he began to write.

He held a *book* in his hands.

A book that chronicled her torture.

Four days later, she was at the perimeter again. They had gassed her every day since, but when the mask had been removed, Sinnia had recovered consciousness to find herself alone, still chained to the bed by her circlets. Though they monitored her reaction to the gas, no one seemed to be observing her in the cell.

They didn't know she drew comfort from the circlets that were the secret strength of the Companions. Whatever the gas had done to her, and it had done *some*thing, it hadn't stripped her of the Claim. Over time, her use of the Claim had weakened the links of the chains. She snapped them with a surge of renewed strength, taking a moment to breathe.

The chamber reeked of the gas. Her skin smelled fetid and damp, a mix of the strange compound of the gas and the odors of sweat and blood. She knew now why the men of the Crimson Watch wore masks. They were shielding themselves from the consequences of their macabre experiments. The terror the masks invoked was a side effect of their work.

Sinnia ran a hand over her neck, feeling the tender areas where the nozzles had raised the skin. She shuddered to think of her disfigurement, but she tried to focus on the door. Each time she escaped, they added another padlock. She could see them now from the hole at the top of the door that passed for a dreary window. She had yet to see another inmate, but she sometimes heard painful, muted whimpers as she sidled past the other cells.

She should try to use the Claim to free the others. She doubted the strength of her skills; her failure might bring them to the same fate she faced—a renewal of the attentions of those who gassed her. She considered the risk and decided against it. She pictured her whip and bow in her mind and formed a resolution.

If she *could* discover a way out, she wouldn't forget the desperate halls of Jaslyk. She'd find a way to return and do some damage, a vow she made to herself.

The red eyes of the watchtower settled on Sinnia again. Horns sounded like heralds of a hastening end, a palpable assault on her hearing. The scars on her neck began to throb in anticipation of the agonies of the mask. The guards dragged her by the arms, their studded gloves scoring her shoulders with dozens of bloody strikes.

She sang out verses of the Claim—the music of it seized up in her throat.

She had asked herself this question many times. Why did the Claim deliver Arian from every difficulty while she was able to summon it only in small bursts? What did this say about Sinnia as a Companion or as a member of the Council? Was she not worthy of the Claim? Had the Negus of her country chosen her as his emissary to Hira in error?

She made her body as heavy as possible, forcing the guards to drag her by the heels. They barely slowed their pace as she bumped along the bloodstained floor, pausing for a moment to study the shattered padlocks. Sinnia fought with all her physical strength, aggression and panic rising together as she heard the sound of the cart rattling down the length of the corridor.

She made a temporary break from the arms of her captors, leaping across the hall and crashing against the door of another cell. She fastened her arms on her circlets, holding fast to the strength of the Companions. She choked out one verse of the Claim, then another. For the briefest moment, the actions of the Crimson Watch were suspended—the cart held still, the guards with their bloody palms motionless in the air.

A moan sounded from behind the door. Sinnia glanced up. A man was standing at the hole for the window, his hair matted and wild, his thin face bloody. His eyes burned like two black coals. They fell to Sinnia's circlets.

"Sahabiya," he gasped. "You've come to us at last."

At his words, there was a murmuring along the length of the hall. Other faces came to the doors of the cells, eager hands reaching through bars.

It was Sinnia's turn to freeze. She should have fled during this strange suspended moment, but this was the first time she'd seen the other prisoners. "Who are you?" she whispered to the wild man. She was stirred by a fierce determination. "How do you know who I am?"

"You came for me." His powerful voice filled with conviction. And then an urgent warning: "Sahabiya, behind you!"

The frozen moment ended. One of the guards caught Sinnia by the neck, squeezing down on her throat. A second man reached for her arms. He'd taken off his gloves to unlatch her circlets.

"No! Don't touch them!" It was the man in the cell who called out. But underneath his words there was more—a strange, low thrumming through Sinnia's veins that carried the sound to her heart.

Another guard rapped on the door of the man's cell. A disembodied voice echoed through the mask. "Get back, all of you! And you there. Still alive? That will change," he promised.

He shoved the cart toward Sinnia, pushing her back into her cell. Her leaping, twisting body was subdued by a company of guards. The cart was wheeled to the side of her bed. She looked at its surface in terror, only to notice that the dark green canister was missing, as was the mask with the hose. In its place was a tray that held a gleaming array of instruments, polished to a shine. The sound-touch inside her veins intensified—her heart rate began to slow.

The disembodied voice spoke again, the man in charge moving to Sinnia's side. He held a long thin spike in his hands. "She's ready for the white needle."

Sinnia forgot about the sound. All she could do was scream.

THE DOUBLE CUPOLA WHERE ELENA WAS TO MEET LARISA WAS ABAN-
doned, its twin domes feathered with bird's nests. A step at a time,
Elena crossed Ahdath lines, weaving in and out of the city of
the dead. The soldiers were quartering the Hazing. If she hadn't
known its shadowed passages better than she knew her own scars,
the Ahdath would have captured her by now.

The Hazing sloped down a hill to an abandoned alley that
branched off into several paths that led deeper into Marakand.
One path led to the Wall, one to the cemetery of the Russe, another to the Registan. Fires burned on the ramparts, glowing from
the Wall like the baleful eyes of demons. The night was dark and
cold, and the Ahdath were armored against it.

The First Oralist may have burned down the Registan, but she
hadn't defeated the army at the Wall. Instead, she'd left the people
of Marakand to the Ahdath's bitter revenge. Screams sounded
from the alleyways as families were dragged from their homes and
accused of giving shelter to the Companions. Elena could hear the
sound of furniture being smashed and the crack of boots against
bones.

She waited for a patrol to cross the Tomb of the Living King. There was a small marking on the door that signaled the Basmachi had passed on her orders to abandon the necropolis. Basmachi often sheltered in the crypt below the tomb. It was a sacred site in the Hazing. Even the Ahdath had not dared to despoil it. The forty steps known as the Ladder of Sinners led to the underground depths of the tomb. Those who submitted to the One were to count the steps descending and ascending. If they missed a step, their pilgrimage to the tomb was incomplete, and the gateway to paradise was barred. Richly inscribed lapis lazuli paneled the tomb itself. The third level of the tombstone was tiled with a warning that gave the necropolis its name.

NEVER CONSIDER DEAD THOSE SLAIN IN THE WAY OF THE ONE. NAY, THEIR LIFE IS ETERNAL.

Elena shook her head. Why had Larisa risked meeting her here? She was the one who'd taught them an overabundance of caution. Now she'd broken the rules she'd prescribed for a stranger she scarcely knew. Perhaps she'd been misdirected by the use of the Claim.

Elena passed the door to the tomb to take a step closer to the double cupola that housed the Mausoleum of the Princess. At the slight trace of sound—boots scuffing against stone—she turned to seek out her sister. She was caught by surprise by an Ahdath blade at her throat. The Ahdath clearly believed Elena was one of the Companions: he was ready to slit her throat to prevent her use of the Claim. The hand that caught at her wrist fumbled over her bracelets. For a moment, the soldier stilled. Then he shoved her into the mausoleum. She was pushed against a wall, her face turned into the stark light cast by the moon.

"Basmachi," he said with satisfaction. "Even better for me."

He was broad-shouldered and powerful in the manner of the Ahdath. With her arms twisted behind her, there was no way Elena could overcome his strength. He shoved a knee between her legs; Elena spat in his face. He slashed his blade across her torso; she fought back a scream of fury. The wound bled freely, darkening his hands, but it wasn't enough to defeat her.

This wasn't Jaslyk—she could fight him. She just had to wait for her moment. She sagged in his arms, forcing him to take her weight.

Another man entered the cupola and she groaned. One she could fight off. Two or more, and it was over.

"Who do you have there?"

"Join me," the first man grunted. "She's not one of the Khanum's doves, but she'll do."

"Do you know who you're speaking to?"

The Ahdath who'd slashed her across the torso swiveled halfway around, his right arm blocking her throat. He stiffened as he recognized the newcomer. "Captain, she's a Basmachi fighter—she bears the signs of the Usul Jade. I was bringing her to the Wall."

The captain's eyes stayed on his man. "So it seems."

The Ahdath relaxed at the captain's note of humor. He shrugged. "I have no access to the Gold House."

"Nor I," the captain said. "Let's have a look at her, then."

"She's not much to look at," the Ahdath said.

"No," the other man agreed.

A horn sounded in the street behind the cupola. Though she should have been thinking of herself, Elena's heart sank. Had they captured her sister as well? Both men turned at the sound, and Elena seized her chance. She bit down on the Ahdath's arm, sinking her teeth to the bone.

He dropped his arm with a roar of pain. Elena brought up her knee to shove him in the groin. She connected, but his leather was too thick. He slammed her back against the wall with both arms, her head crashing into brick. Stars danced before her eyes. A moment later she was slumped on the ground.

She didn't see what happened next. Instead, she heard the sounds of movement: the ring of steel, a hiss of surprise, a thud. Then the sound of something being dragged.

For a moment the world was suspended upside down. Elena felt herself raised as easily as a child; she smelled sweat and felt the scrape of a man's rough beard against her face. She was tossed onto his shoulder and carried away from the mausoleum, into the shadows of the Hazing.

Behind the mausoleum, the captain of the Ahdath set her down on a broken tombstone.

Her head reeling, Elena muttered, "Is it your turn now?"

"Take a moment," the captain suggested, "before you lacerate me with your tongue."

"I'll scream," she warned him, unable to see his face in the shadows.

"Then you'll bring a patrol right to your sister's hiding place." His tone was matter-of-fact.

Elena went still. It *couldn't* be. Of all the Ahdath who could have tracked her to the Hazing, it couldn't be the one who knew she'd rescued the First Oralist from the Gold House, delivering one of the Khanum's doves to this Ahdath in her stead.

The man stepped out of the shadows, showing her his face. A pang of terror struck at her heart—she had walked into an ambush. This Ahdath had come for their heads, using her to trap her sister.

But the captain from the Gold House spoke to her with unexpected kindness. "It's not what you think, Anya. I came *with* Larisa to find you."

Elena stood up, backing away from the man. She gave him a careful nod, wondering if she could outrun him even with the knife wound at her ribs. "Captain Illarion, you've made a quick return from Black Aura. I'd appreciate your escort to the Gold House."

Illarion smiled at her, a rueful smile that didn't lighten his cold blue eyes in the least. "So you can cut my throat on the way? I know who you are, Anya. Larisa asked me to find you—that's the reason I'm here."

Like a tiger of the Shir Dar, Elena sprang at him. Her hand snaked to the knife at his hip. A second later it was at his heart. "What have you done with my sister?"

He stood still, his arms at his side, his palms spread wide. "She's safe, I swear it to you."

Elena pressed the tip of the blade through crimson armor. "Liar."

Illarion was much taller than she was. He seemed bemused by her actions, staring down at her, his blue eyes wide. "Anya—"

"Where *is* she?"

"Here, Elena, I'm here."

Elena didn't move at the sound of a new voice. She switched out of the Common Tongue to the secret language of the Basmachi. "Is this a trap?" she asked.

"No, let the Ahdath go."

Larisa jumped down from the rock wall behind the double cupola, one hand on the sword at her hip, the other shielding her face from the white glare of the moonlight. She was unfettered and alone. "Let him go," she said again.

Elena shook her head. She pressed the blade deeper into the Ahdath's breastplate. His breath hitched in his chest. He held the same nonthreatening pose until Larisa moved between them, removing the knife from her sister's hand.

"The only good Ahdath is a dead one," Elena said, not taking her eyes off Illarion.

"I know. But he's not Ahdath. He's . . . something else."

Illarion fingered his ruptured breastplate.

"Don't be stupid. With Araxcin dead, *Captain* Illarion is now Commander of the Wall." Elena's eyes narrowed. "Let's take him. Let's ransom him for some of ours."

It was Larisa's turn to shake her head. "You know the Ahdath won't ransom our fighters. They're on a killing spree even now."

Elena's face tightened. "Then why did you call me to the Hazing? And why did you bring him with you? You've put us both at risk."

"I need your help, Elena. I need to break a prisoner out of Jaslyk." She said this in the Common Tongue despite Elena's furious glare.

"What madness causes you to share your purpose with the enemy?"

"We have to hurry," Illarion cut in. "It won't take them long to find us."

Elena's rage boiled over. How *dare* this Ahdath speak of himself as one of them when he knew they shared no common cause? The violent urge to bury her blade between his ribs renewed itself. She spun around to face him. "Why aren't you at Black Aura, Captain? I saw you leave for the capital myself."

He shifted on his heels, scouting the Hazing with his eyes. "You were mistaken, Elena. I never went to Black Aura." He stressed her name to emphasize that he now understood her earlier deception. "I turned the Khanum's prisoner over to my men for escort.

Then I arranged for your friends to travel safely through Black Aura Gate."

"What friends?"

Larisa answered for him. "The First Oralist." She seemed to search for words. "And her consort, the Silver Mage."

Elena's lips formed a snarl. "You watched the First Oralist abandon Ruslan, yet you risked yourself to deliver her *consort*? I don't know you anymore, sister."

Tears formed in Larisa's eyes. "Yes, you do." Her voice cracked. "Do you imagine Ruslan's death is a loss you suffer alone? Do you think the Companion of Hira doesn't have a list of losses as long as your right arm? A man she loved was blooded before her eyes."

Elena faltered. "Blooded?"

"Yes. Her grief brought down the Registan."

Elena remembered her primary mission. "And the Gold House?"

Illarion answered. "The Gold House wasn't harmed. The Claim knew who to destroy."

Elena repudiated his words with a wave of her hand. "Were you there? Did you see it?"

He nodded, waiting. Elena's breath caught on a sob. "Then the Claim *couldn't* have known, could it? Not if there's a single one of you left to walk on this earth."

The bitterness and grief in her eyes held him long after she'd turned away.

Larisa drew Elena into the shadows. Moonlight spilled over the curves of the double cupola's domes. Beneath the chipped and feathered bricks of the domes, blue-glazed tiles formed calligraphic patterns that swam in the play of shade and light. The faintest breeze disturbed the shoots of grass sprouting from the brick. It stirred the hair at the back of Illarion's collar. He watched as the sisters muttered to each other in secret. He'd wanted to smile when Elena had suggested taking him captive, but her rage was too raw to suffer his condescension. He rubbed a hand over the bruise on his sternum. He wouldn't misjudge her again.

He was due back at the Wall. And he was due to report to the Khanum. But before he could do either of these things, he needed to get these sisters out of the city to Jaslyk. Though Jaslyk held other dangers. They would have to face down soldiers of the Crimson Watch. They would also be risking a run-in with the Technologist—the madman who supervised the prison.

But if there was a chance to save the Companion, Sinnia, the risks they were taking would be worth it.

Doubt gnawed at him: Could the Companion still be alive? And if she was, did Larisa and Elena stand any chance of successfully bringing about a rescue?

Larisa interrupted his thoughts. "Come with us," she said. "We know how to circumvent the patrols. Unless you think you'll be missed."

He studied the two sisters standing side by side, each with a knife in one hand and a sword in the other. Larisa was by far the comelier of the two, but it was Elena he couldn't look away from, Elena who burned with a volatile fury that reminded him of the First Oralist raging against the murder of her friend with a fury that had fired the sky.

"I can spare a day or two before I must return. The Authoritan will send a regiment from the Ark led by Captain Nevus. Nevus is to assume control and command of the Wall. If I'm not there to receive him, it will raise suspicions."

"That sounds like they don't trust you."

He raised an eyebrow, as if to remind them both that his presence in the Hazing at their side gave the Ahdath reason to doubt him.

Elena snorted, then pressed on.

Illarion followed the women through the double cupola, where the body of the soldier he'd killed lay hidden in the shadows. He prodded it with his foot. "They'll take it for a Basmachi kill."

"As it would have been," Elena snarled at him. "I didn't ask for your rescue."

Illarion ignored this. His stomach had lurched at the sight of the man's assault upon Elena. She'd been helpless, a fact she wouldn't admit to him. Or to any man, he suspected, though she had let her sister tend to her wound with an indifference that spoke to what the sisters had endured.

He focused on answering Larisa as she led the way down the hill, moving in and out of the shadows of the Hazing's once-graceful mausolea. She stopped for a moment at the Tomb of the Living King, adjusting a floral decoration on its faience. It rotated east without a betraying sound. He wondered if the Tomb of the Living King held any significance for these sisters beyond a place where they left messages for the Basmachi. He'd seen grown men fall to their knees crying at the door to the tomb, pressing their lips to its inscriptions. For himself, he was a man without religion. When everything was holy, nothing could be holy.

"Nevus is the Authoritan's man. It was the Khanum who chose me as second to Araxcin. The Authoritan prefers his own men in command, but the Khanum will call me soon enough."

"Then go to her." Elena's scowl was fierce. "We have no need of your escort."

So she *would* go to Jaslyk. Despite the rift with her sister, somehow Larisa had managed to persuade her to rescue the Companion of Hira. "I'll see you safely to Jaslyk," he answered, keeping his voice even.

Elena gave a mirthless laugh. "We know Jaslyk better than you ever will." She spat again at his feet, narrowly missing his boots. He suppressed the urge to yank her by the hair and offer her her blade in kind. But Larisa Salikh was watching him, her narrow eyes pale and intent.

Nor was Elena finished. "If you make it to Jaslyk, Ahdath, you won't be leaving alive."

The message Larisa had left wasn't to abandon the Hazing. She trusted Illarion no more than Elena did, but he'd told her something she hadn't known, something he wasn't aware that he'd betrayed.

He didn't have command of the Wall. And the new commander, Nevus, wasn't due to arrive for another day or more.

She knew what the Ahdath were capable of. She was equally aware of their deficiencies.

For a day at least, the Wall was undefended, the opportunity she'd been waiting for—a chance for the Basmachi to weaken the Ahdath's defenses from inside their own stronghold. A task she couldn't accomplish on her own—not if she was headed to Jaslyk with Elena. She tipped her head to one side, weighing the risk against the gain. Strike too soon or miss the chance altogether? Success depended on timing. Her mission was to rout the Ahdath without allowing the Talisman to overrun them, exchanging one set of masters for another. To weaken the Wall as she hoped to, she'd have to take the risk.

She sent a message to Zerafshan. And prayed his men were ready.

5

"WELCOME TO THE EAGLE'S NEST, EXCELLENCY. I TRUST YOUR RIDE across the mountains was not too arduous, and that your treasure remains undisturbed."

The Black Khan stirred from his perusal of a message delivered to him by hawk. His sister, Darya, had sent news of events at Ashfall, along with her wishes for his safe return. He read loneliness in her words, her genuine affection for him—an affection he used against her without the slightest remorse. To do so did not trouble his conscience: such was his right as Khan. More than that, it was his duty as Prince of the Khorasan empire. He'd risked the dangerous ride from Black Aura to the Eagle's Nest in order to fulfill that duty. Darya's desire to see him again was the least of his concerns.

The man who now addressed him remained a mystery to Rukh. He was dressed in a shapeless brown robe belted at the waist, with a hood that covered most of his face. A lantern burning in the limestone chamber illuminated his jaw and the bleak white line of his smile. He was known simply as the Assassin, and he might have been thirty or sixty. Rukh had never seen the Assassin without his hood.

He'd yielded the throne in the chamber to the Black Khan as soon as Rukh had arrived. The Assassin wasn't one for the accoutrements of power; in this way, as in so many others, he was markedly different from the Khan—a difference that Rukh had never bothered to examine. It was enough that the Assassin was his, as loyal in his own way as Arsalan, the commander of the Black Khan's army. He stowed the scroll inside the medallion at his collar, giving the man his attention without rising from his chair. It was for the Assassin to make an obeisance.

The man in the robe didn't hesitate. He bowed low, hovering over the Black Khan's onyx ring without kissing it. "Excellency," he said again, "my fortress is yours."

The Black Khan's men advanced a step to either side of the throne. The commander of his army always rode at his side, and now he moved closer to the Assassin, who backed away from him, a smooth smile edging his lips.

"Hasbah," Rukh greeted him. "Does the Eagle's Nest stand ready to aid me at this hour?"

The Assassin nodded. In all his transactions with Rukh, he'd made only one request in return: that the Black Khan should never attempt to determine his true identity. The name he permitted the Khan to use in the presence of others was a cipher, giving nothing away of his origins. It was a reasonable price to pay for the skills of a man who would execute on command any of the Black Khan's enemies.

The Assassin beckoned Rukh to a window that overlooked the valley below. Both men ignored the boy trussed up and gagged at the foot of the Black Khan's seat. He whimpered behind his gag. The Black Khan nudged him aside with his leather boot.

"What do you see, Excellency?"

Rukh studied the valley in the moonlight that washed the glade. The Assassin had made some improvements. The climb to the top of the mountain formed a natural barricade against invaders, but Hasbah had taken steps to camouflage his position. The stone quarried up the path was the same smooth limestone of the fortress, indistinguishable from the landscape below.

Rukh strolled to another of the chamber's windows, this one facing the river behind the fortress, a second natural barrier. Hasbah had terraced the fertile plains below, growing and storing his own crops to prepare the fortress against a siege. The storerooms that wound down into the mountain's subterranean channels could have rivaled those of the capital at Ashfall.

"The Eagle's Nest is an impressive fiefdom. Do you govern the north from here?"

The Assassin's answering smile was bland, as if to say there were no borders that could contain him. "Up to a point," he said.

"As long as you remember that you do not command the West."

The Assassin raised two gloved hands in protest. The arms of his robe fell back, the strange black gloves that rose to his elbows fastened by the silvery laces of a fabric that seemed too insubstantial to hold them together. The laces were another of the Assassin's peculiarities.

"Command does not interest me," Hasbah answered.

"But power does."

Hasbah nodded. "The power of words."

One of the Assassin's servants held up a lantern and swept its light around the chamber. Rows of shelves had been carved into the limestone walls, each holding a selection of manuscripts inside a film of the same insubstantial fabric that laced the Assassin's gloves.

The uppermost shelf held a new treasure bound with the same gossamer material. There was a note of anticipation in the Assassin's voice. "Twice now I have brought it to you."

"Your trap was well laid," the Black Khan agreed. "It was boldly done."

The Assassin preened at the Black Khan's praise. "I could have rid you of the First Oralist once the deed was accomplished."

At his words, the trussed-up boy whimpered.

"Be silent, boy," Rukh said, not unkindly. "I haven't harmed a hair of her head." He shook his head at Hasbah. "She's more powerful than you suspect, old friend." He gave an elegant shrug. "And I've no wish to attract the wrath of one such as the Silver Mage."

The Assassin's posture conveyed his surprise. "I could have dispatched him as well, Excellency." A note of doubt crept into his voice. "*You* are the Dark Mage. The Mages are natural allies, your magics are closely bound."

A reasonable interpretation of folklore, though not necessarily true at present.

What was true was that the Assassin knew too much about his affairs. Rukh suspected him of intelligence-gathering. The Assassin must have missed, though, that when the Conference of the Mages had last been held at Ashfall, it was Rukh's half-brother Darius who'd acted as the Dark Mage. It was a birthright the brothers shared, though Rukh himself had had no luxury to study or awaken those powers. Nor would he humble himself before the other Mages. He'd attempted a rapprochement with the High Companion of Hira—Ilea, the Golden Mage. But she'd met those advances with scorn. He wouldn't belittle himself again. Now that he had the Bloodprint in his hands, the others would bow to him.

A small smile curled the edges of his lips: how little they knew of his schemes.

What he needed was to make his way to Ashfall. With that in mind, he'd come to the Eagle's Nest to seek the help of the Assassin. The Talisman had cut off the road to his capital, under the thrall of the One-Eyed Preacher, whose animus against the written word had become the law of the land: an ignorance the Talisman sought to extend across Khorasan, under their bloodstained flag. The Talisman were marching on his capital to burn his scriptorium down. They would take the women of his city and sell them to the north as slaves. Unless he found a weapon to wield against them— and he fiercely believed that the Bloodprint was that means.

Now with the Bloodprint under his protection, he needed a safe route home. He also needed men—men who would relish taking the heads of those Talisman commanders who sought to bring his city to ruin.

The Assassin had those men in legions.

Hasbah snapped his fingers. Servants scurried to do his bidding. A carved table was brought into the chamber, numerous dishes arranged on its surface. Sherbet was poured into golden goblets. The Assassin himself placed a chair for the Black Khan at the head of the table.

Rukh nodded at the boy. One of the servants moved to undo the boy's gag. The Black Khan passed him a goblet and a plate. "Your name is Wafa, yes? Prove your loyalty, then. You will dine, then I and my men." His eyes sought out the Assassin beneath his hooded robe. "And when the boy has tasted my food, you will tell me what you seek in exchange, old friend. Currency, coin, or women? Whatever you ask shall be given, but I must reach Ashfall before the Talisman assault."

Hasbah took the chair opposite the Black Khan. He steepled his gloved fingers, watching the boy eat with a ravenous hunger, oblivious to the fact he was tasting the food for poison.

"My needs are simple, Excellency. While you provision your men for the journey ahead, I require a candle's length of time to read in this room on my own."

Wafa stopped chewing, his mouth half-open, his amazement clear that here was another who could read.

The Black Khan signaled for the return of his goblet. He tipped it toward the light to study the liquid inside. "And what will you be reading, old friend?" He asked this even though he knew the answer.

The Assassin wanted an hour with the Bloodprint.

"Excellency, if you honor my request, I would offer a gift in exchange." The Assassin indicated another wall of the chamber. Its shelves were broader and held a selection of treasures displayed in open boxes: gemstones, talismans, astrolabes, sextants. A silver light pulsed from a slender box at the far end of the room.

"What does that box contain?"

"The tokens of the Silver Mage. I . . . liberated . . . them from his safehold in Maze Aura. Would you like to take them for your own?"

Rukh fingered the symbol of empire on his hand: the onyx ring carved with a silver rook. It was token enough for him: whatever his reputation, the Prince of Khorasan wasn't a common thief, though it intrigued him that the Silver Mage had set aside the symbols of his rank. He remembered the other man's self-contained strength with a scowl, admitting to himself that perhaps the Silver Mage had no need of his tokens at all.

"I have no use for the trifles of the Silver Mage, and I am satisfied with the bargain we have struck. Take your hour, Hasbah. Then I must hasten to Ashfall."

He looked to Arsalan, his closest adviser, who stood behind Hasbah's seat, his hand on the pommel of his sword. But Arsalan's state of alertness was futile. If it came to it, even Rukh's fiercest commander would not succeed at besting the Assassin.

No one ever had.

6

A NEST OF SNAKES MADE THEIR PRESENCE KNOWN IN HIS CELL, BUT THEY left the Silver Mage to bleed in peace in the dungeons of the Ark, a desperate place called the Pit. Its blood-smeared walls were riddled with alcoves the Authoritan had converted into cells. No light penetrated from the great hall above to the dungeons that sloped beneath the palace, but some of its passages accessed the air aboveground, an ever-present torment to the Basmachi suffering below. The agonizing sound of Arian's screams had floated through the passageways during his first week in the Pit, and he had nearly gone mad—powerless to reach her, ablaze with an incandescent fury matched only by his abject desperation. His fingers had scored the walls of his cell, the unyielding muscles of his shoulders bruised by his efforts to break free. He'd gained nothing from those efforts except the terror that followed from hearing Arian's cries fade away.

Had the Authoritan killed her? Had he given her to the Ahdath? What did she suffer alone in the darkest reaches of the Ark?

He needed to clear his mind to resolve upon a path of escape. But Arian's anguish made it impossible to succeed. He found himself floundering without agency, bound by the borders of the Pit, his ability to endure worn away. Then after a week had passed, Arian's screams had ceased—leaving him free to focus on the depravities of the Pit, with none of his torments assuaged.

The humid air carried the stench of boiling flesh to the deepest corners of the pit, a scent further corroded by the odors of waste and blood. Then in the last hour of a man's strength, a hint of peach blossom would drift through the Pit's passageways like a promise of salvation. Peach and pomegranate and hope—false promises all.

Daniyar grunted, shifting his body along the wall to the bars that looked out along the passage. A handful of Basmachi were held in the other cells. He'd managed to speak with them over the past few days, learning what he could of the Ark. An emaciated youth with hopeless eyes had been the one to tell him about the healing effects of the loess that coated the walls. He hadn't believed the boy at first, but after his first lashing, he'd been willing to consider any means of healing his wounds. Each time he was bled by the whip, he rubbed his back against the golden loess. As he did so, his pain decreased and the marks of the whip ceased to throb. When Nevus slashed his palms with a blade, the loess healed his hands in a night.

"It's the secret of Marakand," the boy said. "It may be the only one the Authoritan doesn't know."

A blessing in a place of despair.

The boy's name was Uktam, and he'd been imprisoned in the Pit much longer than the others. He was kept alive because he was useful to the Authoritan as an informant against the Basmachi. He'd seen many of his compatriots come and go from the cells, each cursing him as a traitor. Daniyar set his distaste at the boy's actions aside, as he needed information. So he asked Uktam questions, but shared no intelligence of his own, warned by the others to watch himself when Uktam was summoned to the palace. Not that he needed a warning—the proof of Uktam's betrayal could be seen on his body. The boy may have been beaten and starved, but his back had been spared the whip.

Daniyar groaned to himself. The loess was less effective with each new flogging he suffered. Night after night, Nevus escorted him to the throne room for a display of the Authoritan's sadism. It was Nevus who whipped him, a cold satisfaction in his eyes, and Nevus's arm was powerful. The six-tailed whip was unlike anything Daniyar had experienced. Its filaments seemed to strike his most vulnerable places at once. The tails of the whip were barbed. They scored his skin with dozens of agonizing bites, mocking the strength and endurance he had honed since he'd come to manhood.

Perhaps worse than the whip was his degradation—his punishment had become an entertainment for the court. Ahdath bartered with Nevus to take a turn with the whip. On occasion, pretty young girls from among the Khanum's doves would plead for a chance to bend him to their will.

Their blows didn't land with enough force to hurt him. They couldn't compare to the memory of his first night at the Ark, when the Authoritan had taken the whip into his hands, strengthened by an unholy magic.

Daniyar had tried to summon his knowledge of the Claim to meet the Authoritan's brutality, until Arian's screams had shattered the Ahdath's merriment, and their attention had shifted from him. In that moment, his will had foundered. Chained to the wall, he hadn't been able to see her. But he'd heard the sounds of Arian being subdued. She had fought the Ahdath like a wild thing, and when she could fight no longer, she had screamed for his deliverance, begging the Authoritan with a furious desperation, pleading with the Khanum to put an end to his torment.

Daniyar hadn't been able to master himself. He'd shouted at the force of the blows, at the insidious incursions of the whip's barbed tails. The whip had been devised to inflict maximum damage. At the end of it, he'd hung suspended from his chains, unable to support his own weight, his face wet with sweat and tears, the muscles of his back sectioned by trails of blood.

And with every breath he had summoned, he'd heard Arian's broken pleading. "Leave him, leave him, take me."

Better not to have betrayed their feeling for each other before the eyes of the Authoritan, but he couldn't have done anything differently. If the whip had fallen on Arian instead, he would have gone mad with rage.

Gathering himself, he had turned his head to try to glimpse her. His token effort had failed. He'd offered her what comfort he could, speaking in the dialect of Candour, an undertone of the Claim murmuring through his words. "Da zerra sara, I can bear this, but I need you to be strong. I cannot also bear your tears."

"Jaan," she had whispered in reply. It was all she'd been able to say. He'd heard the sounds of her struggle, but he couldn't see the collar being fitted over her throat, suffocating Arian in the cruelest manner possible—the First Oralist, silenced and chained.

Then he'd felt the cool touch of a woman's hand on his shoulder, her nails trailing through his blood, spreading it across his back in a pattern he couldn't see. "Collect it," she said to a servant at her side.

A vial was placed at the base of his spine, its warmth nearly intolerable against his ravaged skin. The Khanum was collecting his blood.

Briefly he closed his eyes.

She moved closer so he could see her, her lead mask reeking of poison. She dragged her bloodied fingers across her lips, staining her white mask red. "You taste better than I imagined." Then she kissed him on the lips.

W hat can you tell me of the First Oralist of Hira?" He used the bars of the cell to support his weight, asking the question of Uktam, who was slumped against a wall of his cell.

Uktam's head lolled in Daniyar's direction, his eyes bulging from within his hollow skull. He raised a hand and let it fall. "The Khanum keeps her at her side. The collar prevents her use of the Claim. The Khanum has enchanted it somehow."

Daniyar nodded. Though Uktam told him the same thing every night, he had yet to comprehend the full extent of Lania's powers.

"She hasn't been put to the service of the Ahdath?"

The possibility filled him with terror. The Authoritan threatened him with it each time Nevus whipped him, but he hadn't seen Arian since that first night in the throne room. And Lania had refused to enlighten him, relishing the power of her silence.

He was devastated by the thought of Arian being given to the Ahdath: as the man who'd loved her for a decade, and as the Silver Mage of Candour. The violation of a Companion of Hira was a sacrilege, but he'd learned a critical lesson from the threat: no laws of honor bound either the Authoritan or his consort.

Yet Lania was Arian's sister. Could she truly bring herself to give Arian to the Ahdath? Without her use of the Claim, Arian was defenseless against them. With the power of speech restored to her, he knew she would bring down the Ark, just as she'd razed the Registan.

No wonder the Authoritan feared her power. No wonder he sought to claim it for himself.

He focused on his questions for Uktam. "Why don't they take the First Oralist to the throne room?"

Uktam was too weak to shrug. With an effort underscored by the Claim, Daniyar slid his bowl across the passage between the cells. Two of the yellow snakes raised their sleek heads with interest. Daniyar murmured to them; they lowered their heads again.

"Take it," he said to Uktam. "You need it more than I do."

Uktam's fingers scrabbled weakly between the bars. He found the bowl and scooped up the rice it contained. Daniyar let him finish, then asked his question again. Uktam licked the bowl clean before he answered. "I shouldn't have taken your ration."

"You're at the end of your strength." Daniyar didn't add that he held something of his own in reserve, despite his nightly sessions in the throne room. Since the Talisman's ascent, he'd lived a hard, demanding life. He'd spent years honing his skills, testing the reserves of his strength against a desolate landscape. Though his trials at the Ark were brutal, he was confident he would be able to endure them. But if Uktam was an informant, it was wiser to keep this knowledge to himself. "Please," he said again. "Tell me what you know."

Uktam considered. "The Khanum is jealous of her sister. She does not wish the Companion of Hira recalled to your mind when she is present."

"There is nothing they could do with the whip that would cause me to forget her." That much was common knowledge.

Uktam nodded. "She is well aware. But she has some purpose for your blood."

"Do you know what that purpose is?"

Uktam stared at the empty bowl as if it were an oracle that could divine the truth.

"Don't trust him," another voice whispered from the darkness. "He tells you that which the Khanum wishes you to know."

Uktam scowled. "I would not betray the Silver Mage," he said with dignity.

The other prisoner snorted. "You've betrayed each one of us in these cells. You've been kept alive these months for a reason."

"And what of you?" Daniyar intervened. "You've been here some time yourself." He needed Uktam on his side.

"A day before you, my lord. Tomorrow they execute me, but this one will still be here."

Uktam slid the bowl back across the passage to the Silver Mage. His head fell back against the bars. "Even if I lied to you, I follow the Usul Jade. I'm a student of the teachings of Mudjadid Salikh. He trained many generations in the Claim—which is why the Authoritan destroyed him. But what he could not destroy was the flame of knowledge he lit, and now his daughters carry that light forward. With what I owe Mudjadid—my sanity, my life, my unsundered belief in the Claim—I would *never* betray the First Oralist."

Daniyar read the truth of it in his words. He hadn't told these men of his skills as Authenticate; he wanted them to speak to him freely.

And he wondered about Salikh, whose daughters Larisa and Elena had helped Arian to find the tomb that had led her to the safehold of the Bloodprint. Would Larisa and Elena Salikh be willing to aid them again? He kept the thought to himself, the merest hope in his chest.

Uktam was speaking again, and he forced himself to consider the boy's advice. "You could use the Khanum's interest to your benefit," he suggested. "She is taken with more than your blood. You need not endure the whip. I do not know how you bear it."

Daniyar softened his voice. "You were kind enough to tell me of the loess; it has served to ease my pain. I am grateful to you, Uktam. If you know a course of action I might take, I am willing to hear it."

"No, my lord!" The cry came from a prisoner Daniyar couldn't see. "You cannot trust him. You *must* not trust him. He is the Khanum's man."

"Who better, then, to know the Khanum's mind?" He turned his silver gaze on Uktam. "What does she want?"

This time Uktam managed a shrug. "She wants *you*, my lord. But you will need to prove yourself to her."

"And how do you suggest I do that? With the Authoritan's eyes on us both, and Nevus's hunger for the whip yet to be fulfilled?"

And my bond with Arian plain for all the world to witness, as we suffer each other's torments?

"The Authoritan enjoys your pain. You must find a way to turn that to your advantage. You must divide the Khanum from her consort. Then she will rally to your cause."

My cause is Arian. It will always be Arian.

But if there was a path to Arian through Lania—*if Lania could be seduced,* if her message to him through Uktam was that she would welcome proof of her powers of enthrallment—he would be a fool not to pursue it when here at last was a chance. A chance to break free of the Pit, and also to discover the reason that Lania hunted his blood.

"What must I do? Speak plainly."

Uktam's head lolled on his shoulders. As the boy dropped his tired eyes, Daniyar heard the truth in his voice. Uktam did not deceive him. "You must fight for her," he said. "You must fight the Ahdath."

7

"Come watch me, sister." The Khanum of Black Aura seated herself on a golden stool whose seat was inlaid with pearls. It was placed in front of a pearl-encrusted mirror before a table that held an apothecary's treasure in colored jars, a mixture of paints and ointments and dozens of sweet-smelling oils. Filmy curtains stirred in the breeze from a pair of windows that looked out over Black Aura. Sentries patrolled the ramparts in the distance, but this side of the Ark was spared the grisly remains of prisoners or the stench that hung over the square.

Layers of blues shadowed an evening sky that blossomed with clusters of stars. Now that the Authoritan had finished for the day with Arian, a fragile peace existed between the sisters.

"'Black Aura Blue,'" Lania said with a smile. "The name of a song my doves sing to the Ahdath in the evenings, a song of our twilight skies."

Arian knelt on the ground beside her sister. When they were alone together like this, Lania removed her collar. She had no need to fear Arian's use of the Claim: Daniyar's life was bought with her compliance. Then too, Lania was gifted with her own magic, a dark sorcery she conjured to keep Arian in her place.

Now Arian pondered the opposite fates of the daughters of their house, daughters who were gifted in the Claim. They had been taught by parents who cherished the written word, linguists who had curated their own small scriptorium, guarding a treasury of manuscripts. When the Talisman had come to their door to proclaim the law of the Assimilate, her parents and brother had been murdered, and Lania stolen away. Only Arian had been saved by her mother's quick action and by her deliverance into the hands of a Talisman captain named Turan. Turan had come to her aid again during her pursuit of the Bloodprint. And he had paid the price for riding at her side, when Lania—with her powers as the Khanum—might have chosen to save him.

But short of the darkest sorcery, Lania could not revive the dead. If Arian's struggles with the Claim had taught her nothing else, this much she'd witnessed for herself. And she wondered with a pang of dread how Lania's distortion of the Claim had caused her sister to lose her way.

Now Lania sat before her mirror, shorn of her intricate head-dress, her silky hair brushed over her shoulders, her face bare of the wraithlike mask. Her slender fingers picked up a brush. She dipped it in a pot of lead inscribed with thick-lined calligraphy. It was charmed with incantations that promised power and protection. She settled in to paint her face.

"Why?" Arian asked. "Why do you wear this mask? Your face is beautiful unadorned."

"You compliment *yourself,* sister," Lania said coolly. "The mask is my shield. It warns my enemies to be wary of my power."

They studied each other in the mirror. They shared the same felicitous arrangement of their bones, the same delicate hollows at the temple, the same quick mannerisms captured by a tilt of the head. Lania's green eyes were flecked with spears of gold; Arian's were darker and deeper. And where Lania's pale skin had been unnaturally preserved by the mask, Arian's bore the glow of frequent exposure to the elements. They looked of an age, but on closer inspection, one would never be taken for the other. And from the grim twist of Lania's bare lips, she wasn't pleased by the contrast.

Whereas Arian's heart ached to find the mirror of her sister in herself.

She tried to urge Lania again, seeking a point of connection. "Come with me, Lania. Escape this place with me. Help me save you. Help me save myself."

She'd made the same plea each night, seeking a means to return to her companions, desperate for deliverance from the misery of the Ark, wanting to find herself clasped in the safety of Daniyar's arms. And to embrace him in turn, cleaving hard to his strength. She knew that she had squandered the time she'd been blessed to be given at his side, a lesson too painful to bear. She took an audible breath, reminding Lania that she waited for an answer to her plea.

With one last stroke of her brush, Lania's mask was in place. The illusion of familiarity vanished: a stranger's face looked back at Arian, remote and formidable with secrets.

"What do you imagine I need saving from?" Lania asked idly. "I am queen of an empire. Why would I seek deliverance?"

Arian hesitated. This was a new response. Though Lania fussed over Arian like a pet, she rarely provided answers. The question Arian's words had brought to light might yet move Lania against her, a risk she had decided to accept. As it stood now, her future encompassed only two possibilities: her continued captivity or her public execution. To free herself from the misery of the Ark, she needed Lania to give herself away—to give her something she could use. To put an end to Daniyar's suffering and the daily misery it evoked.

Lania's silky reproach interrupted the racing of her thoughts. "I have many gifts, Arian, but reading your mind isn't one of them."

Arian forged ahead, sketching the outline of a plan. "You are queen because you are consort to the Authoritan. Do you not find your duties . . . onerous?"

Repellent, she wanted to say. Grievously injurious to Lania's spirit, and hardly bearable to one once destined to be a Companion of Hira.

Lania understood her meaning without her judgment being voiced. Within the painted mask, her tilted eyes were cold. "The Authoritan does not importune me. He is beyond such desires."

What Arian had witnessed in her decade of liberating slave-chains told her this couldn't be true. She had hunted every kind of man, from the pious to the sadistic, and they had all desired to inflict their lust upon women. And in some cases, on children. The thought reminded her of Sartor—and of Wafa, stolen by the Black Khan.

Convinced of her conclusions, she asked, "If the Authoritan does not desire women, why does he barter with the Talisman for slaves? What of your dovecote? What of the Tilla Kari?"

What she most wanted to ask was if Lania would stand with her against the Talisman's enslavement of women, given her first-hand knowledge of their trade.

Lania took her time choosing another pigment from the colored jars. This time she applied a searing crimson to her lips, in preparation for her nightly blood-feast. There was a purpose behind the bloodrites that Arian hadn't fathomed, and she had very little time to work it out. She needed something to break her way, and it wouldn't happen by chance.

As if sensing her urgency, Lania spoke up. "You presume a perfect equality between the Authoritan and me, and that is your own illusion. You understand nothing of how he rules."

"Then teach me! Teach me what I do not know. Help me understand why you are here, when you could be at Hira, if you chose. You *must* have the power to free yourself."

Lania whipped around from her mirror to face Arian on her knees. "You *dare* to describe me as a captive when you know nothing of what transpires here at the Ark!" Her long eyes narrowed. "And do not speak to me of Hira. Where was Hira when I was taken? Where was the Citadel Guard when I was sampled by Talisman commanders before I was sold behind the Wall? He killed every man who touched me, did you know? It was slow and cruel and *beautiful,* and he encouraged me to watch."

A bitter smile lifted the corners of her crimson lips. "He has never touched me himself. If an Ahdath looks at me, he kills him on the spot. He taught me, he trained me—and he placed me above every member of his Ahdath, even the Crimson Watch. He saved me as Hira declined to do, when the High Companion abandoned me to my fate. Now I am his forever."

There were so many things Arian could have said in response, so many dreams that had materialized into loss at Lania's words. She had guessed at the fate Lania described. But she wondered at the construction Lania had placed on the Authoritan's actions. Surely her sister could not believe that the Authoritan was responsible for her deliverance.

"*I* did not abandon you," she said after some thought.

"Yes, I know." Lania came to her feet. She rang a bell on the table, and two of her doves came to do her bidding. They brought her heavy gold robe. She raised her arms, standing slim and straight so they could close it over her dress. Her hair was arranged in an imperiously high coiffure, a selection of pearls woven through it. The headdress came next, fastened to her chignon and supported by the weighty collar at her neck. One of her attendants attached a veil to the headdress; the other took up a brush to darken her mistress's eyebrows.

Lania held herself still throughout. A trace of affection underlined her words. "I know you defied the High Companion—you nearly broke with Hira because of your love for me. Each Talisman soldier you killed was a man you imagined had harmed me. Each woman you freed from a slave-chain was to atone for not having saved me. You blamed yourself for being rescued while I was taken by wolves."

Tears shimmered in Arian's bright eyes, turning them to crystal.

Lania's smile sharpened. "You are beautiful, indeed, little sister." She didn't offer her approval.

"How do you know this?" Arian asked. "How *could* you know any of this?"

Lania reached up a hand to adjust the feathered plumes of her headdress. "You forget what you have learned here, Arian. The Authoritan told you himself. He trained me as his Augur."

Arian took a breath. As much as she sought a weakness in Lania as a means of escape, she was entrapped by her memories of her sister. She needed to untangle the past. "If you *knew*—if you envisioned my search through your Augury, why did you never come for me? Why didn't you let me know you were safe behind the Wall?"

Lania turned back to her mirror. Satisfied with what she beheld, she dismissed her attendants with a wave. From the table, she picked up Arian's collar and measured it between her hands.

A ring-bedecked finger beckoned Arian closer. "You still don't understand me, little sister."

She snapped the collar in place, choking off Arian's gifts.

"You searched for me because you loved me. But I have always hated you."

8

RUKH REFASTENED HIS ARMOR, NODDING TO HIS CAPTAINS TO LEAD THE way. He glanced at the Assassin, who kept pace at his side. The man's movements were stealthy, dangerous, his footsteps making no sound and leaving no trace behind him.

"Will your men not accompany me to Ashfall?"

"You do not require them at Ashfall, Excellency. What you require is a means to break through Talisman lines."

The Black Khan and the Assassin climbed to the top of the Eagle's Nest for a vantage point over the Talisman army. Both men were cloaked in black, camouflaged against the night.

"You give me only a dozen men. I asked for ten times that number."

"They are assassins," Hasbah said, as if that were all the explanation needed.

Rukh's snort of exasperation communicated his dissent.

"They will not be leading a charge through the enemy's ranks, Excellency."

"No?" The sky held little light, the campfires of the Talisman flaring up like matchsticks in the distance. The air was cold, its bite cruel, with turbulent clouds massed in smoky clumps over-head. The Black Khan feared for his horses. "What is their task, then?"

"I have dispatched them to their task. Twelve men for the twelve encampments spread across the plains. They will assassinate the commanders. It will throw the Talisman army into disarray. Your road ahead will be clear." His gloved fingers stroked his bare chin.

Rukh considered his words. "I know your men are skilled, but you set them a fatal task."

Hasbah bowed. "That is their mission. They will not fail."

"They will die!" Rukh snapped. "Your best-trained men, used as so much fodder." He wished he could see the other man's eyes, to read his mood or his certainty. He wished he could believe that he hadn't consigned the safety of his city to a devil.

"I have many others," Hasbah answered him. "Trained with the same skills, loyal to the same end, loyal to me and this fortress."

Rukh reined in his anger. To expose his emotion was a weakness—better to think and plan with cold, determined purpose. He needed the Assassin, and perhaps there was some viability to his plan. He had never failed the Black Khan, and yet . . . "The dead have no loyalty, old friend. The dead cherish only themselves."

"You need not fear," Hasbah said. "There is a thirteenth man as well."

Rukh flashed the Assassin a sharp look. "What purpose does *he* serve?"

"The thirteenth man is an archer. He will bring down their hawks before they call for reinforcements."

It *was* a good plan, he thought. It helped that he had witnessed firsthand the fanaticism of Hasbah's followers. Whatever com-mand he issued—even to the detriment of their own lives—they followed without hesitation. Perhaps Hasbah's indifference to such recklessness should have troubled him more than it did, but he couldn't afford to reconsider. The situation in Ashfall was perilous: the sooner he bore the Bloodprint back to the safety of his capital, the sooner he could begin his defense of the west. Hasbah's hour with the manuscript had elapsed. The Assassin had done nothing more than study it, his gloved hands leafing through its pages, until he came to a verse that held him spellbound.

Another puzzle. What knowledge did Hasbah possess of the Claim? Was he an assassin or a librarian? Or both—the needs of one weighed against the deadly skill of the other.

Rukh thought of the trove of manuscripts in the limestone chamber. He hadn't asked to see them, and Hasbah hadn't offered him the choice. He wondered now if his lack of curiosity had been a mistake. Had he missed something that could be turned to his own advantage? His men were gathered at the base of the mountain, provisioned and impatient to be off. He had little time to wait on the answers he needed to find, but he ventured a question. "What did you seek in the Bloodprint?"

The Assassin clasped his gloved hands at his waist. "I sought a key, Shahenshah."

The Black Khan frowned. Perhaps Hasbah meant to divert him with the title King of Kings. He enjoyed flattery as a commonplace due to a prince, but he kept at the forefront of his mind the favors the flatterer sought. "A key to what, precisely?"

Again that fleeting smile touched the Assassin's lips. "Your enemies are my enemies, Shahenshah. Thus I sought a key to the Rising Nineteen."

Rukh subdued a sense of panic. "The Rising Nineteen—why?" He knew well enough that the Nineteen were a force who'd overrun the Empty Quarter: another variant of the Talisman, influenced by the One-Eyed Preacher's teachings, invested in an arcane numerology.

Above all these are nineteen.

An esoteric riddle of the Claim that the Nineteen worshiped like a cult.

A small sigh escaped the Assassin. Resignation? Or deceit? Rukh could have used the gifts of an Authenticate, but he suspected the Assassin would not be easy to read even had he possessed the ability. And he refused to consider his gifts inferior to those of the Silver Mage, who had made himself over into a guardian of rabble. He thought of his princely city with a fierce, possessive pride. What could compare to its grandeur? Certainly not the ruins of Candour.

Hasbah indicated the army on the plains—the threat he must now contend with. "You think of your eastern border, Shahenshah, and the threat your eyes are able to perceive. My scouts have returned from the west."

"And?" Now Rukh could not conceal his apprehension. His army of Zhayedan had been ordered to defend the eastern front.

"You will confirm it for yourself upon your return to Ashfall. The Rising Nineteen have launched a force from the west. They will arrive at Ashfall almost on the eve of the Talisman."

Rukh had left his family undefended in the capital, tarrying too long on the road. The Khorasan Guard would not suffice to protect them. A lack of foresight on his part, swayed by the judgment of the High Companion, who had urged him to seek out the Bloodprint. His jaw tightened with anger: if she had deceived him with Ashfall trapped between two armies, she would pay the price for her betrayal.

His journey suddenly urgent, the Black Khan strode to the

carved stone steps that descended from the keep, Hasbah chasing at his heels. "You must send more men to Ashfall, men who follow after, for I cannot delay." His voice firmed. "And you must come *yourself*. I cannot do without your assistance now."

In the limestone chamber at the heart of the Eagle's Nest, he ordered two of his men to gather up the Bloodprint and the boy. This time Wafa was left untrammeled.

"We are going through Talisman lines," he warned the boy. "Any sound of betrayal will send you straight into their arms."

Wide-eyed with fear, Wafa nodded his understanding.

Rukh grasped the Assassin's arm. "Will you come?" he demanded. "Can I rely upon you?"

Hasbah quoted the Claim. "'*Whoever rallies to a good cause shall have a share in its blessings. Whoever rallies to an evil cause shall be answerable for his part in it.*'" He nodded at the Bloodprint, wrapped in its gossamer fibers. "Do not discard the protection I have sealed it in. It will have its uses upon my arrival at Ashfall."

The tightness in Rukh's throat eased; the Assassin was a man he could depend on, a man who would not leave him to fight the battle for his city alone. And with so much else to worry over, the Assassin's support was critical. For though Rukh publicly scorned the Talisman's brute strength, in truth he was gripped by fear by the unknowable nature of the One-Eyed Preacher, too formidable to defeat on his own. What bolstered him was the aid of men like the Assassin—and the belief it served no purpose to doubt himself. Not when he was armed with the weapons he'd risked so much to secure.

"I will count on every friend I have," he said. "And when I have sent my enemies to ruin, you may ask me for whatever you wish—it shall be granted at once."

The Black Khan had played many games with allies and enemies alike, acts that had kept him in power, his promises as elusive
as the wind. This time he meant every word.

The Assassin's head dipped in the direction of the Bloodprint.
It was a gesture he checked, but not before Rukh had seen it. He
glared at the man behind the hood.

Hasbah hurried into speech. "And what of the other task you
assigned me, Shahenshah? You wished me to return to Black Aura,
to deliver the First Oralist from ruin."

Arian, so proud and delicate and sweet . . . with a spine of
steel forged in flame. He had wanted to tame that fire, to taste
her willing surrender. But he wanted the Bloodprint more, and
there was no woman in all of Khorasan who would stand between
him and his empire. She was a prize, not a means. And no prize—
regardless how sweet—was worth more than his own ambition.

"Forget her for now," he said. "Her fate is out of our hands."

DANIYAR DIDN'T HAVE TO PRETEND HE WAS WEAKENED AND IN PAIN. As
Nevus chained his hands to lead him from the Pit to the great hall,
his steps faltered down the corridors of the palace. Nevus pushed
him along with a callous hand, propelling him before the Authoritan's dais, half-naked, bloodied, and weakened.

A murmur of interest sounded from the Authoritan's collection
of courtiers and courtesans, a gathering of Ahdath commanders
and beautiful girls. He thought of what a single strike at the heart
of the Ark could accomplish. Tension tightened his broad shoulders.

His eyes scanned the throne room, their silver brightness
dimmed.

There was still no sign of Arian. What had Lania done with
her? The sight of the painted face in the mask of white lead, so
similar to Arian's yet so utterly unlike, pierced him with a savage
sense of helplessness. He was bereft—bereft of Arian, bereft of
the Candour, bereft of his honor as a member of the Shin War.

But if Arian was alive, as Uktam had promised, there were
worse fates. He thought of Turan, blooded at the Gallows, and

Wafa stolen away to be used as bait. And of Sinnia, taken to Jaslyk, a prison Larisa had described with bleak and terrifying candor.

Sinnia, Wafa, Turan, and Arian. He'd failed them all as Silver Mage.

He raised his head, his thick dark hair matted with sweat and blood. He faced the Authoritan with hatred in his eyes.

Seeing it, the Authoritan raised one finger with a weightless gesture of his hand.

An unbearable pressure was brought to bear against the insides of Daniyar's skull. His eyes and ears began to leak blood, settling in the hollows of his bones, causing his skin to itch.

Lania quickly raised a hand of her own. If he'd thought she would aid him, he was mistaken. She was making her own preparations for the bloodrites that passed in the throne room. Each night he'd observed that a vial of his blood was presented to the Authoritan to drink—not only to strike fear in his enemies' hearts, but as the means to a fiendish end. The Authoritan used the blood to replenish his dark magic—and the blood of one so gifted as the Silver Mage was said to be an elixir that would hasten him to victory. Many of the Ahdath abased themselves before their master in hopes of earning a taste of Daniyar's blood. But captains of the Ahdath were fed on the blood of the Basmachi, while the lower ranks were permitted only the taste of the blood of swine. An act meant to darken and degrade, yet even this, the Ahdath welcomed as a means of notice from their lord. These strict boundaries of rank were insisted upon by the Khanum, and it was Lania herself who jealously guarded the administration of his blood to her consort.

Now at the Khanum's summons, a beautiful young girl with honey-colored hair perched on her tiptoes before him, one hand braced on his chest. She looked abashed for a moment, transfixed by the physical presence of the man she held at her mercy, her gaze slipping to the hard curves of his mouth. Then her free hand raised a vial to his chin, capturing his blood as it trailed down his face. He shook her off with a roar. The vial shattered on the throne room's marble floor. The girl scooped up the shards, throwing a look of terror over her shoulder at the Khanum.

"No matter," the Authoritan said in his high, thin voice. He lowered his finger and the pressure inside Daniyar's skull subsided. He had a moment to think before the pain struck again. The Authoritan's magic brought an association to his mind he wished he could ignore.

Was this how the Claim served Arian? With these manifest and multiplying tortures?

"Leave him, girl. We'll have blood enough for the bloodbasin before the night is out. The Silver Mage begins to weary me."

Through the pain the Authoritan inflicted, Daniyar struggled to recall Uktam's counsel. He was finding it impossible to breathe, realizing the six-tailed whip was more bearable than the spasms caused by the Authoritan's dark magic. "Lania," he managed. "Lania, *please*."

He remembered Uktam's words. "This dishonors us both," he bit out. "You have the Silver Mage before you. I would serve you, if you asked."

Lania took the Authoritan's hand. Again the pain subsided, this time the respite longer. Tears mingled with the blood that had leaked from Daniyar's eyes to mat in his ragged beard. He was helpless to prevent this humbling before the court, scorched by the Authoritan's malevolence. He prayed that an interval of time would return the strength to his limbs.

"You will address me as Khanum." Her eyes were bold and

curious, fixed on the proud lines of his face. "*How* will you serve me? You are the sworn defender of the First Oralist, I believe."

Uktam's counsel had provided him with an advantage. If he hadn't guessed before, with the pain in his skull in abatement, he could read what the Khanum wanted from him, the depths of her sensual interest in the Silver Mage as a man. The test was to make her believe that he could desire her in turn. And Uktam had given him the key.

"Khanum." He used the title to flatter her, caressing it with his voice. "I do not deny your words; my vows bind me to the First Oralist—it is for her sake you may command me. Set me to any service you wish. I plead with you for her safety."

He thought he would find the words difficult to speak. But he was learning that all things were possible on Arian's behalf, this stinging humiliation the least of what he would endure.

The Khanum's eyes gleamed with a mischief that sat oddly within the painted mask. "I would see you on your knees, then."

Nevus shoved him face-first to the ground before Daniyar could obey. For a moment he was consumed by rage, unable to think of anything save his desire to destroy the Ahdath who had taken such pleasure in his torture. His breath rasped from his chest, his powerful muscles shuddering beneath Nevus's harsh grip. Then Nevus dug a knee between his shoulder blades, setting fire to Daniyar's scars. There was no pretense in the sound of agony that fought free from his lips. He let the tears fall from his eyes, raising his face to the dais.

Struggling to remember his purpose, he whispered, "Please, Lania, I *can't*—"

The Khanum blinked. After an uncharacteristic hesitation, she clapped her hands. Two of her attendants bowed before the pearl throne. "Bathe him," she said. "It does not please me to see the Silver Mage in this state."

Daniyar remained still as basins were brought to his side by two exquisite young women from the south. His face, his chest, and his back were bathed, washing away the stink of the Pit and easing the bloodmarks of the whip. Inadvertently, he glanced at the six-tailed whip hanging over the dais; the Authoritan's laughter mocked his fear. Lania's lips tightened.

"Soothe him," she said to the attendants. The travesty of a smile edged her lips, her eyes tracing Daniyar's face. Glancing at him demurely, the Khanum's doves ran delicate hands over the ruined flesh of his back. The salve they used brought him a measure of relief. After a moment, his thoughts cleared. "Khanum," he murmured, "I would dress."

Her crimson lips stretched wide over her sharp white teeth. She waved a hand and her attendants whirled to obey her in a rustling commotion of silk.

"Not just yet, I think." She rose from her throne and descended from the dais, nodding at Nevus to bring the Silver Mage to his feet. When she reached him, she trailed one scarlet-tipped hand down the expanse of his powerfully muscled chest, exploring its dips and ridges. Her hand lingered just beneath his ribs, tracing the hard planes of his stomach.

"You please me, Daniyar," she said. She glanced up into his eyes and murmured beneath her breath, "You would please any woman who witnessed the gifts you offer." Her explorations grew more intimate, her movements concealed by the outspread wings of her robe.

He could have mistaken her voice for Arian's speaking his name, but he could never mistake her caress. When Arian touched him, he was brought to his knees by the honesty of her desire—by the trust in her eyes when she reached up to kiss him, aflame with an unexpressed love. But Arian's bright innocence and shimmering hope were missing from Lania's touch; what she offered him merely a shadow. She read the thought on his face and her sensual trespasses ceased. Her scarlet nails scored his chest, and grudgingly, he groaned.

She tilted her head back to meet his eyes, the plumed headdress swaying with the gesture. "Would you fight for me, Keeper of the Candour? Though my touch offends you?" She didn't wait for an answer. "Fight, then." She let her hand fall, climbing the dais with an imperial majesty. She spared a cold smile for the Authoritan, who had watched her actions throughout.

"The whip no longer interests me. I would have the Silver Mage dance. Nevus," she snapped at the Ahdath captain, "give the Silver Mage a sword and clear some room for him to fight." She paused, directing her next words at Daniyar, an enigmatic warning in her eyes. "He is said to be skilled with his hands, though my sister will not answer to the point."

A wave of laughter rippled through the room.

Daniyar didn't rise to the bait. He felt a sense of relief mixed with an elation he tried to tamp down. With a sword in his hand, he was on his own ground again. A chance for deliverance at last. A chance to strike at the Authoritan, here at the heart of his citadel.

But he'd mistaken Lania's intent.

She motioned to Nevus to choose a fighter to stand against him. The man who stepped forward loomed over Daniyar, twice as heavy in muscle. He wore his fair hair long, his features obscured by an overgrown beard. He brought up a double-edged sword, his eyes steady and watchful.

Daniyar extended his chained hands to Lania, searching for any sign that his life was of value to her. And regretting now that he'd missed the chance to express his response to her touch. "If you would have me fight."

A peal of steel-edged laughter escaped from Lania's throat. At her side, the Authoritan smiled. "My lord, do you mistake me for a fool? Would I unchain the Silver Mage even if I had a company of soldiers to stand against him, as I do?" Her smile hardened on her face, and any resemblance to Arian's luminous beauty was erased. "No, my lord. You wished to fight for me, so you will fight. Exactly as you are."

Daniyar tested the sword in his hands, running one hand along the blade to see if the contest was otherwise equal. The edge was sharp, the sword balanced in his hands. When he looked at Lania to signal his thanks, he sensed her apprehension.

"Your sword is well suited to your hand." There was something in the words besides her honesty, yet he couldn't deduce her meaning.

She nodded at the Ahdath. "You may begin, Spartak. Do not underestimate the Silver Mage."

Anticipation whispered through the throne room. Spartak recited the ritual words of the challenge, and Daniyar echoed them back reflexively. He touched his sword to Spartak's; they drew away from each other. With a surge of power, Daniyar raised his sword. He retreated a step and Spartak followed, silent and persistent, his own sword raised in one hand. He lunged and Daniyar ducked, missing his footing and stumbling into Spartak's path. Spartak's sword slashed down, glancing off Daniyar's left arm. Spartak brought it around, slashing Daniyar's other arm with his blade. Sweat broke out on Daniyar's forehead. He retreated again, the pain of the wounds burning through his thoughts. Spartak stalked him across the floor, pushing him back toward the wall where the whip was poised below the Authoritan's motto:

STRENGTH IS JUSTICE.

Daniyar knew he would lose this battle unless he could get the other man to speak. "What kind of warrior takes a double-edged sword into battle against an enemy who is bound?" He raised his voice. "How much protection does an Ahdath require against a prisoner?"

A rumble of anger met his words. Spartak nodded, accepting the gibe. "These are not *my* terms, Keeper of the Candour. But then, where is your Candour now?"

The anger melted into laughter. The Authoritan nodded his appreciation of the insult. A hiss of excitement filled the room as Spartak advanced again, pushing Daniyar back against the dais. Their swords met in the air, steel clashing against steel.

His tone conversational, Daniyar considered Spartak's insult. "I suppose the Candour *would* be insignificant to an illiterate."

A rustle of feminine laughter answered the words. Angry now, Spartak shoved Daniyar against the dais with a powerful thrust of his arm. "I read your death in your eyes."

Now Daniyar had what he needed. Spartak had said he'd seen Daniyar's death, but in turn the Silver Mage had read his opponent, discovered his vanity and arrogance, and understood his weakness. He called the Claim to answer it, his nearly soundless hum slowing Spartak's speed, giving him the chance to meet each new parry of his sword with an answering feint of his own. They danced as Lania demanded, and Daniyar's confidence grew.

But his enemy was not easily bested. He swung his weight around, one leg tripping the Silver Mage, forcing him back against the wall to recover his balance. Daniyar's arm brushed the hitch of the six-tailed whip even as Spartak's sword arm skimmed his throat. The crowd of courtiers gasped. The Silver Mage no longer had the space to maneuver.

Daniyar dropped his sword, backing up against the dais. Spartak raised his arm for the killing blow, a gloating pride in his eyes, the victory assumed before the battle had concluded—a hubris that served him ill. Caught by surprise, Spartak staggered back as Daniyar's chained hands flexed against the wall, unmooring the six-tailed whip. A quick flash of his wrists coiled the tails around the other man's throat, just above his armor. With a sharp yank, backed by all the strength his weakened body could muster, Daniyar collapsed the Ahdath's larynx.

Spartak dropped to his knees, sputtering for air. Daniyar kicked their swords aside, yanking the whip tighter. He flashed a look of contempt at the Authoritan. The room fell as silent as the giant warrior before him. "Is strength truly justice?" he demanded. He eased his grip on the whip.

"No!" Lania called. "Do not release him, my lord. In the Ark, we observe the rites of Qatilah. One or the other must die. Here our custom is the sword. Bury it in his chest."

Daniyar looked down at Spartak, humiliated and defenseless at his feet. *Could* this be the custom of the Ark? Had the Authoritan corrupted the High Tongue? For in the High Tongue, Qatilah meant "murderer."

He knew he'd forsaken his honor to get himself to this point, but he would not kill without purpose. He threw down the whip, Spartak gasping at his feet.

"Do you dare to defy the laws of Qatilah?" The Authoritan glided to his feet, his robes whispering in the silence. He pointed a bony finger at his captain. "Bring her," he said.

Daniyar waited, watchful and wary. Nevus disappeared, and in his absence the throne room seemed to hold its breath. He returned minutes later, thrusting Arian before him, and Daniyar drew a quick breath, joy hammering his heart. Then he realized she was dressed in transparent silk that bared her loveliness to the court in a manner he had never seen. It inflamed him—his desire warring with an anger fueled by the Ahdath's speculation.

His emotions consumed him for the span of a breath, until his attention was claimed by a sight that shattered him. Fitted about Arian's neck was a leather collar that tightened about her lower jaw and throat, leaving her face half in shadow. The exterior of the collar was studded with spikes and linked to her wrists by iron chains.

They had dressed the First Oralist of Hira as a slave, debasing her rank as Companion. Demeaning the Council of Hira. Demeaning the woman he loved.

He raised his head, his silver eyes pinning the Authoritan in place. Calmly he said, "This Ark will burn and you along with it."

The Authoritan's rigid expression didn't alter. An unholy glee lit his eyes. He raised a narrow white hand in reply, tightening it into a fist. And unimaginable pain burst through Daniyar's skull.

"No!" The curt command came from Lania. "The rules of Qatilah must be observed." She lowered the Authoritan's hand with her own, her skin whispering over his like the rustle of brittle parchment. "We will suffer no insult before our court. Pick up your sword, my lord."

Reeling from the pain, Daniyar was unable to comply.

"Nevus."

At the Authoritan's command, the captain of the Ahdath unsheathed his dagger. With a calculated flourish, he pressed its tip to Arian's heart, his fingers lingering on the soft swell of her breast. A smile stretched the tattoo on his face. "If the Authoritan should grant me this prisoner, I will tattoo a matching bloodmark on her breast, so all might know who owns her."

Propelled by a staggering rage, Daniyar threw himself at Nevus. He was brought down by half a dozen Ahdath.

The Khanum spoke again. "Bring the Silver Mage to his feet and place his sword in his hand. If he will not observe the Qatilah, let him taste the First Oralist's blood."

A pair of Ahdath dragged Spartak before the Silver Mage, forcing the Khanum's champion to his knees. Daniyar's eyes met Arian's over Spartak's head. A silent message passed between them, each offering solace to the other. Arian's eyes blazed with purpose. And seeing her undiminished fire, desire set fire to his veins in a raw conflagration of need. There was no trial the Authoritan could devise that would keep him from reaching her side.

As if she'd heard the vow from his lips, her eyes became heated and dark. She made him a promise in turn. *My love, these torments will pass. We will find each other again.*

His gaze dropped to Nevus's hand, with its cruel hold on Arian's breast, and he knew there would come a time when he would sever it from his arm. Shaking off the grip of the Ahdath, he scowled at Lania on the dais. "You permit this offense against the First Oralist? With your insistence on protocol? I thought better of you, Khanum."

Now he brought the full force of his attraction to bear, using the thrall he suspected he cast over Lania's thoughts. The Claim hummed between them, turbulent and bold, urging her to remember herself as a girl stolen from her home, to be ravaged by Talisman commanders. The strength in her voice faltered. Her eyes locked on Daniyar's, she jerked Arian free of Nevus.

Satisfied, Daniyar raised his sword. He murmured a prayer of the people of Khorasan. *"From the One we come, to the One we return."*

He plunged the sword into Spartak's chest, stepping clear of the path of the blood spray.

"Prepare the bloodbasin." The Authoritan's command didn't penetrate the reality of what Daniyar had just done. What he *would* do, night after night, to purchase Arian's life. He didn't have time to upbraid himself for his choice; a strange white foam began to bubble at the corners of Spartak's mouth. His breath rattled from his body on a gasp, his limbs twitching in their armor. The bloodbasin shattered at the first touch of his blood.

Daniyar had driven the sword tip-first into Spartak's body. Aghast, he stared up at Lania.

A smile vanished from her lips so swiftly, he wasn't certain he had seen it. In her weakness for him, she had meant to confer an advantage.

Your sword is well suited to your hand.

The tip of the blade was poisoned.

10

LARISA AND ELENA CLIMBED A TOWERING RED DUNE, FEELING THE SAND shift beneath their feet. Shapes loomed out of the darkness, their edges limned by the light cast down by thickly tangled stars. The strange shapes shifted against the patterns of the desert as if they crested gold-flamed waves.

To the north, a giant nothingness claimed the horizon, a vast black pit whose farthest edge was outlined by a wraithlike blue, starlight reflected in a surface that shimmered like a huge silver mirror. It was an improbable note of beauty against the bleak walls of the prison.

Both women had covered their faces to protect themselves from the grit of blowing sand. Now they lowered their scarves to speak.

"What are they?" Larisa asked. "Some kind of weapon?"

"Ships of the old world, run aground some time before the wars of the Far Range."

"Ships? Then that blue—"

"It was once a lake. Ruined by the wars. What do you think he does down there?"

Elena brought a spyglass to her eye and scanned the rusted hulks of the ships. As light skittered over the helm of one, she caught a trace of movement against the night, a black shadow that darted between the keels. A circular light flashed against the bulkhead of a ship. A tangle of dead vines ran down one side, and rusting underneath it was a baffling set of runes.

"It's Russe," Elena told her sister. "They used to name these ships."

Larisa looked at her curiously. "How do you know this?"

"It took months of preparation to break you out of Jaslyk. The Crimson Watch was loose in its talk." She frowned as the shadow dipped under the hulk of another ship. "I should be down there, not him. I know the sands of the Kyzylkum better than he ever will."

"You don't know that," Larisa answered. She was weary of defending a man she barely knew, a man she relied on only because the Silver Mage had used his gifts at the Registan to assure her Illarion could be trusted. "*We* don't know that," she amended. "We don't know who he is or where he came from, or whose purpose he serves."

The gritty fall of sand warned her they were not alone. Illarion had returned. He held out a canteen, encouraging the sisters to drink. Larisa took it from him with thanks. Elena turned away, striking a timbaku root, sheltering its burning end with her palm.

"It was right where you said it would be—stowed in the hold of the ship closest to the lake. They haven't discovered your cache."

Ignoring his words, Elena drew smoke into her lungs. She had yet to speak a word to Illarion on their journey, communicating solely with her sister. The peppery scent of timbaku wafted over the dunes, too remote from Jaslyk to betray them.

The sisters made an exchange, the canteen for the roll of timbaku. Just as Elena had done, Larisa sheltered the tip of the roll from giving away their position.

"Do you smoke?" Larisa asked Illarion.

"No. You shouldn't either. Timbaku is a poison. It just kills you slowly."

He waited for Elena to pass him the canteen, though she looked as if she had no intention of ever considering his needs. Larisa prodded her sister. "Elena, I'm sure the captain would like to ease his thirst."

Not bothering to look at him, Elena held out the canteen. She held herself still as he brushed her hand in the exchange. He drank with evident thirst, then offered it back to Elena.

"Thank you, Anya," he murmured.

She glared at him. He knew her name was Elena—he was taunting her with a reminder of their first encounter. She demanded the roll from Larisa and took another puff.

"You will ruin your beauty," he warned her.

"You said I have no beauty to ruin."

"True," he agreed with a smile.

Larisa watched them, disquieted. The tension between her sister and the Ahdath augured uncertainty for their attempt to rescue Sinnia, now at Jaslyk ten days. But she needed them both if their plan was to succeed—a paradox she'd have to reconcile.

Even if Elena and Illarion were in accord, the rescue could still go awry. She knew from her own experience that the Technologist would have been summoned, and if that had happened, Sinnia would be in no position to assist them. If she'd had the Claim at her disposal, she would already have freed herself.

"Will you present us as your captives?" Larisa asked Illarion. "Will you say you've brought the daughters of Salikh for the Technologist's trials?"

"No." With a casual movement of his hand, Illarion flicked the timbaku from between Elena's fingers and ground it out beneath his boot. "I'm known as Araxcin's second. They'd know I wouldn't be escorting prisoners on my own—there'd be a full patrol with me. We should go under cover of night, if Anya is certain of the route. We can't afford a mistake."

"Worry for yourself, Ahdath. Whether you return from Jaslyk is of no importance to me." She spoke to her sister, impatience rising in her voice. "I won't show him the passages. We must protect the resistance at all costs, and I won't risk the Basmachi on the word of an Ahdath who survived the fall of the Registan. I doubt he was even there."

Derision colored her voice; Illarion stiffened at the imputation of cowardice. He turned to Larisa. "I don't need you to guide me in. I'll say I was sent by Araxcin to assess Jaslyk's security after the attack on the Registan."

"Impregnability, not security." But Elena wasn't speaking to him. The words were prodded from some distant memory. She brooded over the sight of the prison, its black walls rising like a cliff against the night. Here there were no traceries of stone or iron, no glazed tiles or patterned bricks. No vegetation grew along the high stone walls, no creepers abloom with desert flowers. Jaslyk was a place whose ugliness couldn't be borne, a place of unremitting death. And she knew each watchtower, each guard, each passage the Basmachi had tunneled underground like others remembered a lover's face. The memory of it was suffocating.

They discussed the plan once more. Finally Illarion said, "Let's go."

But as they picked their way down the dune, he was left in no doubt that it was Elena who was in charge.

11

Sinnia no longer needed the restraints. Her limbs were filled with a wondrous languor, and the dark skin she prized was outlined with radiant flares of gold. Her arms were weightless. She was floating above the world, buoyed on a wave of inaudible sound.

She smiled at the man in the gas mask, trailing her fingers along the tray of needles. The floor of her cell was crimson and gold, colors and patterns bobbing along the Sea of Reeds. Her hands were filled with delicate spiny shells. She flung them to the shore with a smile.

"Please," she said to the man in the gas mask. "It's wearing off. I need more."

A thunderous sound filled her ears. It was Salikh and the others banging against their cell doors. Salikh's oddly insistent murmurs whispered through Sinnia's mind, shattering the needle's delights. She knew the others were jealous. They craved the white needle as she did—they'd do anything to steal the tall man's attention, but she was the prisoner of choice.

Her full lips pouted. She was—what was she, again?—the words seemed difficult to recall. A woman of the Negus. A Companion of a stronghold on the banks of the High Road. She wore a pretty silk dress and—intricate bands on her arms. She tossed her head. It didn't matter. Why should any of it matter when she was black and gold and weightless? She would soon be cast upon a sea of languid bliss. If she could ignore Salikh's imperceptible cautions in her mind.

"The needle," she begged again. "Give me the white needle."

The tall man in the mask moved his head from side to side. He had three heads, each equally beautiful. He stroked a gloved hand down Sinnia's arm, setting her on fire. When he grasped her upper arms, the tiny barbs on the palms of his gloves felt good. They scored a path on the place on her arms that had lately come to feel bare. Scarlet drops were added to the pattern of black and gold that engulfed Sinnia in an airless cocoon. Her dazzling smile indicated her sense of transcendence. But was it the white needle? Or did some other power soothe her senses? A power that was inexplicably familiar, as though rooted deep in her soul. She could feel it flickering before her—she needed to reach for its promise, knew it offered her salvation.

"More," she said. "Please, more."

A new sound reached her ears—not the clamor of the other prisoners. Nor was it Salikh shouting strange names at her, as he did with such persistence.

"Companion, remember yourself. Remember Hira! Remember who you are!"

It was the horrible sound, the sound that intruded on her daydreams: the sputtering hiss of the hose. The tray of needles was gone, replaced by the canister she had come to know with horror. She returned to her body with a thump. She gazed at the tall man in confusion. Now there were other men with him. Three men instead of three heads.

"What's this?" she asked. "What have you done with the needle?"

A hollow voice echoed through the gas mask. "This is a test," it said. "The white needle amplifies the effects of the gas. Some die on its first application; others last for months. We are attempting to accelerate its effects."

"No," Sinnia whispered. "Give me the white needle. Can't you see that I need it?"

"Oh, yes, I can see." She heard a sickening anticipation in the eerie throb of the tall man's voice. "But this is my first experiment on a Companion of Hira. I want you to live through the night."

12

An inhuman scream pierced the walls. It rebounded through the prison's courtyard, followed by a flurry of activity and noise. It sounded like an animal, twisted and broken in the savage rites of death. But Elena knew the scream—she'd heard it from her own throat, as a source of infinite horror, and also from Larisa, a sound that had almost killed her.

The Technologist had come.

The scream sounded again. It was a woman's scream; it could have been one of the followers of the Usul Jade.

But in her heart, Elena knew it wasn't. She *knew* it was the Companion of Hira, the woman she'd never met—a woman she was risking their lives for. All at Larisa's bidding, while Illarion paced like a hungry jackal at their side.

"What's that noise?"

Elena looked at him with hatred in her heart. "That noise is *you* and everything you stand for. The Ahdath, the Crimson Watch. Torturers who now inflict their savagery on a Companion of Hira."

Illarion stared back at her, his clever face unreadable.

"Go," she muttered. "The lights will sweep from the tower in thirty seconds. If we run out of time, you must divert their attention at the door."

"I know what I'm doing, Anya. Whether you believe it or not."

Larisa and Elena waited in the shadows as Illarion crossed Jaslyk's courtyard. Torches flared at the gate, men's voices ringing out. Illarion showed them something from his pack. A pass? A document? Elena couldn't guess.

"Now."

She tugged at her sister's hand, guiding her through the barricades in the courtyard, the secret hiding places, the small patches of cover, ducking out of the path of the lights. Dogs began to howl in the distance. A patrol shifted on the perimeter, doubling back to the gate. The Salikh sisters moved forward, darting ahead under the great weight of the ominously pooling shadows.

The courtyard was as vast as the prison itself. Neither sister could look at its walls with anything other than despair. How many members of the resistance had been broken at Jaslyk? Drug-addled and pain-ridden, they had told the Crimson Watch everything they knew before they had died, painfully, pitilessly rendered from themselves. Based on their confessions, new prisoners had been captured, Basmachi hunted through the Hazing, and still there was no shortage of screams to shatter the sightless eyes that watched over Jaslyk.

One day she'd burn the prison down.

But not this night. She had no fighters or armory at her disposal. All she had was Larisa, and she could see Larisa was faltering, overcome by the memory of her time at Jaslyk. Both sisters had been drugged, raped, and tortured; both had suffered the full range of the Technologist's experiments. Both had lost their ability to hear the Claim. Though the loss of it had once been unbearable, for Larisa's sake, she had pretended to a strength she didn't possess.

"Don't think of it, Larisa."

Another high-pitched scream scraped against the walls, spurring Elena on. The sisters found their way to the door that fronted the basin of the lake. There were dogs at the door, accompanied by guards. They had picked up the sisters' scent, and now they began to howl.

"Hurry."

Behind the outer rings of its walls, Jaslyk was composed of irregular shapes designed to maximize the interior space, while giving guards and staff the ability to transition easily between the courtyard and the prison blocks. This allowed the Crimson Watch greater vigilance. It also reduced the possibility of escape. Elena and Ruslan's mission to rescue Larisa, a year ago, was the last time a prisoner had left Jaslyk alive.

But the diamond-shaped construction of the prison also concealed a weakness. The Basmachi had been able to dig tunnels beneath the transition areas, and the Crimson Watch couldn't cover them all, particularly as more and more men were being summoned to the Wall.

The sisters skirted the barricades that had been erected over Larisa's escape route.

It was meant as a feint, of course. Elena pressed her sister's hand, holding a finger to her lips. She had no intention of using the same tunnel. One of the dogs barked, closer than she expected. She stumbled against the barricade. Her hand pulled something from the pack she carried—a scented powder that she flung over the risers. The dogs began a frantic whining. She pulled Larisa around a corner. "Let *them* cover their ears for once."

She led Larisa along the south wall, away from the patrol. As they'd planned, the torches along the southern perimeter had been redirected to the gate, where Illarion engaged the guards. It was the first sign to suggest that perhaps Illarion could be trusted.

Feeling her way along the wall, Elena stopped when she came to the stone she had etched with Basmachi signals. She'd imprinted each of the prison blocks with a series of directions, distinguishing the Technologist's Wing from the others. She picked out the command center at the intersection of the blocks, a heavily guarded nexus she knew they needed to avoid.

"It's here."

Elena dropped to her knees, running her hands along the stone base of the wall. She looked over her shoulder at Larisa. "What's our mission here?"

She knew the answer; she was making sure Larisa understood the cost of what they were leaving undone: their friends in the resistance left behind to face the Technologist.

Larisa hesitated. Then she confirmed her choice. "The Companion of Hira. Her safety is paramount now."

Elena shifted a stone. A narrow and airless passageway opened beneath it. She'd heard a dozen rumors about the fall of the Registan, yet she still didn't know which of the rumors were true. "Why? Because you swore an oath to the Silver Mage? Did his comeliness bewitch you?" This had been rumored as well.

Larisa slid into the tunnel first, Elena following behind, careful to shelter her ribs. She'd smoked timbaku to dull the pain inflicted by the Ahdath's blade in Marakand, something she'd withheld from Illarion. She wasn't in the habit of confessing weakness, especially to an Ahdath. Once they reached the corridors of Jaslyk, her injury would be the least of her concerns.

"Don't insult me," Larisa answered. "You know what I think of men. I swore my oath to the First Oralist. And I would do it again." She turned to face Elena suddenly, a cold and deadly warning in her eyes. "We have one purpose, Elena, *one*. And that is to free our sisters, a mission the First Oralist shares. Do you understand me?"

Elena nodded, satisfied that Larisa hadn't led them on a fool's mission. Her sister was still committed to their cause.

They moved along the tunnel, swallowed by the dark.

13

ILLARION WAS ESCORTED TO THE COMMAND CENTER BY THE WARDEN OF Jaslyk, a stooped-over man whose wisps of white hair covered his scalp like a crown. The Warden's vision was distorted by a pair of goggles. From behind the goggles, his blue eyes scanned the room. He dressed in a long white smock, cinched at the waist by a thick metallic belt sectioned into chambers. As a functionary, he wore no crimson: he wasn't a member of the Ahdath.

Illarion scanned the command center. It was staffed by eight men, all members of the Crimson Watch, each with an area of jurisdiction patrolled with relentless regularity. Each man was junior to Illarion in the Ahdath's hierarchy, and each accorded him the necessary signs of respect. He briefed them on the fall of the Registan, concluding by asking, "Could it have been orchestrated by prisoners held here?"

"There have been no escapes and no communications, as far as we are aware. But a prisoner has just arrived from Marakand. Marat can tell you more." The Warden nodded at the man responsible for the Technologist's activities.

The soldier named Marat saluted Illarion. "Captain Illarion. Or are you Commander of the Wall now?"

"No. The Authoritan sends Commander Nevus from Black Aura to take command. We expect him any day."

The men in the room straightened at the mention of Nevus's name. It was a name they feared more than Araxcin's.

"He won't be coming here," Illarion clarified. "Unless he has some reason to suspect your prisoner's involvement in the attack on the Registan."

Marat considered this. "Perhaps he does. She was taken to the Technologist on arrival. She's due to be moved to the Plague Wing tomorrow."

Illarion straightened. He placed his hand on the pommel of his sword. "When? If she's who I think she is, she will need to be interrogated."

But the men in the command center had their own sources, and another man spoke up. "She's not the First Oralist. The First Oralist and the Silver Mage were captured some days ago in Black Aura. The Authoritan has them now."

"I know that," Illarion barked. "But your prisoner may be a Companion of Hira. She must have had some knowledge of the attack."

"She is," the Warden conceded. "I thought as much—two members of the Council of Hira would not make their way behind the Wall without a purpose. If there's anything to know, the Technologist will have the answers for you tonight." He nodded at a heavy-lidded pewter bowl on the table behind him.

"Why tonight?"

The Warden lifted the lid of the bowl. "The Companion of Hira took longer to break than one of the Basmachi. But once we removed her circlets, she fell to the persuasion of the needle."

He did not touch the objects in the bowl, even though he wore gloves. Illarion had no such qualms. He gathered the golden circlets in his hands. He'd seen them once before, on the arms of the First Oralist. This pair must be Sinnia's. "A pretty prize to take to the Wall."

The Warden grabbed his arm. "The Technologist hasn't finished with them."

Illarion shook off the Warden's hand. His voice was low and dangerous. "I will present them at the Wall. If you wish otherwise, you may explain your wishes to Commander Nevus."

The guards in the room glanced at one another. No one intervened.

His face pale with alarm, the Warden cleared his throat. "What is it you wish?"

"I wish to be taken to the prisoner. You, man." He snapped at Marat. "You will show me the way." He slipped the circlets beneath his breastplate, taking the measure of the Crimson Watch. At last his gaze came to rest on the slack-mouthed Warden. "You may accompany us."

"The Technologist is in the midst of an experiment. You cannot enter the room."

Sinnia's earsplitting scream sounded through Jaslyk again.

"I'm well aware." He jerked another object off the table behind the Warden. A mask with goggles larger than the Warden's own. He tossed a second mask at Marat.

"You're coming with me. Before her mind collapses, I want to know what she knows."

14

DANIYAR RESTED HIS HEAD AGAINST THE RIM OF THE GREEN-MARBLED tub. He was soaking in a bath prepared for him by two of the loveliest women he'd ever seen, slaves from the northernmost regions of the Transcasp, their skin translucent, their hair and eyes golden, their luxurious flesh softly rounded. They murmured to each other in dove-soft voices, and he recognized their tongue as the ancient tongue of the people of Russe.

His bath was scented with rose petals and a luminous gold powder that worked its way into the tissue of his deepest scars, easing his pain and healing his damaged skin. His forearms were wrapped in a soft leather binding, protecting his wounds from the water.

The Khanum's maidservants hovered on either side of the tub, passing him lotions and oils, offering to scrub him from head to toe. He dismissed them with a frown, yet the instant they left, he missed their raillery, their utter absence of malice when everything else the Ark had to offer promised him unrelenting pain. And if he was honest with himself, the gentle feminine interest expressed by the doves' attentions was a respite he welcomed as a man pushed too hard and too long by his trials.

He was forced to fight in the rites of the Qatilah, sometimes with a sword, sometimes with a club, oftimes bare-handed, falling back on his limited abilities with the Claim. Though each night's trial concluded in hard-fought victory, his battered and bloody body was dragged back to his cell, his limbs aching from the effort it had taken him to resist, his thoughts inevitably darkened by the killing of so many men.

To be shifted from the Pit to Lania's luxurious apartments was a contrast that weakened his resolve, testing the extent of his honor. He held fast to one thought in his mind—if he responded to Lania's overtures, perhaps he might lure her to his side. If he could make her believe he was drawn in by her allure or her resemblance to Arian, an opportunity might arise: a chance to escape the Ark with Arian at his side.

He was half-dressed when Lania called him. Moving less stiffly now, he let her pull him down beside her onto a chaise cushioned in silk. Her feline eyes grew heated as she viewed his state of undress. She leaned close to him, resting a hand on the sculpted planes of his chest. "Another man would not deny himself the pleasures my courtiers offer."

He met her gaze, his voice courteous but firm. "We've discussed this," he said. "These girls from the north of the Transcasp are slaves. They're compelled to your wishes by their servitude. I am the Guardian of Candour. I have never touched a woman against her will."

Lania's laughter sounded, low and quiet. When she was alone with him like this, she relinquished the adornments of the Khanum. She wore a plain silk dress and had left her face unpainted, her gold-flecked eyes soft and clear. She looked younger and more vulnerable, freeing the silk of her hair with a graceful movement of her arms. A traitorous thought slipped into his mind. He imagined her slender arms gilded by Arian's circlets. Bound though he was to Arian, it was Lania who held his attention at this moment. Indeed, she looked so much like Arian, defenseless and unafraid, that his yearning and sense of loss expanded. Here was a woman who would grant him what he wanted, with a warmth he could take if he wished. She would gladly end the self-denial he'd chosen to endure too long, a temptation he'd thought himself immune to.

"You underrate yourself, my lord," she answered him. "You would not need to compel my doves—they would attend to you gladly." She moved from the chaise to kneel behind him. When he couldn't see her face, she added, "As would I, if you asked."

Her hand came to rest upon his bare shoulder, moving to the base of his throat. The air between them was fraught. He knew she could feel the racing of his pulse.

"Am I not teaching you?" she urged him. "Do I not gift you with the Claim and share with you the secrets of the Authoritan? Do I not heal your wounds with the mysteries I know?"

Daniyar tipped back his head. Their eyes met in a dangerously slow seduction. His glance raked over the unpainted curves of her mouth. He caught a handful of her hair in his hand and used it to tug her closer. An answering spark lit her eyes.

"The Qatilah is rigorous," he murmured against her lips. She kissed him, and he let her feel his response, heat stealing through his blood.

"The Authoritan insists on it," she said when she had the chance. "He is jealous of my . . . interest . . . in you. He takes his revenge through the Qatilah."

"And you, Lania? Do you seek to punish me as well?"

She slid onto his lap in a whisper of silk, fastening her arms around his neck. "Does this feel like punishment?" she asked.

He kissed her again, the kisses slow and rough, her rich curves pressed against the hard lines of his body, appreciating anew how different she was from Arian—the pampered softness of her flesh distinct from Arian's strength, the calculation behind her response instead of Arian's honesty. He pushed the thought of Arian away and kissed Lania more deeply, grasping her head with his hand. When she was pliant in his arms, he murmured the question on his mind—the question he'd waited to ask.

"Your attentions to me are not as marked at the Qatilah. Do you fear the loyalty of the men who bring me here?"

Surprised but too languid to stir, she answered, "No, these men serve only me. Just as the doves are mine."

"Then what *do* you fear? If the Authoritan does not claim you as his own, what is it that he wants?"

Irritation crept into her voice. "What does any man want? Territory."

He traced his hand over the silk of her dress, gently squeezing. "Is this not territory enough? As it would be for me."

Suspicious now, she asked, "Do you play with me, Daniyar? Or do you offer the truth?"

He sensed the uncertainty behind her words—her longing for his regard, and a deeper yearning yet to take him for herself. But he didn't know if it was the man she wanted or the legend of the Silver Mage. Or whether she was more damaged than he knew, and she sought to strike at Arian where she knew it would hurt her most. Because unlike Arian, when Lania was in his arms, she resisted the chance to surrender. Beneath the luxurious entreaty of her kisses, she maintained a conspicuous control.

"You are an Augur, Lania." He used her name to mitigate her mistrust, urging her to believe he respected her sorcerous gifts. "How could I hide the truth from you?"

Suddenly alight, she searched his face for confirmation. "Would you have me think you have given Arian up in the face of this tri-fling temptation?"

He took her hand and dragged it down his body, forcing her to acknowledge the evidence of his desire. "Do not disparage your-self. And do not think me a fool unable to see who you are."

For a moment there was silence as Lania caressed him, push-ing him back against the chaise. She leaned over to whisper in his ear, her artful tongue flickering inside. "I think you are a man who does not forsake his bonds, though why you have chosen Arian when she is beholden to Hira, I cannot understand. What power does she possess that you practice this self-denial?" Her eyes be-came hazy and slumberous, occupied by the work of her hands. "Why beg for crumbs from her table when I offer the banquet en-tire?"

Her clever, caressing hands nearly stole his resolve—it took him a moment to remember his purpose in this room. He shifted her off his lap on the pretext of stretching his back.

"I will fight for you," he vowed. "But not for the pleasure of the Authoritan. Think of how he diminishes you, while I would be eager to serve you. If I am to stand at your side, why spend my strength at the Ark?" He dropped his voice to its lowest register, growling the words in her ear. "Don't you wish me to claim the Wall?"

Lania drew away, as if something in his eyes made it impossible for her to hold his gaze.

He pulled her back, curling a hand around her neck, letting her feel the potency of his desire. She needed to believe he would fight at her side, unconquerable in his strength—her partner in all things.

"I see a man at the Wall," she answered. "And that man is not the Authoritan. More than that, I cannot make out." Her voice grew cool. "There is a woman at his side . . . a woman who commands the Wall."

But Lania wasn't certain, and Daniyar read the truth of this as well. "The woman must be you."

"She is dark and fights like a man."

She misread his frown, drawing away to stare out the window. Daniyar followed her, conscious of his state of undress. He needed to press her now—or all he'd risked to persuade her would be lost, his commitment to Arian forfeit.

"The man at the Wall *could* be me—it feels as though it should be."

She touched her forehead to his. Daniyar misjudged the action, hurrying into speech.

"To stand at the Wall at your side, I would need the magic of the Bloodprint. Every moment hastens it away. Flee Black Aura with me. Set me on the Black Khan's trail."

Lania went still, in no doubt now of his intentions. With an angry grimace of dismissal, she freed herself from his embrace, spearing a quick glance at the upper galleries of the room, screened by lattices of stone. "I cannot betray the Authoritan. Not after everything he's sacrificed for me. Besides which, the Bloodprint would not serve you. Why do you imagine the Authoritan was willing to trade it away? He was High Priest of the Bloodless. He studied it so deeply he twisted its meaning beyond recognition. He has mastery over the Claim. You cannot use it against him."

But Daniyar didn't believe this. Why else would Arian have been subjected to the humiliation of a slave-collar? The Authoritan feared the powers of the First Oralist of the Claim. Which meant that the Claim could still be used against him. He pressed her for an explanation. "Then why did you summon Arian here, if not to make use of her gifts?"

"I do not require Arian to teach me what she once learned from me," Lania snapped. "I asked her to tell me of Hira." She studied him, sensing something of his reaction to her use of Arian's name—the longing that he was never completely able to suppress.

"Of Hira? Why?"

"It was the seat of my childhood. It was everything I aspired to. Can you not fathom that I have missed the sisterhood of the Companions?"

Daniyar schooled his thoughts. She was lying, an undercurrent of hate feeding the words. And though he couldn't think why, there might be a way to use it. "Come to Hira, then," he said. "Arian would aid you in any way you wished. If you help her against the Talisman, she will stand at the Wall by your side."

"That is *not* what I have Augured. There is one man, one woman at the Wall. And I know I shall never leave Black Aura." She said this without self-pity.

She left him and he knew he'd lost her. When she turned back to face him, she was robed in the premeditated power of the Authoritan's consort again, his betrayal of Arian for naught.

"Are you imagining I would cede command of the Wall when I labored all my life to secure it? Can you possibly believe I would swear my fealty to yet *another* man, dependent on his intercession to save me from being ravaged by his soldiers?" She spat her next words at him. "Black Aura is mine; these are *my* men, *my* slaves, *my* prisoners. You will take your place among them. Or not, as you decide." She let the words burn through him.

Daniyar bowed his head. He had moved too soon and lost.

She called her guards to take him to his cell, speaking with perfect indifference. "You will fight in the Qatilah tonight. I will send Arian to watch you."

Daniyar risked another question, knowing he had nothing to

lose. "What of my blood, Lania? Why do you collect it for the Authoritan? What use does he make of it?"

She moved to stand before him, raising her hand to his chin to tilt down his head. She gazed into his eyes, focusing her attention on the silver pinpoints. "Yes," she murmured. "You have the birthright of the Silver Mage, just as the Black Khan shares the mark of the Dark Mage. I have often wondered how a Mage is chosen and marked. Your eyes give your birthright away. They are remarkable. They gift you with your powers. They keep you alive in the Qatilah."

But that was only part of it, and Daniyar knew better than to share with her the rest. How he too had some small knowledge of the Claim to aid him in unobtrusive ways.

She smiled a secret smile suggesting she already knew. "Your blood is magic," she said to Daniyar. "And *you* are magic, my lord."

Though he needed to know how his blood was usurped, she told him nothing else.

How beautiful and lost she was, he thought.

As he had nearly lost himself.

15

THE TECHNOLOGIST EXAMINED THE SUBJECT ON THE TABLE. SHE HAD passed out, her exquisitely dark limbs lying limp. Some of his men had asked to use her, but she was not a prize to be squandered on the base desires of rabble.

There was something about this Companion.

Though she craved the needle, the gas affected her differently than it did the others. When he gave her a respite, she thrashed with all her strength against her restraints, her liquid-dark eyes sharp with rage. She became clearer, more powerful, more certain of who she was. And though she couldn't speak, her eyes promised him a savage revenge.

It was intriguing. It was *exciting*.

He bent over her, his barbed fingers tracing the thin white circles the mask had outlined on her tautened flesh. She was nothing like the women of the Tilla Kari, cosseted and indulged. Her limbs were lean and muscular, capable and well formed. A delicious sense of possibility curled through his awareness. What use could he make of this creature? How could he bend her to his will? How long would it take to wrench the beauty of the Claim from her throat?

He pressed his thumbs against her larynx. How easy it would be to silence her for good. He very much wanted to, but there was more to learn from the gifts of this Companion from the Negus. To her credit, between her screams she'd tried to calm herself by murmuring verses of the Claim. He'd increased the volume of the gas, and her voice had fallen silent, but it still preserved the strength the Companion contained within.

But perhaps this *was* too much too soon. He wanted to see everything the gas could achieve. He wanted her to know what she was losing.

He wanted to take from her, but he also wanted her to surrender everything she had to him. Everything she *was,* this remarkable, undamaged creature. He felt intoxicated by the thought.

He reached behind him for the tray, collecting an instrument he'd designed especially for members of the Salikhate. A generation ago, this had been the name taken by Salikh's compatriots. The Basmachi were a far cry from what the Salikhate had once been, illiterate and ill schooled in the Claim. This Companion was different. He could feel the Claim shivering through her, its flavor musky and sweet. A frisson of pleasure spiraled through his body.

How excellent it had been to have both Salikh's daughters under his care. How much he missed them now! Larisa he'd taken more easily than planned, but Elena—ah, Elena had resisted with a rare and beautiful fire. The memory of her impotent fury warmed his thoughts, just as her loss was like a winter of the soul.

But now he had another young woman under his care, a woman from the lands of the Negus, a Companion such as he'd never known, and he felt reborn, fire lighting his blood. If he could keep the Companion alive, and if the Khanum would send the First Oralist to Jaslyk, he would be able to use them against each other, just as he had used the sisters Salikh.

The Technologist held a peculiar double-pronged instrument up to the light in the room. His men shifted a step or two away from him—they knew the Malleus would reduce the Companion to a frothing mess of blood. They knew what the Technologist was capable of.

This Companion would soon be at his mercy. He bent closer to Sinnia's head and applied the curved blades of the Malleus to her ear.

"You will learn," he whispered.

16

THE HOWLS OF THE DOGS HAD SUBSIDED, THOUGH ELENA COULD HAVE wished now for their barking to cover the sound of their bodies wriggling through the tunnel. The space was narrower than she remembered, or perhaps it was only that she was better fed, fitter, and stronger than the last time she'd used the tunnel for safe passage.

Larisa found the end of the tunnel, pulling her sister up and out into the darkness of the prison block's silent wing. The sisters worked without light, feeling their way along the walls. There would be a pair of guards at the end of the wing, but the guards would have grown lax in the absence of resistance. They knew the inmates the wing housed were too drugged to be capable of rebellion. Elena held her bow in her hands, a knife strapped to her leg. She anticipated using both. She passed ahead of her sister, using a hand signal to mark Larisa's palm. The tunnel had led them a level or two below the place the screams originated from. Those screams had fallen silent now, and both women feared the reason for it. They had to find the stairs, quickly.

Elena brushed by the window of a cell. A prisoner within murmured at her. It was too dark for him to see her, but somehow he'd sensed her presence. His calls became more insistent, drawing the attention of the Ahdath.

Cursing to herself, Elena crossed to the ward with Larisa, and waited for the Ahdath to approach the cell. Both drew their bows, but only one man came. The sisters exchanged another signal. Larisa slid to the head of the ward while Elena put away her bow to use her knife. When the Ahdath rattled the door of the prisoner's cell, Elena slipped up behind him and slit his throat. Before his body could fall, Larisa had loosed her arrow on the guard at the head of the ward.

A prisoner's face showed at the bars of the cell. "Free me," he begged.

A grim anger invaded Elena's thoughts at the pitiless nature of her choices. She shook her head. "Not yet. Wait and be quiet."

He sobbed to himself as they left him.

Pain struck her hard and deep. Were she here for any other reason, she would not have been able to bear leaving the prisoner behind.

This Companion had best be worth it.

Elena slipped after her sister, helping her drag the Ahdath to join his friend. Another signal passed between the sisters to indicate the passage to the stairs. They were careful with the heavy door, climbing the stairs in the dark.

They had reached the prison's upper level, and now they could see the torches lit at the watchtowers. The ward was periodically swept with minzars, modified starscopes angled to face the upper levels of Jaslyk. They were stationed along the ramparts that linked the towers. This was the Technologist's Wing. Sinnia's screams had come from here. Elena's thoughts flew to the Companion.

You must bear this. You must *survive until we reach you. Else I risked my sister for nothing.*

The guard was doubled on this ward, two members of the Crimson Watch positioned at either end. Two more were guards stationed outside a door in the center of the ward. The Salikh sisters crouched low, inching their way along the wall. If the guards on either end of the ward turned, the sisters would be caught in a cross fire. They needed to take the guards by surprise.

They never spoke of their fears or their memories of Jaslyk, but each action they took now was weighted with their determination to protect each other from the consequences of failure. The two women were at their strongest, single-minded with purpose. They had no choice: as leaders of the resistance and as sisters bound to each other's survival, they couldn't afford self-doubt.

Larisa and Elena separated. Each moved in a different direction, their bows strung. They waited a heartbeat for the minzars to sweep the ward, then came to their feet and whistled. The guards at both ends turned. Two pairs of arrows found the weak spots in their armor. But they couldn't catch the men at the door, who wheeled and drew their swords. The sisters were soon engaged in close combat, and they fought as they always did, back to back, using back-alley tricks against the size and strength of their opponents, utterly without fear.

Elena grunted as a sword thrust nearly slashed her ribs. Larisa took her weight, flashing a sharp knife up and under Elena's arm, stabbing the guard in the chest. Elena whirled around, taking her sister's place.

The minzars swept the ward again, catching the fierce and soundless tussle. Horns rose in warning. Two more men spilled from the inside of the cell guarded by the Crimson Watch, pressing the sisters back. It was Larisa's turn to cry out. She dropped her knife as her sword arm was slashed. Elena stabbed her blade through the assailant's eye. They were losing ground, losing strength. The Ahdath forced them back toward the stairs.

A loud metallic clang rang inside the cell.

Sinnia's scream pierced the air again—edged with something new—something bold and eerily familiar.

Prisoners came to the doors of their cells, shouting and banging at their doors, distracting the Crimson Watch. Elena tripped one man, then rolled with his momentum to stab through his armor with the full weight of her body. She lay on him for the space of a breath, wiping the sweat from her eyes. Boots stamped down an intersecting corridor, the sound drawing closer.

In the courtyard below, the dogs began to howl.

A guard grabbed Larisa by the hair, yanking back her head, his knife at her throat.

A minzar's light found her face, and the guard who'd seized Elena's knife arm staggered around, Elena struggling in his grip.

"Stop!" he shouted. The other man stilled.

"Look at her," he went on. "Look at *them*. Don't you know who they are?"

Now the ward was filled with soldiers, half a dozen members of the Watch clambering up from the level below and from the corridor that linked to another block. Larisa and Elena stood panting.

Men shouted all around them, prisoners, guards, adding to the noise coming from inside the cell—a gurgling noise that petered out.

Illarion appeared at the head of the ward, escorted by a handful of men, just as the door of Sinnia's cell was thrown open. Elena caught a glimpse of the woman on the table. She was unrestrained. Somehow she had snapped the hose attached to a dark green canister. Blood leaked from her eyes, ears, and nose, glistening and sticky against her mulberry skin.

What she'd attempted had nearly killed her, yet when she raised her head, her eyes blazed with a contemptuous conviction that said there was no man who could defeat her.

A man taller than any of the others stepped out of the room, a nightmarish mask covering his face. Elena shrank in her captor's arms, suddenly unable to breathe.

Illarion strode to meet him, and the tall man unhooked his mask with sleek and raptorial movements. His face emerged into the sharp light cast by the sweep of the minzar. Beneath the mask, his ghastly skin was waxy, his lips without blood. His colorless eyes bulged from their sockets, a disfiguring effect of the mask.

At the sharp clap of his hands, two of the guards lit torches.

The tall man bent to look first at Elena, then at Larisa. A smile spread over the cadaverous planes of his face. He clapped his hands together lightly. "How beautiful," he said with delight. "I've missed you." His natural voice rasped like the spike-edged barbs on his gloves.

Elena's sob caught in her throat.

The tall man noticed Illarion. "Captain."

"Technologist." Illarion nodded in return.

Elena's frantic eyes sought out Illarion's face. The teasing warmth he'd shown her earlier had vanished—the mask he'd worn over his purposes as a soldier of the Ahdath, as a tool of the Technologist's will. His high-planed face was set and hard. She hadn't believed she had anything left to lose—anything to hope for or believe in—yet a savage sense of betrayal pierced her thoughts, and hard on its heels, a passionate, volatile fury. She would kill him with her bare hands.

But Illarion had dismissed her without a glance, his eyes fixed on the Technologist.

"You're a man of your word," the Technologist praised him. "You delivered the sisters as promised."

Illarion nodded curtly. "It was easy enough to deceive them—they were desperate to believe."

Elena made a throttled noise in her throat, thrashing against her captors, her hands scrabbling for a blade to plunge deep into his heart.

"What beautiful misery," the Technologist said, his smile deepening to a leer.

"And now I require what you promised me in turn," the captain said. "The talisman. The one that unlocks the Plague Wing."

17

MEN, DOGS, PRISONERS SHOUTING, WEAPONS BEING SHEATHED—THERE
was so much noise in the ward and along the watchtowers that
at first Elena didn't hear it. She'd failed her sister so completely,
she couldn't fathom it. She was swamped by a wave of panic and
dread, watching the men who'd captured them now handle her
sister with careless, bestial ease. A roar of outrage broke from her
throat, climbing rapidly to hysteria.

And then beneath it, she heard the sound again, strange and
oddly familiar, a sound she remembered from childhood. It seemed
to be coming from two places at once. From a door on the other
side of the ward—she had a brief impression of wild eyes and
matted hair—but also from behind the Technologist in the room
with the shattered canister, where an instrument with curved blades
lay twisted and deformed on the floor.

It was the Malleus, a tool the Technologist used to sever the
hearing of the followers of the Usul Jade, its tiny blades burrowing
into their ears, tunneling ever deeper.

The otherworldly sound grew stronger. Larisa's head snapped up.

She was hearing it too. And like Elena, some part of her recognized the sound.

The sisters looked at each other. Larisa's hands flickered with a subtle signal; Elena's mirrored the gesture.

Kill me, Larisa said. *Kill me now, end it here.*

Elena gave her word.

The sound warned her not to do it. The sound was lyrical and clear, poetic and soft, pliant yet also urgent. As dire as their circumstances were, some of Elena's panic eased. She was able to think calmly, observing the men who had captured them. The Technologist and Illarion she marked off as dead men, but neither they nor the Crimson Watch appeared to hear the sound.

Untroubled by it, the Technologist issued an order. "Strip them and take them to the Plague Wing. It's time for me to chart their progress."

The Crimson Watch were slow to comply, the sound from the cells growing louder.

"The talisman," Illarion repeated, the words rasping in his throat.

The Technologist tried to reach something covered by his robes. He frowned when he found he couldn't. His bulging eyes moved from Illarion to the cell the captain was blocking.

"Is this your doing?" he called. "I thought the white needle had silenced you for good."

A cell door slammed behind him. No member of the Crimson Watch moved, held in thrall as a dark arm snaked around the Technologist's neck. The Technologist lurched forward a step, but was yanked back by the arm.

A beautiful, throaty voice answered. "No, you monstrosity, it's mine."

Elena found she was free, the guard who'd held her captive sinking to his knees behind her. She whirled around, scooped up her knife, and stabbed the back of his head. The movements of those who tried to fight her were sluggish and disjointed. Her blade found their unprotected necks, one powerful thrust after another. The two men who'd hurt Larisa, Elena stabbed through the heart.

Larisa grabbed her sword from the floor. The prisoner in the cell behind Illarion took hold of him by the arm. He didn't struggle in the prisoner's hold, standing firm and strong.

"Where . . . is . . . the . . . talisman?" he choked.

The Technologist watched the sisters' actions, a sneer frozen on his lips.

The wild man in the cell spoke up. He whispered to Illarion, and the Ahdath captain went still.

Sinnia's grip tightened around the Technologist's throat. "Does this one matter to you? Because I'm planning to snap his neck."

"No!" Larisa and Elena shouted together.

The horns on the wall sounded again, summoning reinforcements.

Larisa raced into Sinnia's cell. She came back with the Malleus gripped in her hand, her young face hard with rage. Elena reached for the Malleus—Larisa held it out of reach. The sisters stared at each other for a lethal, weighted moment; then slowly Elena nodded.

"No!" Illarion shouted. "Ask him where he keeps the talisman!"

Without pausing to answer him, Larisa drove the Malleus into the Technologist's brain. He slipped feebly out of Sinnia's hold, his body sagging to the ground.

Elena kicked at his robes. "It's not enough," she said. "It will never be enough."

Elena yanked out her broadsword and severed his head with a stroke. Then she advanced on Illarion, tossing her words over her shoulder.

"The Technologist was yours, Larisa, but this one belongs to me."

Illarion met her eyes, a bewildering despair in his own. "Mudjadid, please tell them."

The hands gripping his throat slid back into the cell.

Elena's sword flashed up. Illarion blocked it with his arm. She reared back and lunged again, and this time Illarion grabbed both of her arms and forced the sword from her hand. Then he pulled her close as she struggled, seeking out Larisa over Elena's shoulder.

"How *dare* you use that name?" Elena spat at him, as Larisa asked more calmly, "Where did you learn that name? Who do you call Mudjadid?"

The prisoner in the cell came to the window. The minzar swept across the ward, throwing his features into sharp relief. His blazing eyes and craggy face were obscured by the tangled growth of his beard. A moment later the light from the minzar was gone, and neither Larisa nor Elena could be certain of what they'd seen.

A mirage, a ghost of the past, a specter of a man they'd known and loved.

The oddly familiar sound thrummed through the ward again. Sinnia stepped over the Technologist's body, a transparent mist emanating from her mouth. It echoed the sound coming from the wild man in the cell. Was it a memory, or was it real? And if it was a memory, how could the Companion of Hira know it?

Elena fought her way free of Illarion's hold. "Break this door. Do it now." She was half-sobbing, half-pleading.

Letting go of her, Illarion smashed the lock with a thrust of his sword. If he'd been hobbled like the Crimson Watch, his strength was unfettered now.

The door to the cell unlocked, the prisoner within staggered out into the ward. A soft chant rose from behind the doors of the cells that lined both sides of the ward.

"*Mudjadid. Mudjadid. Mudjadid Salikh.*"

The wild man stared at Elena and Larisa, tears sliding into his beard, the Claim abating in his throat. It had done its work. It had called them here, and it had unshackled the gifts of the Companion of Hira, allowing her to acknowledge him as a teacher of the Claim and to accept his direction of its use. He'd subverted the workings of the needle to Sinnia's great advantage. An advantage he'd whispered ceaselessly in her mind, expanding her knowledge of the Claim.

Illarion sank to one knee, his fair hair falling around his face. A palsy gripped the wild man's hand. It shook as he raised it to Illarion's hair. Illarion grasped it in his own and kissed the jade ring the man still wore on his finger.

Larisa gasped. "Who are you?" she asked in a strangled voice.

Sinnia stared at the sisters in disbelief. "Don't you recognize your father?"

She reached for the old man, fastening her arms around his neck, ignoring the soldier at his feet. "Thank you, Mudjadid. Thank you for saving me."

His thin frame trembled in her grasp, but he raised his head to meet Sinnia's radiant eyes. "You freed yourself, sahabiya, with your mastery over the Claim."

18

LARISA TOOK HER FATHER IN HER ARMS, UNABLE TO COME TO TERMS with his rebirth. For so long she and Elena had believed that their father had met his death at the Authoritan's hands. Searching his haggard face, she knew that his survival had been purchased at an inordinate cost. The far-seeing eyes were the same—kind and inspirited with belief—but something vital was missing. Perhaps that same element that had hardened inside Larisa after her detention at Jaslyk. Perhaps her father was looking at his daughters and telling himself the same thing.

I don't know who they are anymore.

"You've come," he choked out. "I told Captain Illarion I would see you again one day."

Larisa's face had lost all color. Her limbs trembled with disbelief and her voice was hoarse as she spoke. She looked like a woman who dared not believe her eyes, who dared not cling to hope.

Elena stayed quiet, the personal toll of discovery too wrenching for her to fathom. Her father was a ghost. He was nothing but a memory, a dream of what Marakand might be.

And who *was* this Ahdath who called her father Mudjadid? He had betrayed them—he might still betray them—or had she been wrong to doubt his loyalty all along? She was swept up in an excess of emotion, unable to separate her feelings.

Had she finally met a member of the Ahdath who'd earned something other than her hate?

She brushed a shaking hand across her eyes, unwilling to face Illarion—to witness his compassion at how deeply she'd been harmed by the knowledge of his treachery. His blue eyes were alight with concern, but she turned her face away.

"I was in the Plague Wing," her father said. "The Technologist kept you away from me—I would never have let you suffer had I known. After you escaped, he transferred me back to this ward. He took pleasure in describing all that my daughters had endured."

Her hatred so great that it engulfed her like a living skin, Elena drove the heel of her boot into the Technologist's severed head. She heard the grinding of his bones with a savage satisfaction.

Illarion flashed her a glance but didn't interfere. He crouched down on his knees to search the Technologist's body, coming away with a small object that he tucked into his belt.

"I heard you," Larisa murmured, disbelieving. "I heard the song of the Claim—the song of our childhood. I didn't think I ever would again."

Salikh kissed the top of her head, his pale, rheumy eyes leaking tears. He hugged his daughters close, his thin frame shuddering with sobs.

"*Nothing* is stronger than the power of the Claim. No matter the gifts of the Authoritan, he cannot override it."

She wasn't sure she could believe that, despite what she'd heard firsthand, but there was no time to discuss it further. Reinforcements from the Crimson Watch were already on their way.

"Free us!" The prisoners in the cells called out to their improbable gathering of allies.

Sinnia moved to obey, but Illarion turned to Salikh. "What is your command, Mudjadid?"

"If you unlock these cells, you will never reach the Plague Wing as you hoped. You must leave us at once."

"Must I also leave you, Mudjadid?"

"I could only hinder you in your plan."

"Then flee with your daughters to the graveyard of the ships."

Salikh's pale eyes were kind. "I cannot leave my followers to suffer when they've done everything I asked. And there is more to accomplish."

He spoke to the men in the cells in the dialect of Marakand— his instructions deliberate and fierce. "You've done so much of what I've asked, but my daughters must go free. Forgive me that we must remain."

He was using the Claim. The men in the cells grew calm.

"As you command, Mudjadid," promised one.

Larisa's protest was firm: she refused to abandon her father to his fate at the Ahdath's hands. That she had found him was a miracle surely granted by the One; she wouldn't leave him behind. "If you won't come with us, Father, neither will we leave. We'll make our stand here together."

Salikh shook his head, unable to explain his will or to describe his purpose. He gestured weakly at Illarion, who spoke in a cutting voice, to return them to the urgency of the moment.

"Your father knows what he's doing. You need to get out of Jaslyk while you can."

"You won't make it to the Plague Wing alive," Larisa warned him. "Come back with us to the graveyard of the ships."

Illarion shook his head. "I can't. Not now that I have the talisman." He turned to Sinnia. "Companion, follow them to Black Aura, where the First Oralist has been taken prisoner. She sent me to deliver you from Jaslyk, and now she has need of you in turn."

Sinnia nodded at him briskly, taken aback by this news.

"Yours is a fool's errand," Larisa persisted. "They will hunt you into the ground. Better that *you* escort the Companion safely back to Black Aura."

"I can't," he said again. "I have a mission to complete. You needn't worry—anyone who could betray me here I've already killed." He touched the crimson splash at his throat. "This will get me into the Plague Wing."

Elena cleaned her sword on the Technologist's smock. "What is it you seek to find?"

His eyes met hers, a banked flame in their depths. "Did you never learn why these prisoners submit to the Ahdath's tortures—why these Basmachi in particular were captured by the Crimson Watch?"

She frowned at him, unwilling to admit her ignorance of anything concerning her men.

"They keep the Technologist focused on themselves to draw him away from the Plague Wing. Each man here volunteered. Each has a loved one who suffers the torments of the Plague Wing. It's what keeps them here, deflecting the Technologist's attention."

Her voice softer now, Elena asked, "And what of you, Ahdath?"

Illarion shrugged without meeting her eyes. "They have my sister. It's why I joined the Salikhate. Now go. You've delayed too long as it is."

Elena's voice was matter-of-fact as she gathered up her weapons. She had shut her father out of her mind, to force herself to focus on their plan.

"Take the Companion to Black Aura," she told Larisa. "Father must decide his course for himself, and you know the way back, so you won't be needing me. I'll meet you in Marakand. This Ahdath won't make it to the Plague Wing on his own."

Illarion's eyes jerked to hers. "What? Anya, no—"

"My name is Elena," she said. "And no one knows Jaslyk like me."

WINE, MARE'S MILK, HONEY, AND BLOOD. THESE WERE THE LIBATIONS that flowed from the silver tree at the center of the Authoritan's court. The Ahdath and the doves were gathered in the great hall, as an audience for a program arranged for their amusement.

The Ahdath commanders who had gathered were eager to prove themselves in combat against the Silver Mage, hoping to earn the Authoritan's trust, or to impress the coterie of doves whose favors might be won by their display. The Ahdath drank the wine freely; the doves tasted only mare's milk. A few among the more exclusive ranks of Ahdath were served the blood libation in tiny golden cups. Nevus was among these, his eyes fixed on Arian. When he'd captured her at the Bloodprint's mausoleum, he'd paid her scant attention. He was a man more focused on his enemies than on the pleasures of the court. But ever since Arian had been collared and dressed in the seductive manner of the doves, his attention had strayed from the Wall. She was kneeling on a stool beside the Khanum's throne, staring out at the display from the dais. In this ignoble position, she was a curiosity to be marveled at, and marvel the Ahdath did. Their lascivious interest reminded Nevus of the Khanum's first appearance at the Ark.

The Khanum had once been the most beautiful woman in Black Aura, but the mask of lead had sapped her vitality and diminished her physical allure. When she'd first come to Black Aura as a gift of the One-Eyed Preacher, she'd been a broken thing, powerless and abused. The Authoritan had made her over in his image, raising her to the throne as his consort—and this without ever tasting of her blood. The Authoritan had been wise: she'd repaid his clemency a thousand times over. Her gifts of Augury were the one thing Nevus knew to respect. They kept him in command of Black Aura.

And now her attention had diverted to this Companion, the First Oralist of Hira, who knelt on a cushioned stool in a position of great discomfort, her arms bound behind her back, in a pose that displayed her beauty. She was a pet on the Khanum's leash more than a plaything of the Ahdath, though her flesh had felt firm and enticing under his palm.

Dressed as she was now, in pale green silks patterned with gold, her hair dressed with jewels and her soft skin shimmering, he knew he would have her and soon. The Authoritan recognized his value. He had never constrained Nevus's private vices. He had *earned* this Companion for himself.

When the First Oralist's troubled gaze strayed in his direction, he raised his gold cup and knocked back a draft of blood. He touched his fingers to his lips and then to the blemish on his face. When she shivered at the gesture, he knew she understood.

He smiled, blood staining his teeth and lips.

The Silver Mage waited for Lania to speak.

"It is time," she said.

"Where do you take me, Lania?"

"To dress. Tonight you observe the Qatilah against the fiercest warrior of the Ahdath. Either you will kill him or these . . . encounters between us will come to an end."

"If you unchain me, perhaps it stands some chance of enduring."

The Khanum smiled. Tonight she was dressed in an excess of luxury, wearing the crimson robe he'd first seen her in. The robe was cinched with a belt of gold. Twelve sprays of rubies that descended from the belt matched the stones in her headdress. On each arm she wore gold cuffs that reached from her wrists to her elbows. These were worked with verses of the Claim inscribed on the cuffs in delicate enamel. Her hair was set high in the front, anointed with a half-crown of pearls that flashed from the long hair trailing loose at the back. Her elaborate plumed headdress was poised upon a pedestal in the center of the room.

"I foresee you will lose this fight, my lord." She said it with a smile.

"If you unchain me I could use my talents as the Silver Mage," he urged again. When she didn't reply, he went on, "Who am I to fight?"

"Nevus. And there is to be a prize at the end of this Qatilah."

"What prize?"

"Whoever wins will be gifted with my slave—the First Oralist of Hira." And at his look of outrage, she added, "She is mine to dispose of as I wish."

"She's your *sister*, Lania. She's spent her life seeking to deliver you. Is this how you repay her sacrifice?"

She shrugged. "Perhaps you will win the Qatilah, after all."

"You've already Augured my loss. You *must* unchain me if you are offering up Arian. You cannot let her fall into Nevus's hands. He will brutalize your sister."

Lania shrugged, pearls rippling through her hair. "You will find the daughters of my family are much stronger than you imagine. And did I say I wished *you* to have her? The talents of the Silver Mage would be wasted on my sister. I thought we had agreed that *I* am your natural equal. *Khawateen!*"

She summoned her doves with a sharp snap of her voice. The beautiful girls of the Transcasp hurried to do her bidding. Daniyar felt himself caressed by many hands, hands that traced and bathed his wounds, clothing him in armor.

When he was half-dressed and without his breastplate, the Khanum clapped her hands and the doves retreated, kneeling in expectation of her next command.

"Bring it."

The girl with honey-colored hair rose to offer a mother-of-pearl shell to the Khanum. She placed it in the palm of the Khanum's hand.

"Let her see this."

The Khanum's doves drew back a curtain that shaded an alcove in the room. The lantern that hung from a brace threw a gilded light over its inhabitant. Daniyar's breath quickened in his chest. Arian was seated on a tall stool, her arms held behind her back, her circlets polished, her dress exquisitely molded to her body. Was it transparent, or did the light make it appear so? He could not take his eyes from her beauty or from the need in her eyes. Never had she appeared less like Lania—he was struck once again by the knowledge of all he stood to lose.

"Arian."

She couldn't answer. She was wearing a collar that bound her mouth and throat inside the rough clasp of leather. He read in her gaze that this was a stratagem of the Khanum's. And he could not promise her there and then that her suffering would soon be ended. If he defeated Nevus—and Lania had foretold he would lose this next Qatilah—he would still have to face an army of Ahdath, along with the Authoritan, a man who could break him by raising a pointed finger in his face. And that was assuming he could trust to Lania's promise. Or that any of his efforts at seduction had swayed her view of his worth.

What could he do? What *would* he do?

He looked into Lania's catlike eyes and knew the answer was clear: he would do anything he had to.

Lania circled him, the mother-of-pearl shell held aloft in her palm. A delicate gold dust filtered through the air as she lifted the shell to his chest.

"You begged me to spare him, so see how I tend him now. I know you will thank me, sister."

She dipped one hand into the shell, coating her fingers with the powder. Then she smoothed it over his skin. Though her palm was soft, her nails left a mark. At first he thought she caressed him to provoke a reaction from Arian, seeking to cause her pain. She had loved her sister once. Her time with the Authoritan had eroded that bond—but had it severed it completely? Even his gifts as Authenticate could not read the riddle of her heart.

He looked down at the hand on his chest and dared to hope. She had spread the powder in a pattern: an invocation of the Claim. She was standing in the shelter of his body, his much larger frame blocking a view of her actions from the gallery, where her glance seemed to stray.

"He bloodmarked you," Lania said in a low voice. "I mark you with its opposite."

She circled him again, studying the lash marks on his back. "Do these pain you, my lord?"

Her hand began to massage the golden dust into the wounds.

He felt his body relax all at once, agility invigorating his limbs. Whatever her powder contained, it was more concentrated than the loess on the walls of his cell. The burning sting subsided. It was possible to bear her touch. And to realize that she *wanted* Arian to witness the intimacy of this act. He had been wrong to hope: her pursuit of him *was* driven by her desire to cause Arian pain.

Close your eyes, he mouthed, but Arian's eyes remained steady on his, her self-assurance unscathed. She seemed as delicate as a lily poised upon its stalk, yet her posture radiated strength.

And he knew then that Arian had always been stronger than he, able to deal his love away in the name of a greater good. The knowledge struck him like a wound, swift and secret and deep, his tension apparent to Lania, whose hands still caressed his back.

"Does this infringement matter more to you than to Arian, my lord?" A cajoling note crept into her voice. "I have tried to show you what you need, instead of what it is that you seek." She smiled over his shoulder at Arian, lightly licking his ear.

"Fight for me." One hand splayed over his chest. "Win for me and Nevus shall not have her. Do otherwise and it will not matter. My influence with the Authoritan does not extend as far as you think."

Poised between the woman he loved and the woman he needed to persuade to his side, Daniyar took the space of a breath to decide. "Will you dress me in suitable armor and give me the poisoned blade?"

"You shall have anything you desire, if you kiss me and make me believe it."

His voice rough, he answered, "Close the curtain, then. Arian doesn't need to see this."

Lania took his face in her hands. He could smell the lead on her cheeks. Her tongue darted out to moisten her crimson lips, lips he had claimed for himself, though he loathed himself for it now.

"But she *does* need to see, my lord. That is part of our exchange."

She angled her mouth over his. Brutally he gave her what she sought, and she flamed to life beneath his lips.

"Hold me," she muttered, and his arms came up to embrace her. In another minute or two, he would be forced to fight Nevus in the rites of the Qatilah, but the real test was here with Lania. When he raised his head, she bit at his lips and drew blood. She sighed her satisfaction, casting a feline glance at Arian.

"The Silver Mage tastes like no one else. I wonder you haven't tasted him yourself."

Daniyar's eyes met Arian's with a mix of reluctance and shame.

She sat silent and composed on the stool, her head tilted away from Lania, to all appearances unmoved. But the radiant fire of her eyes laid bare her passionate fury. She had claimed Daniyar as hers. She would never deal him away.

Daniyar was dressed in battle armor by the doves while Lania assumed her headdress. She took a seat next to Arian, running her hand over Arian's circlets, rearranging the folds of her dress.

"You are breathtaking, sister. You will draw every eye. You would draw the Authoritan's eye, were he bound to earthly pleasures. You should count yourself fortunate in your escape."

Arian frowned. It was clear she was thinking of Nevus.

"He is not as harsh a man as you envision. He will not brutalize you for the sake of doing so. My doves have taught the Ahdath finesse. And if you bend to his will, you will uncover his weaknesses in time." Her eyes darkened. "I would not give you to him of my own accord, but the Authoritan will have his duel. He sweetens it with you as the prize."

Lania ran her finger along the lip of Arian's leather mask.

"It is a pity to mar your beauty this way, but your desperation may drive you to use of the Claim. And as you would not share its secrets with me . . ." Lania shrugged, causing the plumes of the headdress to sway, its feathers brushing Arian's arm. "You will not be permitted to use its potency on others. What would you seek? I wonder. To flee Black Aura with the Silver Mage *after* he has shared my bed?"

Arian didn't believe it. No matter his desperation, Daniyar would never betray her. It was time to make Lania understand that Arian couldn't be manipulated into losing faith in Daniyar. But when she tried to move the muscles in her throat, working them against the tightness of her collar, her voice refused to respond. Lania patted her knee.

"Did you think me a novice in the Claim, sister? I learned its cadences long before you did; I learned the use of its many meanings. Why did I not use it against my captors?" She brooded over this for a moment, one hand straying over a gold cuff. "The Talisman are a brute and primitive force, and I was not as strong then as I am now. You must have learned how desperation unlocks deeper reaches of the Claim."

Rage flickered across Lania's face at the flicker of compassion in her sister's eyes. She grabbed Arian by the throat, ignoring the bite of the collar's barbs. Arian tried to twist away from the pressure, the muscles of her throat cramping. Lania held her fast.

"Do you think you are the first adherent of the Claim to be contained by this collar? It has been tested on members of the

Salikhate—I used it on Salikh himself. Do you remember learning of his teachings at our mother's knee? If I could break *Salikh* with it—sister, you are nothing."

"Don't harm her!" Daniyar called out. "I go into battle as you ask. I've said I am yours to command."

Lania bent to her sister's ear. "Do you see? You will be given to Nevus, and I will take your lover for my own."

Instead of despairing as Lania intended, Arian whispered a prayer of thanks. The Qatilah ended in death. If Lania spoke the truth, Daniyar's life would be spared.

20

Nevus made his obeisance before the Authoritan and the Khanum. He looked taller and stronger than Arian remembered, no trace of levity about him. He nodded at Arian, poised on her stool and bound by the leather mask. He considered the satiny flesh exposed by the neckline of her dress.

"You're too beautiful to be marked." He moved his head so she could better see the blemish on his face. "But I will take pleasure in doing so regardless."

Though she couldn't speak the words aloud, Arian recited a vow of reprisal to herself: the Claim was her sword, the Claim was her shield. She need only wait for her moment.

Missing the deadly promise in her eyes, Nevus turned to the Silver Mage, who waited with his blade poised between his chained hands. Their swords touched before the dais. Nevus recited the oath of the Qatilah, a bleak inversion of the Claim.

"Die now and die again, unto a world without end."

Daniyar echoed the words back to him, and the heft of the rage he kept tamped down simmered through the vow. He didn't wait, lunging forward and striking first.

Nevus stepped back, drawing Daniyar out. "I will mark her as the Authoritan marked me. Do you know how it was done?"

Their swords met, flashing up and away. They circled each other with care.

"The Authoritan has a brand." His tone was conversational. "It is composed of dozens of silver needles and bathed in the blood of his enemies. Then it is fired and set to the skin. But the brand does not burn; it discolors." He dashed a hand at his blemish. "It is a mark of utmost honor. Every one of the Ahdath seeks to earn it." He drove his point home with a lunge at Daniyar. "The Claim cannot work against it."

A cold smile curled Daniyar's lips. "Then you've nothing to fear from the First Oralist. Why not remove her collar? Or is Nevus of the Ahdath powerful only against warriors who are bound and women who are silenced?"

He had the other man's rhythms now—Nevus was not a man for idle taunts or vainglory. As Daniyar had done in subtle ways with the Claim, Nevus was using his words to unsettle his opponent.

Now the men fought in earnest, steel ringing against steel, one man pursuing, the other feinting out of his path. Nevus was battle-tested, forcing the Silver Mage to give ground with each powerful press of his arms. A nervous anticipation filled the room. Members of the Ahdath shouted encouragement to their captain.

Only the Authoritan was silent as the Qatilah pressed closer to conclusion.

Nevus was right. Daniyar's subtle invocation of the Claim had little effect on his enemy. Nevus struck his armor twice with painful force. He struggled for breath and then was on the ground, tripped up by Nevus's superior footwork. The sword of his opponent came down, narrowly missing his head. He rolled to one side, pushing himself to his feet, straight into Nevus's path. A slash at his shoulder, another quick thrust at his neck that he dodged. He fell back panting and Nevus smiled. He didn't bother with a mocking display of superiority or seek the recognition of the Ahdath, as Daniyar's other opponents had done, exposing themselves to the efficiency of his sword.

Rather, he was tiring Daniyar out, his attention focused on his enemy. Pressing, always pressing, and making effective use of Daniyar's previous wounds by striking at them again. Daniyar hadn't landed a blow with the poisoned tip of his blade. Nothing seemed to slow the other man's advance.

Which meant the answer was to meet him on his ground. So Daniyar plunged forward, leaving his chest unprotected. With a quick feint under the other man's guard, he leapt at Nevus's sword, tangling it in the chains that bound his wrists. He jerked the sword straight out of Nevus's grip, in the process losing his own. Both men scrambled for their weapons. Nevus recovered his first. He slashed at Daniyar's chest and it was over. The Silver Mage was brought to his knees.

The great room exploded into noise.

Nevus raised his sword for the final blow. "Die and die again, unto a world without end."

"Hold, Captain Nevus."

The Authoritan and the Khanum rose as one. Arian strained against her leash, her eyes urgent upon Daniyar's face. But even her great need in this moment couldn't unlock the verses of the Claim seething in her mind, as it had done at the Clay Minar.

What could she do? Her thoughts leapt quickly over options.

She had been this powerless only once before in her life—when the Talisman had raided her home. The sight of Daniyar forced onto his knees portended a grief as severe—an endless reckoning of loss she knew she would never be able to face.

She watched in desperation as Nevus drew back, panting from the effort it had taken him to win. He made a quick bow before the Authoritan, then said, "Khagan, the rites of the Qatilah have not been completed."

A smile passed between the Authoritan and his consort. "I am changing the rites."

He nodded at Daniyar, bound and on his knees, held there by two soldiers. "The Khanum has persuaded me of the Silver Mage's value." He snapped his fingers at another soldier. "Bring the blood-basin."

"Khagan, you dishonor me." Nevus's voice was tight. He was unused to being refused any privilege he sought. *He* was the Khagan's commander in Black Aura.

"Would you bloody the hands you would use to bring the First Oralist to bay?" The Khanum pushed Arian to her feet. "Take your prize and go. The Silver Mage is mine."

His eyes aglow, the Authoritan swiftly rebuked her. "He is *mine*, Khanum. Every blade of grass behind the Wall belongs solely to me."

Lania made her voice soothing. "Of course, Khagan. That is what I meant."

She took the bloodbasin from the Ahdath's hands to present to the Authoritan. It was a bowl carved of gold, an occult incantation inscribed upon it in a lajwardina glaze. It was deep enough to hold the blood drained from a man's body.

"Have what you will of the Silver Mage," she said. "I have tasted his blood and know its potency for myself. I know it will augment your strength."

Nevus grabbed Arian by the arm. She held herself aloof.

"Do you grant her to me, Khagan?" He spoke directly to the Authoritan, a subtle yet unmistakable sign of disregard for the influence of the Khanum.

The Authoritan dismissed him with a flourish, smiling with a calculated power. "If you do not wish to observe the blood rites, then go. But do not remove the collar—you would find yourself unmanned."

Nevus curled a hand around Arian's circlet. Though he'd been bested by the Khanum, the First Oralist of Hira was not an insignificant prize. If he could not end his enemy's life in battle, the taking of this woman would inflict the ultimate wound. When Arian tried to resist, he lifted her struggling body in his arms.

"No!" Daniyar shouted. A soldier's blade drew blood from his throat. The Khanum descended the stairs in regal, gliding movements. She held the bloodbasin to the edge of his wound.

"Cut him again," the Authoritan said, power raging through his voice. "Cut him deeper. This takes too long."

With one hand, the Khanum detached the silken veil from her face. She gazed up at the Authoritan.

"Khagan," she insisted again, "taste his blood tonight. See how it empowers your use of the Claim. As the First Oralist will not yield, his blood will give you the weapon you seek. Do not spend it all in one night. You will need it again before long."

But this was too open a communication from the Khanum. The Authoritan flicked his hand in her direction, his crimson eyes blank and considering, his power held in reserve. With a painful grimace, she fell silent.

"I know what it is you seek of him," he hissed at her. "I know of his visits to your chamber." A strange intonation wound its way through his voice, and with it an intimation of madness.

"Khagan—"

"Be silent."

Daniyar's blood dripped into the bowl, a scarlet oozing against the incantation. Hazily he tried to read it. What was the significance of these arcane pronouncements and rites?

He thought of the Verse of the Throne, of molding it into a weapon and using it as Arian had used it. If he could aim it like a dagger and fling it at the Authoritan's throat—

"Blood will be shed. Blood will be shed."

The Ahdath assembled to watch his defeat began to murmur, the sound of the chant rising like a wave.

"There is no one but the One, Alive and Self-Subsisting."

But his voice was too weak, and he wasn't able to shape the words as Arian had done. He wasn't an Oralist or a Companion of Hira. He was simply a man of faith.

He tried to remember the verse Arian had recited during their long journey north.

A throne to comprise the heavens and the earth.

The words echoed back to him in the silence of his mind.

It was Arian—easing him, soothing him, as his lifeblood drained from his body. She was thinking of him, even as she faced her own peril at Nevus's hands. He shuddered at the thought of the blood-marked tattoo and of what Nevus would do.

He felt the steady flow of his blood, his strength beginning to leave him.

He offered the words again. There would be power in them—they wouldn't set him adrift.

"A throne to comprise the heavens and the earth."

He raised his head to face the dais, finding a repellent fascination in the Authoritan's crimson-tinged eyes, as hypnotic as a viper of the steppes. He wondered at the distinctive commingling of bloodlines that had caused this transformation in the Bloodless.

Then he said, "It isn't *your* throne. It isn't *your* dominion over the heavens and the earth."

A gasp from Lania drew his eyes to her. A secret gesture of her hand warned him not to challenge the Authoritan. But he was no longer at her mercy.

"Cut his wrists."

The Authoritan's command was heeded by his men. Blood discolored the chains at Daniyar's wrists, defining the corded muscles of his forearms. Lania moved the bloodbasin to encompass this new flow of his blood.

He could taste the anticipation of the Ahdath, revenged for their humiliation at his hands. He could feel the Authoritan's consciousness probing dagger-sharp through his mind.

He thought of his great trust, the Candour, and the letters that gleamed on its surface.

حق

Haq.

The Candour had burned before his eyes, but its teachings were present in his mind.

Qala fal haqqu wal haqqa aqool.

Wearily he said, "This is the truth and the truth is what I utter."

His defiance failed to strike at the Authoritan, who hovered above him on the dais. Daniyar sagged at the knees. Lania caught him by the arm, one hand slipping under the chains to press the knife wound at his wrist. She did the same with the other hand, her movements so subtle and stealthy, he couldn't be certain of her actions.

"Khagan," she called, "you must taste the blood while it is fresh."

She produced a tiny vial from a pocket within her robe, using it to decant a minimal amount of blood. The Authoritan summoned one of the Ahdath to bring it to his throne.

The words pressed against Daniyar's mind.

A throne to comprise the heavens and the earth.

Arian. Arian, my love.

A sharp stab inside his skull brought him fully to his senses.

He met Lania's eyes. They were filled with a strange despair.

Did she love him? *Could* she love him? She knew his love for Arian now—and that he'd deceived her to that end.

Think of me, a cool voice said. *Think* only *of me, Daniyar.*

It was *Lania* who spoke in the once-pristine silence of his mind. *Lania*—not Arian.

The Authoritan drank from the vial of blood, tipping back his head to expose the articulated column of his neck. His parchment-like skin was transparent, the viscous fluid oozing down his throat.

Daniyar shuddered again, slipping to his knees, though Lania tried to hold him, tenderness in her touch.

"You were right." The Authoritan spoke to his consort, a hint of surprise in his voice. "The blood of the Silver Mage is unlike anything else I have tasted. It renders me unassailable."

He raised the vial high above his head, his crimson eyes alight, his thin lips stained with Daniyar's blood as he glided to and fro. He toasted his Ahdath.

"Blood will be shed," they roared.

"Everything south of the Wall will burn." He examined the

crystal vial in his hand, holding it up to the light, where it pulsed like an orphic heartbeat. Then he pointed at Daniyar.

"*This* is the truth and the truth is what *I* utter."

Daniyar glanced up at Lania, still holding him in her grasp. And caught the subtle smile that edged her lips.

21

ARIAN FOUGHT NEVUS EVERY STEP OF THE WAY TO HIS CHAMBERS, DI-vided between the urgent need to consider her own safety and the sight of Daniyar bleeding to death at the Authoritan's pleasure.

She needed to use the Claim. But the more she attempted to do so, the tighter the leather collar squeezed the muscles of her throat. Her larynx was swollen and raw. She didn't know if even freed from the collar, she'd be able to recite at need. She wasn't deterred by the thought of failure: Arian intended to try.

She intended, as ever, to fight.

Nevus dropped her onto a narrow wooden bed, scarcely large enough for two. She scrambled back against its headboard, try-ing to get her bearings. She was bound and painfully gagged. She searched the room with her eyes for anything she could use to delay or subvert the inevitable confrontation. The room was smaller than she'd expected—hardly the opulent quarters of a captain of the Ahdath. The air was unscented by incense or aromatic oils, with an absence of silk curtains hanging about the bed. It was sparsely fur-nished and without ornament, the room of a disciplined man who spent most of his time at the Wall and rarely engaged in frivolities.

A narrow window looked out over the courtyard of the Ark. From the void beyond, she heard the call of soldiers giving orders from the Wall.

Nevus turned his back to her, engaged in the task of removing his gloves. Arian slid off the bed, moving closer to the unbarred window. There was nothing she could use to anchor herself, to slip below to the courtyard—and even if she were able to reach its safety, she would be at the center of a company of Ahdath. She needed another way out. She turned her gaze back to Nevus.

He had paused before a table, unlatching his crimson breast-plate. He set it aside on a chest at the foot of the narrow bed, exposing a blue-glazed table to her view. It was the only note of beauty in the room, a table embellished and inscribed, profligate in the use of verse. But these were not verses of the Claim, and Arian couldn't make out the script.

Her resolve firmed as she examined the items Nevus had placed on the table. A collection of stiletto blades was arranged over a runner of white silk, laid out from the blade with the thinnest tip to the widest. Each had an ornamented haft worked in filigreed silver. At the far end of the table, a group of delicate decanters surrounded a bowl painted with a lajwardina varnish. It was a miniature version of a bloodbasin, and on seeing it, Arian felt her determination flare anew. She could not let herself be blooded. She *would* not.

As another piece of his armor came off, Arian moved closer to the table, plotting her escape. The crystal decanters were filled with liquids in different jewel tones. One was clear and transparent; another was filled with mare's milk. A thin gold ladle rested in the center of the miniature basin, traces of blood staining its lip.

"You needn't worry," Nevus said behind her. "I have other uses for you."

Arian's palms searched behind her for one of the stilettos on the table.

Nevus's smile distorted the bloodmark on his cheek. Arian watched it ripple against his skin. There was another item on the table, an item whose purpose she guessed. It was a silver brand with a leather grip that would fit inside a man's palm. The brand was in the shape of a square, with dozens of sharp silver needles. She couldn't contain a shiver at the thought of the needles pressed to her skin.

Nevus laughed, then rang a small bell beside the door to his chamber.

He advanced on Arian, removing the blade she had gripped behind her back with little effort. His touch was light. He used no more force than was necessary to restrain her.

"Sit here." He led her to a narrow bench placed before the window. A breeze drifted through the curtains to stir the waves of her hair.

Nevus seated himself on a corner of the carved wooden chest. He studied Arian's face in the light that flickered from a lantern by the window.

"She looked like you when she first came here, and I thought to have her, as I now have you." His tone was conversational. "The Authoritan kept her to himself. He trained her, he raised her up, and soon the notice of an Ahdath captain was beneath the Authoritan's consort. She lost no opportunity to make that clear to me. Are you much like her? I wonder."

He unfastened his leather greaves, then removed his boots.

Arian shook her head, persuading him with a softening of her eyes. She could do nothing as long as she was bound, so the first necessity was to convince him to remove the collar.

"You think to speak to me? To answer my questions? The Authoritan warned me against it." He moved closer to the bench, reaching behind Arian to unfasten the chains that linked her wrists together. He sat back on the chest, giving a slight nod of his head at the daggers on the table. "I do not like to see you constrained, but I warn you, my aim is unerring."

Arian nodded her understanding, the movement tightening the collar. She winced, gingerly stretching her arms to ease their ache. Sensation flooded back to her upper arms, throbbing under her skin. Carefully she put her hands up to the collar and gently massaged her throat. When tears slipped from her eyes, it was a ruse intended to soften Nevus, aided in part by the tumult of her imprisonment at the Ark. Her inner purpose was undeterred.

Nevus braced his hands on his thighs. His bloodmark rippled, as a muscle tightened in his cheek. With a careful hand, he brushed a lock of hair over Arian's shoulder. He touched the same hand to the moisture on her face.

"Who do you cry for—the Silver Mage? Or do you cry for yourself as the reward I earned for besting him in the Qatilah?" His hand traced the path of the collar, working its way from the outline of her jaw to her throat, too lightly to feel the bite of the silver spikes. He brushed the front of her dress, molding the silk to her body. Deliberately, Arian brought up both hands to still the movement of his.

"Do you think you can delay this?" Nevus asked. "Do you imagine I will not claim you as my own? I wouldn't have forsaken the bloodrites for anyone other than you. Your magic is powerful; its essence will renew me. But I need not be cruel to you. I am not a man who is savage with women, though there are many of that ilk among my soldiers."

He took one of her hands in his, kissing it lightly before letting it go.

He resumed his seat on the chest, watching her for a reaction. Arian crossed her arms, gripping her circlets with her hands. A subtle strength flared from their inscriptions, reminding her that she had brought down men more powerful than Nevus, often unaided by the power of the Claim. She gave him a measured smile, probing out his weaknesses.

His words were gentle, his touch careful on her skin, but what he discussed so calmly could not be mistaken for other than what it was. This night in his chamber wasn't a seduction. And the threat of sexual violence—to herself, to Sinnia—had been present whenever they had disrupted a Talisman slave-chain. She had learned to set it aside, or the fear would have paralyzed her abilities. She remembered that now and used it to draw strength into her body. She focused her attention on the man who held her captive, the man who thought her powerless. She cast a demure glance at him, and even that was edged by covert invocations of the Claim.

She raised one brow in an imitation of her sister. Offering him her obedience in a glance filled with promise, she raised her hands to the latch at the back of her collar.

Watching her, he reached for the smallest of the ornamental blades. His gaze drifted to her breasts, outlined by the silk of her dress.

"I am warning you," he said thickly.

Arian slid the bolt from the lock that held the collar together. It came apart in her hands. She held it out to Nevus, docile and utterly harmless.

"You have no need of this," she assured him, arranging verses of the Claim in her mind. Her voice rasped against her throat, each word painful. She forced herself not to think of Daniyar, pressing ahead to a single end. She made her words careless, lightly mocking.

"Is it me you seek to use or my sister? Was *she* the prize the

Authoritan denied you when you'd sacrificed so much in his service?"

Nevus took the collar she held out and dropped it to the floor, its silver spikes striking the marble. He pulled her into his arms and fastened his mouth to the bruises at her throat. Arian went lax in his grip, demonstrating submission. His attentions grew more urgent, and only then did she try to slow him.

"Wait," she said. She stroked a hand over the bloodmark on his cheek. "I will submit if you do not use me roughly." She pushed him away, reaching for the cape fastened to the back of her dress. When she released its clasps, it whispered to her feet.

Nevus set the stiletto back on the table with the others.

His voice cool, he said, "There is time enough for that." And at his casual promise of violence, Arian knew she had not misjudged him.

He motioned at her arms. "First the circlets, then the dress."

She had moved to comply when a knock sounded behind him at the door. Without waiting for an answer, a page entered the room bearing a jug and a matching set of silver cups.

He was gaunt and skinny, and he wore his hair in a cluster of riotous curls.

"Leave it and get out." Nevus kept his eyes on Arian. "Continue."

The page stumbled at the sight of Arian in a state of undress, bumping into the chest and spilling the ruby wine from the jug. Nevus's arm shot out. He grabbed the page by the throat, forcing him to his knees. The violence he'd been containing had found a more immediate target, giving Arian the opening she'd been waiting for.

She lunged past Nevus to the table, scooping up two of his blades. Nevus loosened his grip on the page, leaping after Arian.

He caught her by the waist, using the heavy silk of her dress against her. She whirled, both blades shifted to one hand, but they were at too close quarters. She could do no more with the blades than score his palm.

One hand gripped her throat and squeezed; the other tightened around her wrist, forcing the blades from her hand. Arian cried out in pain. The stilettos crashed against the marble and skittered across the floor. Now Nevus ripped the dress at Arian's shoulder, wrenching it down her arm. It caught on one of her circlets.

He kicked the page with his boot while he wrested Arian closer to the blades.

"I wasn't going to bleed you," he said. He wasn't out of breath; he had subdued Arian with minimal effort. "But you have shown me disrespect, and now you must answer for it."

Arian's hands scrabbled against the table. She was losing air from the bruising pressure of his grip. He shoved her head to one side. "There. Do you see what I will do?"

With a mist rising over her eyes, Arian focused on the brand on the table.

"After you are bled, the brand will be fired and coated in the magic of your blood."

He wrenched the silk of her dress aside and squeezed the curve of her breast.

"Here. This is where I will brand you, for all the Ahdath to witness."

Whatever he would have said next was choked off, his grip eased from her throat and breast. He staggered away as he cast about the room.

"Sahabiya, run!"

Arian whirled around. The page was still at Nevus's feet, one of the stilettos in his hand. A trail of blood leaked from the back of Nevus's leg. The page had slashed him at the heel, severing his tendon. Now the young man grabbed Arian's hand, pulling her to the door.

Nevus shouted after them, blundering against the table. He swept up the remaining blades and fired them with lethal swiftness at the door. Six of them lodged in the door's wooden planks. The seventh found its mark in Arian's back.

She staggered forward from the force of the blow, dragged from the room by the frantic hands of the page. The door slammed shut just as Nevus sounded the alarm.

"Hurry."

But in her condition, she couldn't keep his pace. The page was forced to drag her along the passageway, ducking into an alcove that crossed another passage. With a gasp of horror, he noticed the crimson stain spreading from the blade buried in her back. He pulled her aside, finally meeting her eyes. She recognized him now.

"Alisher!" Despite the pain from the knife wound, Arian's voice was steady, even welcoming. She could see that the poet she had met at the Clay Minar needed his courage bolstered. His hands were trembling with fear, his handsome young face tearstained. "Do not worry about me, there isn't time. I can continue on."

Alisher swallowed and nodded, then grabbed a satchel from a darkened corner of the alcove. From its depths, he unearthed a fabric pouch cinched with a leather tie. This was followed by a thick cotton wrap that he wound about his forearm.

In spite of her brave words, Arian sank down to the ground, pain radiating from her back to her nerve endings. Fiery streamers of pain pulsed beneath the bruises at her throat.

"Forgive me."

Alisher blushed as he drew the torn silk of her dress over her naked skin with a clumsy pass of his hand. He reached over her shoulder and yanked out the blade, dousing Arian in sweat.

He drew out the contents of the pouch—a thick gold paste that shimmered in the dark. He plunged his hand into the wound, smearing the paste over it, his other hand covering the scream that rose from Arian's mouth. As soon as it was done, he dropped his hands, muttering his apologies. Now he used the cotton wrap to stanch the flow of blood at her back.

"Can you walk?" he whispered, and she nodded. "This way, then."

Ahdath horns sounded through the upper gallery of the Ark. Boots thudded along the corridors.

"Can you mask our passage?" Alisher murmured. Arian shook her head. Her throat was still on fire, her senses overwhelmed by pain. She struggled to place one foot in front of the other, desperate to reach Daniyar before it was too late.

"No matter. I will take you through the rooms of the doves."

"Alisher—the Silver Mage! The Authoritan bleeds him in the throne room."

"You'll never make it there in time. I'll go myself after I find a place to hide you."

Nothing would have been sweeter than to rest. Everything hurt—heart, body, spirit. But her last glimpse of Daniyar had been of the Silver Mage being prepared for the bloodrites.

She forced herself to focus on how the Claim might serve her now.

Because a ragged poet who had fled the Clay Minar could not stand against the Ahdath on his own.

"Here," Alisher said. "Wear this."

He'd brought her a pair of women's boots and an outfit similar to his own, along with a hooded cloak of the Ahdath's. She felt a sharp sense of relief at stripping off the torn and bloodstained dress that clung to the sweat on her body. She dressed quickly at the threshold of one of the rooms of the doves. In the shaded intimacy of the room beyond, an Ahdath soldier had failed to heed the alarm. He was wrapped in the embrace of a dove with a beauty mark on her cheek. Her eyes met Alisher's over his head, and she nodded, motioning to him to hurry.

Arian and Alisher slipped away.

"Who is she?"

"Just someone I know."

Alisher knelt down to help Arian drag on the boots. He pulled the hood up over her hair, noticing the bruises on her neck.

"Sahabiya!" It was a whisper of dread. "Can you— Is it—" He stumbled over the words. "Are you bereft of the Claim?"

Bereft.

The word struck through to her heart. She was bereft of everything that mattered.

But she wasn't about to share that with her only ally.

"We must go."

Nodding, he guided her along. As they moved through the palace, Alisher reached back into his pack for the leather pouch with the paste. They stopped again along the upper gallery, just out of sight of an Ahdath patrol, crouching behind the marble panels.

"Sahabiya, may I?" Alisher gestured to her throat. Arian nodded, blinking back tears. His air of diffidence at the prospect of touching her stood in marked contrast to Nevus's violence.

With a featherlight touch, he applied the gold paste to her bruises. The pain from the knife wound in her back had eased, no longer burning with every step. She prayed the salve would work as well on her throat.

A patrol crossed behind them to the far side of the gallery.

"Come," Alisher said. "There is a way down. The doves use it to assure the privacy of their dalliances with the Ahdath."

Arian followed him down the secret staircase, taking care to step lightly in the boots. She drew back in alarm as one of the Khanum's doves intercepted their path. Alisher flashed her a look of reassurance. He nodded at the dove, who touched his hand as she passed up the stairs.

"Alisher, these doves are the Khanum's spies. You must know you cannot trust them."

A bittersweet smile touched his lips. "I'm *alive* because of these doves. The girl who passed us on the stairs is my sister. The other was my betrothed."

22

She had come to the Damson Vale dressed in white silk, her thoughts and her love only for him. She touched him with a soft hand, a hand that no longer gripped a sword raised to strike, and her soft lips were smiling. He had seldom seen her smile.

"Did I deceive you?" he whispered. "Or is the Damson Vale as I promised?"

She placed a hand over his lips, urging him not to speak. "Rest now. You will be with me soon."

He was dying, weaker with every sip the Authoritan took from the vial of his blood. Lania tried to ease him with her touch; he saw only Arian.

He wasn't afraid of death. Others would rise to take up his burdens. Another boy would be born to the inheritance of the Silver Mage, even if Daniyar would be the last to discover the secrets of the Candour. He'd always thought he would yield his trust in the glades of the Damson Vale. He would die there peaceably, at Arian's side.

No man knows in which land he will die.

Arian had said this to him once, cautioning him against their deepening attachment. But he had once had more faith in their prospects for joy.

If misfortune touches you, know that misfortune has also touched others.

The words of the Claim flitted through his mind and made him angry at himself. He would bear misfortune gladly, his share and Arian's, to spare her any suffering. And now she was in Nevus's hands, defenseless without the Claim, while his lifeblood slipped away—from his neck, from his wrists, from two delicate slashes at his ankles.

Whatever is in the heavens and earth surrenders itself to the One.

I surrender, he thought, his heart squeezed by regret.

Lania bent to kiss him. *No,* she said. *You mustn't.*

Has he passed from this life, Khanum?" The Authoritan summoned Lania to his side.

She responded coolly, her headdress swaying as she ascended the dais. "You bled him too swiftly. He was not long for this world."

The Authoritan's hand tightened around her wrist. "Is that a rebuke, my love?"

He didn't utter it in the accents Daniyar used with Arian. Lania tried not to flinch.

"I wished to strengthen you, my lord. I would have delayed the bloodrites to that end."

Whatever he would have said in reply was cut off by a stridency of horns. The Ahdath left their places in the hall, forming into patrols. The Authoritan nodded at a stalwart soldier, whose hair was held back from his face by a leather tie.

"The First Oralist causes difficulty. Find out what Nevus wants." He turned to Lania. "You didn't warn me of this." The strength of his grip was bruising, the ashen skin of his cheeks stretched in a grimace of rage.

"I did not foretell it, Khagan. You know the sight comes to me. I cannot call it forth."

The Authoritan wrenched the headdress from her head. It fell back heavily, striking the dais, pulling at the curtains of pearls in Lania's hair.

"What I know is you begged me for your sister, so I gave her to you as a gift. You claimed your powers would be strengthened by her knowledge, yet you failed to achieve mastery."

Lania rubbed the back of her head. Without the mystery cast by the headdress, the lead mask was brittle and rudely exposed. "You collared her," she muttered. "My sister's voice was damaged."

The Authoritan raised his forefinger with a snarl. The lead mask cracked in two.

"Could she not write? Do you not read?"

He moved his finger twice more in the air. The ruby sprays on her belt snapped off. Inexorably the belt tightened. She stared at him in horror.

"I gave up the Bloodprint in exchange for her gifts. You deceived me, Khanum. It was *not* the First Oralist you sought—you wanted the Silver Mage. And out of lust for him, you hoped to deny me his blood."

Lania's fingers groped at the belt, trying to unlatch it.

The Authoritan flung open his hand. The heavy crimson robe was torn from Lania's shoulders. But the belt remained in place, biting into her ribs.

He was stripping her of rank, stripping her of her place at his court.

Did he intend to replace her with Arian? But he'd given Arian to Nevus. He'd insisted on the gift. So what did his fury portend?

"Did you foretell *this*?" he asked cruelly. "Did you imagine for a moment your machinations had escaped me? That I sent no spies to your rooms? Yet you gave yourself to the Silver Mage. After everything I did for you, everything I *was* to you."

In her silk underdress, Lania began to bleed. The belt sliced through the silk, tearing strips from her flesh. "Khagan, I am yours. I have served only you."

"Once, perhaps you did. But not, I believe, any longer."

Unnoticed in the tumult and horror, Daniyar lifted his head.

The Authoritan's control over Lania was complete. Was it an occult magic? What could he do to help her, given that he could scarcely help himself—

With a start, he felt his strength slowly return to his limbs. His blood had long since clotted, sticky on his ankles and wrists. It no longer flowed from the five-point wounds of the bloodrites. The realization confounded him. Through the ebbing tide of pain, he considered the nature of the ritual Lania had enacted. What precisely had she done? What advantage might it yield him now? He struggled to clear his thoughts, his hand groping along the floor for a sword. No one was left to guard him. The Khanum's doves hovered before the dais. The Ahdath had fled to seek their captain. And the Authoritan was occupied in the punishment of his consort.

Again, Daniyar was confused. Why did he punish her? She had given Arian up, and she had allowed the Authoritan to drain him of his blood. How had she shown her disloyalty? Or was it her noticeable favoring of Daniyar that had earned her the Authoritan's displeasure?

A dove bent over his chest, her hand bringing up a cloth to wipe the blood from his throat, an act that might have been taken for the preparation of the dead. He felt the hard edge of steel in the folds of the cloth. She moved it next to his wrist, her golden head tipped to one corner of the hall.

Daniyar peered in that direction, his silver eyes searching the shadows. What did she warn him of?

Shouts sounded from the upper gallery. Swords were drawn. Boots pounded down each of four arcades, another set down stairs that led into the hall. These were followed by a slow and painful thumping.

Nevus lurched before the dais. "My lord!"

The Authoritan's hand dropped from Lania's face, moving limply to his side. "What is it, Nevus? How did a woman bound and chained escape you?"

Now Daniyar saw a trace of movement in the alcove. It was a hand. It beckoned him to run. But Nevus stood between Daniyar and the alcove.

Even with his path cut off, a wave of relief swept over him.

Arian wasn't with Nevus.

With the Authoritan distracted, Lania twisted the belt from her ribs and cast it upon the dais.

Terrifying, trenchant verses of the Claim spilled from her lips, notes of broken glass that clawed the air with blanched and bloodied fingers. It slowed the approach of the Ahdath.

For this brief moment, she and Daniyar were able to face down the Authoritan and Nevus unimpeded. She passed a signal to him, she spoke—she murmured the recitation she had daubed in gold on his chest. Power surged through his body, his mind starkly free of pain. She *had* been disloyal, then.

And now she needed his help.

He gathered the cloth-wrapped blade in his hand, easing it from its folds. He moved his hand just as Nevus thought to look down at his feet. Striking with the swiftness of an eagle, Daniyar slashed Nevus's other tendon. The captain went tumbling to the ground, bracing his sword before him.

Now the Authoritan turned on Lania with full force. His white hair streaking out around his skull, his crimson eyes scorched her face. He raised both hands in the air, stabbing her with malevolent strikes. Strips of blood smeared her torso, soaking the gold silk of her dress.

"No!" Daniyar shouted.

The Authoritan rounded on him—a raised hand struck him down. He fell to his knees and met Nevus braced on his. Both men raised their weapons.

"Was this why your Augury failed you? You *meant* to replace me with your pet?"

The Authoritan gathered the white staff in his hand. Step by rapacious step, he advanced upon Lania. Crimson fire flared from the finial at its top. The words on the staff began to bleed. And Lania bled with them.

Catching sight of her, Daniyar was amazed. She was drenched in her own blood, yet she faltered not at all—the blood loss hadn't weakened her.

Was this why she had claimed his blood?

Did it empower her as it empowered the Authoritan?

Nevus lunged at him and missed. Daniyar pushed him back, his knife finding its way to the captain's throat.

"Where is she?"

The knife pierced Nevus's flesh.

"Here!" It was a low, hurried cry. Then he saw her—Arian, his golden companion, his heart—wounded and in pain from the bruising at her throat, her eyes radiating joy to find him still alive.

His throat under Daniyar's blade, Nevus managed a smile. The bloodmark rippled like a wave. It rendered the Ahdath monstrous.

"Her chastity was sweet," he said. "I claimed it as my own."

Daniyar crushed his throat with his knee.

Nevus's head lolled back and went still.

Raising his sword with grim purpose, Daniyar severed his hands.

He staggered to his feet in time to meet the fire that blazed from the Authoritan's scepter. His armor disintegrated with a touch. But his flesh did not burn or bleed.

Instead, the script on his chest flamed to life. It rose before him like a shroud, a garment of protection.

Lania curled a hand in his direction, words pouring from her lips in a raging torrent of fire.

"If the One should sustain you, none can ever overcome you. But if the One should forsake you, who can sustain you after? In the One, then, let the believers place their trust."

Her eyes blazed at the Authoritan with a mixture of triumph and compunction. "It is as you taught me, Khagan. Blood *is* power— *my* power—just as you always promised. *I* have ascended to the throne."

The Authoritan raised his staff at her, impotent sounds of fury issuing from his lips. Lania blocked him with a word. "Die."

The Authoritan spat out a response. "I *cannot* die. I am fed on the blood of the Silver Mage—the bloodrites render me immortal."

She raised a careless hand in Daniyar's direction. "Look at him," she said, a tender note in her voice. "Does it seem as though I bled the Silver Mage?" She pointed at the scepter, dissolving it into flame. "I fed you the blood of swine, collected these many months for this purpose." She narrowed her eyes at him. "Does it burn, *my love*? Does it render your power wretched?"

"Lania—"

The Authoritan choked out her name, blood flecking his lips. Crimson streaks bled through the harsh white lines of his skull.

She tilted her head to one side. Even bereft of her headdress, her power and majesty were terrifying to behold.

"It *does* burn. I'm so glad." She held up the vial she'd hidden under her robes. With a delicate fingertip, she repainted her lips with traces of Daniyar's blood. When she had finished her gruesome task, she pursed her mouth. "It was time, Khagan. You have ruled the Wall long enough."

She paced around him in a circle, watching him try to cough up the tainted blood. He clutched at the sudden hindrance of his robes, suborned by the heft of his bones, heavy and graceless again.

"I weakened you." She trailed her bloody fingertip along the pale expanse of his forehead.

"And I healed myself, Khagan. What did you imagine those trials with the bloodbasin were? They were *my* bloodrites. They aided my Augury; they made me strong. I brought my sister and the Silver Mage here, the Silver Mage—who could not be defeated by the Talisman in Candour. And I sent the Bloodprint to safety. All this I have done, and I did it with what you taught me."

The Authoritan was driven to his knees by the tip of Lania's finger.

"Why?" he gritted between his teeth, stripped of his invincible aura. "I was your protector. I was once your *savior*."

"No," she spat back at him. "I was traded to the Wall *because* of you. I was ravaged at *your* command. How could you imagine I wouldn't be revenged for that? You will die, Khagan. I have suffered you long enough."

Now when Lania sang, her voice was eerie with pronouncement. It conjured up images of death.

"I bring forth the dead out of that which once was living."
Daniyar stared at her with dread.

This was how Lania conjured the Claim. She occulted each word with its opposite meaning. It was a darkness so grand and terrible, he felt the reaches of his soul shrink back from it. Had she learned it from the Authoritan—or had she *taught* it to him?

Again he felt a traitorous, ignoble thought stray across his mind: With her occult abilities, she could have prevented the burning of the Candour. But she'd been playing her own game, reluctant to give away her hand.

Leaving ruin in her wake, as she unraveled her grand design.

The Authoritan's breath rattled once from his chest and was still.

The weight of his body collapsed inward. When only the shell was left, Lania hissed a final word. The bones of the High Priest of the Bloodless shattered, leaving behind a white powder. At Lania's sharp look, two of the doves hurried to collect the fine white dust in a bowl.

He gave her one last look, not sure if what he expressed was pity, admiration, thanks—or all three—then stood ready to join Arian.

With the Claim silenced and the Authoritan destroyed, the Ahdath patrols faltered into the hall. None drew a sword against the Silver Mage. None attempted to recapture Arian, or Alisher cowering at her side.

Instead, they assembled in formation. Two of the commanders whispered to each other. Lania marked them out. She hissed the arcane word at them. In a breath, they fell down dead. A murmur passed through the officers' ranks and just as quickly subsided.

Lania held up her palms. One faced the Ahdath, and to them she said, "I command the city and the Wall. If any man disobeys, he will meet the Authoritan's fate. Is that clear?"

None ventured to challenge her.

With her other hand, Lania beckoned Arian close. "Did Nevus harm you, sister?" she asked. She had her answer when Arian moved nearer, exposing her injuries to the light.

Lania's palm slashed the air. Nevus's head rolled neatly from his shoulders.

"You should have taken his head as well as his hands," she said to Daniyar. "But you're too measured a man for that." Her voice was touched with a note of wonder, though she meant the words as a disparagement.

Her eyes narrowed as Daniyar stepped over Nevus's body to gather Arian into his arms. Arian clung to him with a strength that surprised them both. They sought out each other's wounds, each appalled at the suffering of the other. Tears streaked Arian's cheeks at the sight of Daniyar's blood, spilled in such excess that he wore it like a second skin. She tried to give him her cloak, but he wouldn't allow her to remove it or to unlatch her arms from around his neck. He kissed her as if he were a dying man drinking from a gold-strewn river.

Turning her head away from the sight, Lania spoke to the man skulking in the shadows. "Come forward," she said. "Tell me your name."

Trembling, Alisher skirted the waiting Ahdath. He hovered just under the Authoritan's whip, casting a chary eye upon it. His knees shaking, he bowed low before the Khanum. "Alisher, Highness. It's Alisher, your tutor."

"Alisher?" She struck her hands together in a self-mocking gesture. "You I did not Augur. You were nowhere in my reading of the bloodrites." Her voice sharpened. "I thought you dead. The Khagan sent you to the tower. The verse you wrote displeased him. I believe you wrote it for your beloved—see how the Khagan repaid you."

A grimace of pain twisted Alisher's face.

"Recite it for me now."

With her cracked face and her lips as red as a demon's, Alisher dared not meet her eye. He mumbled the verse to himself.

"Louder."

He cleared his throat, repeating himself while the Ahdath watched with manifest disfavor.

"I would give up Black Aura and Marakand / Just for the mole on your cheek."

Lania smiled her cold, red smile. "You were my favorite tutor. You should have taken more care."

Alisher cast a quick glance at the Ahdath, unwilling to trust to Lania's mastery. He hastened to agree. "It was presumptuous of me. I thought it would amuse him, as my verse often did. But he said Marakand and Black Aura were not mine to gift, and all for so trifling a sum. I told him he could see my exorbitance had left me in a state of poverty. The Khagan wasn't amused."

"He wouldn't have been. Black Aura and Marakand were the treasures he held closest to his heart. He admitted no other's dominion. Not even in foolish verse."

"I learned that to my cost."

Lania took the measure of the hall. The Authoritan's silver fountain had run dry. Behind the military arrangement of the Ahdath, her doves waited for instruction.

"You." Lania indicated the captains. "Assemble at my sighting chamber in the Sihraat. I will instruct you there. I will Augur any attempt at disobedience. Instead of Basmachi, yours will be the skeletons strung up over the gates. The rest of you, to the Wall."

An Ahdath with a portentous face stepped forward. "Khanum, it was Commander Araxcin who held the Wall. Who commands in his absence?"

Lania spoke the word she'd occulted again. It pierced the man's heart like an arrow. This time when Lania snapped her fingers, Ahdath came forward to bear away the bodies of those who'd dared to doubt her. The rest scattered on her command.

Lania spoke to the doves. "Go. See that my orders are carried out. Except for you," she said, pointing.

Half a dozen girls of the Transcasp came forth. They knelt on either side of Alisher, their glances stealing to the Silver Mage, who held Arian fast in his arms.

Lania returned her attention to the poet, compelling him to meet her eyes. "I did not Augur your presence here, Mudassir, and this puzzles me." Her use of his former title startled him. "How did you come to be with my sister?"

"I—ah—chanced upon the First Oralist," he managed. "I was rescued from death at the Tower of the Claim by the courage of the Silver Mage."

"Yet you stole back into the Ark, using my doves against me," Lania told him. "It was the last time, Mudassir. Do not return again."

Alisher bowed low, his ill-fitting breastplate banging against his knees. "It was my honor to teach you, Highness."

A faint smile shimmered through the ruins of her mask. "Didn't you know, Mudassir? It was always *me* teaching you."

Alisher hesitated. He dropped to one knee, adopting the posture of the doves. "Khanum," he said, "what of Pari and Donyanaz? May I take them with me?"

Lania ignored the request. She spoke to two of her doves instead. "Find the one called Gul. I will need her at the Sihraat."

At the mention of Gul's name, Arian's head came up. For the first time, she looked at her sister—at the destruction of the dais and the silent emptiness of the great hall. What had seemed insurmountable to Arian, Lania had destroyed in moments, taking control of the Ahdath and the Wall, the Authoritan burned to dust.

In a hoarse voice, Arian asked, "Was this what you always intended? Is this why you brought me here? To use me to defeat him?"

Lania's face didn't soften. "You still think it was you? After I let him give you to Nevus? No, little sister." She glanced at Daniyar, a sudden softening in her face. "It was the Silver Mage. *His* was the blood I needed. He was *everything* I needed. You were merely a pretext the Authoritan could believe. He wasn't my savior," she said thoughtfully. "The Authoritan was my destroyer."

She turned away from the warmth of Daniyar's eyes—from his limitless compassion.

Hesitantly Arian continued. "Did the blood of the Silver Mage change you? Did it truly make you stronger?"

Lania's answer was fierce. "Blood changes everything." And at Arian's troubled look, she said, "Do not ask what you do not wish to know." She ignored Arian's confusion, her gaze sweeping the hall to take the measure of her victory. She snapped orders at those who had yet to leave the room, evidence not only of her abilities, but of the single-minded ferocity it had taken to get her to this moment. The gestures of her arms rippled with power and purpose.

Arian went to Lania and embraced her. Impatiently Lania suffered the embrace, though her hand was gentle on the wound at Arian's back.

"It will be cleansed," she murmured.

Arian drew back to look at her. "You are free of this now," she said. "Come with me. Come back to Hira where you belong."

Lania pushed Arian aside, her gilded green eyes ablaze with a violent satisfaction. "You seem to forget that I command an army—I now command *everything* north of the Wall."

"And what will you do with your army?" Daniyar asked. He reached for Arian's hand, pulling her back to his side, his gesture possessive and bold.

Lania's eyes darkened. She took note of his silent allegiance with a peremptory nod of her head. She spoke in a brittle voice. "What does it matter to you, my lord? Your destiny calls you away."

"You told me I would die tonight."

"I said you would *lose*—and lose the Qatilah you did." She pointed to the Authoritan's shattered scepter. "But it was never my intent to let you die. Not when your blood is so precious."

Daniyar looked at her steadily, reading the things she didn't say, the unvarnished emotion that she tried to disguise. "Am I your prisoner, then? You told the Authoritan my blood would renew him *if* you kept me alive. Is it the same for you, Lania?"

Her eyes closed at his gentle use of her name. With a blind gesture, she indicated the powder collected by her doves.

"I have no need of you now. Your blood has served its purpose in my rites. Take my sister and go."

Arian let out a sound of protest. "You could still come to Hira."

Lania's reply was cold. "You understand me not at all, sister."

Arian persisted. "If you won't save yourself, think of your doves. They were brought here by Talisman slave-chains. Will you not act against that? Will you not aid me in this?"

"The doves are none of your concern, sister. Stay if you will; go if you choose. I must take my Ahdath in hand."

"To what end, Lania? *Why* do you seek this war?"

"Why do you think? The Authoritan has answered for his crimes. Now I unleash my army on the Talisman and on anyone who stands in my way."

"Then we fight the same battle. We serve the same cause."

"No, Arian—we do not."

They stared at each other, so closely bound together, so alike in coloring and expression and countenance, yet so different at heart and in experience, the older face a ruined echo of the promise of the younger.

Sensing she had lost, Arian pressed a hand to Lania's cheek. "I came to save you, Lania."

"I know you did, little bird." Gently she removed her sister's hand from her face. She studied the lines of Arian's palm closely. "I Augur a difficult road for you, Arian—what waits for you beyond the Wall will cause you a suffering unlike anything you have known."

Arian stared at her, stricken. Lania knew her inadequacies as First Oralist better than anyone else. If *she* thought Arian would fail . . .

She tried to hide her uncertainty, but she knew that Lania had seen. Blinking swiftly, she said, "What is to come, Lania? What do you foretell?"

Lania shook her head, amused. "You are First Oralist of Hira. You do not believe in Augury. You certainly cannot sanction it."

They stared into each other's eyes, loss and love passing between them in a language neither sister could speak. The long years Arian had spent searching for Lania, raiding slave-chains, cast out from Hira, impelled by a love that was truer in memory than reality—to find Lania so distant, so twisted by darkness . . . so changed. And yet still with that infinitesimal spark of love buried beneath the ruins of her charade as the Authoritan's consort. Lania's love for Arian hadn't died. Neither was it enough. And Arian—so gifted in the Claim, so powerful in her own right as a child of Hira's magic—couldn't find a way to persuade her or to reach her sister's heart. Lania's refusal to speak a word of affection to her, to offer Arian anything deeper as an explanation of her choices, told Arian as much.

The links that had bound the daughters of their house—the daughters of Hira—had long since been sundered by suffering. There was nothing else Arian could do.

Feeling the weight of her disillusionment, Daniyar pulled Arian back into his arms, determined to shield her from everything still to come. "We must go," he murmured in her ear. "The Bloodprint cannot wait."

Lania nodded at her sister. "Go with him, he is yours. It is you he loves, no other."

Daniyar glanced at her dress. "You still bleed, Lania. Let me do what I can to aid you."

With a proud lift of her chin, she waved his hands away. "Do not presume to handle me. I cannot bear your touch."

Her voice faltered over the lie, and Daniyar registered the truth. She had wanted him, she had grown to care for him, and so she had sought to protect him . . . though what moved him most was that she had hoped he would yearn for her in turn. But his love for Arian was unmistakable, *undeniable* . . . and he looked at Lania with regret for having deceived her to this end. Outraged, she strode across the dais, searing him with a look. She snapped her fingers. One of her doves brought the six-tailed whip to her hand. She curled it around her fingers. Cracked, stripped, bleeding, and defaced, she seethed with imperial power. Holding Daniyar's gaze, she took her seat on the Authoritan's throne. "*This* was your gift to me."

Alone in the throne room, Lania dipped a finger into the bowl of white powder. She extracted the vial of Daniyar's blood to add it to the bowl, stirring it with her finger. When the mixture had thickened, she lifted the bowl to her lips and sipped. Then she set down the bowl and took up the six-tailed whip, easing back onto the throne.

The tails of the whip were stained with Daniyar's blood.

She remembered how he'd looked, beaten and bloodied by the Ahdath, his face strained in agony, his fierce will unbroken. How much pain the Ahdath had caused him. How much he'd been willing to suffer on her sister's behalf. She touched her lips to the whip, kissing the traces of his blood.

Then she destroyed it with a word.

23

THE BLACK KHAN'S PARTY HAD BEEN ON THE ROAD FOR TWELVE DAYS and had changed their horses twice. They were close to Ashfall, having ridden through the night, to discover the first of the Talisman's preparations against the city. With the attention of their main army focused on Ashfall's outer defenses, the Talisman had dispatched a smaller force to block both sides of the approach to a narrow pass that led down to the plains, where the Talisman army was camped, south and east of the city's ramparts. The lowlands that surrounded the city were deep and fertile, sectioned with dozens of glimmering blue tributaries, yet anything that could have given sustenance to Ashfall had already been set to the fire or claimed for the Talisman's own use.

Because the passage ahead was cut off, a confrontation would be necessary for the Black Khan to reach his seat of power. He'd been a long time away, and the Talisman had been on the move, a wave of infantry, patient and determined, readying themselves for combat against the Black Khan's army, the forces of the Zhayedan.

Seldom used to fighting in the open, the Talisman were a guerrilla force, skilled in ambush from the cover of their mountains.

As Ashfall's mountains lay too far to the south for the Talisman to use for this purpose, the only advantage their infantry possessed was in numbers. And the Talisman had bolstered those numbers by recruiting men from towns and villages they had conquered on the central plains. Approaching from the east, their forces expanded west and now had Ashfall in their sights. If the Black Khan was unable to harness the power of the Bloodprint, his capital was doomed to fall.

But he had other weapons at his disposal—plots he had laid, allegiances he had won—and he would strive to make use of them all before the battle was done.

Looking down from the pass, to the battle lines far ahead, he dismissed the sight of the Talisman's forces with a disdainful sniff. Each weapon he commanded, including the Bloodprint, *would* respond to his need.

And once he unlocked the magic of the Bloodprint, he would scrub the Talisman from his lands. He would extend his protection to the lands farther west, as far as the gates of Hira. With the magic of the Bloodprint at his fingers, he would realize his long-sought goal: Hira would become a protectorate of Ashfall, unable to stand on its own. He would ensure its survival. In turn, the sisterhood's gifts would be placed at the service of Ashfall—*his* service—*if* he could rout the Talisman approach. Then he would turn his attention to his talents as the Dark Mage. How high he would rise—how much more he would be able to achieve—all of Khorasan would witness. And the One-Eyed Preacher would have no choice but to fear his will.

Rukh summoned Commander Arsalan, the general of his army, with a whistle.

A man with glossy back hair and exceptionally refined features rode to the Black Khan's side. He was dressed in sharp black with no betraying traces of status about his armor. His face was covered with a transparent mask, similar to the Black Khan's own. He was broad-shouldered and strong, of a height with the Khan, and he sat his horse like a king.

"Excellency?"

"The path through the wetlands is cut off by barricade ahead. You'll need to retreat to skirt their encampment. Once you do, send back a troop of Zhayedan to help us break through the pass. They won't anticipate trouble from behind—we'll attack from both sides. I'll expect your return by midday."

The commander nodded. "I'll send two of my best at once."

"No." Rukh frowned. Ahead on the ridge where the Talisman had set up their barrier, two soldiers changed over their patrol. "Go yourself, Arsalan. You're the fastest rider among us."

Arsalan placed a familiar hand on the Black Khan's arm. Rukh covered it with his own, drawing Arsalan closer. "You cannot refuse this," he said.

"I swore an oath not to leave your side, Rukh. I don't trust your safety to anyone else. Khashayar rides as well as I, and he thinks for himself besides."

Arsalan held up his spyglass, scouting a path a lone rider might risk. It was his turn to frown.

"It's too late, Excellency. The men on the ridge are sending out scouts of their own. But not ahead to the walls—they're doing a sweep back toward our approach—perhaps they've had news of the Assassin and want to cover this road. We'll have to make our stand on our own."

"How many men all told?"

"Forty."

"And our company is twelve."

"Yes, Excellency. Two archers and ten who ride to battle. There is also the boy."

"What is your counsel, then?"

"To take the pass ahead, we'll need to face them here before they summon reinforcements."

Rukh was reassured by Arsalan's air of calm, though he'd long since learned his general was ready for any scenario that might confront them.

"We need to draw them in, then," Rukh concluded.

Arsalan nodded. "I'll send Khashayar to lure them."

"They'll be cautious—they won't come all at once—which would be better for us."

"Khashayar will be wearing the Cloak."

The Black Khan's eyes widened in subtle appreciation of Arsalan's strategy. Of course the Talisman would come if Khashayar rode into view wearing the Sacred Cloak. They were hunting for the Cloak. They were preparing their siege against the Citadel to retrieve it; they had no notion it was in the Black Khan's keeping—the first of his betrayals of Hira.

"Well done," he said to Arsalan. "But if we should lose this skirmish, do not forget your oath."

A signal passed between them—a reminder he impressed upon Arsalan that was met with a hostile silence.

"I have forgiven you many things, Arsalan," Rukh said. "I wouldn't forgive you this."

Arsalan's lips tightened. "You ask the impossible of me."

The Black Khan smiled—a slow, seductive curving of his lips that had disarmed many an opponent in the past. He had used it last on Ilea.

Arsalan's eyes settled on the smile for a moment before he

turned away. "Don't waste your efforts on me." His voice was colored by an emotion he didn't name. "You know I will keep my oath."

An oath they had forged in blood—never to dishonor the empire by yielding to the Talisman alive. Arsalan's dagger in Rukh's breast was preferable to a public beheading.

And rather than let them take possession of it, Rukh would burn the Bloodprint.

Y ou, man, what do you have there?" a Talisman scout called out. "Don't tell me you don't know." Khashayar's certainty mocked the Talisman. An angry response followed.

Khashayar had donned the Sacred Cloak, another stratagem of Arsalan's. Now he clutched a handful of the cloth in his hand for the Talisman soldiers to see. Some distance back, Rukh recognized the soldiers' insignia, the black stroke against the field of green. These were not Talisman rabble, they were men of the Shin War, and Rukh had not enjoyed his last encounter with the foremost member of their tribe, the Silver Mage.

Rukh remembered the sound of betrayal in the Companion of Hira's voice, the fragile and beautiful First Oralist.

How unworthy you are of the Bloodprint.

And he'd mockingly replied, *I am unworthy of anything less,* though the man who was truly of worth had been standing chained at her side. The Silver Mage, the Authenticate. A name to induce hope in the broken city of Candour. He'd left the Silver Mage and the First Oralist to the Authoritan's care, and it bothered him now that he dwelt on whether it had been right to do so.

The deed was done. And nothing he chose to do now could undo it. They were likely already dead.

But there was still the possibility that Ashfall would survive, and the survival of his city was worth any compromise Rukh had been forced to make. He wouldn't second-guess himself when he knew he would make the same choice if pushed to the same hard edge.

Seeming to catch his thoughts, Arsalan gripped his arm. "Are you ready for this, my lord?"

Rukh smiled at Arsalan again. He was the prince of an empire. He was never anything but ready.

He took up his spyglass and nodded.

"Tell Khashayar to make his move."

24

THE BLACK KHAN TRIED TO MOVE AHEAD ALONG THE PASS, BUT ARSA-
lan blocked his horse as a matter of course, his sword held aloft
in his hand. There was no higher ground on which to position
archers, but two of his soldiers were in the vanguard of their party,
their bows strung, their horses narrowing the entrance to the area
protected by the overhang. These were the Zhayedan's elite archers, the Teerandaz, an all-female company who trained apart
from the rest. They would cut down the Talisman's numbers before they engaged at close quarters.

Arsalan used his body as a shield to protect the Black Khan.
Rukh would have found Arsalan's protectiveness amusing . . . if
it didn't diminish his authority before his men. But he'd chosen
not to address the tension between Arsalan and himself, reluctant
to call his commander to account. At this moment, it served his
purpose to allow Arsalan to have his way. He needed to minimize
the risk to himself, as the Bloodprint was hidden in his saddlebags.
The manuscript was his trust—it was the sole hope of Ashfall
against the One-Eyed Preacher's conjurings.

They waited for something to break, the air close and cold around them, their horses restless on the higher ground. Wind whipped along the pass, bitter and cruel as it found the openings in their armor. Wafa whimpered as it found him unprotected. The Black Khan sniffed at this evidence of his fear. The boy feared a return to his Talisman masters, when what he should have feared was the destruction of his world.

With his spyglass, the Black Khan could see Khashayar taking liberties with the Sacred Cloak, stroking its folds with possessive hands.

"This is mine," he called out. "I assume lordship over Talisman lands. *I* command you now."

He experienced a moment of anger at Khashayar's presumption, even though he knew Khashayar's actions were directed by Arsalan—the Sacred Cloak was *his* and no other's—and then all at once, he smiled.

If it enraged the Black Khan to see Khashayar in the Cloak, the Talisman's fury would be greater.

Indeed, the Talisman gave chase. Khashayar outpaced them, drawing them back toward the overhang, a slew of arrows raining down in his wake. Then a voice bolder than the rest commanded, "Hold your fire, you fools. Take him without harming the Sacred Cloak."

It was a strange voice, rolling in rhythmic cadences—the words layered over each other, then layered again, a hundred men speaking in one voice.

The Black Khan's heart began to race, powerfully compelled by the sound.

Ahead of him on the path, Arsalan's horse pawed at the ground.

Arsalan held his mount with a hand. He shot a glance over his shoulder at his prince, a glance warm with reassurance. "There is nothing to fear, my prince. Khashayar will draw them to us."

But as the dismal tones of the voice rang out, Rukh felt a stirring of dread.

Arsalan didn't share his prince's doubts. He waited with a steady hand, and when the first group of Talisman appeared around the bend, they were taken by the Teerandaz. Then for long moments all was confusion and sound, underlined by the impatient fury of the hooves of the Zhayedan's horses.

The archers gave way to the men behind them, and in moments combat was joined. A second wave, a third, their fate invisible to the party of men who held their positions ahead at the barricade. The Zhayedan's fearless efforts cut the Talisman's numbers in half.

No other Talisman ventured forth. And though none had slipped beyond the Black Khan's party, there were still enough men to bar the road to Ashfall.

Khashayar gained the safety of the overhang. He let the Sacred Cloak ray out like a banner of war.

The Black Khan stayed his action, pointing to the Cloak with a deadly warning in his eyes. "Don't forget yourself, Khashayar."

Abashed, Khashayar paused to remove the Cloak, bowing before the Khan. "I wear it only in your service." He hastened to fasten it over the Khan's armor, and Rukh gave him an autocratic nod.

"Stay with His Excellency," Arsalan commanded.

Rukh contradicted him at once. "I will ride to the barricade with you. We need every man to fight. None should remain, except the Teerandaz. Send the archers through the wetlands to Ashfall. The army cannot do without them."

Arsalan nodded at the helmed and masked archers. They wheeled their horses around and descended.

"Stay here, Rukh. I have a plan."

Arsalan didn't wait for the Black Khan's permission or the forthcoming rebuke at Arsalan's impertinence before the Zhayedan. Instead, he took his cavalry and rode full speed at the barricade. Arrows flew out from behind it. Two of his riders fell. Now the Zhayedan numbered seven, but they had succeeded in closing the distance. They fought the Talisman at close quarters, their horses bearing down the barrier. Though the margin of victory was narrow, the Zhayedan were the superior fighters.

Hope bloomed in Rukh's chest, firing him with bold purpose.

Then a terrible sound pierced the night—pulsing with a thousand overtones, a twisted, occult rhythm, unhallowed and unearthly in tone. The horses of the Zhayedan faltered, and the Talisman wrested the riders to the ground to face a more equal combat. Unhorsed, Arsalan doggedly pressed ahead, roaring for his men to follow. There were seven, there were five, and then there were only three.

They matched the handful of Talisman who remained, but the noise emanating from behind the barrier was a weapon they couldn't fight. It attacked from all sides, straight to the heart of them, dulling the precision of their swords.

The Black Khan waited no longer.

Arrayed in the Sacred Cloak, he rode forth on his steaming black, gathering up the reins of Arsalan's horse as he plunged ahead. Nothing could be allowed to happen to his general.

"See me," Rukh called to his men. "See the Commander of the Faithful!"

If they responded, Rukh couldn't hear—the Cloak was a barrier against the sound. It streamed behind him as he rode. His stallion plunged over the barricade, seeming almost to fly. Arsalan caught the reins of his horse from Rukh and flung himself back into the saddle.

Abruptly, the sound ceased, the valley below now quiet. Arsalan and Khashayar were to either side of Rukh, dispatching the men who were sheltered behind the barricade. Khashayar vaulted from his horse, striding through bodies, checking each man for signs of life. Arsalan stayed at Rukh's side, seeking others along the winding path, sword at the ready in his hand.

"What was that?" Arsalan muttered, craning his head around the overhang.

Rukh shook his head. He couldn't say what he'd seen—the illusory image so closely aligned to the sound, smoke rising high above the barricade. And from the smoke and shadows, a piercing annihilation had issued.

He shook his head to banish the image. Whatever he imagined he'd seen, it hadn't been able to defeat them—they'd left no Talisman alive. Khashayar and Arsalan gathered the bodies of their comrades and sent them ahead on their horses. Now there was nothing between the Black Khan and the safety of his city. The dead would be received by their own, along with weapons they had taken from the Talisman. His archers would send soldiers to assist them.

They rode back to their shelter, the Black Khan surprised to see the boy hunched over his horse, his face wet with tears, his feeble shoulders shaking. He had left the Bloodprint to the boy with a murmured instruction to defend it, and the boy had chosen not to flee.

When he saw the Black Khan seated on his black, the boy gave a shuddering sob. To Rukh's surprise, there was a look of relief in his eyes. He passed over the manuscript without a word. His teeth were chattering with fear. His hand brushed the Sacred Cloak, and he stared up at the Black Khan in wonder.

"You wear my lady's Cloak. You took it from my lady."

Khashayar laughed, the notion of a woman assuming the Cloak of Commander of the Faithful an impossible, untimely jest.

The Black Khan didn't join in his laughter. He eyed the boy, who had not been present at the Council of Hira—how could he have known about the Cloak? Surely the First Oralist would not have shared its secrets with a Talisman slave.

"It saved you," Wafa continued. He pointed down the path. Rukh felt the first pang of pity at his wide-eyed fear. What had this boy's life been? And what other terrors waited for him ahead? "It saved you from *him*," he choked out.

Now Rukh glanced back over his shoulder, trying to make sense of his words. The road ahead was empty, the smoke dispersed, the barricade borne away.

"What do you speak of, boy?" Arsalan asked. "We left no man alive."

As the boy's mouth went slack with shock and he snuffled back his tears, an intimation of dread rose in the Black Khan's soul as he guessed what the boy would say.

"Didn't you see him?" Wafa asked. "Didn't you see the One-Eyed Preacher?"

25

THEIR SMALL COMPANY NOW TOOK THE SOUTHERN ROAD THROUGH THE
wetlands, riding hard and fast. They skirted the plains of the
salt lake, taking care to ride along the shoreline, where the waves
would erode their tracks. As they crossed the plains and found
entire villages about their business with no sign of preparation
for the Talisman offense, the Black Khan's mood grew grimmer.
When they reached the outer defenses, they were met by a party
of riders. The rest formed an honor guard that rode at the Black
Khan's side.

At the approach to the ramparts, the Black Khan reined in his
horse. Arsalan halted beside him. A series of horns sounded the
return of the Khan to his capital. His standard, a black rook on a
silver field, was raised above the walls.

Arsalan scanned the ramparts, a hand shading his eyes from
the stark glare of the sun. "The soldiers I set to regular patrol are
absent from their duty. I left strict instructions for the city's defense, yet look at the ramparts now."

A single soldier was stationed at a bell tower. Above the gate,
where the heaviest concentration of Zhayedan should have been

positioned, there were only two members of the Teerandaz, and those were the women who had ridden with the Khan.

Arsalan frowned. "I gave the Teerandaz no orders to guard the gate."

Rukh considered this before he answered. "They would have seen what we're seeing now and acted as they deemed necessary."

Arsalan's stallion cantered a short distance away, allowing the Black Khan to take the full measure of Ashfall's defenses.

"We aren't ready. We are nowhere near prepared for the Talisman assault. Send a courier to the Eagle's Nest. I require the Assassin's immediate attendance."

"I wonder if your trust in him is misplaced."

"I wonder if it is my trust in the Zhayedan that is rather at error." He ignored Arsalan's swift frown. "Send for him at once. Boy—do not wander off." As Wafa's mount sidestepped nervously, the Black Khan reached for the horse's reins. "You will be in my city soon enough, and there you will have to earn your keep."

Another signal passed between Arsalan and Rukh, and at the look, Wafa choked back a sob.

The Black Khan dropped the reins of his horse. "I am not a pederast, boy. You *do* have other uses. You will share with my Nizam what you know of the One-Eyed Preacher."

If anything, Wafa looked more afraid of this.

The Black Khan made an effort to soften his voice. "Do you imagine you've returned to the care of your cruel masters when you've escaped to a land of grace? You will not be brutalized here."

He made the promise carelessly, a hard knot of certainty in his chest that if it was necessary to do otherwise, he would not be bound by his oath.

Wafa's gaze dropped to the hands he'd fastened around the pommel of his saddle. It was clear to the Black Khan that the boy trusted only to the kindness of the Companions. When it came to men, the boy had learned he would always be at their mercy.

As were they all, he thought.

"Rukh." Arsalan's horse cantered back to Rukh's side. "We must hurry. Messengers should have been sent to the villages that lie outside the protection of the outer walls. I would know why my orders have been gainsaid."

"Whoever disobeyed your commands will be stripped of rank at once."

Arsalan shook his head, his counsel more measured. "If that were the only danger, there would be little to fear."

Rukh looked at him sharply. "Why? What is it you foresee?"

Arsalan reached over and patted the saddlebag that held the Bloodprint. He frowned at the barren ramparts. "What if the Qaysarieh Portal has been breached?"

26

THEY CLOSED THE DISTANCE BETWEEN THE OUTER RAMPARTS AND THE city walls, Wafa straggling behind, too unskilled to match their pace. Impatient with the boy, Arsalan pulled up and shifted him onto his own horse, leaving Wafa's mount for his soldiers to collect. Wafa sat frozen and anxious before him as they swept past fields of orchard grass bordered by red clover. The path for their horses was a wide avenue, smooth and well worn, unlike the rutted tracks or hardscrabble landscape of the lands to the west. Astride Commander Arsalan's elegant white horse, Wafa was no longer jostled in the saddle.

A second set of horns sounded at the entrance to the city walls. The walls were built of rectangular blocks of smooth white stone, with guard towers at regular intervals. A turquoise frieze decorated each tower, depictions of ancient battles fought for the Black Khan's capital.

The walls seemed to stretch beyond the horizon, bursts of hot bright sunlight casting a dazzle on the stone. The radiance of the stone was blinding, standards mounted and flown along its numerous crenellations.

Then they were at the gate, a gate wide enough to admit the entrance of an entire regiment. A symbol was grafted on the shining silver of the doors: the black rook, emblem of the Khan, and of the ancient nobility of his line.

The gate was opened to the sound of the most beautiful music Wafa had ever heard: he didn't know what could have produced such a sound—gliding wings, gold-tuned strings, the plaintive cry of a throat—but it seemed as if all of history had been captured by the soaring notes.

Their horses passed through to the capital of Ashfall, the gate closing behind them with the same soul-stirring sound. And here Wafa didn't know where he should look first. He'd seen nothing of the beauty of Marakand, terrified by his ordeal at the Blood Shed. But he didn't believe for a moment Marakand approached the magnificence of the sight he beheld now.

They had entered Ashfall from the southern gate, bypassing an opulent house of worship that lay just off the city's axis. As they crossed the gate into a public square built on a scale so massive it dwarfed Marakand's Registan, it became apparent that the facade of the house of worship was visible from each of the three major structures situated on the perimeter. On the western facade, the royal palace entered by the Illustrious Portal. To the east, an exquisite dome presided over a private house of worship reserved for the family of the prince. And to the north end, the Qaysarieh Portal, its doors guarded by archers stationed at a pair of towers.

The square itself stretched out as far as the eye could see, gardens interrupted by fountains, and then laid out again within squares of mulberry and plane trees, a series of orchards framing the whole. Broad thoroughfares dissected the square: the main avenue dedicated to the Khan's army; others for carters, merchants, and ambassadors of state. A pearl-strewn path was reserved for the royal procession.

The square was organized into an outdoor bazaar, with lanes allocated to artisans and jewelers, brocade weavers, armorers, porcelain-casters, papermakers, gardeners, sculptors, painters, and draftsmen. A separate area, farthest from Qaysarieh, was populated by those recruited to provide entertainment to the court: animal tamers, jugglers, jesters, acrobats, dancers, musicians, and poets.

Music drifted through the orchards, a whimsical breeze carrying the scent of lemon trees. The fragrance of roses from invisible gardens perfumed the path taken by their horses. Wafa's head swiveled from side to side in wonder.

R ukh observed the boy's wonder with a mix of amusement and pride.

"Ashfall is half the world." The Black Khan said it with a hard satisfaction in his voice.

One of Alisher's more popular verses had recounted the inestimable grace of the cities of Black Aura and Marakand, a verse that had become popular in Ashfall's alleys and bazaars. But the Black Khan had heard it with contempt.

The holy cities entire could not purchase a single of Ashfall's glories.

Arsalan didn't share his contentment. "Rukh. This is not a city that prepares for war." He nodded at the smooth expanse of grass that bordered the Qaysarieh Portal. A course of equestrian jumps had been set up for a group of riders who were putting their thoroughbreds through their stately paces. "I left instruction. Only one man may countermand my wishes."

Rukh frowned. "He would not do so without reason, Arsalan. Perhaps his scouts have returned to him with news the advance has slowed."

Arsalan did not contradict Rukh, though it was plain that he didn't agree. The two men drew up to the gates of the Qaysarieh Portal. The portal was copiously tiled in blue, the Black Khan's symbol appearing at regular intervals with a grace and artistry that suggested a belonging to rather than a conquering of the surrounding environs.

Wafa was taken from Arsalan's horse by two of the palace's pages. At their inquiry, Arsalan shook his head. "No, he is not meant for Qaysarieh. Dress him and bring him to the Divan-e Shah. Send the Black Khan's personal guard to meet us."

Arsalan and Rukh passed under the portal to the palace of the Black Khan. Here the mystery of the perfume of unseen roses was solved. In the skillfully laid gardens within, masses of white blooms crowned the arbors that framed the stairs.

The riders relinquished their horses to the care of grooms. The Black Khan took the manuscript of the Bloodprint into his own hands and carried it before him. Inside the palace, he was met by a reception. Long-lashed women dressed in pearls and patterned silk held up trays filled with jasmine and rose petals. At the Black Khan's entry, the petals were scattered over the men's hair, and pious and heartfelt devotions for the prosperity of the Black Khan were murmured. He felt a momentary easing of strain, his sense of homecoming deep and profound with Arsalan at his side.

A sweetly swelling sound rose from a trio of setar players centered in the reception hall. Attendants scurried forth, bringing trays of glasses filled with sherbet, platters of apricots and peaches, and basins of scented water.

In the custom of the Black Khan's house, Arsalan and Rukh

paused to wash their hands and faces. When the ritual was complete, the Black Khan dismissed the women.

Arsalan summoned a page. "Find the commanders of the Khorasan Guard. Send runners to the outer ramparts, the city walls, and the Qaysarieh Portal. I want to see them at once."

Their preparations were interrupted by the sound of a glad cry. A young woman ran to meet them from across the vast entrance hall, her slippers tapping on the black-veined marble floor. She threw herself into the Black Khan's embrace, looping her arms around his neck. "Rukh! You've come at last! Your place at court has been empty."

The Black Khan hugged her close for a moment, then set her on her feet, detaching himself from her embrace.

"Princess, you're looking well."

Rukh's use of her title was a reminder to his sister of the stringent etiquette of court. Her warmth faltering, she took half a step back. She corrected her posture, standing slim and straight, presenting herself for his inspection. Her dress would have made it apparent she was a princess of the royal court, her resemblance to him even more so. Her hair was silky and dark, its natural curl tamed, her black eyes full of mischief and life. Yet she was not entirely at ease in the ceremonial dress of court, the dozen layers of lustrous silk captured at her waist by a thick embroidered belt, matched by a series of veils that framed her hair. She was also burdened by jewels in a pearl collar too heavy for her neck and gold armlets that extended from her wrists to her shoulders. She wore a pair of jeweled anklets that he had given her. They chimed when she moved, and had been chosen for that reason—so that he would have forewarning of all his sister's movements. Most marked in her attire was an enormous white pearl that hovered in the space between her well-shaped eyebrows. It signified her rank as princess, yet she still gave the impression of being dressed in someone else's clothes.

"I'm glad to see you have prospered in my absence." Rukh nodded at Arsalan. "I am not the only one who merits a proper greeting, Darya."

His sister blushed, a splash of apricot against her sun-warmed skin. "Commander Arsalan."

Bowing her head, she murmured a series of courtesies without meeting Arsalan's eyes. He responded in kind, nothing in his demeanor suggesting she delayed him in seeking his commanders. Rukh did not permit any neglect of the courtesies of his court, no matter the urgency of circumstance. He was watchful for it in Darya, whose loving and whimsical nature resisted his efforts at discipline.

"Where is the Nizam, Darya? It isn't like him to be remiss in his welcome."

The Princess faltered at his tone. Her manner became consciously formal.

"His grace Nizam al-Mulk awaits you at the Divan-e Shah. He will relinquish his trust in person, Excellency."

"He has not been out at the ramparts?"

"Not since you left, Excellency. Is anything the matter?"

Arsalan cut across her words. "What of the Qaysarieh Portal? Has the Nizam visited Qaysarieh, child?"

Darya's painful blush greeted this form of address. Rukh had made no secret of his desire that she marry the commander of his army. By calling her a child, as he so often did, Arsalan was making it clear that he did not view her as an equal.

Studying the rings that adorned her fingers, Darya answered, "Nizam al-Mulk oversees his Excellency's commands in the Divan-e Shah. He does no more or less than the Black Khan asked of him.

May I ask the reason behind your questions? And your summons of the Zhayedan?"

While Arsalan hesitated over his response, Rukh brushed his sister aside. "This is not the time, Darya. Go on ahead—tell the Nizam I have come."

Darya bent her head again. "Excellency."

Of the two men, only Rukh observed her departure.

Arsalan caught him by the arm. Rukh wheeled to face him with a look of menace.

"She's your sister, not your subject."

"She is *both*. She forgets herself, Arsalan. In the absence of our mother, the stature of the court rests upon her shoulders."

"Darya wasn't meant for the frivolities of court—you *know* her talents lie elsewhere. She is wasted in the role of princess."

Rukh addressed this coldly. "It is not a 'role.' It is her *duty*. Her pretensions are an insult to the court. To prefer the asceticism of Hira to the privilege of her life at Ashfall . . . Marry her, Arsalan, and put an end to these wayward dreams."

"I will not marry a woman against her will. Even if that woman is Darya."

Rukh's laugh was mirthless. "You think her unwilling? It is because you neglect those pretty attentions that women require that her thoughts ever turned to Hira. Had you not made your rejection so plain—"

"She's a child, Rukh."

"She's a woman. You choose not to see it."

"You know why. There is nothing about Darya that attracts me. I cannot help that."

A hostile, weighted look passed between the two men, an unaccustomed tension in the air. Rukh studied Arsalan intently, his narrowed eyes tracing the proud lines of his face—a contrast to the warmth and affection he had always found in Arsalan's strik-ing eyes—absent from them now as Rukh pushed him without re-morse.

"Come closer," Rukh said, testing him. "Look me in the eye as you refuse."

A low growl sounded from Arsalan's throat, a rare glimpse of his displeasure. Angered, he stepped closer, pinning Rukh against the wall with a strong arm at his throat, warning him he wouldn't be trifled with. He looked his prince dead in the eye.

The silence between them held.

Finally Rukh said in a carefully neutral voice, "Don't force me to make this a command. Marry her before the week is out—*before* Ashfall falls to our enemies."

He spoke with utmost seriousness, his dark eyes candid and soft.

Breathing heavily, Arsalan shifted his arm from Rukh's throat and punched his fist against the wall. He took another breath, then stepped back. When he looked at Rukh again, all emotion was wiped from his face—replaced by the same hard calculation Rukh knew could be read from his own.

"I would protect her with my life, regardless."

A half measure. It would not serve with Ashfall at the edge of collapse.

"That is *not* why I demand it. Do you refuse the honor I confer? Do you dare refuse a princess of Ashfall—and one who loves you, besides?"

"Would you truly have this of me? Would you do such a thing to your sister?"

Arsalan's voice was harsh. Rukh ignored his rebuke.

As idly as if he had nothing at stake, he replied, "Yours is an honorable bloodline, Arsalan. If my brother's machinations succeed, there is no one else I would trust to see to Darya's safety. The marriage could not be set aside—she would be safe from Darius's brutes."

"Darius would have me beheaded at Qaysarieh. Then Darya's state of widowhood would offer her as much protection as if we hadn't married at all."

"Then you *do* refuse your prince. I didn't think this day would come."

Rukh knew he was pushing Arsalan too hard, just as he knew he'd been left with no other choice.

For the sake of the empire . . . for his sister . . . even for the friend he loved . . .

Suddenly weary, he rubbed a hand over his eyes. He expected no reprieve from the difficulties ahead, but he'd believed that Arsalan would stand with him until the calamitous end. He opened his eyes to find Arsalan watching him with an unexpected softness in his face.

And then he had what he'd sought when Arsalan yielded all at once. "I have never refused you anything. I will not begin now."

He was shaken by this proof of Arsalan's allegiance, but it was a weakness he could not betray lest Arsalan change his mind. He shook back his hair from his face with an insolent tilt to his head.

On a sly note of mockery, he said, "I trust you will find a way to rise to the occasion. Darya has her . . . charms."

Arsalan checked him with a hard shove of his shoulder. "What transpires between the Princess and myself is none of your concern."

27

In the throne room, Darya conveyed the Black Khan's message to the Nizam, who expressed no surprise at the news. He removed himself from the throne, taking the seat of the Grand Vizier.

Her message delivered, Darya retraced her steps, seeking the comfort of her brother's presence. She came to an abrupt halt in an alcove along the long hallway that led to the Divan-e Shah. Her brother and his commander were speaking of her in low voices.

It was too late to retreat. She melted into the shadows where she couldn't see them, thankful her dress was dark.

But as she continued to listen, a tide of humiliation washed over her. Her brother was threatening Arsalan—coercing him to a course he clearly did not want. And to hear Arsalan say the words . . .

There is nothing about Darya that attracts me.

She drew in a harsh breath. How well she knew the truth of it.

When the Black Khan had first set his seal on her betrothal, she'd listened to the news with an incandescent joy. If she'd doubted her brother's love of her, his choice of Arsalan as her husband had chased away her fears. There was no man she would rather have chosen for herself than Arsalan, commander of the Zhayedan. He was charismatic and powerful and all that a princess of the court could hope to find in a partner. She'd spent long hours dreaming of a future at his side, her heart beating faster whenever she was in his company.

And though he called her a child and spoke of her as one, he was the one man at court who treated her with respect. When she was present in the Divan-e Shah, Arsalan sought out her opinion and pointed out the wisdom of her counsel. He'd been an advocate and an ally, though she'd never thought to ask him to intercede on her behalf. She had no claim over the Zhayedan's commander; she couldn't ask him for favors. But if he was her betrothed, she knew things would be different. There was nothing she might not entreat from Commander Arsalan now.

And what Darya wanted with her whole hopeful heart was the chance to study at Hira, where she might be instructed by the Companions she so deeply esteemed. She knew Rukh feared the Council of Hira's influence over his only sister, but what she found difficult to accept was the fact that his wishes mattered more than hers. He wielded his power so completely, yet Darya had dreams of her own. Rukh had dismissed her dreams out of hand. She hoped Arsalan would be kinder.

Thus heedlessly joyful at the news of her betrothal, she'd cast aside good sense and sought out Arsalan's company. She'd interrupted him at his task of overseeing Ashfall's defenses, bringing him a garland she'd woven with her own hands.

He'd dismissed the men in attendance to grant her a private audience. In the euphoria of the moment, she hadn't seen that his demeanor was anything but lover-like or remembered that he hadn't expressed the slightest interest in courting her. All she'd seen was the commander of the Zhayedan, attired in his finest uniform, treated with deference by the legions of men under his command, and loved without question by her brother—an immeasurable, respectful love that won her heart anew.

Rukh and Arsalan had grown up as childhood playmates for each other. Together they had learned to ride, to fight, to read. Later, as they'd grown older, one had been chosen to govern an empire, the other to command that empire's army. There was no one her brother trusted more, not even his Grand Vizier.

To be married to a man held in such esteem by the Prince of Khorasan—there could be no greater honor for Darya. Nor was it a marriage contrived strictly for reasons of state, because Darya was wildly in love. And yet in the mad exuberance *of* love, she'd thought to extract from Arsalan the promise her brother had denied her, reserving his right to command every aspect of her life.

High up in the Maiden Tower, she'd offered Arsalan the jasmine garland and broached the subject dearest to her heart, blushingly unable to meet his eyes.

"My lord, I wondered if I might ask a concession of you."

When she'd bowed her head, the pearl amulet that indicated her rank had slipped to one side of her forehead. Mortified, she had pushed it into place.

"Princess." He had bowed in turn, a hint of surprise in his eyes at the offering of the garland. "If it is in my power, I will grant whatever you ask."

She had seen this as the declaration of an ardent lover, and—daringly—she had placed a hand on his wrist, looping the garland over their joined hands.

"Though your offer of marriage honors me, it has always been my wish to study at the Council of Hira. My brother does not approve, thus will not grant me his leave." She had smiled up at him then, a becoming dimple emerging from her cheek. "I wondered if you might seek his permission—he is far more amenable to your counsel than to mine."

Surprisingly, his hand had jerked in hers, crushing the garland's petals. Shocked, she'd eased her grip.

"Please don't mistake me, my lord. I assure you I anticipate our marriage with joy. I would study at Hira for a short term— perhaps for the few months it would take for our wedding to be arranged."

She hadn't been able to read the expression in his eyes, but when he still hadn't spoken, she'd added softly, "A wife learned in the wisdom of Hira would be an asset to the honorable commander of the Zhayedan. I ask only that you consider it."

Embarrassed, Arsalan had released himself, the garland drifting to the ground. It would have been easier for him to turn his back to her, but instead he'd met her gaze, his handsome features grave.

"Forgive me, Princess, you have me at a disadvantage. I made no such proposal. It is not my wish to marry."

Unabashed by his directness, Darya had persisted. "I cannot be mistaken. My brother told me just now that our marriage has been arranged. I assumed it was at your urging. I came to share my joy—to thank you for honoring me so."

A terrible empathy in his eyes, Arsalan had answered, "Princess, I regret that it was not. My responsibilities are too onerous. I have never thought of a wife."

And in that horrible moment, Darya had seen her reckless presumption . . . her eager self-betrayal. Scalded with shame, she had frozen in place, just managing to choke out an apology. "Forgive me, Commander. I've worried you without cause. I fear I've disgraced myself."

She would have fled the tower in tears, but Arsalan had taken hold of her arm. With his other hand, he'd raised her chin to force her to meet his gaze.

"There is no disgrace in your affection, Princess—you have honored me by thinking of me in so favorable a light. Please believe my refusal is a source of regret to me."

Though words had trembled on her lips, Darya hadn't been able to speak. She had wished herself locked away at Hira, never to set eyes upon any man again.

But he wasn't finished with her.

"If you wish it, I will speak to your brother about your desire to train at Hira. It is a noble endeavor, and one well suited to your talents."

She made herself thank him, but his touch had become unbearable on her skin. When he released her, she escaped on trembling legs. Halfway down the tower, she'd collapsed on the stairs and wept. She had climbed the tower with such anticipation, on the wings of her radiant dreams. But she'd been forced to retreat in defeat.

Now she experienced that same humiliation, and she raised her fist to her mouth, fighting back any further display of weakness.

With a shuddering breath, she gathered herself, a sense of resolve stiffening her bones. She wouldn't impose herself on any man, even a man she loved. She made her way to the Maiden Tower, to puzzle through her choices on her own.

To escape damaging them both, she would need to find her own way to Hira. She would have a purpose at Hira—her words would be valued there. And she would know a freedom she'd rarely experienced at her brother's pleasure-seeking court. Lost in these half-formed plans, she startled at the sound of footsteps approaching from the tower door.

The Princess whirled around to face Arsalan, not quick enough to hide the longing in eyes that were brightened by the glimmer of the lamps. The night contained a subtle ingredient: the warm brush of the air against his skin, the smoky tang of watch fires, a tangle of velvet vines creeping up the white stone of the tower. The great square was in the process of being cleared, the last faint notes of the musicians awakening a memory of the halcyon days of the court when art and beauty were pursued at heedless cost.

His head disturbed a cluster of satiny flowers. Their petals flew over his armor like falling stars. He plucked one to offer to Darya. Choosing a safer course, she tried to ease past him without speaking.

"Princess." He didn't touch her, holding her with his voice.

"Commander."

"Don't go just yet. I need a moment to speak to you."

Her eyes found his. He read the flicker of hope in her expression before she turned away, leaning her elbows on the parapet. The city lay quiet below, the slumberous sky above threaded with galaxies of stars. Darya didn't speak or move, the bells at her ankles silent.

"You spoke to me once of marriage—I was discourteous in my refusal and have had reason to change my mind."

Darya went still, her slight figure hunched in on itself. She fingered the heavy cuff at her wrist with evident discomfort. "There's no need to apologize, Commander. You were everything that was gracious."

"Please, Princess. Permit me to reconsider."

As he looked at her delicate profile, he caught the sheen of tears in her eyes. She was young, he thought, and easily overwhelmed. But her answer took him by surprise.

"You mustn't allow my brother to compel you against your better judgment."

"Princess—"

"*There is nothing about Darya that attracts me.*" She repeated his words back to him, her shrug a not-quite-careless gesture. "I'm sorry, I know I trespassed upon your privacy. But a marriage that was forced on you would not avail either one of us. You would find yourself unable to forswear the marriage. And I—"

She fell silent.

"And you, Princess?"

Her throat moved convulsively. "It is not what I wish for, either—to constrain a man who doesn't want me."

There was nothing Arsalan could say to this, though he was moved by her demonstration of pride. It spoke well of her. Yet neither the Princess's awakening self-worth nor his own painfully buried desires could be allowed to stand in the way of the inexorable needs of empire. Though he had no wish to marry Darya, his deepest allegiance was to Rukh.

Unless he could determine a more significant means by which to serve his khan. "Do you still think of Hira?" he asked her.

Surprise cleared away the hurt he'd seen in her eyes, to be replaced by a flare of hope. "My lord?"

"Were you to achieve your desire to study at Hira, would you still serve the needs of Ashfall? Would you think of what was due your brother?"

Darya turned away. In a defeated undertone, she murmured, "I had thought that at Hira, I might finally think of myself."

Arsalan bit back an angry retort. The outer ramparts were ill equipped for the urgently needed defense, the Talisman would overrun the intervening distance by nightfall, yet *these* were the thoughts that occupied the Princess. His bitter disappointment in Darya found its way to his tongue. "Then perhaps you are right, Princess. A woman who would think of herself when her city is at the edge of ruin would not be the woman for me."

Darya whirled to face him, an anguished cry on her lips.

At his involuntary movement toward her, she staggered a few paces back.

"I knew I couldn't please Rukh." The tears in her eyes spilled over. "But I didn't know how deeply you shared his contempt."

"Princess . . ."

She put up a hand to stop him from saying anything more, the frantic chime of the bells at her ankles echoing her distress as she fled.

The Talisman drums sounded a warning across the plains.

And Arsalan let her go.

28

THE RAIN SOAKED THROUGH THEIR OUTER CLOTHING IN MINUTES, THE hooves of their horses sending splashes of mud up along their boots and legs. Even in the rain they rode at a furious pace, Alisher charging ahead. They rode through the night over dry hills and dusk-dark ridges, the path lit by the fires of Talisman encampments. Alisher knew the location of each one of these camps. When they had passed through the Wall and over the Amdar River, he'd gained confidence with every stride, ignoring the city that lay behind them—a city alight with confusion and activity as the news of Lania's coup spread behind the Wall.

The night sky pressed low and heavy against their passage, filled with the cries of birds and the strange growls of unseen predators. There was no shelter to be had, the landscape bare of places where they might have gained a respite. There was nothing ahead but an open road where Talisman scouts could appear at any moment.

Two days of hard riding passed, their bones chilled by rain, before they reached the city to the south. The city had been left in ruins after the Talisman assault: sand-colored dwellings drifted into the landscape, a cluster of buildings sheltered under a barren ridge, stripped of the Marakand loess by an infelicitous pattern of winds.

They slowed their horses on the approach, taking note of a fiery trail of scorch marks and the ruined fields of the harvest. The orchards that ringed the city had been felled. Broken stones littered the path.

"We'll find shelter on the other side of this ridge where it's safe," Alisher said.

"How do you know?" Daniyar asked.

Arian didn't speak. She knew the answer, her knowledge fortified by her long campaign in the south.

Alisher's horse began its slow ascent of the ridge, its hooves slipping in the mud. After some time, he confirmed her thoughts. "The Talisman have already been here. They have no reason to return."

He pointed to an odd structure on the other side of the ridge. It resembled the waters of a fountain, if the rising play of water had been etched in cool gray stone. It reached upward, a hyperbolic cone, its many-planed surface intersected by panels of sky. The stone was inlaid with lapis lazuli tile, Nastaliq script smashed by hammers in a furious outpouring of hate.

A standard had been planted at the entrance to the structure. It was sodden with rain and twisted by the wind, but Arian discerned its dismal emblem: a bloodstained page across a torn white flag.

Apart from the stone structure, the house of worship, the garden of the tomb, the small surrounding enclosures embellished by tilework in a woodland of blues—all had been brought to the ground, the gravesite trampled over and burned for extra measure.

Arian studied the scene: what was left to beautify the complex was the aching blue of the sky as the rain clouds began to drift away. She looked over at Alisher. Though his face was expressionless, his hands were clenched in fists.

"You've brought us to Nightshaper," she said in wonder.

"The Poet's Graveyard," he answered. "It's where I was trained."

They took shelter inside the structure. Daniyar lit a fire, the Talisman at too great a distance to worry if its light would give them away. Their small party was in dire need of warmth. Alisher produced provisions from his saddlebags and shared them out, noticing both of his companions were slow and careful in their movements.

"Do you heal, sahabiya, or should I apply more of the salve?"

Arian finished her small ration of fruit. The orange glow of the fire had illuminated the inner planes of the poet's mausoleum— for this is what the stone structure was, and what the Talisman had destroyed were the poet's legendary verses. Above her head, a resplendent array of blues asserted a perfect geometry intersected by the dull light of stars, silver picked out on a field of deepest indigo. The poet's verses were known to the people of Khorasan; this monument was a tribute to his brilliance at mathematics.

Alisher cleared his throat to remind her of his question. She nodded at Daniyar.

"The Silver Mage needs your medicine more than I do. The Authoritan bled him, and the bloodrites have taken their toll."

Daniyar brushed this off. "Lania's bloodrite was a ruse to deceive the Authoritan; she alone tasted my blood."

Arian's head came up at Daniyar's use of her sister's name. There was a softness to his voice that belied the horror of their experience at the Ark. Did he *feel* for Lania? Could he possibly wish their places were exchanged, so that he traveled with a seductive, provocative woman at his side, instead of what Arian was—a damaged and distant Companion? She had never considered the possibility that Daniyar might find her wanting, and now her throat burned with pain at the thought, a bitterly divisive emotion that she struggled to contain.

Alisher turned back to Arian, throwing the straw he'd collected onto their dwindling fire.

"You were scarcely there for a fortnight, sahabiya. Yet in that brief time, you brought the Authoritan down, when none believed he could fall. I still can't accept that he did."

Not I, she thought. *It was Daniyar . . . and Lania. I had nothing to offer save my false recollections of my sister.*

Interpreting her silence as pain, he gestured at her throat, setting the jar that contained the salve before the fire. "Are you certain I cannot tend you?"

"You have already done more than anyone could ask. It was you who changed our fate, Alisher. You were there when we needed you most."

"It was Lania who changed all our fates." Daniyar spoke over her, echoing her thoughts. "You and I safe from the Ahdath, the bloodrites, the doves—it was all done by Lania. Lania brought the Authoritan down, and Lania let us go."

A bitter seed sprouted in Arian's heart. Collecting herself, she said, "You speak well of my sister, my lord. Her seduction must have pleased you."

Alisher sat rooted before the fire, afraid to look at either one of them.

Daniyar motioned with a hand, and Alisher disappeared.

Arian met Daniyar's eyes across the glow of the fire. From the way his eyes sketched her face, she knew he was trying to read her. She raised her chin. She didn't have anything to hide.

"Now you know," he said, his silver eyes molten in the firelight. "Now you know how jealousy burns—how it injures every sentiment, everything in which you've placed your trust."

Arian flushed, both in shame and anger. "Daniyar—"

"My love," he said steadily. "Do you think so little of me? I kissed Lania, yes. I would have paid any price to keep you from the Authoritan or his men."

Arian couldn't help her response. "It didn't seem to me you found her attentions burdensome."

"Perhaps I didn't." His honesty was a whip that cut across her face, both a rebuke and an insult. His voice became bitter in turn. "I do not aspire to sainthood, and you have long denied me your warmth."

Arian's mouth twisted. She came to her feet, clad in the linens she wore beneath her armor. The gold light of the fire danced off the surface of her circlets. She would have left him then, but Daniyar rose to meet her, taking hold of her arms and pulling her close against his body. She resisted for only a moment. Then she said with a note of regret, "When we find the Bloodprint—"

He cut her off. "You're in my arms, yet all you can think of is the Bloodprint?"

"No." Arian's voice was low. She reached up a hand to trace the outline of his jaw through the soft fur of his beard. He held his breath at her touch; he rubbed his face against her palm, moving closer to catch her quiet words. "I thought there was nothing worse than seeing you in Lania's embrace. But then I watched you suffer in the bloodrites."

"No," he echoed, touching his forehead to hers. "There was nothing worse than seeing you gifted to Nevus and hearing him tell me he'd hurt you."

Neither needed to say more. His arms tightening around her,

Daniyar sought her mouth with the thorough, sensual movement of his own. He pressed his lips to her throat with care, testing the bruises left by the collar. Arian burned beneath the tumultuous fire of his kisses. The sky, the stars, the cool and windless air— all of these were as nothing. She wanted him to kiss her until the world around them had narrowed to the shelter of his arms. He was breathing heavily, his features drawn tight as she strained to get closer, her hands tracing over the harsh restraint of his limbs. He was holding his will in check, but when she opened her mouth to taste him, his silver eyes went black and he took control of the kiss with a fierce and desperate ardor. A helpless cry of desire escaped her; his kiss became wildly reckless.

A caustic voice cut through their quiet rapture. "It's good to see the pair of you have finally come to your senses."

Startled, they broke apart, Daniyar's face taut with unrelieved tension, his eyes a silver blaze in the austere beauty of his face. He couldn't tear his gaze from Arian's surrender as he strove to master what he'd given away of his own exorbitant desire. Time seemed suspended between them . . . *precarious* . . . *limitless* . . . as bright with possibility as the infinite symmetry of the stars. But only an instant passed before he was able to recognize Sinnia.

Arian's response was an uninhibited sound of joy as Sinnia's eyes flashed at them in the dark with a brilliant, taunting fire. She was the same in every way—the same Sinnia who'd ridden at Arian's side, her strong right arm, her dearest friend, the woman she loved more than any of the Companions, the sister whose unknown fate had been a source of unspoken anguish. The two women embraced each other, laughing and speaking eagerly over each other's words.

Then Arian noticed other things: Sinnia was thinner than she'd ever been, and there was a weakness, a wasting in her arms, and a gauntness beneath her eyes. She was struck by a pang of dread. She had made the wrong choice in Marakand. She should have gone after Sinnia and left the Bloodprint to its fate.

"Sinnia, what—"

"We've no time to linger," another voice said. "There are Ahdath riders on our trail. I'm afraid we brought them here."

"Larisa!" Arian whirled around to face the leader of the Basmachi with a startled cry of welcome. They had last seen each other in the Registan, where Arian had stood at a crossroads and faced the most difficult decision of her Audacy—a choice between searching for Sinnia at Jaslyk or chasing after the Bloodprint as a means of saving them all. She had looked into the eyes of Larisa Salikh and known that Larisa was someone who would fulfill her oath. Now there was something new in Larisa's face—beyond the hard alertness of a fighter whose strength was honed to the edge—a flicker of light or perhaps hope . . . as if she'd seized upon something momentous, but hadn't yet puzzled it through.

"First Oralist," she replied, her gaze scanning the surround. "There's a boy skulking in the graveyard on the other side of the ridge. Friend or enemy?"

"He's not a boy." Daniyar intervened. "He's a poet from your city, Black Aura. He led us here to Nightshaper."

"My city is Marakand, my lord, but I take your point. Come," she said, with an air of command. "Don your armor, douse the fire."

There was no time to speak further, though Arian would have welcomed a moment alone with Larisa to express her sense of gratitude. The weight of grief that had lifted from her heart at the sight of Sinnia was a gift she could never repay. But Larisa was already moving, bringing their horses while Arian dressed and Daniyar kicked over the traces of their fire.

"Give me a moment," Arian said, thinking of Alisher. She climbed the ridge to search for him. He was resting inside a circle of trees the Talisman had left unburned. He knelt before a grave marker, a slender white stone with an image engraved on its surface.

"It's a miracle they didn't find this," he said.

Arian examined the marker. A broken rose with a drooping head was etched into the stone. "Whose grave is this?"

"My teacher's. She taught me to write and trained me in the art of verse. She was young to be so gifted. She died too young as well."

Though Arian felt the press of the Ahdath's pursuit, she wanted to know more. "How, Alisher?"

"Just as you would imagine. She was brought to the Authoritan's court so that he might bleed her knowledge from her in the bloodrites. Her body was returned to Nightshaper to be buried with the others, at the Khanum's request."

"What others?"

Alisher rose to his feet. A wide sweep of his hand descried the downslope of the ridge.

Arian took a step forward, looking out over the edge.

Tombstones were arrayed in motionless waves along the crest of the hill, fanning out in endless rows, each marked with a broken rose, the symbol of a young woman's death.

There were thousands of the stones.

Arian choked in horror. "Alisher—"

"The Khanum's doves," he said. "After the Authoritan bled them."

Daniyar brought Arian's horse and helped her into the saddle with careless grace, betraying no sign of his damaged back or the five-point wounds of the bloodrites. His hand lingered at her waist, testing her supple strength. She turned her head and met his gaze, sinking into his touch. His silver eyes caught fire, mirroring the heat in hers. He reached one hand up to the back of her neck, to urge Arian closer. Sinnia rode up beside him, dark and powerful and fierce. Her sparkling eyes slid between them.

"Another time," she said as a warning. "The Ahdath won't wait for this."

Daniyar shook his head at himself and left the Companions of Hira to each other's company, to join Larisa ahead.

Larisa circled the ruins, edging forward on a path southwest of the Poet's Graveyard.

"This was once a holy place. Many of our teachers were born here, including my father, the Qari of the Claim." There was a curious inflection in her voice at her mention of her father.

Daniyar set it aside for the moment. "How did you know where to find us?"

"You left chaos behind you. In the capital, no one could speak of anything else." She gave him a respectful nod. "You defeated the rites of the Qatilah, you brought the Authoritan down, *and* you escaped the Khanum. Your legend is not just a legend, my lord. Your deeds outshine any fable I have heard." Returning to his question, she added, "A few of the Khanum's doves are in the service of the Basmachi."

Daniyar shook his head at this. "Does the Khanum not Augur who among her doves are traitors to her schemes?"

"The Khanum's augury is a curious thing. No one fully understands it." If she knew more, she chose not to share it with him. "I will take you to shelter before I return to Jaslyk."

"We could use your sword at our side."

She shook her head. "My sister is at Jaslyk. Our resistance is in our own lands. With the Authoritan defeated, this is our moment to take the Wall." There was something more that urged her return to the Wall, but he couldn't discern her secrets.

"The Khanum holds the Wall now," he said instead of pressing her. "You shouldn't underestimate her ruthlessness." Yet even as he said it, Daniyar was thinking of how Lania had released him from the Ark—how she had honored his desires instead of seizing upon her own, a selflessness he hadn't expected.

"We have no other choice but to face her. This moment won't come again."

Larisa pointed ahead to a deeper blackness that formed an irregular shape on the horizon. "We can take cover there until the Talisman pass. Or we can use it to set up an ambush."

"What is it?"

"The entrance to the Nightshaper mines. You cannot have forgotten."

But he *had* forgotten—he hadn't been north in some years. Now memory returned. Just as the Sorrowsong mines yielded lapis lazuli, the mines of Nightshaper had long supplied turquoise to the capitals of Khorasan. Marakand, Black Aura, Ashfall, Maze Aura, even the Citadel of Hira—their fountains, domes, and houses of worship were adorned with the turquoise mined from Nightshaper's depths.

"The mines are dry," he said.

Larisa jerked her horse's reins, guiding her black mare down a rock-studded slope. "That's what makes them safe for our use. They're wide rather than deep, so the shafts won't frighten our horses. The main problem is the entrance to the mines: the mud will give our presence away."

"Then what do you suggest? What other means do we have of disguising our presence?"

Larisa frowned at him. "Why do you worry when the First Oralist rides with us? She brought down the Registan with the Claim. Surely her gifts will serve to aid our present need."

"The Authoritan damaged her throat. She hasn't recovered her use of it."

This news didn't faze Larisa. She'd been fighting at the Wall long before they'd come to Black Aura. It was Larisa who'd guided Arian to safety in Marakand. And he'd do well to remember it was Larisa who'd delivered Sinnia from Jaslyk.

She responded with a firmness enhanced by years of self-reliance.

"I suggest we do what we're best at, my lord. I suggest we fight."

THE HORSES WHINNIED AS THEY PACED THE TRACKS OF THE MINES' INTE-rior, a series of tunnels that riddled the hills surrounding Night-shaper. The air inside the mines was dank, yet strangely pleasant after the lingering stench of the bloodrites at Black Aura. Their passage into the mines was through tunnels crafted from sand-stone and limonite walls, the scaffolding staffed by abandoned bar-rows and threaded with skeletal ropes. Bits of feldspar and quartz glinted through dark veins of stone, but there were no remnants of the stone of victory—the *firooz* turquoise of the mines. Daniyar's recollection had been accurate: the mines of Nightshaper had run dry, depleted by centuries of kingly demand.

Arian joined Larisa, their voices a low murmur that left the sandstone tunnel undisturbed.

"I have no means by which to thank you for your courage."

Larisa noted the changed timbre of the First Oralist's voice but refrained from commenting on it.

"You've advanced our cause beyond measure: sundering the Registan, shattering the Authoritan to dust. You've given us rea-son to hope."

"Did you face opposition at Jaslyk?"

"Yes." Larisa's face was set in lines of unholy satisfaction. "Another of the gifts you gave us. The chance to destroy the Technologist. And there was something more."

In a hushed and disbelieving voice, she told Arian of her reunion with her father. "They made us believe he was dead. They thought our despair would break us—we who were students of Salikh, students of the Usul Jade." She snorted at the thought.

"He was your father," Arian said gently, leaning forward on her horse. "You were told he was tortured to death. It must have been hard to accept the proof of your own eyes."

"Or our ears. We were also told we'd been sundered from the Claim." She turned her horse down a tunnel. "It was one of the Technologist's tricks. My father made me hear it again."

Larisa recounted her efforts at Jaslyk. Of the many questions that crowded Arian's mind, the one she decided to ask was "Where are Elena and Illarion now?"

Larisa cast an uneasy glance over her shoulder at Alisher. She lowered her voice further.

"Illarion's sister is held at the Plague Wing. And though the explanation seems simple enough, Illarion seeks more than his sister at Jaslyk."

A stray bit of memory came to Arian. When she had left Hira in search of the Bloodprint, Psalm, the Citadel's general, had taken Arian into her confidence.

Ilea sends the Citadel's senior commanders to the north—she sends them to the Plague Lands. I know not for what purpose. All I know is that no one has returned.

A leap of intuition showed her the connection. "This Technologist you mentioned—he experimented on those the Authoritan exiled to the Plague Lands. Isn't that what gives the prison ward its name—the Plague Wing?"

They had come to a wider opening in the mines. Larisa looked over at Arian in surprise. "No, First Oralist, that isn't it at all. I thought you understood the nature of Illarion's mission—my father sent him to burn the Plague Wing."

"*Burn* it?" Arian whispered, aghast. "What of the prisoners held there?"

Larisa shook her head. "There's no hope for them. When the plague from the wars of the Far Range burned out, the Technologist *revived* it. The Plague Wing is where he tests it. This is the secret of Jaslyk."

30

SHOUTS FROM THE AHDATH SOUNDED AT THE ENTRANCE TO THE MINES. They were determined to be revenged. What else had transpired in Jaslyk after their escape, Sinnia couldn't say, but in the graveyard of the ships, she and Larisa had put up a fight worthy of a woman of the Negus. They had armed themselves from the prison's armory, and Sinnia had felt her strength redouble with a whip and knife in her hand. More than that, her enormous respect for Larisa Salikh had flourished from that battle.

For Larisa wasn't just skilled at the use of a sword; she was also a strategist who mapped out the outcome of any step she took, planning against each one. When she and Sinnia had fought in the shadow of a ship teetering over the sand, cornered and outnumbered by a troop of the Crimson Watch, Sinnia had learned that the ship had been chosen for a reason.

Larisa hadn't been ceding ground to the Ahdath.

She'd been leading them into an ambush.

At a shouted word of command, Basmachi archers rained arrows upon the riders. Only one of the Crimson Watch escaped, riding to Jaslyk to call for reinforcements, a Basmachi arrow in his shoulder and two fighters on his heels.

With a quick moment to regroup, Larisa had sent her men to Jaslyk in aid of Elena, on horses she had wrested from the Ahdath. Her swift, decisive victory had been a thing of beauty. And Sinnia thought of what she would give to see the rest of Larisa's schemes come to swift and certain resolution. For it was Larisa's intent to conquer the Wall and bring the Ahdath to their knees.

Flashing a smile at her rescuer, Sinnia had proclaimed, "What a joy it would be to sail one of these beauties to freedom."

Larisa's response had been curt and to the point. "There is no freedom to sail to anywhere in all of the lands of Khorasan. Come, I will take you to the First Oralist."

And then for the briefest moment, Sinnia had thought to question the fact that she'd been tortured in Jaslyk for nearly a fortnight and Arian hadn't come to her aid. What could have been more important when Sinnia had risked her life for Arian time and again? What lesson could she learn from this of the substance of Arian's love? She remembered the reproaches the Silver Mage had made.

Arian had deserted them both.

She quashed the traitorous thought, swamped by a sense of shame. The Audacy Sinnia had been assigned at Hira was to defend the First Oralist with her life. The Audacy Arian had vowed to undertake was to pursue the Bloodprint at any cost and bring it safely to Hira.

What was Sinnia's life when weighed against such a charge?

She forced herself to brush the thought aside: Arian had *not* forgotten her. She had sent Larisa and Elena Salikh, leaders of the Basmachi, and they had succeeded at freeing her—what greater proof of Arian's love did Sinnia need to see?

They would tell each other everything once they had the chance, though Sinnia wasn't ready to speak of Jaslyk in any depth. The pernicious nature of her torture had taken something from her, no matter what Salikh had given her in exchange. She felt less than the woman she knew herself to be—the woman who had trained long months to ride at Arian's side. Sinnia—the sole Companion from the lands of the Negus—had not been without her resources. She wouldn't allow anyone to assert that her strength was in any way diminished. Instead, she'd make light of her trials so Arian would laugh at her stories of their ambush of the Crimson Watch.

Unaware of the doubt and confusion rolling through Sinnia's mind, Arian looked over at Larisa. "Command us," Arian said. "You know their tactics best."

A hard smile edged Larisa's lips. "One day when I engage the Talisman, you'll return the favor."

Arian smiled a matching smile. "Sister, you have my word."

Larisa jerked her head at the entrance. "They'll be expecting an ambush like the one we set up at the ships. They'll try to smoke us out of hiding, but they don't know that there is a way out of the tunnels that will take us around the ruins. We'll emerge on the other end of the Graveyard of the Rose."

"And if they follow?" Daniyar asked.

Larisa's eyes ranged over their faces. "Can *any* of you use the Claim?"

Arian and Sinnia glanced at each other in alarm. Each asked the other silently, *Have you been severed from the Claim?*

"Not in a way that would help us now," Daniyar said.

"And you, First Oralist? Or Sinnia?"

Sinnia shrugged. Her cloak fell back to reveal the stippling on her arm. She fingered the marks the gas mask had left on her throat. "You know about the white needle. My powers are unreliable."

But the mystery of what had been done to her had changed the timbre of her voice. And for the first time she looked away from Arian's penetrating sight, troubled that she now had a secret she felt the need to protect.

Larisa nodded briskly. She led them down another shaft, deeper into the gloom. Their horses balked at the blind path ahead. Daniyar murmured a reassurance that kept them moving.

Arian leaned closer to Daniyar. She spoke urgently in his ear. They could hear the riders of the Crimson Watch entering the mines, a level or two above. Larisa had guessed their actions correctly. They were lighting a bonfire at the drift mouth, and soon the tunnels were filled with plumes of smoke that caused their eyes to tear in the dark. There were other sounds as well, the movement of horses that suggested the Ahdath knew better than to wait for Larisa to return to the opening of the mines.

"They're following us," she said. "If we don't take them here, they'll be able to track our escape route, and that's something we cannot give away. I'll offer myself as bait—they won't be expecting you."

In moments, the pursuit was joined. With less care than Larisa's company had taken, the Ahdath's horses thundered down the slope. They could hear the captain shout out orders: he'd left men to guard the bonfire—there was no chance of doubling back.

"Come on," Larisa called.

Without light, their pace was halting. Larisa looked for an opening only she could see. When they arrived at it, they found themselves before a pit, their horses skidding to a halt. A platform was suspended above the pit. Though its balance was skewed, it was broad enough to support a company of men. Behind the platform, two tunnels led off the circle.

"The tunnel on the left is the path that will lead us out. Take my horse ahead with you."

Before they could stop her, Larisa had dismounted, gathered herself, and taken a running leap onto the platform. It teetered until she found her balance.

"Go!" she shouted, and the Ahdath came.

Sinnia didn't hesitate. She slipped from her horse and vaulted onto the platform. Now both women struggled to find their footing. Then they drew their bows, Sinnia with a cynical lift of her brow.

"I'm guessing that since we're on this platform nearing our doom, you're not planning to fight hand to hand."

"Just don't miss," Larisa answered.

Arian and Alisher moved ahead, leaving Daniyar behind. Larisa signaled to him to go, but he shook his head, his shield raised before him, his hands otherwise unencumbered.

"He listens only to Arian," Sinnia warned. "He's a beautiful, dedicated fool."

Larisa had no time to be astonished at this characterization. The Ahdath had entered the circle around the pit, nudging their horses along the narrow ledge, whorls of smoke chasing at their heels. Sinnia and Larisa loosed their arrows. But even in the light from the Ahdath's torches, both women missed their targets. They fired again, missed again, and this time the Ahdath fired back, the arrows whizzing over the platform. As they ducked, the platform shifted and they lost their footing, tumbling over to the edge. As Larisa slid from the platform, Sinnia threw herself flat, her bow still clutched in one hand.

Larisa grabbed her hand as arrows fell like rain through a blossoming cloud of smoke.

Then there was a counterattack—not from the Silver Mage, as Sinnia had supposed, but from Arian, who had returned. She had taken Alisher through the tunnel and made her way to the opposite rim of the pit. She sat calmly astride her horse, facing down the Ahdath, her bow strung with careful finesse, oblivious to the swirling smoke.

Two of the Ahdath riders fell from their horses but didn't retreat from the fight. They grabbed instead at the chains that held the platform suspended. Ahdath riders found the space between Daniyar and Arian and came up on the other side of the pit, reaching out for Larisa.

Instead of drawing them away from the platform, Daniyar began a slow, steady murmuring in a language no one recognized. There was a note of reproach in the murmur and, just as gently, a hint of encouragement. And before anyone could perceive Daniyar's objective, the Ahdath closest to the Silver Mage were no longer in position to assist the others. Their horses had reared up on the ledge, sending their riders into the pit. The horses found their way to the tunnel on the left and pounded away out of sight.

On the platform, Sinnia pulled Larisa to safety as they swung back toward the Ahdath on the opposite side, whose weapons were poised in their hands. Sinnia leapt at them, the knives in both hands flashing down. Another soldier bounded onto the platform to seize Larisa with a powerful lunge. They battled fiercely through the smoke, the platform swaying on its chains. Larisa freed herself by stabbing the Ahdath's hand. He let her go with a cry, staggering away, and she used the platform's momentum to launch herself at his legs, bracing herself on his thigh to leap up and grab the chain.

She climbed as high as she could, then jumped back to the narrow rim, nearly tumbling into the pit.

Arian caught her before she fell, coughing as smoke rose over their heads.

On the far side of the platform, the horses of the Ahdath refused to move ahead, despite the command of their riders or the vicious spurs they sank into their flanks.

The Silver Mage raised a hand and motioned them back. One by one, the horses responded to the sound of his voice. Realizing their efforts were futile, the riders abandoned their mounts, racing to the edge of the circle, and now Daniyar faced them, sword in hand.

Sinnia dispatched her opponents and looked around, using her hood to cover her mouth. Seeing Daniyar in danger, she circled around behind the Ahdath, wrong-footing two who went sailing into the pit. When the rest turned to face her, she realized the odds were against her and vaulted onto the platform as it swung back into view.

There she uncoiled her leather whip. As the Ahdath pressed the Silver Mage back, the whip snaked across the open chasm, coiling around their boots. One by one, she jerked them over the edge, sending them flailing into the pit. But she wasn't quick enough to save Daniyar. From the corner of her eye, she saw an Ahdath slash at the forelegs of Daniyar's mount, tumbling Daniyar to the ground, his sword tangled in the stirrups.

The Ahdath's sword plunged toward Daniyar's chest.

And then the Ahdath's arm halted mid-descent and he reared back, his mouth open in a soundless O as he toppled into the pit.

The noise and confusion died down, leaving only the sound of the platform swinging through the dark, with the steady whoosh of wind.

Peering through the smoke, Sinnia glanced over her shoulder.

Arian sat poised on her horse, the strings of her bow still quivering from the arrow she'd fired with such precision. Her eyes met Daniyar's as he raised himself up on his elbows.

She offered his words back to him in a tone unlike any Sinnia had heard from her, hard and devoid of music. "I will suffer no man to touch you. For you are mine alone."

31

THEIR PROGRESS THROUGH THE TUNNELS WAS QUIET. WHEN THEY emerged on the other end into fresh, unpolluted air, they were at the perimeter of the graveyard. They looked up the hill, where the white stone markers seemed to bear down upon them, evoking a sense of dread.

Arian and Sinnia dismounted to kneel at the bottom of the incline, facing the long line of graves. They pressed their hands to their circlets, echoing each other's voices in a recitation of the Claim. It wasn't the twisting magic of the Claim: this time they used the Claim as a graceful benediction.

"May the clouds comfort you with their shade. The One shall aid you with a thousand angels, following rank upon rank."

Their circlets seemed to glow. They raised their hands and swept them over their faces.

"Come unto that tenet that you and we hold in common."

They rose and embraced, the tracks of their tears visible on their smoke-tinged faces.

Larisa and Alisher watched them wordlessly, stricken by the sacred rites of Hira. When they'd finished, Larisa asked in a diffident voice, "Do you weep for my sisters, First Oralist?"

"All of Hira weeps. These are our sisters too."

Larisa's eyes scanned the crowded graveyard. "Then you know why we fight this war, and why I must leave you now. I must return to the Wall."

Arian took Larisa's calloused hand into her own. She reached for Sinnia's hand and covered Larisa's hand with both of theirs. "The One save you from the dangers of land and sea, Larisa."

Sinnia echoed the words, her whole heart behind them. She would never forget what Larisa had risked to free her from the torments of Jaslyk.

Arian continued. "We have had no Companions from beyond the Wall in centuries. When we've won this war, we would be honored to welcome you to Hira."

Larisa looked down, brushing something from her eyes. "I'm a Basmachi," she said. "All I know is killing. I'm not fit to be a Companion. I'm too often in the company of death."

"Then you've met one of the chief requirements," Sinnia offered with a grin.

Arian touched a hand to her lips and then to her circlet. She held the hand palm upward to Larisa, who hesitantly touched it with her own.

"Come unto that tenet that you and we hold in common."

Larisa's struggle was a mirror of Arian's, its consequences just as profound.

"You will know when it is time."

They embraced and said their farewells. Soon Larisa's horse was a speck on a desert-red ridge.

32

"Where is Wafa? What happened to you after I was taken in Marakand?"

They were camped beside a narrow tributary of the Amdar River, its blue-black water bleeding into the hills. Alisher had found this shelter on their southern route to the Black Khan's lands, circumventing the Talisman's strongholds along the way. The air was quiet and still, and dusk had transformed the landscape so that earth, sky, and river seemed to meld into low-lying strips of blue. They were sore and tired from their battle with the Ahdath, but mostly they were hungry. Alisher and Daniyar had gone to hunt, leaving the two women by the fire.

Sinnia listened as Arian unfolded the story of her captivity at the Ark. The darkness in her eyes deepened as Arian described the agonies the Silver Mage had endured, her hands clenched tightly in her lap. As Sinnia listened to the recital, compassion bloomed in her chest. She had suffered violence against her mind—a violence leavened by the golden glimmer of the Claim—but Arian had been *collared*. Collared and exposed without the Claim. At the mercy of the Authoritan's whim, forced to endure the suffering of the man she unquestionably loved. That much was clear to Sinnia. Despite the commandments of Hira, Arian had bound herself to Daniyar. And in doing so, she had made herself vulnerable in a way she'd never been before.

Just as Sinnia had been vulnerable to the predations of the white needle, helpless to seal her deepest self away from the ravaging of her mind. She and Arian had been sisters in their strength; now they were sisters in the act of being unmade. A less-than-honorable fate for two Companions of Hira.

Her mind had wandered. Arian was speaking of the treachery of the Black Khan and his long-planned theft of the Bloodprint. Now she listened with singular attention. From their first meeting at Hira, Arian had suspected the Black Khan's motives, whereas Sinnia had been beguiled by his manifest allure.

Friends could be enemies, she realized. And then she thought of Illarion's stratagems at Jaslyk: enemies could also be friends. The trick was to know which was which.

But as Arian continued to speak, the horror of the Black Khan's deception was balanced by the finding of the Bloodprint.

The sacred manuscript was real.

Arian had touched it with her hands. She had *read* from it.

And it held the promise of deliverance.

Sinnia's eyes blazed with triumph, her injuries set aside. Salikh had told her—he had promised her—and now his promise was fulfilled. Their sacrifices would have some meaning. Turan murdered at the Bloodshed. Wafa stolen by the Khan. The tortures she and Arian and Daniyar had endured. The Authoritan's forces had tried to break them . . . *but none of them had been broken*. Instead, they had found a means by which to bolster their belief. For the first time, they had reason to hope.

Nothing could conquer them now.

And then Arian spoke of the Khanum and her fate at the Authoritan's hands. *Lania* was the Khanum, and Lania now held the Wall. A disclosure as shattering to Sinnia as the revelation had been to Arian.

A long and futile quest come to its conclusion at last.

Arian had found the sister she'd searched for all these years, the sister she believed she'd failed. And perhaps to punish herself for the failure, she had given up Daniyar.

Given Arian's choices, would Sinnia have done the same? Was her calling as deeply rooted? But she had more than her calling to consider—she bore the trust of the Negus and of all the people of her lands. Their pride in Sinnia's call to Hira was something she couldn't set aside. She wouldn't abandon Hira, nor would she betray herself.

To assert her own ascendancy, Lania had done something neither Arian nor Sinnia would ever contemplate, as neither would yield the things that had made them who they were. *What* they were—Companions of Hira who viewed their calling as a trust.

Her blood thundering in her veins, Sinnia looked at Arian and knew that no matter the hazards that oppressed them, they were still sisters of the heart.

Silence filled the campsite. Arian began to strip off her armor and linens; Sinnia followed suit, both welcoming the chance to bathe. Arian didn't want to think of how she had been perfumed and displayed for the pleasure of the Authoritan's court. She shuddered to remember the look in Nevus's eyes as his glance had stripped her bare, or worse, his hand upon her breast. Even the subject of Lania was less painful to her than this, for Nevus had sought to tear away her sense of personal sanctity. It was the same thing she'd faced in her years of fighting the Talisman—the disavowal of her humanity based solely on her status as a woman.

The way in which Lania had known the same truth was more than Arian could bear.

Sinnia's voice interrupted her bleak thoughts. "Was Lania looking for you, just as you were searching for her?"

Arian shook her head. "Only as a means to the magic of the Silver Mage. It was Daniyar she needed, Daniyar she *wanted*."

There was a curious hitch in her voice that spoke of her unsettled emotions, but Sinnia didn't press her. They submerged themselves in the river, letting the waves wash away the blood and grime, along with the tang of fear and the persistent darkness of their memories.

Arian's hair drifted long and loose in the water. She felt a momentary freeing from herself, from all that made her First Oralist of Hira. Now that her search for Lania had ended, how easy it would be to leave it behind her.

Then she remembered Larisa giving no quarter to the men behind the Wall. Larisa had fought in the Hazing, she'd returned to the scene of her nightmares at Jaslyk, and then she'd fought in the maze of tunnels that led through the Nightshaper mines. Larisa would never yield.

She knew the same was true of Sinnia. Just as she knew Sinnia had permitted her the barest glimpse of what she'd suffered. Setting her torments in Jaslyk aside, Sinnia had focused on the Bloodprint, stubborn and determined in her faith.

Gradually Arian's sense of loss and defeat faded, to be replaced by an urgent, pulsing anger. Anger at Lania, anger at the Ahdath, anger at the Talisman's desolation of the south, and a burning, rising rage against the man who'd taken the Bloodprint and left her to the Authoritan's care. The Black Khan—who had promised his loyalty to Hira, to betray them all in the end.

She sensed the untapped power of the Claim surging up in her throat. She looked over at Sinnia, whose dark skin seemed to glow under the dreamlike caress of the water. How beautiful Sinnia was—though she had been marked by Jaslyk. White scars stood out against her skin, a circle stacked on two others, within the confines of a star. Her movements were tentative, gingerly testing out the limits of her strength.

"Sinnia," Arian said suddenly, "Nevus attempted to misuse me at the Ark. Was it the same for you? Did the Ahdath oppress you?"

Sinnia's eyes drifted closed. She scooped up a handful of water and let it slide over her face. To Arian, the drops resembled tears—a silent accusation she had earned.

Hesitantly she said, "I led you into danger without thought of the consequences to you."

Sinnia's eyes snapped open. With a proud tilt to her head, she said, "Don't belittle me, Arian. I make my own choices; I take my own risks. You mean it kindly, I know, but I am used to governing myself."

Arian's eyes widened, admonished by the queenly lift of Sinnia's head. Struggling over her response, she said, "I would still value your forgiveness."

Sinnia tilted her head back in the water. "I wondered why you didn't come." She raised one hand from the water, pointing to the bruises at Arian's throat. "But I didn't know of the Black Khan's betrayal or of the tortures of the Ark." A shiver whispered over her skin. "If you consider *my* Audacy, Arian, I didn't come to your rescue either."

This was a new thought for Arian—that she would hold Sinnia to such an exacting standard that Sinnia would blame herself in turn. In truth, they had both been savaged by forces beyond their control. It was a lesson in not bearing blame that wasn't theirs to take on. They were sisters to each other: they needn't be martyrs besides.

In that same quiet tone, Arian said, "You still haven't told me of the Ahdath. *Did* they oppress you at Jaslyk?"

"They have another wing for that. I was in the Technologist's Wing, under his personal care." Stumbling over the words, Sinnia recounted the torments of the white needle . . . and what it had felt like not to know her own mind. "I still don't feel like myself—I don't know what the needle did to me, though Mudjadid Salikh told me it granted me greater power over the Claim."

Arian shuddered. "Any control we have is an illusion. It's the Claim that masters us, though I cannot quite see how." She returned to the subject of the Technologist. "Larisa and Elena spoke of a dependency created by the needle. Have you experienced the after-effects?" She reached over for Sinnia's hand, warmed by respect for her friend. "Are you able to command yourself now?"

They floated side by side in the water, their clothing and circlets on the riverbank, the clouds parted above their heads to disclose a sliver of moon.

"Larisa told me. She warned me that my body would fight itself. She said I would sweat on the outside and bleed on the inside. She said I'd beg and plead and cry for the needle, that I'd do anything to gain it—including give myself to the Ahdath." Her voice became grim. "I think the Salikh sisters have not told us half of what they endured behind the walls of Jaslyk."

She rose from the water to dry herself and dress.

"You still haven't answered me, Sinnia. Is it something you cannot speak of?"

"The gas was terrible," Sinnia said. "And I was desperate for the needle—Larisa and Elena were right. But in that last encounter, when they left me alone on the table, Salikh used the Claim to reach me. I didn't understand what he was doing at first—but from the moment he saw me at Jaslyk and realized who I was, he was whispering the Claim to me, opening up my ability to reach it and reclaim it for myself. His power was immense, augmented by the voices of his followers—or should I call them prayers? Whatever it was he did, each time I thought I would slip over the edge, his followers pulled me back. And then the moment came when I no longer needed their help. I wasn't weak and besieged—I had powers I'd never had before." She flexed her wrists, strapping her bow to her back. "I cannot say exactly what he did. I know only that it is Salikh's *choice* to remain imprisoned at Jaslyk. His knowledge of the Claim runs deep and vast—he works his own purpose with it. May the One grant that it be of service to Elena and Larisa now . . ." She shook her head, experiencing the emotion that had flooded her senses in the cell—transformed for an instant by its brilliance. Then the incandescent memory slowly ebbed, and she nodded at Arian's clothes on the bank, recalled to the present moment.

With a quick smile and a return to her air of mischief, she teased Arian. "You should dress before the Silver Mage returns. Unless, judging from what I witnessed earlier, you would welcome him finding you like this."

Arian sputtered at the thought. She splashed a handful of water at Sinnia. And smiled when Sinnia laughed at her in response.

33

ELENA WOUND HER NECK SCARF AROUND HER HEAD SO ONLY HER NAR-
row blue eyes were visible. She led the way from one axis of Jaslyk's
diamond-shaped formation to another. The passage that linked
them should have been guarded, but the Crimson Watch had been
summoned to put down the chaos in the Technologist's Wing.

In his crimson armor with a gas mask covering his face, Illarion resembled them. Why wouldn't he? He was one of them.

"Grab a mask, Elena. You won't survive the Plague Wing without it."

"Then I die, Salikhate. I won't wear one of their masks again.
Do you have the key to the doors of the Plague Wing?"

He held up an amulet in the shape of a pentagon, his face expressionless behind the gas mask. He tucked it behind his breastplate, a gesture Elena noted. If there came a moment when he
proved to be leading her into a trap, she would know where to find
it after she'd killed him.

He's one of mine, her father had said in the brief time they'd
had together. *Illarion is a brother to you.*

She had no brothers. And with Ruslan dead, she had no lover

221

either. Whatever game this soldier of the Salikhate was playing, he would never lay hands on her—either as lover or enemy.

Disproving the thought as soon as it passed through Elena's mind, Illarion jerked her roughly behind him. "Fall back," he muttered. "There's a patrol ahead."

They found one of the doors along the passage unlocked and crouched behind it, waiting for the sound of the Ahdath's boots to pass.

"They'll kill the prisoners we left behind. They'll kill my father."

"No, they won't. Trust me."

But she didn't trust him—she never would.

Illarion pulled her out of the room as soon as the Ahdath moved on. She yanked her hand away with a scowl he couldn't see.

"I don't need your protection, Salikhate. I'm a leader of the resistance. *You* should follow *me*."

He said nothing. He simply gestured at her to lead on.

They crept down one staircase and along another corridor where torches had been lit, avoiding the sweep of the minzar.

"The minzar reaches this area every forty-five seconds. That's how much time it takes to sweep the entire prison. Their protocols haven't changed."

"How do you know this, Anya? Just how long were you held here?"

Elena shifted her daggers into her hands. She ignored the question. "Open the door, turn right. I'll follow behind."

Illarion's eyes glinted through the mask. "I trust those daggers won't end up in my back."

"That depends." She snaked past him, weaving her way from one corridor to the next, until they came to the staircase at the end of the hall. The door was chained, the ward deserted. A fine gray dust powdered the railings along the wall.

"On what?" He used his sword to untangle the chain, wincing as it clanged against the door. Elena caught the slack on the chain and pulled it taut.

"On whether you do something stupid like that. Are you *trying* to give us away?" She yanked the scarf down to cover the fringe of hair on her forehead. "Maybe you are. How do I know you have a sister in the Plague Wing? My father's been driven mad by this place; it could be his madness that trusts you."

Illarion jerked the links of the chain apart with a powerful thrust of his sword. Gathering the length of chain in his hands, he looped it around his waist. They slipped through the door, leaving behind traces of their passage in the dust. They couldn't avoid it; they had to press ahead.

"Don't tell me about your time in Jaslyk and we won't talk about my sister, agreed? And in terms of your father—" He glanced at her over his shoulder, taking the lead again. "I was a student of Mudjadid's before he fell into the Authoritan's hands. So were all the members of the Salikhate."

He was moving so swiftly, his movements rhythmic and powerful, that she was panting with the effort to keep up.

"That's not the way. There's a full patrol stationed at the main door. We have to come through the laboratory."

She broke away from him, crossing a much wider hallway filled with broken pallets and twisted metal implements. A peculiar scent assailed her nostrils—a chemical odor mixed with the metallic sweetness of blood. This was underlined by the tang of something unfamiliar and unpleasant. She found herself gagging at the smell.

Illarion caught up to her. He grabbed one of the gas masks from a pallet on the floor and passed it over. "You haven't been here before. You'll need this."

Still gagging, she grabbed the mask from him and fitted it over her head, tying her scarf at her neck. They stared at each other, their disembodied voices floating through the masks.

"You'll need the amulet. It opens the laboratory doors as well."

The pipes in the ward began to gurgle. A hollow banging punctuated the hissing of the pipes. Illarion drew the amulet out of its hiding place. He moved to the thick-paned windows that provided a glimpse of activity in the Plague Wing. Gas-masked men in long black smocks prowled between dozens of occupied beds. At the far end of the ward, the room opened off to another space, occupied by hundreds of the beds.

At the opposite end, closer to Illarion and Elena, a tall bronze door was sealed so air couldn't pass from one chamber to the next. Three stacked circles were stamped onto the door in a faded bleary crimson.

Though Elena was familiar with the tunnels that connected the wings of Jaslyk, she'd never been beyond the tall bronze door. She assumed Illarion's sister was one of the twisted near-corpses in the dozens of narrow beds or in the giant workroom beyond.

She choked back a sudden stab of despair. What if she'd ended up in the Plague Wing? The Technologist's personal attentions had been difficult enough to bear, but the women she could see on the cots were grossly misshapen, their limbs bent, their skin mottled, their eyes bulging from their sockets. Each was a symptom of the Technologist's experiments with the plague: there were others as hideous and cruel.

One of the occupants of the beds reared up against the chains that bound her, her malformed head lolling toward the door. A red-and-white froth bubbled from her mouth. She raised a manacled hand to the door.

Illarion pulled Elena away from the window just in time to

avoid being seen by one of the plague doctors. He spoke a sooth-ing formula through his gas mask and the prisoner on the bed subsided.

Elena didn't want to push Illarion, but she had to. Every min-ute was costly. "Is your sister one of them?"

Illarion shook his head. Elena gestured roughly at the tall bronze door.

"Is she on the other side? I didn't think that door led anywhere."

"It doesn't," Illarion said. "Not to anything that lives. It's the door to the waste disposal system. *Human* waste disposal."

Elena's hand hesitated on the outer door. She remembered the strange odor. "Incineration? Do they burn plague victims there?"

Illarion looked away, pressing the amulet between his hands. He examined the lock on the door—a cavity indented by numeri-cal markings. He placed the bronze amulet into the depression.

"Not incineration," he told her. "They liquefy the dead be-hind that door. They use the liquid to refine their poisons. If you weren't sent here, you were lucky."

Elena's eyes went blank behind the mask. Her time in Jaslyk was a closed subject; she didn't intend to discuss it with Illarion.

"What's the plan?" she asked.

"Take out the doctors," he said. "Let me search for my sister."

He turned the dial of the amulet until its numbers aligned with the markings on the depression. Then he pressed it down. The door gave way. Elena didn't hesitate. She leapt into the room, her knives coming alive in her hands, flashing between the pallets, stabbing through the plague doctors' smocks, slashing the hoses at the back of their necks.

She'd reached nearly all of them when from the corner of her eye, she saw Illarion sprint past her to the wider chamber beyond. He didn't stay to help her, diagnosing that the doctors posed no threat to her skillful use of her knives. He was right. One by one, the plague doctors fell, but before her knife caught the last one, he staggered to the wall and into the minzar's searchlight. He raised both hands in warning before he slumped to his knees.

The searchlights swept back to the Plague Wing, trapping Elena in a hot burst of light.

"Salikhate!" she called. She followed him into the other chamber, keeping her gaze from the misshapen figures on the beds. "The Crimson Watch know we're here!"

If she'd thought he'd abandoned her, she was wrong. There were a dozen doctors in the larger chamber, and two of these were making their way to the main doors of the Plague Wing. Illarion was engaged with the rest—puncturing their masks with blunt thrusts of his sword, stabbing others where they attended the women in the beds.

Elena chased down the pair headed for the doors. She caught the first with a knife in his back, the second against the door. But she was too late. His pounding fists alerted the soldiers on the other side.

"Elena!"

She wheeled around in time to catch the chain Illarion had looped around his waist. He didn't need to tell her. She used the chain to secure the door, knowing the glass was too thick for the Ahdath to break with their swords.

But the chain wouldn't hold for long against the weight of their strength.

Paying no heed to what Illarion was doing, she sprinted back to the antechamber. Her hands fastened on the amulet in the door and yanked it from its cavity. The doors closed behind her, locking them inside the Plague Wing. She raced back to the other room to jam the doors. If she could insert it into the depression on the inside of the doors, she could prevent the Ahdath from unlocking the main entrance to the room.

She saw them on the other side of the door, each gathering up a gas mask. Her fingers clumsy and sweating, she jammed the amulet into the cavity, twisting it counterclockwise. As she'd hoped, the mechanism on the outer door failed. Now it wasn't a matter of breaking the interlocked links of the chain. The Ahdath needed a way to rework the amulet's mechanism.

But her actions were not enough to save them. She had locked Illarion and herself in a wing full of plague victims, barring the only way out. And the entrance from the rear could be breached by the use of a second amulet. From the shouts of the Ahdath beyond the door, she knew they'd reached the same conclusion. Men were dispatched to find the Warden.

Illarion had reached the far wall when the searchlights swept the room again. He was going from bed to bed, turning the plague victims over. Would he recognize his sister like this?

Elena forced herself to look at the women chained to the beds. Not all of them were as deformed as the women in the antechamber. These women were in the early stages of the disease; they hadn't experienced blindness or the wasting of their flesh.

"What does she look like?" Elena shouted, running to the opposite end of Illarion's row, working her way toward him.

He waved a hand at his hair and face. "Like me. She has a scar above her left eyebrow."

Elena moved quickly, skipping over the women with dark hair, turning over the rest. The women's eyes were blank—they were either drugged or had been blinded by the disease, she couldn't tell. Their faces were screwed up in pain, their limbs warped within their chains. It was a terrible sight, worse than what the Technologist had done to Elena.

As she proceeded down the row, neither she nor Illarion found his sister. They moved to the next row, then the next. The fifth row farthest from the wall, less than a third of the way down, Elena found a pale-haired woman with a jagged red line just above her eyebrow. Though her face was twisted in lines of pain, Elena could tell she was just a girl.

"Salikhate—here."

He hurried to her side, taking the girl into his arms. He pushed back the cloudy hair that drifted over her forehead. It came loose in his hands, leaving her scalp partly bald. Ripping off his gloves, he traced the scar above her brow with gentle fingers.

Alarms went off in the Plague Wing. The Ahdath had brought a battering ram. As soon as they destroyed the amulet, they would be through to the chamber.

"Illarion," she muttered, using his name. "Hurry. Whatever it is you're going to do, do it." She raised one of the girl's twisted arms, showing him the chain. He ignored her.

"Lilia," he murmured softly, keeping his agony at the sight of his sister from his voice. "Lilia, it's me. It's Illarion, your brother."

The girl didn't stir in his arms. Elena pushed back a strand of her hair to uncover her ears. She whispered a forgotten prayer when she saw Lilia's ears were undamaged.

The amulet snapped free with a sharp pinging sound. The Ahdath rammed the door. With their second attempt, the chain looping the door's handles started to come undone.

"Illarion. We can't stand against them all."

He came back to himself with a jolt. "Find her a gas mask," he urged. "And get her to the door we came from."

Elena cast a frantic glance back to the antechamber. "We can't get out that way. Ahdath followed our trail. They'll be here any second."

"The gas mask," he insisted. "Trust me, Elena. I know what I'm doing."

She was risking everything for a man she didn't trust. But she had seen him with his sister, his large hands cradling her face with an inexpressible tenderness. Could a man who would risk his own safety for his sister be capable of such deceit? She found the mask, fitted it to Lilia, and used her dagger to work the manacles free. She jerked the girl's limbs straight, hoisting her across her shoulder.

The girl had been starved of everything except the Technologist's drugs—she was weightless on Elena's back. Elena moved away from the beds where other women were stirring, their pleading eyes turned to hers. She heard the sibilant sound of Illarion drawing his sword from its sheath. There were Ahdath coming at them from both sides of the Plague Wing now.

"Illarion," she said. "There's no other way out."

He raised his sword high and aimed it at the black pipes that ran along the walls of the Plague Wing.

"Are your masks sealed?"

Wide-eyed and fearful, she nodded. "Illarion, what—?"

The chain on the main doors snapped, bearing the battering ram into the room with the force of the Ahdath's momentum.

Illarion's sword crashed down, severing the pipes. Ten feet away, the unmasked members of the Crimson Watch grasped at their throats with their hands. Illarion backed away, grabbing Elena's wrist and pulling her along in his wake. He threw cots and pallets in the Ahdath's way, slowing down the handful of soldiers who were masked.

"This way!" he shouted.

But there was nowhere to retreat to, even in the antechamber. The rear doors had been breached by another group of soldiers. A bilious yellow gas rose from the ruptured pipes, rising like a haze in the room.

The women on the beds choked and sputtered, blood spewing from their mouths as their bodies twisted like grotesqueries. Those of the Ahdath who were unmasked experienced the same symptoms. A handful of others pursued Elena and Illarion into the antechamber, stumbling over bodies and beds.

Illarion threw his weight against the heavy bronze door. It needed no amulet to open.

The horrifying odor of liquefaction permeated the wing. This close to it, Elena choked at the stench. Her knees buckled, Lilia falling with her. Illarion grabbed her in time. He pulled Elena to her feet, shifting his sister's weight onto his own shoulders. Keeping hold of Elena's hand, he dove into the gas-filled chamber, pulling her past giant steel vats that bubbled with ghastly purpose.

"Don't look," he warned, yanking her forward.

She couldn't. She was too busy putting one foot in front of the other without retching inside her mask. She felt a tug from behind. An Ahdath grappled at the hose of her mask. Focusing on the immediate danger, she buried her knife in his shoulder.

As soon as his flesh was rent, the blood in his arm began to foam. He fell back. Elena disappeared into the growing fog in Illarion's footsteps.

"Don't leave me here," she choked through the mask, anxious for his reassurance.

His mask bobbed in her direction. "Don't worry, Anya. You still owe me for the Gold House, and I promised to collect."

She followed him through the haze. Behind her, choking sounds mingled with the susurrant ripple of liquefaction. Head down, she blundered ahead until they came to another door. This one was sealed from the outside. Illarion tried to budge it without success.

It was the door that led to the courtyard. He shifted his sister to the ground. Freeing up his sword, he tried to break through the seal. There was no space to wedge his sword into the frame.

They looked around, searching for another means of escape. Between two giant cauldrons, Illarion spied a small square hatch. With his gloves on, he felt around its edges.

"Wait!" Elena choked. "That's not one of the Basmachi's tunnels. I don't know where it leads."

Illarion showed her the pipes that disappeared into the wall on either side of the hatch. "These pipes are emptied outside the prison, into the desert wasteland."

"The Plague Lands, you mean," Elena muttered. She was beginning to distrust the known history of the Plague Lands. The Wall had been erected to create a boundary between the Plague Lands and the rest of the north. But what had poisoned those lands to begin with? She had heard it was the alchemical effects of the unending wars of the Far Range. Whatever poisons those wars had unleashed, the Technologist had put them to use.

"Perhaps." Illarion found the opening to the hatch with his fingers. It was rusted through and difficult to maneuver. Elena shouldered him aside, jabbing at the rust with her knife until the lever that opened the hatch came loose. She yanked it down. The hatch was a chute of some kind. It sloped downward into a constricted space obscured by a nebulous gloom. The pipes that ran beside it burbled through the walls. A terrible stench permeated the chute. It reeked of human waste. She choked behind her mask.

"Are you sure about this?" she asked.

"I'll go first. With Lilia."

The thought flashed through her mind that this would allow Illarion to leave her in the room with the cauldrons.

"It's too narrow for you. You won't be able to take your sister."

Before he could protest, she said, "I'll take her—I'm smaller than you, I can carry her on my back."

He hesitated at the proposal, a flash of anxiety on his face. Whatever else this Ahdath was, he clearly loved his sister. She gathered Lilia gently from the floor, linking the girl's arms around her neck.

Somewhere on the other side of the door they'd entered through, she could hear the sound of the Ahdath's voices echoing through their gas masks.

"Hurry," she said. "They'll track us here any moment."

Illarion didn't need to be told twice. He wedged himself into the hatch, feeling the sides with his hands, measuring the distance ahead. The hatch sloped down and then sharply dropped off. He looked back at Elena, taking Lilia's weight on her shoulders, waiting to climb up after him.

A whiff of burning smoke rose through the empty cylinder of the chute. What if Elena was right and this was the route to an incinerator? Would she have time to turn back with his sister? But what would she have to return to? The further horrors of testing that sloughed the skin from her bones? Even if fire awaited them at the other end of the chute, it was a kinder fate than the manifest cruelties of the Plague Wing.

He said a prayer Mudjadid had taught the Salikhate and dove headfirst through the chute. Moments later he was in free fall. There was nothing to support his weight. His body arrowed down through darkness, a fall that didn't seem to end. He put his arms out and encountered empty space. The scent of smoke died away, the vastness of the dark purifying it. He tilted his head up, searching for Elena as he fell. He could just make out another shape against the blackness. And still he plunged through the air, his body received by silence.

He brought his arms back against his body and tucked his knees to brace for impact. He landed on a shifting surface that gave way, knocking him off his feet. He rolled out of the way in time to avoid the impact of Elena's fall. She fell face-first, propelled by the weight on her back, and he feared they might both be injured. Her mask was splintered, and her hose came loose.

He feared she might be dead.

Shaking off Lilia's body, Elena noted the spider-web cracks fanning out from the center of her mask. Feeling about, she discovered the hose had been severed from the mask—her fear became tinged with panic. She scrambled to reattach the hose, her hands trembling at the thought of inhaling the Plague Wing's poison. It could blind her, deafen her . . . *destroy* her.

Then she realized. The air was cool and clear, the blackness in her vision easing to a midnight blue, lightened by the distant glow of stars. They had left the glare of the searchlights behind to reach the boundary of the desert. Far ahead, she could make out the outline of ships cast adrift on the sands.

She wrested the mask from her head, breathing in the air with huge, shuddering gasps, Lilia and Illarion forgotten. The mask dropped from her hand with a strange thud as it hit the sand beneath her feet. She took a step and the sand crunched beneath her boots. She looked down at the sand and faced another horror.

The ground beneath her feet was powdered and littered with bones.

34

WHEN ELENA AND ILLARION HAD CROSSED TO THE SAFETY OF THE SHIP'S graveyard and reached the shelter of a ship, Illarion relinquished his sister's weight, setting her down on the forward deck that sloped into the sand. He drank water from his canteen, passing it to Elena, who was crouched beside Lilia, searching her face for signs of the effects of poison.

"She might still be saved," she said with a note of doubt.

Illarion wiped his mouth with the back of his hand. He shaded his forehead against the wind that raised whorls of dust all around them.

"It's too late. She wasn't masked in the Plague Wing; neither were the others. That means she's been exposed; it's just a matter of time before she experiences the more extreme symptoms."

He knelt beside Elena, taking his sister's hand within his own, a contact of skin upon skin that was infinitely careful. She didn't respond, her head lolling back upon her neck.

"Then why did you risk yourself to free her?"

"Why did you return for Larisa after everything you suffered at the Technologist's hands?"

"You've just answered your own question. Better to kill her myself than let her suffer as I did."

"Yes," Illarion agreed. "That is the only choice."

Elena looked at him with a sudden comprehension of his words. "Illarion—no. I *was* able to save Larisa. You'll do the same for your sister."

He shook his head. "Larisa was never exposed to the plague. Lilia's fate is certain. It's only a question now of how much pain I choose to spare her."

Her troubled eyes searched his face. Behind his studied neutrality was a harrowing weight of sorrow. It sang to her. It haunted her, but she couldn't argue against his choice. Ending Lilia's suffering required the kind of courage very few men possessed.

She looked back at the way they had come where Jaslyk's walls stood tall, the light from the minzars spinning out in pursuit.

"I should have burned it down," Elena said. "Just as I promised I would."

"You saw what I did with the pipes. No one in the Plague Wing will survive that."

With the gas mask discarded, Elena could see the grim decision in his face, and the traces of what it had cost him. Her father had been right, she realized. Illarion's efforts mirrored hers. He was faced with the same harsh choices, and he braved them without regret.

"If I'd known about the pipes, I would have done the same." Her voice was pitiless; she spoke without looking at him. "But it isn't a permanent solution. The Ahdath will bring others to suffer here. The Companion told Larisa as much. The Talisman have been accelerating their delivery of the slaves. And if the slave-chains fail, there are always the Khanum's doves."

Illarion kept his attention on his sister, stroking her hair, easing the lines of pain in her face, his fingertips lingering on her scar.

"You're planning something," he said, his voice rough. "But you've seen Jaslyk. You can't take on the Crimson Watch by yourself."

"Are you offering to come with me, Salikhate?"

"The opposite, Anya. You should come with me to the Wall. The Khanum doesn't know about you. We can use that to our advantage."

Elena frowned. "The Khanum is an Augur—*how* does she not know about me? Or you, for that matter? How did she not foresee everything that happened at Jaslyk and send her guard to stop us? Why weren't they waiting for us?"

She rose to her feet, navigating the tilt of the forward deck with grace. Her hands found the railing: she measured the distance back to the prison.

"I should have told you," he said.

She waited, her tense expression giving little away.

"Your father spoke of you often, but when I met you that first time in the Gold House, I didn't know you were his daughter. I didn't know I could trust you."

Elena's lips tightened in a grimace. "You shouldn't trust me. You *don't* know me."

"I know you follow the Usul Jade. Even if you weren't his daughter, that would be enough for me." He joined her at the railing. One hand reached out to move her hair aside, exposing a tattered ear. She stiffened under the touch. "You thought the Claim had been stolen from you, but the Claim cannot be stolen—your father will recover it for you."

She listened to him closely, her eyes narrowed to slits against the grit of blowing sand.

"His mastery of the Claim is something you can't imagine. He uses it to block the Khanum's Augury. She cannot perceive those who serve him. And since you crossed my path, she cannot see you either."

Elena wasn't sure she believed this, though what else could account for their escape? Or for the continued success of the Basmachi's raids? What reason would the Khanum have for not cutting off the head of the resistance?

"Come with me to the Wall," he urged. "As long as you're with me, you're safe."

It was the wrong thing to say to Elena. She brushed his hand aside, gripping the top rung of the ladder that descended to the sand.

"I'm sorry about your sister, Salikhate. And I wish you well at the Wall. But I am not in need of being saved by you or any man. The Basmachi have work to do." Yet even as she said it, she faltered, no longer quite as fierce in her defense.

Illarion studied her, his eyes bold on her uncovered face. She met his gaze without flinching, giving him back the look, seeing the strength she had mistaken as arrogance.

"What is it, Anya?"

"If you see my father again, tell him—"

"Come with me," Illarion urged. "If only because he needs you."

Elena was surprised. "Needs me? He hasn't needed me in all this time. He could have sent word—" She choked off the rest. Illarion wasn't her confidant. Exposing her weakness to him would serve only to make her weaker. "Just keep him safe, Salikhate."

She swung her body over the side and fluidly slipped to the ground, drawing her scarf up over her face.

She lifted her hand in a wave, her thoughts reclaimed by her unfinished mission. "Farewell, Salikhate. Perhaps we'll meet again."

"Come to Black Aura, Anya. If you need me, you'll find me at the Wall."

She didn't correct him this time. She'd come to understand that he used the name as a term of affection, almost as an endearment. She felt an unaccustomed spasm of emotion. As she slipped away over the ridges of the desert, she identified this newest source of pain.

It was a longing for human connection. And a warmth that took her by surprise.

IN THE BLACK KHAN'S PRESENCE, NO ONE ELSE DARED SIT UPON THE Peacock Throne. In his absence, it was the duty of the Nizam to reign on the Khan's behalf. Now at the news of the Khan's return, he descended from the throne to take a position at the head of the reception for the Khan. The Khan's cousins and aunts and nieces formed two rows, each bearing in their hands beautiful enameled trays decorated in the Khorasani style of turquoise blue and green motifs. The trays were burdened with delicacies: rosewater-flavored sweetmeats, sticky orange loops of hardened syrup, layers of flaky pastry studded with pistachios and almonds, trays upon trays of fresh fruit. The Khan's youngest niece bore the tray that held his favorite dish: the ruby seeds of pomegranates piled high inside a chalice engraved with an onyx rook.

The elders of the Khan's family carried garlands of roses in their hands, yet something was amiss. The Nizam realized what it was and frowned at Darya's absence. The Princess should have been at the head of the reception, but Darya had always shown a regrettable lack of respect for Ashfall's centuries-old traditions. It was unsurprising that she'd chosen to do so again.

When the Khan entered the Divan-e Shah followed by his commander, the women began a joyful ululation. They scattered rose petals in the air, and as the Khan bent to embrace the women of his family, each of his aunts raised a garland and draped it over his head.

The Nizam frowned. The Khan was dressed in his armor and still bore the grime of the road. Though he smiled and kissed his aunts on both cheeks, the smile was absent from his eyes. He accepted the rituals patiently, tasting something from each of the dishes proffered and fondly kissing the top of his niece's head before taking a spoonful of pomegranate seeds. He fed her a spoonful in turn, reminding the Nizam that the Khan was prone to these gestures of affection when it came to the women of his family.

Darya was the only one whose behavior unsettled the Prince. She'd earned his suspicion by petitioning for the release of their half-brother Darius from Qaysarieh. And she'd made plain her desire to leave the capital and make common cause with Hira. To the Nizam of the Khan's empire, the Council of Hira was not a sisterhood to be revered: it was a nest of conspirators, one of whom slithered in their midst. He was waiting for his moment to advise the Khan along those lines. He would also have to account for Darya's discourteous absence.

It was at his urging that the Khan had prevented Darya from leaving the palace. He had refused her request to study at Hira, and as a punishment for her disloyalty he had banished her from the scriptorium . . . though somehow Darya managed to slip back into it whenever he was absent from the palace. Now that the Khan had returned, his rules were more likely to be upheld.

The sooner the Princess married Arsalan, the better. The marriage would settle them both, for Arsalan was not a man to permit any wife of his to set foot outside the palace. He guarded his honor jealously. Though why he'd refused the marriage to begin with was a question that not even the spies of the Nizam had been able to answer, though rumors of Darya's visit to the tower had reached the Nizam's sharp ears. The girl had disgraced herself by running to Arsalan to discuss his offer of marriage, an unthinkable impropriety. But hardly surprising when nothing Darya did was in accordance with the etiquette of court. She was a changeling, out of step with the refinement of her cousins . . . out of place in the court of the Khan.

It angered the Nizam that she had laid her foolishness bare to a commander of Arsalan's stature. Another woman endowed with half of Darya's beauty would have had Arsalan eating pomegranate seeds from her palm. Instead, her impetuous behavior had driven Arsalan away. To repair such a breach and hasten the marriage was another source of annoyance and an infringement on his time.

His gaze sharpened. Darya slipped into the Divan-e Shah in the wake of Arsalan and the Khan, retreating to the women's seating area. She should have taken her seat in the front row of the pavilion, showing off her costume and her jewels to the eye of the Khan's commander. Instead, she placed herself on a cushion at the back, tripping over her silks, dwarfed by the collar and headdress she could never seem to manage with anything resembling grace.

All this, not only before the Prince of West Khorasan, but also before the commander of the Zhayedan. Worse yet, in the presence of the intruder from the Citadel.

The Black Khan reached his side. Wrenching his thoughts from Darya, the Nizam made the customary obeisance, which the Khan was quick to protest. The Nizam was his teacher, the Grand Vizier of West Khorasan, and the Khan had always treated him as such.

His boyhood courtesy and solemn respect characterized their interactions. The Nizam treated him like a son.

The Black Khan placed his hand on his chest and bowed to the Nizam. "Nizam al-Mulk, I thank you for honoring my trust and for guarding Ashfall in my absence."

An elaborate ritual of courtesies was observed, the women of the Khan's family hastening to add their praise to the Khan's, extolling the Nizam's many virtues. The Nizam wasn't fool enough to believe in the legend of his own glory: he knew the machinations of the court. Any woman who had his ear knew she had the ear of the Khan and could use him to maneuver for position. They were all engaged in these schemes—every woman, every courtier the Khan paid notice to, and a host of others besides. Even the Begum, the Khan's aunt. As the eldest woman of the family, the Begum presided over the court, her seat at the Khan's side elevated above the Nizam's.

In this, the Khan distinguished himself from the Talisman: the women of his court were independent, exalted in their place and honored by the customs the Khan insisted be observed. Darya was the only exception to his rule, and for Darya, neither the Khan nor the Nizam had found an answer.

"Excellency," the Nizam said, "you have not yet rested from the rigors of your journey. Should you not refresh yourselves after so difficult a ride?"

He indicated the commander of the Zhayedan. Arsalan made the same obeisance the Khan had made, but it lacked the warmth of Rukh's gesture, speaking to his formality at court.

"Arsalan has summoned the commanders of the army. I come to ask you to preside over a council of war. The matter is urgent and cannot wait." The Khan's eyes flicked over the courtiers gathered in the Divan-e Shah. "I've brought a boy in my train from Black Aura. You will need to question him."

The Nizam bowed his head at the honor conferred, noting the discomfort that appeared in Arsalan's eyes. Arsalan was commander of the Zhayedan; he should have been called to preside over the council.

"As you wish, Excellency." Because he could, he placed a warning hand on the Black Khan's arm, nodding to an ostentatious gold chair, positioned at the Khan's right hand. "Before the council is convened, you should know you have a visitor. It would be best to summon her before we discuss matters related to defense."

The fingers that held the Black Khan's wrist moved in a sequence of gestures, a language that allowed them to speak privately before the court. *She is dangerous,* the flicker of his fingers told Rukh. *She must be sent from Ashfall before she can do you any harm.*

"Present her," the Black Khan said.

Darya watched as Rukh strode to the Peacock Throne, unlatching his weapons and handing them to Arsalan, rather than to the page who had sprung up in attendance. If the Nizam of his empire feared this visitor, it was Arsalan he trusted with his sword.

The garlands strung about his neck would have made a lesser man seem absurd. Rukh wore his garlands like honors, his stature regal and imposing, his will enlivening the court, who were struck into calling out his praise. As he took his seat upon the Peacock Throne, a page brought the Shahi scepter—the scepter of the prince—to his hand.

The Nizam retreated to an antechamber. He returned with a

beautiful woman at his side, and Darya gasped aloud. The woman was dressed in blue silk and wore a gold diadem that blazed with a single sapphire. Her white-gold hair tumbled down her back; her golden eyes were clear and watchful. She bowed before the Khan, her silk cape whispering aside, exposing the circlets on her arms.

Cries of surprise sounded in the room. The women of the Khan's family scrambled for a better look. Darya pushed aside the others, hurrying to find a place before the Peacock Throne. In her haste, the heavy gold armlet she wore tore at the silk of her dress. Ignoring the sound of the tear, Darya ran to greet the visitor, taking hold of her by the hand.

"Darya!" A sharp rebuke came from the Begum, whom the Khan had seated with courtesy at his side.

Darya was unheeding. Tears trembled at the edges of her lashes. "High Companion," she whispered, "you honor the court at Ashfall. We have never been so distinguished. You humble us, Exalted."

"Darya!" This time the rebuke came from Rukh. At his sharp nod, Arsalan pulled Darya aside, freeing the High Companion's hand.

Darya kept her eyes on the other woman's face, her own expression hopeful. Then she looked to her brother, her dark eyes widening with joy. "Rukh, did you ask the Exalted to come? Have you changed your mind? Has she come to take me to Hira?"

"Be silent, child." The Nizam intervened before the Black Khan could react. "Do you imagine the counsels of the Black Khan's court are convened with your benefit in mind? Commander, take the Princess to her chambers."

"No, Rukh, please!"

"Darya."

It was all her brother had to say. She knew what it meant when he uttered her name in that cold, implacable tone. She became aware of the court's attention: the majestic displeasure of her aunt, the contemptuous disapproval of the Nizam, the mocking laughter of her cousins. She flushed hot and then cold, her arm trembling in Arsalan's grip.

She'd hoped for an intimation of welcome on the face of the High Companion. But the High Companion ignored her with a dignified restraint. Her head hanging low, Darya allowed Arsalan to escort her from the room.

Her back to the Peacock Throne, she heard the High Companion speak. "Excellency," she said to Rukh. "I have come to reclaim the Bloodprint as agreed. But if it is your wish, I will take your sister as well."

36

DARYA DIDN'T HAVE TO WAIT LONG FOR ARSALAN'S REBUKE.

"What were you thinking, child? You know the customs of our court."

Arsalan's tone was chiding. She heard the pity beneath it and flushed.

"I'm not a child, Commander Arsalan. I meant no disrespect to my brother; I was simply overcome. The High Companion *here*—isn't it a source of wonder? Doesn't everyone at court feel the same? I have so many things I have dreamed of learning at Hira—what I would give to have the chance to ask."

Her dark eyes beseeched him. She was suddenly conscious of the fact that he held her by the arm just outside the door to her chambers. He was close enough for her to feel the heat of his body through his armor. There was strength in the hand that held her, but there was tenderness as well. Though her faults often became Arsalan's burden to bear, she found he was always kind to her. She shut the scene at the tower from her mind and asked herself whether his tenderness might not be a form of love. What did it matter if he'd spoken of her to Rukh with such matter-of-fact disregard—what did it matter that she'd now refused him as he'd once refused her? She should try to change his mind, just as the Nizam had counseled her to do.

He would love you, the Nizam had said, *if you gave him anything to love.*

"Commander Arsalan." She tried to make her voice sound alluring. "You are tired and worn from your journey. May I tend to your needs? I could have wine ordered for you—or anything else you prefer."

Arsalan's head was turned toward the Divan-e Shah, indicating his impatience to return. Now his eyes met the hopeful entreaty in Darya's. With great care, he released her from his hold. "Forgive me, Princess, it was discourteous of me to touch you."

Darya reached for his hand and placed it back upon her arm, just above the embrasure of her cuff.

"Though these hands are hardened from fighting many battles, they are always gentle with me. If you do not desire me, why are you so careful when you touch me? You treat me as though I am breakable, when I'm not."

She unfastened the gold cuff that bound her arm and let it fall to the floor. With an encouraging smile, she drew Arsalan's hand over her arm, emulating a caress. Instead of transferring his gaze to the bare skin of her arm, his eyes remained steady on Darya's.

"This is the lesson you cannot seem to learn. Yes, there was wonder in the High Companion's presence, but you should have stopped to think of what was due to your brother when you abased yourself. Do you not understand the priorities of Ashfall when it comes to the schemes of Hira?"

"Schemes?" Darya drew a swift breath. "This is Hira you speak of. The Council and Companions of *Hira*. I did not abase myself, I gave the High Companion her due."

"And what of your brother?" Arsalan asked. "When will you comprehend the impact of your actions on his rule? Do you think it easy to govern an empire when war is at its gates? He cannot count on allies, so he forges his path alone."

"Why?" Darya demanded. "Why would the High Companion have come if not to offer her help? Why would Hira abandon us? The threat the Citadel faces is just as dire as the army camped beyond our outer ramparts."

Arsalan shook his head, turning back to the Divan-e Shah. "There is no teaching you what you do not wish to learn. You are blinded by your desire to worship at the High Companion's feet. I do not have time to wake you from your half-formed dreams."

Stunned by this rebuke, Darya realized she had nothing to lose. She was driven by a mad excitement: Arsalan had never addressed her with such unchecked passion before.

"Perhaps your kisses would wake me."

Now she had his full attention: she squirmed beneath his black gaze.

"Arsalan—"

He seized her by the waist and lowered his mouth to hers. His kisses were nothing like she'd imagined they would be, his mouth hard and bruising, urgently self-seeking. She struggled in his arms, beating her fists against his chest. When he was satisfied he'd made his point, he let her go.

"Is this what you dream of, Princess? Did it help you to come to your senses? Do you see the danger to Ashfall? Do your brother's needs at this hour ever cross your mind?"

"Why would they need to when they are always on *your* mind?"

She shouted the words at him and missed Arsalan's sharp look. She pressed her hand to lips that were pulsing from his onslaught.

"You will never love me as you do him. I was stupid to think that you could."

She bent to the ground to reclaim her cuff. For a moment she wished she could stay there, sunken in misery and shame. But she was a princess of Ashfall, and self-pity was a luxury even Darya wouldn't indulge. She nodded in the direction of the Divan-e Shah.

"Go," she said. "He's waiting for you. You belong at his side. Your conduct at court is above reproach, which is more than can be said about mine. And since you seem to agree with the Nizam, you should welcome my departure to Hira."

"Rukh needs you *here,* Darya."

She watched in distress as he wiped the taste of her lips from his mouth. She'd mistaken the depths of his aversion. His kindness to her was merely kindness.

She swallowed her realization, determined to hold on to her pride.

"For what purpose? He heeds no counsel of mine. He shares neither his thoughts nor his affections with me. He refuses to allow me to see Darius, whom he confines in the depths of Qaysarieh. And now he has denied me the scriptorium. He will not allow me to read."

She rolled her gold cuff between her hands. "He dresses me in these cuffs that weigh me down, these anklets that give me away wherever I choose to run, and he does not allow me to seek wisdom in the scriptorium. Is this why you think he needs me?"

Two pages appeared outside the doors that opened onto the Divan-e Shah, searching for the commander of the Zhayedan. He dismissed them with a curt nod.

He took the cuff from Darya's hands and fastened it back in place. It locked on her arm with a click, reinforcing the power of her words.

"Your words are treasonous, Princess. Be grateful you speak them to me. The Nizam would send you to join Darius."

He adjusted the wayward pearl on her forehead, touching the jewel without touching her. He was close, so close she could feel the heat of his hands and taste the wild, sweet scent of his breath. Why hadn't he kissed her as she yearned to be kissed? With the reverent and tender care he expressed with every other gesture? Tears fell silently from her eyes, and now he did touch her, brushing them away with his thumbs. The gentleness of the touch undid her, rendering her powerless before him. And she wondered—did she need to be powerful in her dealings with Arsalan? Was everything between a man and a woman meant to be fought like a battle?

"I know what you carry, Princess. I think I've always known." His quiet admission revealed nothing of his thoughts or of his inner struggle. If he regretted his plainspoken censure or his harsh embrace, it was something he didn't confide. And she would be foolish to ask.

"You hurt me," she said at last. "I didn't think you would hurt me."

"Darya—"

She should walk away while she still had her pride intact, and let him return to the prince he wished so ardently to serve—but what if this moment didn't come her way again?

He stood tall and strong before her, a man who had only to speak to be obeyed, yet who wore his command lightly, attuned to the welfare of his warriors, focused on the safety of his city. She wouldn't meet a man of Arsalan's caliber again.

"Darya."

He tipped up her chin with a finger. This time when he pressed his lips to hers, the kiss was soft and unhurried, drawing her from herself, a shimmering sense of delight coursing through her veins. Darya kissed him back, her arms stealing around his neck, eager and vital in his embrace.

"*Afaarin.*"

The single word dropped into the silence. Arsalan raised his head to meet the Black Khan's gaze. Rukh clapped his hands, an unreadable expression on his face. "I didn't think you had it in you to be so bold with my sister. It explains your absence from council, an excuse I suppose I must accept."

He was not as forgiving with Darya, his speech becoming clipped. "You forget yourself, Darya. You are a princess of Ashfall."

Again, Arsalan intervened. "It was I who imposed myself." His tone brooked no further inquiry. "The Princess could hardly refuse me."

"Resist you, you mean." The Black Khan's voice was dry, mocking Darya's confusion. She had not been as quick to recover herself as Arsalan, lost in the excitement of his kiss.

Rukh studied his commander, noting the way he shielded Darya's dishevelment. "I cannot wait on you any longer. I trust the Princess will release you."

Darya's arms were still wound about Arsalan's neck. She dropped her hands and vanished into her room—her moment of joy fleeting, diminished by her brother's reproof. She listened to their voices as they left her behind, until the sounds had faded into nothing.

Just as I do, she thought.

"Why?" Arsalan asked. "Why do you speak to Darya with so little regard for her feelings?"

"Are you her champion now?" Rukh returned. "I was under the impression you found her unbeguiling."

"Do not test me, Rukh. You set me to an impossible task, then censure me for doing it. I'm not an untried girl like Darya. I will not permit you to insult me."

"I will accept that once you accept that you cannot instruct me on matters related to my sister. I will deal with Darya as I choose."

Arsalan came to a halt. "Not if what you choose is cruel disregard. I expect better of you, Rukh. I *demand* it."

Rukh scowled. "You're the commander of my army, not the guardian of my morality. Don't overstep your bounds."

Arsalan's hand shot out to Rukh's arm. He pivoted through a quick movement that brought the Black Khan to the ground. He followed him down, pinning him with a knee to the chest, the heft of his full weight behind it. Rukh looked up at him through narrowed eyes. His arms were braced to challenge Arsalan, yet he knew he couldn't defeat him one-on-one—he'd learned that from a lifetime's practice. Arsalan held him in place, his breathing slow and unhurried, the speed with which he'd brought Rukh down a testament to his skill. Wondering how far he would go, Rukh coiled his muscles to spring, angered by the effortless strength that held him pinned to the ground. He waited for Arsalan's next move.

When it didn't come, he became aware of the quickening of Arsalan's breath, followed by a flare of heat. He allowed his gaze to drift over Arsalan's face before settling on the taut lines of his mouth. Arsalan's eyes became hooded. He waited for an invisible cue. Rukh raised a hand to Arsalan's face. He traced one cheekbone lightly—his touch careful, exploratory, provocative—while Arsalan simply watched him, a searing heat in his eyes. He shifted his hands to either side of Rukh's head, caging him in with his arms. He was tense with anticipation when Rukh dropped his hand to his side.

Neither man uttered a word.

When Rukh said nothing more, Arsalan came to a decision. He eased back a little of his weight. In a voice made harsh by disappointment, he growled a warning at Rukh.

"Act the Khan of Khorasan when others are around, but don't play your games with me. *I* know exactly who you are, and I will not tell you again: *Do not test me, Rukh.*"

He meant every word, but for emphasis, Arsalan dug his knee deeper. Then he sprang to his feet, pulling Rukh up beside him with more force than was necessary.

Rukh eyed Arsalan warily, rubbing the bruise on his chest. "You've made your point, Arsalan."

Arsalan stared back at him, undaunted. "And?"

"And I concede. You are the only enemy I do not care to make."

37

It was worse than Arian had feared. The Talisman encampment stretched from one end of the horizon to the other, the plains dotted by hundreds of fires, the darkness punctured by standards bearing the bloodstained flag. Ahead of the Talisman army, a procession of drummers advanced toward Ashfall's outer ramparts. The standard-bearers were horsed, while the rest of the army traveled on foot, its supply chain at the rear.

The Talisman's purpose was singular. There were no slave-chains in its wake. Instead, their aim was to defeat the Black Khan and thereby conquer his empire. Arian knew what that would mean: Ashfall's scriptorium would burn, its Warraqeen would be slaughtered, and the women and girls of the city would be ravaged and sold to the north.

Unless her strengths were greater than she knew.

"Arian." Sinnia squeezed Arian's hand. "What if they've reached the Citadel as well? Our first duty lies there."

"If we're to make our stand at Hira, we must recapture the Bloodprint. It's the only thing that can save us." She looked at

Daniyar, who was measuring the strength of the Talisman through his spyglass. "What is your assessment?"

"There *is* a passage that is open, but there is a more pressing issue. There are very few guards on the ramparts." He lowered his spyglass, shaking his head. "The Black Khan has left his city undefended. The outer ramparts will be taken before this night is through."

Their horses were lined up on a ridge overlooking the plains, where a chill had descended on the camp.

"What of the villages outside the city walls? Have they been abandoned yet?"

Daniyar scanned the plains again. "Until we pass through the ramparts, there's no way of knowing. If the villages have been overrun, there's no answer for the Black Khan's neglect or its consequences for the fate of Khorasan."

He spoke to his horse, the same gentle murmur he'd used on the Ahdath's horses in the turquoise mines at Nightshaper. He'd used his gifts to turn the Ahdath's horses against their riders. Now he encouraged his own mount against the terror that lay ahead.

"Does the Black Khan wear the Sacred Cloak?" Arian asked. "Can you find him on the ramparts?"

"There is a token force at the outer walls: a handful of archers and a single company of Zhayedan spread out along the walls. I see no sign of the Khan."

"Then we must be the ones to help them hold the outer walls."

Daniyar's eyes ranged over their party: two Companions of Hira and a youthful poet whose trembling hands on the reins of his horse reflected the depths of his fear.

"Unless you can summon the Claim the way you did in the

Registan, we must get to the city without further delay. Can you, Arian?"

His eyes traced the fading marks of the bruises on her throat. "I don't think so—not yet."

They didn't speak of what else Arian had done with the Claim in the courtyard of the Clay Minar—the death she had offered the Ahdath in spades, the wild, secret pleasure she had taken in it. Her remorse had come much later.

"Who leads this army?" she asked him.

"Each Talisman brigade is commanded by an Immolan from one of the Talisman tribes."

"And at the center?"

He knew what she was asking. "Shin War. They command the army."

Sinnia's head whipped around. She couldn't conceal her dismay.

"My lord, this is a quandary you shouldn't have to face." She saw a look pass between Arian and Daniyar and added hurriedly, "Not that I'd expect you to abandon the First Oralist."

She blushed at his knowing smile, but all he said was "Their presence may be an advantage I can use, but it's too soon to tell. Lead the way, Arian. We must consult the guards at the outer wall at once."

Sinnia's horse kept pace with his on their descent down the ridge, the last chance they'd have to speak until they reached the ramparts.

"You haven't been to Ashfall before, my lord?"

"Once," he said. "To attend the Conference of the Mages. I had no need of secrecy then, so I took the open road."

Alisher echoed his words with some amazement. "The Conference of the Mages? I thought the Conference a myth—folktales we were told in childhood."

"I as well," said Sinnia.

Daniyar smiled at Sinnia again. He reached across to her horse and pressed her hand with genuine warmth. "You thought *me* a myth before you met me. Would you not say I'm real?"

Since he offered her the opportunity, Sinnia's bold glance sketched his face with frank appreciation—the chiseled planes, the finely shaped mouth, the glory of the brilliant silver gaze. "Real and unreal, such beauty," she teased.

"I could say the same to you—a young queen of the Negus." He returned her glance with such forthright masculine approval that Sinnia blinked. He smiled at her momentary confusion, and seeing the smile, she shook her head at them both.

"Don't try your tricks on me, my lord. I assure you I'm quite immune."

"Pity." His tone was so indulgent that Sinnia grinned to herself.

"If you're quite finished trying to charm me, tell me about the other Mages."

His voice still soft, he answered, "Ilea, the Golden Mage, leads the Council of Hira. Rukh, the Prince of West Khorasan, has inherited his brother's role as Dark Mage. There is also the Mage of the Blue Eye. The others, I do not know. Perhaps *they* were creatures of myth. What I do know is that each Mage is gifted with some ability with the Claim, though study and practice are required."

"How do you study, my lord? *What* do you study? And what is it that binds the Mages of Khorasan together?"

She was touched when he answered her frankly, as if he considered her worthy of his trust. "In my case, the Candour was my guide. It lists many of the rites of the Mages. Over the years, the Candour led me to other manuscripts that guided me further. But you should know, the Golden Mage has even greater ability than

I, as she has more knowledge of the Claim. She's had a lifetime to study from the treasury of manuscripts at Hira."

"The same must be true of the Black Khan at Ashfall. It is said that Ashfall's scriptorium is one of the wonders of the world."

"I hope so," Daniyar said grimly. "But I cannot speak to the Black Khan's abilities. When a Conference of the Mages is convened, the Claim redoubles its power, and we are able to make of its magic nearly anything we choose—either for good or for ill."

The grim line of his mouth eased a little, as he saw the hope in Sinnia's eyes. She had struggled so long at Arian's side that she had thought the two of them would always be on their own, with no one else to aid them. Now, though . . .

Alisher was listening too, rapt at this review of what he had believed to be folklore.

"This must be why you do not fear these armies," he said. "Perhaps if the Mages wield this power, there is nothing that can defeat them."

Daniyar sighed, shifting in his saddle to stretch the sore muscles of his back. He had given hope to the others and kept his doubts to himself. But a more honest explanation was warranted.

"Those powers are not quite as ascribed by myth. Consider how little they aided me before the Authoritan." He nodded at the Talisman standards in the distance. "Our real power rests in knowledge."

Puzzled, Alisher asked, "What magic does knowledge afford you? Or any of the Mages of Khorasan?"

"Why would the Immolans fear knowledge enough to burn it if it didn't threaten their rule?" Daniyar chose not to elaborate further, glancing over at Sinnia. "Are you well enough to undertake this journey? You would be safer at Hira. You could take Alisher with you."

They had nearly reached the great white plains of the salt lake, the ground rippling beneath their horses' hooves. She waved away his concern, making light of her injuries at Jaslyk. "You know I won't leave Arian's side," she said without apology. "Just as I know what you were prepared to suffer on her behalf. You and I, we are bound to her. Wherever she rides, we ride."

She was answered by a brusque nod of his head.

Perhaps seeking to assert his own commitment, Alisher quickly said, "I may serve a purpose at Ashfall. They say the Khan is an admirer of verse. His interest may allow me to slip inside the city, if other methods fail."

Sinnia clicked her tongue at him. "We are not in the habit of abandoning our friends. We will see you safely to the palace."

They fell into conversation, and Daniyar rode ahead to join Arian. "What is your plan, Arian? I sense you have something in mind."

She was measuring their progress around the salt lake, comparing their speed to the Talisman's advance. Holding her injured wrist in place, she nodded at the outer walls. "We must lend our aid to the company at the wall. If we cannot assist them in holding the outer wall, at least we will gain enough time to deliver a warning to the Khan. Then we must make for the Emissary Gate."

On the eastern front, the Emissary Gate was for ambassadors to the court at Ashfall. The Messenger Gate to the west was named for the Messenger of the Claim.

"And the Claim?"

"Whatever use I can make of it, I will."

"Will you use the Verse of the Throne?"

"Yes. I've taught it to Sinnia as well. And you—do you remember?"

His eyes held hers, a shadow crossing his face. "I remember everything."

"Don't," she said, reaching for his hand. "Don't think about Nevus."

His gaze settled on her bruises, then drifted back to her cheek. "If he had branded you with the bloodmark—"

"He didn't," she said swiftly. "And even if he had, it wouldn't change anything between us." Her voice slowed. "Would it?"

He raised her hand to his lips and kissed it. She fanned her fingers across his beard.

"You know it wouldn't." They nudged their horses ahead, the wetlands giving way to solid ground. The Talisman drums were louder, pounding through drifts of night. "When the Black Khan sold you to the Authoritan, he broke the vow he made to the Council. If he was willing to besmirch his honor, his desperation must have been great. How will you persuade him to cede the Bloodprint to you?"

"With the Claim," she said. She looked across the plains to the gathering of the Talisman's forces. "I will promise my aid in defending his city in exchange for the Bloodprint."

"And if you are prevented from using the Claim? Or unable to?"

Arian's reply was matter-of-fact. "No man will collar me again."

A series of high-pitched whistles sounded above their heads. They looked up, expecting to see Saqar, the falcon that had tracked them from Hira. The sky was dark, but at the ramparts ahead, they caught a flicker of torchlight against the lens of a spyglass.

"They've spotted us." He motioned to Sinnia. "Show them the tahweez."

He found a long match in his saddlebags and lit it against the night. It flared against their circlets before he blew it out. The whistle sounded again—two short, sharp blasts.

"They've understood. Ride hard now."

He spurred his horse a short distance apart from theirs, riding closer to the Talisman encampment. They had the cover of night, but all it would take to discover them was a presentiment of danger and a well-aimed spyglass.

The Talisman had no magic to use against them. What they had was strength of arms. Daniyar's mind raced with calculation. How and why had the Black Khan been so negligent? Had he returned to his city from Black Aura, or had he been ambushed along the way?

And who besides the Shin War directed the movement of this army? The army's formations were too vast and well studied to have been organized by the Shin War. He suspected the maneuvers of a deadlier foe, but he kept his thoughts to himself. There would be time enough to lay additional burdens on Arian. These were disciplined forces, arranged by a division of skill: archers, fire-lancers, engineers, infantry. They lacked horses, a possible outcome of the actions of the warriors of the Cloud Door. The Buzkashi had gathered a vast number of horses from the plains, acclimating them to higher altitudes. By contrast, only a handful of the Talisman's Immolans were horsed.

Daniyar had stayed too long at his mission in Candour, herding the orphaned boys of the city, paying scant attention to anything else. Now the orphans of Candour were on the march to Ashfall, regardless of his efforts. They carried Talisman standards into battle, rough and ready forces who would take the brunt of the Zhayedan's response, their lives expended by their commanders with little thought to their value.

Nearly all sides were ready for the war: the Ahdath, the warriors of the Cloud Door—and here in these lowlands, the Talisman. But where were the Zhayedan—the Black Khan's invincible forces? If Ashfall fell, the west would lie open to the Talisman advance.

The wind was at their rear, pushing them across the salt flats. They reached the bell tower of the outer walls. To the east, there were murmurs of discovery, torches lit in their direction, men ordered to the perimeter.

Arian and Sinnia rode faster, their cloaks flying behind them, leaving their arms uncovered. They were the emissaries to a foreign capital, ragged, injured, and worn from the road, as was he himself. The Shin War crest he had stitched to the cloth at his throat was frayed, his armor Ahdath castoffs from Lania, his weapons not the weapons born to his hand. He didn't have his ring; he didn't have the Candour. For himself, it didn't matter. But Arian should have entered the city like a queen, her black hair arrayed with jewels, her golden circlets ablaze.

Instead, she was covered in the dust of their ride. Wounded and battle-weary, she looked fragile to his eyes. Her face was strained, reflecting what she'd endured. And other trials awaited them at Ashfall. Though the Companions of Hira were not cosseted during their training, they hadn't faced hardships like these. Guessing at his thoughts, Arian's eyes found his, radiating purpose. Once more, he'd underestimated her. She was wounded, not weakened. Her carriage was straight and tall in the saddle, her face calm, her judgment measured. The crucible of Black Aura had left her gifts immutable. She had no more need of jewels and silk than he did of the Candour. It was something *he* wanted for her, his thoughts flashing back to how Lania had dressed her at the Ark, the beauty of her curves shining through her dress, and

he wondered when they would be more to each other than confederates in a cause . . .

When we have defeated them, he thought.

He glanced back at the Talisman army. A small party had detached itself from the host.

He spurred his horse through the gate.

38

"PLACE IT ON THE PEDESTAL. ALLOW ME TO SEE IT FOR MYSELF."

Rukh's men were in the council chamber, engaged in a heated debate manipulated by the Nizam, while Arsalan stood at the foot of the table and listened to the men without comment. Rukh had withdrawn with Ilea to the antechamber off the room where his commanders prepared for war. It was a small and intimate space, lit by candles placed in wall sconces, its surfaces inscribed with Khorasani motifs.

A delicately enameled candle clock shed light upon a gold pedestal modeled after the Peacock Throne. A quintet of black silk curtains separated the antechamber from the council chamber, both rooms opening onto the city walls, with windswept views of the gardens. The city had gone quiet: a series of commands issued by Arsalan had set the perimeter to rights.

The High Companion of Hira cared for none of this. She had come for the Bloodprint, at some cost to the Citadel. She did not explain to the Prince of Khorasan how she'd eluded the Talisman encampments that blocked the road from Hira, and he didn't ask. She suspected he didn't care, impatient to resolve the issue of the Bloodprint and return to his council of war.

At a nod to his page, the silk-wrapped manuscript was taken from its protective folds and placed upon the pedestal. The ancient ink had dulled to a rusted gold. The elongated strokes of the Bloodprint's script lay lightly upon the parchment.

Ilea knelt before it and prayed, her smooth face secret and remote. "Show me the marking," she said.

The Black Khan's page brought a basin of fresh water to him; he washed his hands again. Beset with difficulties and dangers on every step of his journey back to Ashfall, he hadn't looked at the manuscript himself. Too, his triumph was tainted by the knowledge of what he'd traded to achieve it: the First Oralist at the Authoritan's mercy. Though he knew he would make the same choice again, he was diminished by what he'd done.

He reached clean hands to the sacred manuscript and opened it to the page bloodmarked by history. He spread the pages wide so the High Companion might find what she sought from the parchment: the blood that stained the Bloodprint.

There was a slight tremor in the fingers that traced over the staggered marks of blood. It was the only indication the High Companion was moved.

She read the words aloud, her recital different from any invocation he'd heard from the students who studied in his scriptorium, every last one of them male. Her voice fell on his ear strangely, a desolation to twist his heart. The words were deeply affecting. And as always, he wondered how to make use of them.

"*If they believe in that which you believe in, they have been rightly guided. If they turn away, they are only in dissension, and the One will be sufficient for you against them. And the One is the Hearer, the Knowing."*

She looked up at Rukh, the light from the candle clock outlining her hair in gold. She seemed unearthly, an angel with a sword in her hand, except that the sword was her voice.

"He was killed as he recited these words. His blood transformed them in ways I do not understand. Did the First Oralist have the chance to read them?"

"I don't know."

"No," Ilea agreed. "How could you? Your time with her was brief once you delivered her to the Authoritan. It seems your plan came to fruition."

"It was your plan also, Ilea. Or have you forgotten that?"

"No, I haven't forgotten. I yielded the foremost weapon in my arsenal in exchange for this." She traced the bloodstains again. "Yet here it is in Ashfall, instead of at the Citadel as promised."

Rukh gave an elegant snort. "Did you really think I would turn it over when I assumed all the risk? You have—what? A handful of Companions who may be able to read the Bloodprint? I have a hundred trained Warraqeen."

Ilea tipped her head to one side, her hands folded at her waist. "You have trained your Warraqeen for how many years? A decade at most? And you think them able to find within this manuscript the power of the Claim?" She laughed. "It isn't a matter of reading it, Rukh. How poorly you understand it."

She pointed to the Bloodprint. "The Guided One died in defense of its tenets, so you imagine the glory of the Bloodprint is reserved to him. Your Warraqeen are men, are they not, Great Khan?" She shook her head, pitying him. "You hoped to prevent the Warraqeen's defection to Hira, a pointless strategy."

He watched her narrowly, letting her say her piece.

She placed her hands, palms down, on the Bloodprint. A golden energy pulsed from the manuscript and arrowed up into her body. He took a step back, not entirely dismayed.

If there was another way to use the Bloodprint—

She smiled at him as if she read his thoughts.

"It was a *woman* who assembled the manuscript of the Claim. She kept it under her protection until the Guided One called for it to be returned. It is imbued with her secrets and her magic. You wonder what it is I have at Hira. A handful of Companions who are useless in this war? No, Excellency, you've mistaken the power of Hira. I have *Half-Seen* at the Citadel. Half-Seen is the descendant of the collector of the Claim. A thousand Warraqeen couldn't match her in knowledge. Half-Seen alone could bring down your walls."

He didn't doubt it. And now the reasons for Ilea's conspiracy against the First Oralist were illuminated.

"I did wonder how Hira could survive such a blow. To lose the First Oralist—I thought her mastery unmatched."

Ilea's response was dry. "She is not Hira's only treasure. There is also Ash."

"Your jurist?" He raised a silky brow. "But we're not set upon disputations of the Claim when we scarcely know what it says."

"How wrong you are again." Ilea studied the movements of the candle clock, its imperceptible machinery reflecting the workings of a subtle intelligence. "Disputation is precisely the reason Hira has been in search of the Bloodprint. As soon as Half-Seen and Ash begin its study, we will be able to dispute the Talisman's proclamations. The Assimilate cannot stand in the face of the Bloodprint's written proof. It shall be copied and sent to every corner of Khorasan."

The Black Khan shook his head. He drew Ilea away from the

Bloodprint, his hand lingering on the soft skin of her arm, and over to the windows that looked out onto the gardens.

"It would be counterfeited as soon as you sent it. A thousand counter-disputations would arise. Khorasan would know chaos."

"Khorasan would know *redemption* from chaos. Each of our copies would bear the seal of Hira—anything else would be known for a lie. And besides—" Idly, she reached up a hand to stroke the rook at the Black Khan's throat. He let her, capturing her hand with his own. His bemusement with the High Companion hadn't abated. He would willingly take her again. "The only scribes in Khorasan are here or at the Citadel. And do we not seek the same end, my lord? We want the Talisman to burn. Just as they burned everything in these lands."

Rukh bent and kissed the top of her head. His honeyed voice whispered in her ear. "Make your copy and go, Ilea. The Bloodprint is needed here." He raised her arm alongside his, showing her a point on the horizon, under the cover of the clouds. "The Talisman are not the only threat. The Rising Nineteen are rumored to march on Ashfall from the west."

The words seemed to jolt the High Companion. Her slender body went still against his, her gold eyes opaque with calculation. "If this is true, how will you ensure its safety?"

"The Khorasan Guard are dedicated to the protection of the Warraqeen. And an army stands between the palace and the scriptorium, which is more than Hira has to offer in its own defense. There will be time enough for the Companions to dispute the Talisman's Assimilate. We require the Bloodprint to serve our immediate needs first."

It was clear she couldn't persuade him, a possibility she must have known. "Then I concede to your greater need."

"As easily as that?" And he wondered what else she would concede or whether he might seek a momentary oblivion in her arms. But she didn't share his need for consolation—for a temporary stay of the darkness about to beset his rule.

"Not quite. Send me your head calligrapher. I will need some time with the Bloodprint before I leave."

For a moment he thought of asking her to act as Golden Mage, to stay in Ashfall and teach him something of his powers—the secrets Darius knew. His own understanding was deficient; the plots he'd laid had left no time for dedicated study. He knew a few tricks of voice and movement, yet he was Dark Mage in name only. He shrugged aside his weakness. He knew the power of the Mages would not be enough to hold Ashfall.

Only the Bloodprint would.

39

"I GAVE ORDERS FOR THE DEFENSE OF THE CITY, NIZAM AL-MULK. WHY did you reverse them?"

Though Arsalan spoke with a surface politeness before the council, the Nizam was not a fool. He knew the effort it was costing Arsalan to keep his anger in check, just as he knew how to play this game, always flattering the Khan, who was seated at the head of the table within view of the council's chief objects: the table-sized map of the province of West Khorasan, and the armillary sphere at the windows, aimed at a dusting of stars.

"Please answer him, Nizam." Rukh's voice echoed with a deference that Arsalan found galling in the circumstances. He waited at the Khan's side, across from two captains of the Teerandaz, clad in the armor of their kind, embellished at the neck and the arms with arrowheads shaped like silver rooks. The two women had removed their transparent face masks for this meeting. At the sight of them, the Nizam grimaced in distaste.

Dismissing Arsalan's question with high-handed insolence, the Nizam took his time to address the Khan's request. "I did not *reverse* your orders, Commander, I delayed them. You must have known your absence from Ashfall would cause a general panic, yet you chose to curry favor with the Khan. Your lack of foresight in abandoning the city distressed the Warraqeen. And his Excellency left me in no doubt that the well-being of the Warraqeen was to be my chief concern. Was that not so, Excellency?"

Rukh nodded. He did not dispute anything the Nizam had said, nor did he take issue with his rudeness to Arsalan. But Arsalan could play this game as well as the Nizam.

"I fail to see how manning the outer walls and preparing the armory could disrupt the studies of the Warraqeen," he pointed out. "Why should they have suffered discomfort?"

"It wasn't just that," the Nizam said smoothly. "You'd asked for the residents of the outlying villages to be brought within the city walls. The Warraqeen were unable to set about their work. They are noble-spirited. They wished to join the city's defense."

Arsalan's eyes narrowed. "So you thought to soothe their worries by offering *no* defense at all?"

The Black Khan rose from the table. "Enough, Arsalan. The Nizam al-Mulk is correct in all he says. Without the efforts of the Warraqeen, any other defense is moot. They must be shielded from agitation. The Nizam acted for the best."

"The Warraqeen are not the Prince's only charge. Everyone beyond the city walls is at risk. They must be gathered behind our defenses at once."

"You forget the outer ramparts," Rukh chided.

It was all Arsalan could do to keep the anger from his voice.

"*There are no men at the outer ramparts.* A direct contravention of my orders to the Zhayedan—do you dare to pretend otherwise?" His steely-eyed gaze rested on each of his captains in turn. "The gravest dereliction of duty."

The council erupted in noise. The Black Khan listened in silence, a movement of his hand telling Arsalan to let it play out. When the commanders had fallen silent, one of the captains of the Teerandaz spoke, her words concise and certain. She spoke with utter command of herself, assuming control of the room.

"My lord commander, I deferred to Nizam al-Mulk on the issue of the defense of the ramparts, where six of our companies should have been stationed. But we have been preparing, regardless. The archery is fully armored, and we have rehearsed our plan of attack along each line of our defenses." She gave Arsalan a quick nod. "We are ready. What's more, though we were not permitted to send riders to bring our people into the city, we sent messages through our couriers. His Excellency's hawks have sent your memorandum to each of the outlying villages. They know to expect the order to retreat."

"They did not seem in readiness when we rode into the city, Captain Cassandane."

Cassandane hesitated. "The shortcoming was mine, Commander."

Arsalan didn't believe her. "Speak your mind, Captain. You've never been afraid to do so."

"My lord, the Nizam assured the villages they were under the Khan's protection, even if they chose to remain outside the city walls."

A rare fury blazed from Arsalan's eyes. He moved to confront the Nizam, heedless of Rukh's attempt to restrain him. "*I* command the Zhayedan, Nizam al-Mulk. With what authority did you gainsay my orders?"

The Nizam studied his well-tended nails. "You soldiers and your imaginary fiefdoms. It is the *Khan* who balances all our fates in his hands. As *he* did not advise that I no longer govern in his absence, I allayed the fears of the people, as has always been my duty."

Arsalan's hands clenched at his sides, the palpable force of his self-restraint silencing the outcry in the room. His voice dropped, the warning in it low and lethal. "And what protection does your *governance* offer now?"

Now it was the Nizam who moved closer, meeting him on his ground with a fine and sneering disdain. "I have accounted for my actions to the Khan. I need not explain myself to you." He flung a contemptuous glance at Cassandane. "Nor to the woman you hide behind by appointing her to your ranks."

A terrifying expectation settled in the room at this insult.

The moment of reckoning. The moment for Rukh to decide whose counsel he valued most.

Through the fog of rage in his head, Arsalan became aware of Rukh's fierce grip on his arm—and of the fear communicated by the strength of that grip. This wasn't a choice to be forced upon the Khan, not now at this perilous moment. Not with the Talisman hastening to their gates.

He took a swift breath to calm himself. Then another and another, unnoticeable to anyone in the room save Rukh, who still held on to his arm.

He was playing into the Nizam's hands.

And he was giving his prince every reason to second-guess his judgment. He pressed Rukh's hand briefly with his own, his decision made. This wasn't the moment to force a confrontation. His gaze came to rest on Cassandane, who held herself aloof, as he should have done in the first place.

His glance flicked over his men. He addressed himself to them, though his message was for the Nizam.

"I will not tolerate any disrespect shown to the Captain of the Teerandaz." Then he turned back to the Nizam. "Perhaps if we are fortunate enough to survive the Talisman assault, you will be able to persuade me of the merit of your actions. Until then, my concern remains what best serves the Prince of Khorasan and the capital of this empire."

His commanders saluted him as one. Cassandane shot him a glance he couldn't easily interpret—something between gratitude and warning. Rukh's grip on his arm eased, his thoughts hidden as he shielded his eyes with his silky, downcast lashes.

A pulse throbbing in his jaw, Arsalan conceded the Nizam's victory. He turned to the captain of the cavalry. "Send riders now at once. The Talisman approach our walls. And you—" He pointed to another of the commanders. "Double the number of men at the eastern gate. Prepare supplies, man the parapets."

The Black Khan interrupted him. "Set a special guard at the door to the scriptorium. No one is to be allowed through without my express permission. That includes Darya."

A murmur of laughter rippled through the room. It didn't please Arsalan to hear it. The Khan's sister had become a curiosity, one who could be mocked with impunity in his presence. Whose doing was this? The Nizam or the Black Khan himself? Perhaps both men were to blame.

"If the Princess desires to visit the scriptorium, tell the guards to notify me." He relayed additional instructions, sending his men on their way. Cassandane he held back.

"What else have you learned?"

"I sent scouts to the west. Your intelligence was correct. There *is* an army gathered in the valleys of the Empty Quarter. Though the full strength of the army is weeks away, a vanguard is at our borders. We need a better defense." She glanced through the silk curtains to the manuscript on its pedestal. "We need a weapon greater than anything we have in the armory. I would think on that, Commander."

Arsalan nodded. Of all his captains, he relied on Cassandane the most, whereas the Nizam preferred to appoint his own men to the Zhayedan. Arsalan wasn't distracted by personal loyalty. Nor did caste, class, or individual affiliation factor into his staffing of the army or the Khorasan Guard. He trained with the Zhayedan regularly, alert to independent thinking. It hadn't taken him long to place Cassandane in charge of the Teerandaz. In addition to her skills as an archer, she possessed imagination. She spoke up if she spotted a flaw in his tactics, unafraid of his displeasure. She was the kind of captain Ashfall would need to survive the coming Talisman offensive. The Nizam's men, he trusted not at all. They were bound by dual loyalties, too often absent from duty, scurrying back and forth with messages for the Nizam.

Rukh had left the Zhayedan in Arsalan's hands. He was more than the commander of Rukh's army: he was Rukh's confederate and closest friend. It was a bond that meant more to Arsalan than any other, and he knew the Nizam would use it against him, given the first opportunity. The two men the Black Khan trusted were once again at odds.

The Nizam's decisions had left the city vulnerable. The Zhayedan wouldn't hold the outer ramparts for long. The defense of the city walls was uppermost in his mind. He needed to know how quickly the Talisman advanced. He sent Cassandane and a handful of trusted others back to the outer walls to report. He needed more time. Cassandane would buy him that time.

"We've done what we can for the moment," he told Rukh. "We'll know more when Cassandane reports. At least the Nizam has ensured the city is well provisioned. If we can defend the walls, we'll be able to last out a siege."

Rukh listened with half-attention. His hand moved the armillary sphere, scattering the light over its finely worked quadrants. "What of the western gate? It's the weakest point of our defenses."

Arsalan gestured at the Bloodprint. "Send the Warraqeen there. Make sure they know how to use it."

On her stool before the Bloodprint, Ilea listened to the war council. Something was amiss. The Black Khan was passive before his council, permitting others to speak in his place, to advise him against his better judgment. Was it the tension between Arsalan and the Nizam that kept him quiet? Or did he have an agenda of his own the others failed to perceive?

He gave the Nizam a free hand in matters of governance, but the Zhayedan were Arsalan's province. Why did he permit interference with Arsalan's jurisdiction? It was Arsalan who'd installed Cassandane as commander of the Teerandaz, a decision of some perception.

It didn't surprise Ilea that women filled the ranks of Ashfall's archers; the Teerandaz trained agile and adept girls from earliest childhood. Just as the Companions of Hira had their legend, so did the Teerandaz's archers. She was pleased the Black Khan had kept up a tradition that empowered women, even as he suppressed their studies as Warraqeen.

She could fathom the contradiction. He feared the dominance of Hira, though he little knew how much *more* afraid he should be. She smiled to herself. She found him a worthwhile ally, even an alluring one at times. His schemes had borne fruit more than once. Truthfully, she hadn't believed the Authoritan would relinquish his treasure. He'd turned out to be a tyrant no different from the One-Eyed Preacher, one who couldn't conceive of the *nature* of his treasure.

While the Black Khan left her alone with the Bloodprint, she was working out a plan of her own. She wasn't overcome by the knowledge that myth had proved reality. She was heir to Hira's secrets; she had known the Bloodprint was real. It fulfilled her every hope. She memorized each line she read, feeling its power take root.

There were things she hadn't been able to do before, things the Bloodprint would help her to correct. Magic she would be able to seize. Lands that would fall under Hira's command. Everything north of the Wall would be hers, everything west Ashfall's. And when they had merged their two capitals and their bloodlines, she would no longer be High Companion of Hira, the women of the Citadel nipping at her heels. She had freed herself of the encumbrance of Arian; she had dealt with the First Oralist for good.

Everything she had worked for, silent and alone, would be within her grasp. This included the Bloodprint and the Khan.

She made her preparations to depart. The Citadel needed her first.

40

ARIAN AND DANIYAR REACHED THE RAMPARTS AHEAD OF THE TALIS-
man soldiers at their heels. As the gates closed behind them, they
rode up the ramparts into a scene of chaos—orders shouted along
the parapets, signal flares launched from the corners of oppos-
ing towers, a buzz of furious activity as soldiers raced to position
themselves at defenses along the wall. The sense of urgency was
everywhere, a tense command to bar the gate issued by a woman
at the wall.

The woman was dressed as a captain of the Teerandaz, the silver aigrette pinned to her helmet an indicator of rank. Her black
leather armor was feathered at the neck and wrists with a row of
silver rooks. Beneath her pointed helmet, her hair was fashioned
in dozens of intricate braids, her skin as dark as Sinnia's, her hair
and eyes the color of black carnelian, her features that of the people of the Aryaward. She was joined by another member of the
Teerandaz, this one a native of Ashfall, lighter in complexion and
sharp-featured like the Khan.

Both women bore the lightweight double bows and deadly
silver-tipped arrows of their unit, and their bearing was that of

deadshot archers who'd been trained from earliest childhood to join their company's ranks.

The dark-skinned woman greeted them in the manner of the Companions of Hira, one arm extending out and brought back to her chest. She gave a quick nod, first to Arian and then to Sinnia, with a swiftly masked look of surprise. With the Talisman assault gaining speed, she didn't have time to spare, yet she plainly recognized that the arrival of the Companions could serve at this desperate hour.

"First Oralist," she said. "Companion."

"Captain Cassandane," Arian returned. "You hold the outer wall—just the two of you alone?"

Cassandane grimaced. "The Nizam's orders were to gather our forces at the inner walls, to keep the Warraqeen safe. We're here to track the Talisman's advance." She indicated Daniyar and Alisher with a quick jab of an arrow. "Who accompanies you?" Her eyes studied the torn crest at Daniyar's throat as she waited for the answer. Arian motioned him forward. He raised his head and focused his silver eyes on Cassandane. She stepped back a pace with a whistled breath.

"Thank the One," she said simply. "Perhaps the Nizam will heed the counsel of the Silver Mage, as he was once prone to do."

Daniyar crossed the bell tower, looking at the villages that lay outside the protection of the city walls.

"The outer ramparts will be taken, Captain Cassandane. Have your villages received no word of the army on the march?"

Again Cassandane's eyes rested upon his crest, and this time Daniyar took note. He wouldn't get answers from the captain until he'd made his own position clear. "You know I am of the Shin War. And that I do not ride at their head."

Cassandane nodded. "When last you came to Ashfall, you were

dressed as the Silver Mage. Your ring, your sword, the Candour—where are they? Why do you wear the tokens of your . . . less promising allegiance?"

Daniyar hesitated for a moment, then decided there was nothing to be gained by discretion. There were nearly out of time: they needed to come to terms. "I come to you from Black Aura—the Candour was taken from me there."

Captain Cassandane flinched. "I didn't know."

Daniyar's eyes narrowed. "How could you have?"

She weighed her response before answering. "I rode with the Khan to Black Aura, but I wasn't permitted entry into the Ark. I did not know that the Bloodprint had been purchased from the Authoritan at such a cost."

Daniyar glanced quickly at Arian. But she chose not to disclose the Black Khan's act of betrayal or what she'd suffered as a consequence. Focused on the needs of the moment, she reached out for Cassandane's hand.

"Was the Bloodprint brought to the capital? *Has* the Black Khan returned?"

When Cassandane hesitated, she pleaded with her again. "Please, Captain. All our fates now rest upon the Bloodprint. Look below. The Talisman will be at the inner walls soon. Why hasn't the alarm been sounded?"

Cassandane's voice was wooden. "In the Black Khan's absence, it is the Nizam who assumes command. But the Nizam refused to issue any orders for the city's defense."

"What of Arsalan?" Daniyar cut in. "Does he not command the Zhayedan?"

"He rode with the Khan, as he always does. He thought his orders would be followed." Her tone was laced with foreboding. And then, as if realizing she was wasting precious time, she came to a swift decision. "If it's the Bloodprint you need, ride to the city at once. Soon there will be no escape."

Arian shook her head. "When the outer ramparts fall, you'll be needed at the city gates. Let us retreat together."

The second Teerandaz archer was introduced to them as Dilaram; she looked at the Companions with relief. "We've enough to make our report, Captain. We won't be able to hold."

She gestured at the group of Talisman fighters who had reached the foot of the ramparts—four dozen men in all. Others were coming up behind them. They shouted catcalls at the bell tower, followed by the beating of drums.

A shower of fire-lances arced up and across the parapet, disappearing over the other side, setting the grasslands ablaze in pockets.

Daniyar took up a position along the wall, poised with his bow in his hand. But Sinnia responded first. Faster than the Teerandaz could follow, she fired six arrows at the soldiers lounging at the base of the tower. Each of the six found their target, awakening a roar of outrage from the scouts. They took shelter under the cover of their shields.

Cassandane looked at Sinnia with new respect.

Dilaram joined Sinnia, firing arrows deep into the Talisman's ranks, delaying the returning volley of the fire-lancers.

Daniyar used his spyglass to sight the vast distance between the inner and outer walls. He prodded Alisher into the shelter of the bell tower, where a ladder climbed to the sky. "We must send warning to Ashfall. Climb the ladder and ring the bell."

"Those are *not* my orders," Cassandane said sharply.

Daniyar held her gaze. "Then your city will fall. You know I am speaking the truth."

The Talisman shields broke apart. They had fastened two fire-lances together, doubling their capacity for ruin. Before Sinnia or Dilaram could react, the conjoined lances were fielded from below, scattering a rain of fire over the parapet. Sparks fell all around them, brushing their hair and their arms. The lance arrowed over their heads, setting fire to their route of retreat.

"Climb, Alisher."

With a harried glance at the others, Alisher disappeared up the ladder. Cassandane let him go, a faint frown on her brow. Daniyar took that as encouragement.

"Send word to the Zhayedan to hold the gate as long as they can and then to retreat to the nearest village. The people there will need cover, fleeing into Ashfall."

"*I* command the Teerandaz, my lord."

Daniyar's voice remained even as he said, "There is a time to follow orders and a time to think for yourself. Your allegiance is to Ashfall—not to the Nizam, nor even to the Black Khan. What would serve your people best?"

She nodded to herself at the words. "Very well. But *I* determine what happens from this moment on." She gestured at the Zhayedan positioned along the ramparts. "It was hard to win their respect—I won't be seen taking orders from any man other than my commander." She quirked a brow at him. "Not even one as worthy as the Silver Mage."

He made her a bow. "Understood, Captain. Then what are your orders? They've brought a battering ram to the gate. How long will it hold?"

"Not long." She whistled to the Zhayedan, a series of disconnected blasts without a seeming pattern. Yet men raced along the wall to meet them at the parapet, taking note of the new arrivals without comment. Sinnia and Arian focused on the party below, firing until they'd used up their supply of arrows. But their accuracy was no match for Dilaram's unerring aim. Each arrow she released found its target. When her sling was empty, she dodged into the shelter of the tower, where more silver-tipped arrows were stacked in piles.

"You." She pointed to Sinnia. "Can you use one of these?"

She handed over a double bow and passed Sinnia a sling. "Be careful," she warned. "Avoid the tips of the arrows."

Sinnia didn't have to ask why. Below them, the men Dilaram had winged began to stagger away from the gate. Their limbs jerked apart in frenzy.

A handful of Talisman riders were on the brink of reaching the gate. Sinnia aimed at their necks. Her brief smile wasn't a celebration—it was an acknowledgment of her skill.

Dilaram spoke into her ear. "Wherever you come from, we could use you here."

The words reminded Sinnia of the Technologist's dark promise, whispered close to her skin: *I will find many exquisite uses for you.* She shook off the words with a shudder, turning to grin at Dilaram.

The grin died on her face. A Talisman arrow winged through the night, catching Dilaram in the throat. Her blood spattered Sinnia's face. Coughing, Sinnia leapt to catch the archer in her arms. Zhayedan soldiers took their place, sheltering them from the next volley.

A moment later, Alisher reached his target. Ashfall's warning bell sounded over the plains, piercing the night with a loud, discordant clang. He had spun many verses in his time, but none felt as pure as the ringing notes of the bell that echoed toward the city. It rang twice more. By the fourth reprise, an answering bell sounded from the opposite corner of the city walls.

The Maiden Tower. Their message had been received.

"Leave her," Cassandane said of Dilaram, motioning the others to the inner staircase. "She cannot be saved."

Sinnia eased Dilaram's body into the shelter of the tower, unwilling to abandon her. "We could carry her into the city."

Cassandane's answer was grim. "There will be other bodies before this night is through. Go now."

She turned to find the Silver Mage at her side.

"You don't come with us?" he asked.

She smiled, a rare expression on the face of the Teerandaz captain. "I'd heard it spoken of once—the gallantry of the Silver Mage. But though I honor it, I am not in need of your courtesy. I command these walls. I will retreat when nothing more can be done to hold them. Do what you can for our people, but make sure you reach the city." She nodded at Arian, hovering at the edge of the staircase, waiting for Alisher to reach them. "The First Oralist must gain access to the Bloodprint—she is our only hope."

Daniyar nodded at her gravely. "May your aim never waver."

She answered the Zhayedan formula in kind. "May your sword strike bone."

41

The Nizam balanced the Shahi scepter in his hands. It was a good, solid weight, carved of gold and set with rubies, diamonds, and red spinels, some as large as forty carats. He held the weight of empire in his hands, and the weight was pleasing. He bowed before the Black Khan and offered him the scepter. He'd persuaded the Khan to take up his throne to reassure the court of his fearlessness in the face of the Talisman advance.

The Black Khan took the scepter in hand and mounted the Peacock Throne. His mind was otherwise occupied, his regalia of state dismissed: the Shahi sword, abounding with emeralds; the painted enamel dagger with its haft set with Aryaward diamonds; and a heavy gold belt whose central stone was an emerald the size of an egg. This last was fitted over the Khan's black silk tunic, the entire effect one of utter decadence. The Black Khan's official return to court required the accoutrements of power.

Two giant armlets blazed from the Khan's upper arms, each set with a luminous stone larger than a man's fist: the Mountain of Light and the Sea of Light, the latter blazing a fiery pink. The onyx rook at the Black Khan's throat seemed a trifle next to these.

Yet the rook was the emblem the Nizam knew the Khan cherished most. The Peacock Throne and the regalia of state were the symbols of an ancient dynasty; the Khan preferred the insignia of his recent ancestors, patterned in black and silver. And now he wore the Sacred Cloak over his ceremonial dress. The Cloak seemed to ennoble him, enhancing his stature at court.

From the Khan's careless survey of the room followed by his mannerly acknowledgment of the court, no one could have guessed that the Talisman had advanced to the city's outer walls. Captain Cassandane's urgent call for reinforcements had been intercepted by the Nizam and refused, a decision he had made without consulting the Khan. The battle would be at the inner walls—he would not spend the warriors of the Zhayedan on an unfeasible defense. If the outlying villages were taken, it would serve the empire in the end. Ashfall was provisioned for a siege. It would hold out longer if those provisions were free of the weight of refugees.

He wasted no thought on farmers or unschooled undesirables. Ashfall was the glory of an age: the Nizam had something to protect. His mouth curled at the sight of the mongrel boy who'd been made to kneel before the throne. An illiterate, he thought. What use could the boy be to any defense of Ashfall?

"Speak, boy. Tell us what you know of the Talisman."

Wafa sobbed to himself, his head hanging down, his limbs trembling with fear. He was guarded on either side by two soldiers in leather armor, their faces covered by transparent masks. One of these prodded him with the tip of his sword; he gulped back another sob.

The boy was a pitiful wretch.

"Hazara doesn't know," the boy said. "Hazara's use was for the slave-chains." He motioned with his hand, imitating the gestures of a slave-chain's tally-taker. The Black Khan watched him with hooded eyes. He nodded at the Nizam again.

"You must have heard the Talisman speak amongst themselves. You must have heard plans for the assault on Ashfall."

Wafa answered the Nizam humbly, gazing up at him in awe. "I don't know Ashfall." With a shudder, he added, "I didn't know Black Aura."

A whisper of dread chased across the room at the mention of the Authoritan's capital.

"Whatever your life has been, you've been with the Talisman for years. You've *seen* the One-Eyed Preacher. You recognized him on the road. Tell us what you know of him."

Wafa put his hands up to his ears, his memory now made nightmare. "I *don't* know," he said. "I don't know what you want."

The Nizam gestured impatiently at one of the guards. The soldier's fist struck Wafa hard in the back. He went flying, striking his chin on the marble floor. A line of blood trickled from his mouth.

"Speak, boy."

The soldier's boot struck Wafa between his shoulder blades. He didn't let out a cry, which served to irritate the Nizam. The boy closed his eyes and braced his hands, preparing for the next blow.

"Stop this!" A woman's voice called from the end of the hall, her words followed by the tapping of slippers and the chiming of tiny bells. The guard who'd struck Wafa was pushed aside, and the boy was swept up in the shelter of a young woman's arms. The Nizam scowled at her from his seat.

Of course the Princess would find a way to interfere. A second pitiful child to answer the needs of the first.

"What are you doing?" she demanded, her voice surprisingly fierce. "Why are you beating a child for all the court to see?"

"Princess." The Nizam's voice was cold with displeasure. "You have no notion of what transpires here or how useful the information of this Talisman spy may be."

"How could a Hazara be a Talisman spy?" she asked, incredulous. "You know they exterminate his kind." She turned to her brother, not bothering to bow. "Didn't you hear the bell? Why are you receiving the court when Captain Cassandane is calling for help? Shouldn't we be preparing the city against attack?"

Before the Khan could respond, the woman seated to his right rose from her chair. She was a majestic woman, attired like an empress in layers of silk under a brocade robe. Her eyebrows and eyelids were lined with kohl, and despite her great age, her lips and cheeks were rouged. Her headdress and jewels were nearly as splendid as the Khan's. It was clear the woman wielded enormous power. Even the Nizam waited for her to speak.

"How dare you address the Prince in such a manner? How dare you presume to know better than the Khan how to mount his city's defense? How many times have I warned you about your impertinence at court?" She motioned to a member of the Zhayedan. "Take her to Qaysarieh, let her learn her lesson there."

Though her cheeks were red and her voice was faint, Darya managed an answer. "If you send me to Qaysarieh, Begum, at least I'll have the chance to see my brother."

The Nizam seized the opportunity granted by Darya's response.

"I warned you, Excellency. The Princess conspires against you with Darius. Your brother would seize your throne given the merest chance—he grew bold in your absence from Ashfall."

Wafa trembled in Darya's grip. The Nizam smiled to himself, well aware that the boy would not wish to be condemned at her side.

Darya's hands were gentle on the boy's arms, stroking them to reassure him. She shielded him with her body from the Nizam's cruel gaze.

The Black Khan rose from the Peacock Throne, the scepter in his hand. He nodded to the Begum to take her seat, motioning his guards to stand down. Not that the gesture was necessary—none would lay a hand on a princess of the blood, except at the Khan's command.

The corner of his mouth quirked up at the sight of Darya attempting to shield the boy. "Reinforcements are on their way to the ramparts, Darya. Have faith in Commander Arsalan."

"But they're not!" Darya said desperately. "I don't know where the Commander is—"

"Then perhaps your efforts would be better spent in pursuit of him. You are normally certain of his whereabouts."

She blushed at the Khan's mockery, and he sighed.

"I interrogate this boy because I wish to mount the best defense of Ashfall. Can you not see that you delay me?" Rukh surveyed the assembly, the women jeering behind their fans, the soldiers of the Zhayedan, who seemed embarrassed for their princess. His voice hardening, he said, "You disgrace yourself, Darya—and you insult the Prince of Khorasan."

He nodded to one of the guards. "Remove her." And after a pause, "To her chambers, *not* the Qaysarieh Portal." Then he gestured to the other. "Continue. The boy must speak."

Darya fought off the grip of the Zhayedan, holding fast to Wafa. "You *cannot* beat him. Look at him! See the terror in his eyes. Does it not disgrace the Prince of Khorasan to wreak violence upon a child? Is this not a graver offense than my disregard of custom?"

She faced him defiantly, her headdress aslant on her head.

This was the time to crush her, to put the girl firmly in her place. Instead, the Nizam watched in dismay as the Prince waved his guard aside. He looked at his sister and smiled. "What would you have of me, Darya?"

Darya's face brightened with joy. She didn't hesitate. She issued a quick series of orders to the guard who had tried to take hold of her. He looked to the Black Khan, who nodded. A chair was brought for Wafa, along with a basin and cloth. Darya dipped the cloth in warm water and began to clean the boy's face, wiping blood from the corner of his lips.

The hard edge of Rukh's mouth softened. The Nizam knew what he was thinking: the Princess of Ashfall touched a Hazara boy and viewed it as an honorable service. He shook his head at the Khan's belief that a girl with his sister's heart would never conspire to dethrone him. Rukh spoke to Darya gently. "Darya, I *must* know."

Darya whispered to Wafa. "Tell me, please. I don't want them to hurt you. My brother might frighten you, but he isn't needlessly cruel. So please, is there anything you can tell us of the One-Eyed Preacher?"

Wafa licked a trace of blood from his lips. His glance flicked up at the Nizam before coming back to rest upon Darya's gentle face. He must have taken encouragement from the way she refused to desert him.

Gathering up his courage, the boy spoke haltingly, trying to describe what little he knew. He told her of the Talisman's conclaves, of their determination to conquer all of the lands of Khorasan. He told her that though they'd forbidden others to read, they were searching for an ancient script. The Immolans were skilled in the script. They twisted it with their tongues. Wafa had met their master only once, when he'd been sent to serve the One-Eyed Preacher. He pointed to the Nizam, who glared at the boy's presumption.

"He's not a man—not like that."

"What do you mean?" Darya asked. "Not wise, not important? He's not someone of rank?"

Wafa didn't understand. He was shaking his head, confused, uncertain as to how to explain. He moved his hands, sketching a shape in the air—something that seemed tall and vast and ephemeral—almost transient. But the boy didn't know these words and so he didn't use them.

"He's bigger than himself."

"Do you mean he's taller?"

Again, Wafa shook his head. He peered into Darya's eyes, as if he searched for the answer there.

"He's everywhere at once. He can see everything, no matter where you try to hide." He pressed his hands to his temples. "He's here. Inside. And his voice—"

When the boy saw that the Nizam and the Black Khan were watching him intently, he faltered into silence.

"There's something special about his voice?" Darya encouraged him to continue.

Wafa cast a wild glance around the Divan-e Shah for the commander of the Zhayedan.

"The soldier heard it too. He knows."

Rukh descended from the dais and came to stand before Wafa. "What *was* that?" he asked. "You're right, it wasn't a man's voice."

Wafa cupped his hand over the bulge in his throat. "He makes it with his voice." He struggled to find the words to make it clear. "He makes *himself*. He knows words—I don't know the words he knows." His hands made an aborted gesture. "The words *she* knows. They were like her words, but she doesn't use them to hurt."

"Whom do you speak of, boy?"

291

Wafa scowled at Rukh. He hadn't forgotten that the Khan had betrayed the kindest woman he knew.

"The one you left," he said, gathering his courage. "The one you sold to the demon." His hand fluttered at his side. "The lady Arian."

A gasp of disbelief came from the Begum seated on the dais. Did a Hazara boy dare to decry the actions of a prince? Did he call the First Oralist by name? The Nizam watched as the Black Khan studied his courtiers. None would call the Khan to account, but he had not forgotten the circumstances that had set the stage for a coup. The loss of power required only the briefest misstep. The Khan's betrayal of the First Oralist could certainly be counted as such. But in the end, he had brought the Bloodprint to Ashfall, a reminder of his indisputable influence to the scheming members of his court.

Thoughts of the Bloodprint cleared the Nizam's mind. There was no talisman considered as valuable; he felt his tension ease away. He focused on the Khan's response to the boy. He would gloss over the Khan's treachery at the Ark and address the matter at hand.

"You're saying he uses the Claim—the Claim empowers him, just as it empowers the First Oralist. The Claim is the magic they wield."

Wafa trembled with relief. The Hazara boy had managed to make his meaning plain.

"He makes the Talisman afraid. They listen to him—they *have* to listen to him."

"And what happens if they don't?" Rukh's eyes were curious on the boy's face.

Wafa sought comfort from the safety of Darya's arms. Though

the Black Khan was gentle with his sister, he had no such assurance of his mercy.

He described what he knew to the court: the riders in the pass, his struggles in the Blood Shed, his work as a tally-taker in the midst of Talisman soldiers, a slave at the One-Eyed Preacher's heels. Then he choked out an answer to the Khan.

"Then . . . everything is shattered to bright red blood and bone."

The Nizam clapped his hands together, snapping the court out of its reverie. His disapproval plain on his ascetic features, he sneered at the boy. "What kind of nonsense is this? He speaks of necromancy, magic—arcane rites. *No one* has use of the Claim. No one outside of Ashfall has ever *read* the Claim."

The Nizam had forgotten the Bloodprint. He'd forgotten what the Prince of Khorasan had risked to bring the Bloodprint home. And he'd discounted the learning of the Council of Hira. Rukh bowed to him, a gesture of respect meant to mollify his vizier before he openly disagreed.

"You weren't there, Nizam al-Mulk. The boy is right. I saw the One-Eyed Preacher at the pass. I heard—*some*thing. Now we learn it was the Claim, though not the Claim as I knew it." He pointed to the Bloodprint, openly displayed to the court. "I brought it to the Divan-e Shah to bless the city as it readies for battle."

He snapped his fingers at two members of the Khorasan Guard. "Purify yourselves and take it to the scriptorium, where they stand ready to receive it."

A commotion rose at the doors to the Divan-e Shah. The Khorasan Guard hesitated between the Bloodprint and the entrance. A chorus of male voices was answered by a woman, whose speech was decided and firm.

"I thank you for your escort," she said. "You must permit me to address the Black Khan."

Rukh's eyes met the intruder's across the assembly of courtiers. She was flanked by a dark-skinned woman and a man with glowing silver eyes, all three accompanied by Arsalan.

He thought he'd seen the last of the First Oralist.

She'd proven him wrong again.

42

Wafa broke free of Darya's embrace. He darted across the hall, stumbling in his haste. He flung himself at Arian's neck, sobbing with outright joy. She held him fast in her arms, favoring one wrist. She pressed her forehead to his before the court's astonished witness.

"Wafa," she said, a smile in her voice. "My brave and loyal friend. I hope the Prince of Khorasan has treated you with care."

He shook his head, trembling in her arms. Then he saw Sinnia, and his own smile grew wider. He grabbed her at the waist, nudging his head against her collarbone.

"Still alive, you little ruffian?" She hugged him tightly in return, turning him to Daniyar.

Wafa hesitated only an instant. Instead of embracing the Silver Mage, he tried to remember what Sinnia had taught him.

"My lord." He made an awkward bow; then his wide, delighted smile broke out once again. "My lord, the Silver Mage." He pronounced the words with care. Daniyar ruffled his hair.

Daniyar bent to his ear and whispered, "Who at the court can we trust, Wafa?"

Wafa shook his head and whispered back, "No one, my lord. No one except—" His voice trailed off. He pointed shyly at the Princess.

Arsalan moved past them, ignoring Darya and the Nizam. He found Rukh and communicated something to him in a rapid and urgent undertone, his breath stirring the Prince's hair. Rukh's reaction was a slight widening of his eyes. His jaw tightened. He ascended to the throne again and laid the imperial scepter across its arms.

He clapped his hands twice, calling for the court's attention.

"The outer ramparts have fallen to our enemies. The Talisman approach the inner walls. Dress for battle and arm yourselves. Men to the walls, women to the Al Qasr. Arsalan, the city walls are yours." He swept a hand at his personal guards. "The Khorasan Guard must defend the scriptorium at all costs. Khashayar, I charge you with protection of the Warraqeen."

"My lord," Khashayar protested at once. "The Khorasan Guard does not leave your side."

The Black Khan smiled at Arian across the room, his face full of a hard, mocking charm. "You need not worry," he said. "I have all the protection I need."

The court was seized by panic and confusion, heedless of the Black Khan's orders. Courtiers pressed into the Divan-e Shah, seeking reassurance and safety. The vast hall was filled to capacity, nobles jostling one another to reach the Peacock Throne and the ear of the Khan. Neither Arsalan nor the Nizam could bring them under control. The Khan raised his scepter and brought it down hard. Even this had no effect.

Arian detached Wafa's arms from her neck. She nodded at her companions to let her proceed alone. Covered in the sweat of her hard ride across the plains, her armor battered, her hair and face disheveled, she cut a path through the press of courtiers. As her cloak fell away from her arms, her circlets shone in the glow of hundreds of tapered candles.

The courtiers moved to either side of her, falling silent as she passed. The women of the Khan's family surged forward for a better look. Arian crossed the length of the Divan-e Shah to the pedestal that held the Bloodprint. She washed her hands in the basin positioned beside it. To a concerted gasp, she murmured an incantation and leafed through the pages of the manuscript. A look of peace in her eyes, she turned to face the assembly.

"*In the name of the One,*" she said. "*The Beneficent, the Merciful.* Heed this message to your city."

She pressed her hands to her tahweez, taking their light into herself.

"*In the change of the winds, and the clouds that run their appointed courses between the sky and the earth: in all this, there are signs for people who reflect.*"

The Divan-e Shah was stricken into silence.

"*True piety does not consist of your turning your face to the east or the west, but in those who believe in the One, in the Last Day, in the angels of the realm, in Revelation, and in the messengers.*"

"And in you?" the Nizam sneered, unperturbed by her recitation. He wouldn't be. He had secrets and gifts of his own.

"Nizam al-Mulk," she said with great courtesy, "I bring you greetings from Hira."

She raised her chin, her gaze finding the Black Khan. The chance had come at last to repay him for what his treachery had cost her, and yet she could not act as he would have done in her place. There was too much at stake. What she *could* have was this single moment, so she chose a verse of the Claim that would call him to account . . . warning him of the power she could wield against him on a whim.

"The Reckoning that you are promised is bound to come; there is nothing you can do to elude it."

His composure ebbed; when he spoke, his voice was hoarse. "Do you threaten me, First Oralist?"

Was he so arrogant that he thought it impossible she would? "It was *you* who threatened me. I come to treat with you, to ask you to honor the bargain you made at the Council of Hira." Her eyes measured the breadth of his shoulders, covered by the Sacred Cloak. Something else he had stolen from Hira that he had no right to possess.

"Excellency," the Nizam interrupted, the warning plain in his voice. "There are enemies on all fronts. We must respond at once."

The Black Khan's gaze weighed Arian, and some calculation in her face must have given him heart. "I have dealt with my enemies," he said. "Now I would hear my friends."

It was the only apology the Black Khan would make, swift to turn her arrival to his advantage. She told herself to remember that and to deal with him when she could.

She switched her attention to the Nizam, whose expression was wary. She was reminded in that moment of Lania—and of all those who sought to exert power behind the throne, jealously guarding their influence.

Addressing the Nizam directly, she said, "I have never been an enemy of the people of Ashfall. Nor of the members of this court."

Now she took notice of the Begum of the court, the would-be empress, and the members of the Black Khan's family. Last, her gaze dwelt on Darya, a young woman she did not know.

The girl's breath was suspended in her chest as she stared wide-eyed at the circlets on Arian's arms. Her hand moved to touch one of the tahweez before she snatched it back, the pearl on her forehead dancing as she bent her head.

She'd felt the power of the Bloodprint, Arian realized. Her recitation had reached this girl in a manner unlike any of the other courtiers.

A sense of premonition sent a shiver down her spine. She had a sudden image of this girl dressed in white silk, crossing the waters of the All Ways, to swear her oath at Hira.

The girl raised her head, her eyes wide and dark, as if she'd witnessed it too. She knelt at Arian's feet. When she spoke, her voice was low and sweet. "First Oralist, you honor us. Ask and I will serve you."

Arian urged Darya to her feet with a gentle pressure on her arm. She raised her right index finger to the sky, knowing the court of Khorasan would recognize the gesture. The courtiers mimicked her at once. "Kneel only before the One, as I do."

She studied the golden cuffs on Darya's arms. "You are royal," she said. "Yet I do not know you."

"My name is Darya, First Oralist."

"Darya, Princess of Ashfall," Rukh inserted dryly. "Sister to the Khan of Khorasan."

Arian interrogated him with a lift of her brow. She lowered her voice to address him. "Why do you encumber your sister in this manner?"

Darya's headdress was askew, an onerous weight upon her slender neck. She looked like a little girl dressed in an older woman's clothing.

Rukh's eyes grew cold. "Do the customs of Ashfall displease

you? A pity you found it necessary to find your way here from Black Aura."

"We will speak of your sister later. You know why I've come, Excellency. Just as you know why you need me."

She sang out verses of the Claim. And promised the deliverance of Ashfall.

THEY WERE TAKEN TO THE BLACK KHAN'S WAR ROOM. A MAP OF THE empire was spread over a table carved of black lacquer inlaid with mother-of-pearl and highly figured panels of abalone. Globes and armillary spheres were positioned around the room, along with a series of starscopes. Aloft before a pair of windows, giant minzars swept the walls and gardens. One was angled to face the Maiden Tower; the other its opposite, the Tower of the Mirage. Most notable in the chamber was the silver armillary sphere stationed across from the Black Throne, its brass rings charting the ascension of the sun against the gradations of its meridian.

The Black Throne was at the head of the table, and here the Black Khan gave commands to members of the Zhayedan and to the Khorasan Guard. Behind each captain's chair smaller stools were placed for the scribes of the council, none of whom were present.

In fact, no one took a chair around the table. Rukh waited for Arian to speak, his thoughts racing, his calculations half-formed.

"You know why I've come," she said. Her voice sounded

different—lower, richer, hoarser in some way. "We need to discuss the Bloodprint and the Cloak."

"Neither of which I will yield."

"Both of which you must."

The First Oralist's tone was implacable, and here before his Nizam and the commanders of his army, the Black Khan took it as an affront. To be challenged by a woman in front of his men—he was not so lenient as that.

"Have a care, First Oralist."

He felt the flick of silver eyes like a lash against his face. There was no mistaking the other man's anger. The Silver Mage was his enemy.

"If I did not care, I would not have come. Now I ask what possible use the Bloodprint could be to you? It should be at the Citadel of Hira in the hands of those who can read it."

Rukh moved behind the Black Throne, placing his hands on its headrest. "My Zareen-Qalam has trained a generation of students to read."

The Zareen-Qalam was the keeper of his scriptorium, his head calligrapher, a man whose learning was unparalleled in Ashfall. He would be the first target of the Talisman assault.

Yet neither he nor his students were able to use the Bloodprint in a manner that would aid them in time.

"They are novices. With all due respect to the Zareen-Qalam, to read without context is profitless. The text can be shaped into anything. It can be of service to Khorasan only if it is read by scholars of the Claim."

"You refer to the Companions of Hira."

"Yes! We are trained to this purpose—it is all that we know."

He considered the First Oralist's impassioned response. She was breathtaking in her defiance, her beauty heightened by her suffering at the Ark. He could see that she was damaged: her wrist was bandaged, her throat bruised. She held herself with an unaccustomed stiffness . . . yet she still outshone every woman at his court. It wasn't the arrangement of her bones; it was something magnetic in her presence, in her powerful command of magic. Against Ilea's glacial attraction, the First Oralist burned like a flame. He wanted to be consumed by it, inflamed by secret desires. His black gaze fell to her mouth.

The Silver Mage drew his sword. At his action, Arsalan did likewise, shifting closer to his Khan.

Arian glanced at Daniyar. A slight gesture of her hand held him in place, a momentary respite gained. Though Rukh did not fear the Silver Mage, he wondered at his place at Arian's side. They were linked by an emotion that was palpable and fierce. And some of it spilled over. The Silver Mage's antagonism awakened some instinct of Rukh's. Something primitive curled along his senses, hastening his blood. It gave him a curious strength.

"Not all, I think, First Oralist. Hira pursues its own schemes. You are not the first Companion to try to part me from Ashfall's inheritance."

"*Ashfall's* inheritance?"

The Silver Mage cut in. "The Golden Mage was here?"

His question drew the Nizam's attention. He watched the Silver Mage with sharpened interest.

"A few days, hence." Rukh was not oblivious to the Companions' distress at this news. Of course, they would think their Citadel abandoned, as it had been for a time. "She is gone now. Consider this, Arian. If I didn't yield the Bloodprint to Ilea, your entreaty is less likely to succeed." He hinted at the intimacy he'd shared with Ilea, watching the Silver Mage's eyes flare. "But I am not entirely without sympathy for your cause. Stay and teach my

Warraqeen the subtle arts of Hira. When we have routed our enemies, I will give you the Bloodprint as a gift."

But his answer failed to please the First Oralist, who let her temper reign. "How is it no man understands this? The Bloodprint belongs neither to you nor to me, nor to the tyrants of Khorasan. It is not something to be *gifted* from one ruler to another. It is the inheritance of a people—of *all* people. It belongs to each one of us—to every last child." Arian's gaze fell on Wafa. "Like the Cloak you wear, Prince of Khorasan."

Rukh stiffened. He respected Arian's gifts, but even if some part of him wanted to claim her for his own, he would not countenance her censure.

"I wear the Cloak because *I* am Commander of the Faithful. Does any man here doubt my claim?"

The Nizam bowed before the Khan, as did the commanders of the Zhayedan. Arsalan raised a skeptical eyebrow. There was a hint of mockery in his eyes, a touch of indulgence in the quirk of his lips, though neither was a sign of disrespect.

"I wore the Cloak also," Arian reminded Rukh. "I placed it on this boy's shoulders." She spared a smile for Wafa. "Had he not feared its power, he might be wearing it still."

The Black Khan studied Wafa's trembling form. "Women," he said with contempt. "No wonder Hira has never ruled an empire."

Arian swallowed the impulse to show him the use she could make of the Claim. Instead she said, "Be grateful that is not what we seek. I will train your Warraqeen; indeed we will send Oralists from Hira, women skilled in the nuances of the Claim. But now when the need is dire, you must trust me with the Bloodprint."

The Black Khan laughed. "Why would I trust you, First Oralist? Where does your true allegiance lie? Not with the High

Companion—I know what you think of her." His gaze traveled the circuit of the chamber. "With the Silver Mage, perhaps?" The cold fury in the Silver Mage's eyes promised the Black Khan a reckoning. He shrugged it off. "With this mongrel child whom you defend as if he were a son of the Esayin, instead of what he is—a contemptible scion of slavery. If you would have the Bloodprint, swear your allegiance to *me*."

"You expect me to swear my allegiance to the man who delivered me to the Ark? And left me in the Authoritan's care? What have you done to earn my trust besides take up the mantle of the Cloak?" Now Arian did use the Claim to emphasize her rebuke. "Do you imagine that *wearing* the Sacred Cloak renders you Commander of the Faithful? How could that be possible for a man who possesses no faith?"

The Black Khan flung the Claim back at her, a verse he had snatched from the Bloodprint. But he could not use against her what had belonged to her from her first reckoning of the Claim. He could not cause her injury when he held no faith in the words.

Or perhaps it was because he did not *wish* to cause her harm.

She met his words with an inner strength, retrieving their power for herself. "You demand loyalty from me. But who among your retainers has long since left your side? Why were your outer defenses yielded before the war?"

The Nizam struck his hands together, startling the others. "Excellency, send her to Qaysarieh collared. Do not let her speak another word. She poisons your faith in your men."

Arian turned on him, angry at this denunciation of her history of service. "Yes, I know of your fondness for Qaysarieh. You've sent far too many men to die there. But why would the Nizam of the Khorasan Empire detain the First Oralist of Hira? As the

Khan's regent, it is no one's trust more than yours to receive me as Ashfall's ally. Have you forgotten what is due your Khan? Have you forgotten *yourself*?"

The Nizam moved to confront her, but Arian stayed him with a sharp intonation of her voice. Her gaze was implacable and cold, a ruthlessness stirring within. She welcomed it. It was necessary in this room.

"The next man who tries to collar me will find himself dead at my feet. Is that what you wish, Excellency? Is that what *you* wish, Nizam al-Mulk?" She looked beyond them to the Talisman fires. "Should we be fighting amongst ourselves when your empire is at risk?"

His answer was to bark an order to the commander of the Zhayedan. "Arsalan. You heard the First Oralist threaten me. Take her to Qaysarieh at once."

The Silver Mage stepped between Arian and the Nizam, his sword poised in his hand. Arsalan shouldered the Silver Mage aside, sheathing his own sword and holding up his hand.

"You wished for wisdom at your council," he said to Rukh. "Now you have it. I urge you to hear the First Oralist." His eyes expressed his desire to be heeded over the Nizam, just this once.

But the Nizam intervened again. "You fell under Hira's spell because of your witch of a mother. But this empire is not under the sway of a heretical coven."

The insult to Hira—and to Arsalan himself—was surely grievous. But Arsalan wasn't a man to be baited at the spur of his temper. He would deal with the Nizam when he thought the moment was right.

"Yield the Bloodprint to the First Oralist," he urged Rukh. "Who else within these walls has her fluency?"

"The Warraqeen—" the Nizam began.

"The Warraqeen are novices. You know it as well as I do. We must trust the First Oralist now."

Talisman horns broke across their council, echoing Arsalan's words. "The First Oralist could compel you," he added. "But she doesn't. Think on that."

"No," the Nizam snapped. "She will take the Bloodprint to Hira, abandoning this city to ruin."

Arsalan swept his arm across the expanse of the windows. "How do you imagine the First Oralist could break the siege? What route do you know that would see her past Talisman lines?" Impatient now at this long delay when he should have been at the walls, Arsalan nodded at Rukh. "Whatever you decide, Excellency, I will see it done."

The Black Khan took his time to decide, his hawk-eyed gaze moving from face to face until it came to rest upon Arian. "What *can* you do?" he asked her.

Her eyes shone with a crystal-like clarity that made him want to offer her his throne. He followed the graceful sweep of her hand to the silent pages of the manuscript. "I can unlock its magic to bring the Talisman down."

Her shining, seductive use of the Claim wove a spell around the chamber, inspiriting the Zhayedan and infusing Rukh with new purpose. Arsalan listened to her voice with the glitter of tears in his eyes. Then he turned away from the Nizam's perception of his weakness. "*Rukh.*" He urged his prince again, an indefinable note in his voice.

Rukh came to a decision. "I will send the Bloodprint to the scriptorium, where you may study it at will. You will have time for reflection. No one will disturb you there."

The beauty of Arian's smile made a mockery of his objections. He found he could not refuse her. Sensing this, the Silver Mage took her hand, as if he had the *right* to take it in his own, and Rukh felt an internal wretchedness take hold.

"You honor me with your trust, my lord."

Her words urged the sorrow from his thoughts. He felt . . . conscious . . . of his own abilities and of his gift to rule. He drew a sharp breath, meeting the speculation in the eyes of his Nizam. Swiftly, he veiled his gaze.

"Excellency, if I might."

Rukh nodded, still feeling the impact of Arian's voice. He owed his Nizam every courtesy for the wisdom of his counsel. And that included privacy. He arranged for two of his guards to escort his unexpected guests to private chambers to rest. It struck at something in him to witness their close companionship—the unspoken affinity with which they reached for and held each other's hands.

"We will speak again," he assured them. When they'd left, he addressed his Nizam. "When do you anticipate the Talisman assault?"

Arsalan answered for the Nizam. "As early as the next dawn. Certainly no later than tomorrow night."

"Then we still have time for the banquet." Though the Nizam spoke the words quietly, they were as inexorable as a command.

"Have you taken leave of your senses?" Arsalan could not prevent his outrage from escaping his lips.

"Our traditions must not be forfeit." A cruel smile edged the Nizam's lips. "Your mother insisted on them, if you recall."

Arsalan spoke through his teeth. "The city is at war, Nizam. Rukh—*tell* him."

"The *empire* is at war. But not this night, Commander, according to your own advice. We *must* observe the Banquet of the Victorious. You would not wish the Prince to be the first to break with tradition."

"Rukh—" Arsalan's voice was despairing. It was a flagrant

abuse of power to take the time for decadence when the enemy was at their gates—the city would fall. The Khan would be captured and executed. He would do everything he could to prevent it. He would do anything he could—including take on the Nizam.

"Never in the history of Ashfall has a Khan of Khorasan failed to conduct a Banquet of the Victorious. It gives confidence to the people of the city."

Arsalan pressed his fists against his temples. "This is *madness*, Rukh. We should hold the banquet *after* the battle is won."

The Black Khan assumed an expression of hauteur. The Nizam's appeal to his vanity had made its ill-favored mark.

"The banquet commemorates the valor of the Zhayedan. It is given as a leave-taking."

"I will not attend it," Arsalan insisted. "Neither will my commanders. We must be at the walls."

"Make your preparations," Rukh said. "The walls can spare you for an hour—the banquet will be brief."

"Rukh—"

"Arsalan. Do you command, or do I?"

"I would never guide you astray." His burning eyes were fixed on Rukh's face, urging him to belief. Something elusive flickered in Rukh's eyes—something unconnected to his words. Arsalan's heart thundered in response.

"Do you imagine my Nizam would? The Banquet of the Victorious will hold the city together. It will give the Zhayedan a deeper reason to fight."

"My prince, they are ready *now*."

"They abandoned the outer walls."

"At the *Nizam's* command."

"If they are swayed by his wisdom, all the more reason that we *should* observe the banquet."

"You defeat me," Arsalan said, appalled. What more could he say? What more could he *do*?

"I trust you with more power than any commander in the Zhayedan's history. Is that not enough for you, Arsalan?"

It wasn't. It would never be enough. Yet how could he admit this when the things he did want could never be shared with his prince? As Rukh had taught him already. He drew up sharply, conscious of the Nizam closely observing his response. Banking his despair, he renewed his pledge in neutral accents, concealing his state of mind. It was his duty to bolster the others, to give confidence to his Khan.

"Whatever you decide, Excellency, I will see it done."

44

MODELED ON THE ROSE HOUSE AT TIRAZIS, ASHFALL'S SCRIPTORIUM
was the wonder of its age; its design married light and glass to
a symphony of stone. The scriptorium was separated into two
large prayer halls, east and west presided over by massive concave
arches, their colors and patterns orchestrated by the divine. The
plainest arrangement of blue-gold geometry was balanced by diz-
zying motifs: rose-pink sunbursts on lapis lazuli blue, an outer
fretwork of triangles and diamonds spinning through the scriptorium like a hall of endless mirrors. Slender columns supported
beautiful concave arches over a luminous glass floor: when dawn
entered the scriptorium, patterns of stained glass broke upon a
turquoise sea.

A boulevard carpeted in rose-pink silk divided the space between the prayer halls. Here young men clustered at waist-high
tables, dressed in the robes of scholars: each attired in a long black
gown belted with a sash. The sashes were looped with the rings of
wooden spindles; these were kamish pens cut from reeds yet to be
darkened by ink.

On either side of the boulevard, arches ran in rows along the vaulted walls. The arches were lined with shelves where the treasures of the scriptorium were stored. On the east side were those treatises of law, mathematics, and medicine that were the inheritance of Ashfall. To the west, the work of miniaturists, cartographers, poets, and storytellers. Above these both, a row of smaller arches paralleled the rows below. These were the great works of philosophers, accessible to the most learned of the Warraqeen.

The scriptorium's shelves were labeled in a graceful script that read from right to left, each a description of the manuscripts within. In smaller vertical nooks between the shelves, cobalt-blue bottles glowed in the reflected light of lanterns balanced on steel pillars. Candles were forbidden inside the scriptorium. Any of the Warraqeen found using one would be banished from the chamber for life.

A bound manuscript thousands of pages long was spread upon a pedestal carved from the trunk of an ash tree. This was the scriptorium's catalogue. On the far side of the scriptorium, a marble pedestal similar to the one Arian had found at the top of the Clay Minar was reserved for the Bloodprint and sheltered from the light. It was a majestic, awe-inspiring space dedicated to the written word, as hushed as a house of worship. Its heavy outer doors were patrolled. Admittance to the scriptorium was granted by Khashayar, captain of the Khorasan Guard.

Once one was permitted within, the halls were cool and free of dust. Each of the vaulted nooks was sealed to aid in the preservation of the manuscripts. The tables and pedestals were positioned out of the reach of natural light, illumined instead by lanterns resting upon copper stands. Stacked next to the pillars of the stands were numerous parchment scrolls. These were used by novice Warraqeen to practice their skills as calligraphers.

The head calligrapher strolled along the rows of desks praising or correcting his pupils. He paused as the door to the upper gallery opened, tilting up his head that so his gray silk turban nearly slipped from his head. Arian raised her hand in the traditional greeting of the Companions. Accompanied by Khashayar, Darya led her down a spiral staircase to greet the Zareen-Qalam. There was an undertone of urgency to the courtesies they exchanged.

Arian was now attired as Darya had expected to see a Companion of Hira, her clothing and jewelry gifts from the Black Khan. She wore a dress the color of rose dust, and gemstones were strung through the dark waves of her hair. A gold and pearl tiara rested on the crown of her head, and brought out the shimmer of her eyes.

Though her dress was modest and bared only her arms, her beauty shone through it for the scribes of Ashfall to behold. There was a clumsy scraping back of stools from the Warraqeen's desks as the young calligraphers gathered around their master.

Darya stood beside Arian, proud to be the one to introduce her, though she knew well enough that the Zareen-Qalam needed no introduction from her. Still, he made her welcome, and given her recent humiliation at court, she was grateful for his notice.

"First Oralist, you return under this new administration."

When the First Oralist smiled at him, several of the Warraqeen flushed red. "I am honored you recall my first visit, Zareen-Qalam. The scriptorium is lovelier than anything I've seen—even the scriptorium at Hira. Your work here is to be reverenced."

His dark eyes warmed with pleasure. His hand strayed to his pointed beard. "You remember when you first came—how difficult it was to persuade the Khan of the necessity of this effort. Our history would have been lost otherwise. Even at this moment things are changing. Each of the Warraqeen were selected by me, their backgrounds . . . considered . . . for outside influence."

They shared the glance of two who spoke each other's language. A single Warraq with Talisman sympathies could burn the scriptorium down, inflicting ruin without raising a hand to arms.

"You have a new Khan now," Arian said. "And he endorses your efforts. Except that he does not allow women to be instructed in this effort." She motioned to Darya. "I understand the Princess wishes to train as a linguist."

The Zareen-Qalam led the two women across the scriptorium to the pedestal where the Bloodprint was held. Two members of the Guard stood to either side of it, swords drawn, black eyes sharp and suspicious. The Zareen-Qalam bestowed a gentle smile upon them, urging Arian forward. To Darya's astonishment, the weathered faces of the soldiers of the Khorasan Guard softened into warmth.

"Sahabiya," both murmured. "You honor us with your return."

"Peace be with you," she said. "And with the people of Ashfall."

"You are most welcome here," one of the guards said. "The city needs your benediction." They drew away to allow her privacy with the Bloodprint.

"What do you think of it?" she asked the Zareen-Qalam, her own sense of wonder scarcely dimmed. How insignificant the trials of her journey seemed compared to the manuscript itself. Then she remembered Turan, whose sacrifice had enabled her to reach this moment, endowed with the power of the Claim.

"I wept," the calligrapher said simply. "I could not believe it was real. But when I read it—" His voice became a whisper. "Sahabiya, only you could have given us this miracle—you and no other, not even the High Companion." His tremulous hand hovered above the fine vellum of the manuscript. "I confess I cannot read as fluently as I would wish. We have had no means of studying its language."

Arian nodded. She beckoned a diffident Darya forward. The Princess had been waiting to one side, her dark eyes wide, her mouth slightly agape, stunned into silence by the presence of the holy text. Tears trembled at the edges of her lashes, threatening to the fall to the page. She brushed them aside with her hand, staining the blue sleeve of her robe.

"Can this truly be the Bloodprint?" She stared wonderingly at Arian. "Can it be possibly be *real*?"

"Come closer," Arian pressed her. "Decide the truth for yourself."

Darya blinked, bewildered by the suggestion that she could be worthy. Or that the First Oralist might deem her so. Trembling from head to toe, she bent her head to view the strong square script under the mark of blood. As she drew close enough to touch it, a bolt of fire singed her veins. She felt as though she were falling . . . and that she continued to fall, through time and darkness and distance, with nothing to anchor her in place. She heard a welcoming sound—the soft cascade of water rising through rooms of stone—and she saw the image of a woman against the backs of her eyelids—a woman old enough to be her mother, dressed in a long silk dress—looking back at Darya and whispering a single word . . .

Read.

But Darya heard the rest in her mind.

Read in the name of the One, the One who created all there is in existence . . .

She bent to the manuscript to obey. The script danced before her eyes. But the bloodmark on the page began to take the shape of history spiraling out its golden forms—*ah, in the name of the Citadel of Hira—in the name of the glories of the One—the blood of a man spilled at prayer—she shaped the pattern of it in her mind, felt the grief strike clean to her heart—the centuries of loss—one man in a moment on his own—a consecrated script alive with hope on the page . . . it was speaking to her and it was saying, Come to me, come to Me, child . . .*

Darya staggered to her knees at the force of the summons in her mind. It was a long while before she came to herself again, to find she was sobbing like a child, held in the First Oralist's arms, her throat raw with a sorrow she wasn't strong enough to bear.

She was *mourning*. Mourning as if the blood on the page had just been spilled before her eyes. The woman in the white silk dress raised a finger to her lips and turned away.

"Who—" Darya choked out the word. "Who *was* that? What did she want from me?"

The First Oralist didn't answer, her brow marked by surprise, her eyes glimmering like two mirrors reflecting a coruscating light. And Darya recognized the light. She felt it in the leap of her blood—*heard* it in the pulsing of her veins.

The First Oralist hadn't spoken . . . she was radiant with the Claim.

Without answering Darya's question, she murmured softly to herself, "You are a child of Hira. You *belong* to us."

Darya bit back a sob. It was everything she had yearned for—to be wanted, to be taught, to do something of value with her life—and here the First Oralist offered it as if it had never been in doubt. As if Darya mattered to someone, after all this time.

Her voice thick with tears, she said, "I cannot read the manuscript. I dare not even try." She waited for Arian's censure, for the displeasure that would surely result.

Instead, the First Oralist held her close and drew Darya to her feet. Tenderly she said, "I will recite it for you, Darya, until you can read it for yourself."

She separated the pages of the manuscript, covering the blood-stains with a prayer. She found what she sought several pages back, reading the verse to herself.

Her recitation was clear as a bell.

"This is the Book about which there is no doubt, a guidance for those conscious of the One."

An astonished whispering met the words. The Warraqeen inched closer to the pedestal.

"A guidance for those who believe in the unseen, who establish prayer, and who spend out of what the One has provided for them."

She read ahead to herself, experiencing both the comfort and the threat of the succeeding verses. She hadn't been taught to view the Claim solely as a blessing: she had learned to respect its admonition.

"Do not doubt it, scholars of the Warraqeen. This *is* indeed the Bloodprint."

The young men pushed closer, each straining for a glimpse of the manuscript. Without conscious thought, Arian raised the index finger of her right hand to the sky. Each man in the scriptorium did the same.

Darya tentatively raised her hand. "What does your gesture mean?" she asked Arian.

Arian felt a swift stab of anger at Rukh. She stepped away from the manuscript, not wishing to profane it.

She'd witnessed Darya's trance, and she knew, as Rukh *must* have known, that his sister was connected to the Claim—a child of Hira, waiting to be transformed. How could a man in his position have prevented his sister from taking up her calling at Hira? Had Arian not been fighting a war, she would have trained Darya herself.

"It's called the shahadah, Darya. I bear witness there is no one but the One. *There is no one but the One, and so the One commands.*"

The Warraqeen echoed the words in a chant, their voices resonant with the nuances of their training.

"There is no one but the One, and so the One commands."

The sonorous recitation eased the feeling of oppression that had weighed Arian down since her use of the Claim at the Clay Minar. The Warraqeen's was a spiritual recitation opposed to the blasphemy of the Ahdath or the proclamation of the Talisman's tyranny.

"It will not take you long to learn," she said to Darya, keeping her voice even.

"The women of my family are not trained in the legends of the Claim. My brother forbids it." Darya's voice was as wistful as a child's—she had recovered herself. "There is something uneasy in his relationship with Hira." But as her words sounded in the scriptorium, she hurried to correct them. "It is not for me to speak of my brother's concerns. He does what is best for Ashfall under the strain of these times."

Arian couldn't help herself. Whatever the strict rules of etiquette at the Black Khan's court, she knew Darya needed comfort. She needed the grace of self-belief. She hugged the Princess close, speaking so the others could hear.

"You are most dutiful, Darya. You are an honorable reflection of your brother."

"I have always thought so," a masculine voice drawled.

The soldiers of the Khorasan Guard hurried to their stations, offering a ceremonial salute. The Zareen-Qalam moved to disperse his Warraqeen, bowing so low before the Khan that his turban trembled on his head.

"Excellency. Your presence honors the scriptorium."

The Black Khan waved away the courtesy, his black gaze intent on Arian, beautifully dressed and adorned. "You wear my gifts," he said, his dark eyes searching her face.

"Your Excellency was most kind."

"Rukh," he said, reminding her of his name. "Just as I will call you Arian."

It was an echo of their first encounter before the waters of the All Ways. He had held her in his arms at Hira, wooing her with the gift of a manuscript sent from his own scriptorium.

Darya's eyes widened watching the interplay between her brother and the First Oralist. Surely no one spoke to the First Oralist in this manner? And what of the Silver Mage? Was he not the First Oralist's consort? His every glance declared it. Though the women of the court were stunningly lovely, ornamented, perfumed, and jeweled, his silver eyes had never strayed from the First Oralist, covered in the grime of her journey. Darya was even more astonished by the First Oralist's reply.

"Rukh, then," she answered with a trace of humor. "I wish you would adorn Darya as lightly."

Darya had never seen such a smile on her brother's face before. He was roguishly amused, yet there was a tenderness to his expression as well. "Stay in Ashfall," he murmured. "I will carry out your every command."

Darya stumbled over the hem of her robe in surprise, the chimes at her ankles disrupting the silent spell woven between the First Oralist and her brother.

Arian's reply was formal. "We are *all* with you until this battle is over: the Companions of Hira *and* the Silver Mage."

"I don't think the Silver Mage cares to see himself as a champion of Ashfall. Not after what transpired at Black Aura."

"That is your own doing. You provoke him without cause;

you've no idea what he suffered at the Ark." The light in her eyes dimmed at the memory.

"If it pained you, I am sorry for it," Rukh said. "But I did not know you were bound to him. I thought as a Companion of Hira . . ." His voice trailed off, too gallant to make reference to Arian's vow of chastity.

He moved closer without touching her, though Darya could sense her brother wanted to take the First Oralist in his arms. Rukh made no secret of his paramours, but she'd known he would need an heir to secure the future of Ashfall. The eldest daughter of the Begum had relentlessly chased that distinction.

Now to realize that Rukh might be thinking of the First Oralist in this light was a source of delight to Darya. She could imagine her brother softening, relaxing his restrictions on her freedom. She could see him at his ease for the first time on the Peacock Throne. She could imagine beautiful black-haired children climbing on his shoulders and wrestling with Arsalan for the amusement of the court. She could hear her brother's laughter. She could envision the First Oralist at her side in the scriptorium. She would learn to read, she would learn to recite—*she might even be sent to Hira*. She couldn't hide her elation, her hopes shining brightly from her eyes. Her mind crowded with questions, she opened her mouth to speak. Rukh shook his head at her as a warning.

Darya melted away, drawing the Zareen-Qalam with her. The Khorasan Guard remained in place, their swords ready in their hands.

"Arian," Rukh said, "tell me what you need."

It would have been easy enough to tell him *he* was what she needed, to swear herself to him and acknowledge the pull between them. The light from the room's lanterns glossed over the concave lines of his cheekbones, giving him an aura of mystery and an air of bewitching enchantment. She was flooded by a sense of weakness, her gaze drifting down to his lips, remembering now how her sister had tried to seduce Daniyar. Their kiss was seared in her memory—replayed in her mind during her lowest moments; she knew she could never cause Daniyar an instant of such anguish in return. Nor would she seduce the Black Khan to gain an advantage for Hira. No matter the spell he sought to weave, she couldn't forget what his betrayal had cost her at the Ark. Though he dismissed his actions as lightly as if he imagined her impervious to pain. How capricious and remorseless he was.

"Do not say it," he said with regret when her silence had gone on too long. "I would have preferred the charade." He gazed down at the Bloodprint. "But you wouldn't pretend, would you, Arian? Even if I showed you I welcomed it . . . that I *craved* it."

"I would not deceive you, lord."

"Rukh," he said again, his face closed and remote. "At least give me that much, Arian."

"Rukh," she relented, watching his lashes sweep down to rest upon his cheeks.

He touched her shoulder and stepped away with a lithe, coordinated movement, facing her across the pedestal.

"With what I learned firsthand of Ilea, I didn't expect such reticence from you. I should have listened to you at Hira." He studied her bare hands. She wore the jewels he had given her; the pearl tiara, the strings of gems wound in her dark hair. Pursuing the subject further, he asked, "If you are promised to the Silver Mage, why do you wear none of his tokens?"

Arian ducked her head. "It is a private matter between us."

Rukh's glowing eyes slid to hers. "If you were mine, this ring would be on your hand." The silver of his signet ring flashed in the lantern's light.

Arian swallowed. She couldn't help herself. It wasn't just what Rukh offered her—it was the magnetism with which he offered it, the richly alluring certainty of his desire. His eyes burned in his dark, arresting face. There was some element in him that called to her, raising a restless excitement that pierced her like diamond-sharp blades. But to offer her the symbol of his line, the symbol of his own integrity—what had she done to merit it? She offered him the same resistance she'd once shown to Daniyar.

Into her mind flashed another memory: the Silver Mage in the valley of the Ice Kill, offering the Candour to the Lord of the Wandering Cloud Door, giving away the heart of himself in order to serve her cause. Because of her, the Candour had been destroyed. What harm would befall the Black Khan, who claimed to be under her spell?

"Rukh," she said at last, wishing she had the right to speak to him as he deserved or the courage to deny him outright. She was torn in a way she couldn't explain. What value was she to anyone when her life and gifts were bound elsewhere, her deepest allegiance to Hira? She touched the pages of the manuscript, seeking to draw its power into herself, to illuminate her doubts and set them aside for good. His hand shot out to cover hers, letting her feel the vitality that pulsed beneath his skin.

"You need not fear for Hira. The High Companion was here. The Zareen-Qalam transcribed the verses she asked for. She has taken them to the Citadel. Did she send you no message that your Audacy is complete?"

Arian studied the Bloodprint sadly. Had the Talisman not risen, the discovery of the Bloodprint would have heartened all of Khorasan. Instead, each person most concerned with Khorasan's fate conceived of the Bloodprint as a weapon. And never as a consummate gift.

"You were there when I took the shahadah. You know my Audacy will rule me until I am offered release. I've had no word from Ilea. But this isn't what we need to discuss."

"No?" he asked. "It seems to me your first thought is for the Bloodprint. And when it isn't, it is of the Silver Mage. You are dutybound, *consort*-bound. I've come to accept this truth." He faced her with the reckless arrogance she'd come to expect from him.

She flashed him a glance full of urgency, her delicate features beseeching him.

"Such a queen at my court," he mused. "What I would grant you, you can't imagine."

"*You* imagine my choices are painless. Or that I refuse you lightly." She freed her hand from his, sketching an arc that mapped the breadth of the scriptorium. "You gave me a *manuscript* as a gift, a history of my own family." Her breath was coming faster now. "Can you truly believe I am not conscious of what you offer?" She dropped her voice, aware of the Khorasan Guard. "Or that I am not . . . affected . . . by your allure? If so, you mistake yourself, and you mistake me."

Stunned by her admission, it took him a moment to answer. His hooded gaze dropped to her deeply molded mouth, a dangerous deliberation in his face. "I am not the Silver Mage."

"No," she said, standing her ground. "You are not." No man could be what Daniyar was to her—and there was only one man she loved.

"Then why tempt me to forget myself, Arian?" He said it blankly, expecting a rebuke.

Arian made a futile gesture with her hand. "I am asking you to consider that I may have been tempted as well."

He raised his head, his face full of a glittering intensity. "You forget. I've seen you with the Silver Mage. I have no wish for crumbs."

They were at an impasse. He thought of her as an antagonist he could seduce to his side. She had hoped to make him see her as an ally—possibly as a friend—one who could be as loyal to him as his commander of the Zhayedan, as long as they sought the same end: the renewal of the written word.

She'd thought that if she made herself vulnerable to him, he might respond in kind—seeing what she hoped to achieve and deciding it would serve them both. But she would always be the First Oralist to him . . . a tool he hoped to exploit. It was only Daniyar who was able to see the woman behind the myth.

As Rukh's eyes pierced hers, she could sense the distance between them, a distance that increased with his refusal to understand.

"I wasn't suggesting I needed a lover. I hoped you would see me as a friend."

The jet-black eyes flashed at her. "Impossible. When you are a creature of Hira."

Arian set the insult aside. "You refuse to accept that I hold convictions of my own. Don't you see what it is that I serve?"

He gripped her arm with deceptive strength, drawing her close to the hard warmth of his chest. A current of awareness spun between them; he laughed under his breath, a soft, sensuous sound. "You serve a sisterhood of witches. Who knows where you fall in Hira's grand design?"

"I serve the One. I serve the people of Khorasan."

But he couldn't be persuaded. Moreover, he presumed. Not in handling her, though his physical allure was challenging enough to oppose. There was a faint violence in the way he drew her to him—a masculine presumption. He contrived to harness her powers, something she could never allow. In the end, his insistence brought them to the same point. She would have to use the Claim against him, and she would do so as an instrument of Hira's.

"The Bloodprint belongs at Hira. Without it, the Citadel will fall. Our history will be erased."

"What is Hira to the prince of an empire?" He spoke with stunning contempt. "What are the claims of the Companions against those of the people of this land? Stay and defend this city with your gifts. Tonight I give the Banquet of the Victorious. Tomorrow, who can say? Perhaps both Ashfall and Hira will fall."

Arian drew a sharp breath. "Doesn't that hurt you, Prince of Khorasan? All of this lost for good when Ashfall is your trust?"

The hand that held her arm now feathered over her throat, his touch a delicate tracing. A thrill of excitement coiled along her spine; for a moment she was under his spell, a prisoner of his enchantment. She wanted to be held, caressed . . . *cherished*. But not by the Prince of Khorasan, whose heavy-lidded gaze had caught the enthrallment in hers. Heat flared in his eyes, gilding the lean distinction of his face with dark, sensual power. And she knew she'd failed to reach him in any way save this.

His black gaze whipped over her face, a savage edge to his voice. "You know nothing about me, Arian. How I rule, *why* I rule. You haven't the least idea. To use your gifts to track slave-chains . . . how could you serve as queen of an empire when your vision is so constrained?"

Pride stiffened her bones, an agony of feeling so intense, the power of the Claim flamed through her, shattering the spell he wove. She removed his hand with a grimace. "The women of Khorasan are not disposable. Their freedom is the calling I serve. You speak of me as your queen, yet you know a queen wields power of her own, and that isn't what you want at all."

He looked as if he were moved to strike her. She didn't flinch away, holding him in place with the Claim's irrefutable command. When it had done its work, a weary resignation settled in his eyes. He spoke to her without anger, though his words were bitter and quiet.

"You know nothing of what I want. But that is a future beyond us at this moment. At present, we face the same enemy. And in the end, what choice do you have, Arian? There is no route to Hira that would see you safely to the Citadel. So you make a fruitless bargain."

A horn sounded from the walls, its clarion notes reaching the scriptorium. They listened to it in silence. It was followed by the indistinct throbbing of drums, the first herald of the Talisman approach.

"You misconceive my intent, if you think I will not fight for Ashfall at its most perilous hour. But there is a war beyond this battle—and an Audacy I must fulfill. Very soon will come a time when you will have to let me go."

The Bloodprint seemed to pulse on its stand. He gave a disconsolate shrug. "As to that, how could I stop you?"

"And the Bloodprint?"

The supple lines of his mouth tightened.

"Go and rest, First Oralist. Refresh yourself. I would like you to dress for the banquet. If there *is* a tomorrow, we will speak of the Bloodprint then."

45

Sinnia was alone with the Bloodprint. The Khorasan Guard stood a short distance away to give her these moments of privacy. She had welcomed a bath and a change of clothes as luxuries she had almost forgotten. And now she stood before the Bloodprint in a dress lovelier than any she'd had the pleasure to wear, her profile drawing the admiration of the young Warraqeen. It was a reverence she ignored, her attention occupied by the manuscript on the stand.

One hand crushed the gold stuff of her dress; the other she raised to the Bloodprint. Beholding it now, she thought of the oath Arian had sworn to Larisa.

Come unto that tenet that you and we hold in common.

It was the *Bloodprint* they held in common.

Wafa had described the beauties of its encasement to Sinnia, employing a vocabulary unequal to it. Sinnia had gathered the sense of things. An extravagant profusion of gemstones, an emerald to rival anything in the Black Khan's court, diamonds, rubies, sapphires—as with Arian and Rukh, the treasures of the encasement meant nothing to Sinnia at all. The manuscript itself was enough. The manuscript was *everything* to her. She drew a shaky breath and placed her hand on the page.

Believe in that which is beyond the reach of human perception.

She did. Even before she'd crossed the Sea of Reeds, she'd had a profound sense of her calling to the One and of the clarity of the Claim. It spoke to her ceaselessly, its fuller qualities awakened by the Technologist's experiments. During those moments on his table, her heart had become a black stone, adamantine and shrunken, driven by an urge to power. To work the Claim like a miracle of self-ascendance! She could do it. She *would* do it, as she'd planned at Jaslyk.

Until Salikh had reached into her thoughts. He'd helped her. He'd revisited the Claim, unveiling the current of integrity that underlined its words. These discoveries hadn't come to her on that last day when she'd been at the mercy of the Malleus—Salikh had been sowing them in her mind from the moment she'd arrived at Jaslyk, supported by the echo of his followers. He'd shut off that dark impulse as powerfully as the Technologist had chosen to expose it. He'd shown her a place of beauty. And courage had flooded her heart.

Do not fear the Claim, he'd whispered. *The Claim will not unmake you. You are Sinnia, queen of the Negus. The Claim will show you yourself.*

She touched the tips of her long fingers to the bloodstained page, humbled to stand in its presence. The ancient manuscript was plain, yet it gleamed like a jewel from its heart.

She turned its pages slowly, treating the vellum with care. When she reached a certain page, she felt her fingertips ignite. She paused to read the words on the page, her eyes falling upon a single line.

We accepted your solemn pledge that you would not drive one another from your homelands.

A sob broke from her throat like a gasp. She knew what the Claim was telling her; she felt the gravity of her calling.

She belonged by right to the sisterhood at Hira. And she was meant to fight for the consequence of women in the Council of Hira's name.

46

DANIYAR KNOCKED ON THE DOOR TO ARIAN'S CHAMBER. HE WAS HER escort to the Khan's banquet. Even with a city braced to fall, the rituals of the court were carried out. He thought it preposterous, but there were mysteries at this court that he had yet to unravel. If the Khan had assembled the city's luminaries in honor of the First Oralist's visit, then they would have to attend on the chance they might gain an advantage he wasn't able to name.

Even as battle raged around them.

Gifts of dress and tokens of rank had been provided to them all, not excluding Alisher and Wafa. He himself was attired in robes befitting his status as Silver Mage. Though the courtesies of court made Daniyar impatient, he needed allies at the Black Khan's table, allies who could be won through the use of his influence and magic. Abandoning his armor for a night seemed a small price to pay in exchange. Doing so as Arian's consort helped to soften the blow.

Yet when she didn't answer his knock, he nudged the door to her chambers open.

The Black Khan had allotted her the finest rooms available to guests at the palace. The private apartments known as the Khas Mahal were linked by a canal that ran through a passage of marble wreathed in floral motifs. The silky stream of water was a vivid turquoise green. Above it, the sunset burned in a sky that was deepening to a smoke-singed gold.

The apartment opened onto a lush garden through a colonnade topped by sandstone arches. The cornices were limned with a dusty, subtle gold worn away by the wind. Pale curtains screened the pillars, lifting in the breeze from the gardens below. Sheets of bougainvillea hung from the balcony, flinging petals onto the lawn against the fragrant peace of night.

Exquisite furnishings filled the room, patterns of marble and jade playing upon silks and brocades. On every surface, peonies blossomed in shades of rose. The scent of sandalwood and ambergris rose from censers in the room—too musky to suit Arian, he thought. The outer chambers were empty, so he moved past a marble lattice, as finely filigreed as lacework, following the path of the canal. The turquoise waters teemed with silky-soft clusters of jasmine.

Behind the lattice, the marble floor opened onto a deep rectangular pool from which rose a curtain of steam. The pool occupied most of the room, a turquoise gem in a mother-of-pearl setting, framed by a roof that was diamond-patterned in bits of obsidian and jade. It was a sight of such elegance and artistry that for a moment, Daniyar stood there and took it in—the marble colonnade, the figurative arabesques, the tessellation of the smallest nook, the dazzling symmetry of the hall.

Then he noticed Arian, her head resting on the lip of the pool, her long hair streaming behind her onto the marble floor. Her eyes closed, she was bathing in the pool, her body floating beneath a sea of jasmine that shielded her from his view. There was a sheen of mist on her face and her shoulders; her skin was lightly flushed. Her circlets lay to one side of her head; her dress hung upon a mother-of-pearl screen paneled with trifling bits of glass. Beyond this was an inlaid table covered with censers worked in silver, each exuding a scent lighter than those in the outer chamber. A set of treasures rested on the table beside these—a lacquered comb whose teeth were made of ivory, a gold-and-sapphire tiara, a curtain of stones mounted on a gold band. These gifts of the Black Khan were meant to honor the First Oralist. But to Daniyar, they presaged more: together with the jasmine-filled pool and the flowering masses of peonies, they were intended to *entice* Arian—to flatter and pursue her. He didn't like it, but he could fully appreciate the Black Khan's fascination when he was held by a similar spell. She could bring a man to his knees simply by speaking his name, and he wasn't thinking of the coercion behind Arian's use of the Claim. To Daniyar, Arian's graces were unparalleled. With her beauty, her magic, and her rank, it was inevitable that the Black Khan would wish to pursue her as his consort.

He trailed a hand through the sapphire ropes scattered on the table, wondering at their purpose. He moved to a spot where Arian could see him and quietly spoke her name.

She opened her eyes. He was caught in her dark green gaze, a flush upon his skin at the intimacy of his transgression. She waited for him to say more, sinking a little lower beneath the cover of jasmine.

"Take my hand," he said. "Let me help you dress."

She held his gaze, her lips slightly parted. He could read her yearning from across the pool, sense the heavy beat of blood beneath her skin.

"Daniyar." In his name he read denial.

"Let me look at you," he urged, his voice low and caressing.

She shook her head. "I can't. I'm not—" She crossed her arms over her breasts, her shoulders rising from the water.

"You're not what, Arian?"

He held out his hand. She shook her head again, shrinking away from his touch.

He thought she would use the vow she'd taken at Hira as a reason to deny him. Instead, she raised her bandaged wrist to trace the line of her throat.

"I'm not *whole*. My wrist, my throat . . . my back. My hands are callused from the use of my sword." She hurried over the words. "And with the famine in the south—I'm not the woman you knew. I'm damaged."

Nothing could have surprised him more. It pained him that she doubted her physical self. That she felt lessened in her own eyes, a diminishment impossible in his. She was fiercely bewitching to him, more so now that the Claim had made her over, more so with a decade of trial behind her. But his words would not suffice to soothe away her concerns.

So instead he knelt beside her, scooping a handful of jasmine from the water and spilling it over her hair. He held the image in his mind—the gently furled white blossoms caught in her midnight hair, a thing of beauty to set against the darkness.

His fingers traced a path from the gleaming skin of her shoulders to the wound from Nevus's blade, testing the damage beneath. She held her breath, heat flaring under his touch.

"Does this hurt?"

"No."

The stiffness of her voice gave away the lie in her response. For a brief instant he paused; then he lifted her face to his. He dipped his hand in the water, then raised it again, sprinkling jasmine over her face, crushing it against her lips.

Arian reached for him, her arms linked around his neck, her torso twisting to meet him. When they broke apart, blossoms were caught in the full line of his lashes. She brushed them away, caught by a dark excitement. He held her close, tasting the jasmine on her lips. His kisses deepened: he drank the sweetness from her mouth until she was consumed by a shattering delight. Then his lips moved to the shadow of bruising at her throat, each kiss a tribute to her pain. It wasn't enough. Her hands tested the disciplined strength of his back, urging him on with a delicate violence. His mouth closed hungrily over hers.

A brisk knock on the outer door broke them apart. It was Sinnia, come to fetch her.

"Just a moment, Sinnia. I'm not ready." She motioned to the screen, urging Daniyar to move behind it.

"What have you been doing?" Sinnia called.

"Bathing."

Flustered, Arian rose from the pool, petals of jasmine clinging to her skin. She reached for the drying cloth beside her dress, brushing the petals to her feet.

"I'll help you dress. Your arm must be tired and sore."

"No!" Arian said in a strangled voice. "I can manage on my own."

There was silence from the other side of the door. Then dryly Sinnia said, "I'll wait for you in the banquet hall, shall I? As you're not in need of *my* assistance."

Daniyar's quiet laughter reached both women's ears, and Sinnia laughed too as she let herself out of the room.

When Arian was dressed, she took up the ivory comb.

"Let me."

Daniyar's eyes met hers in the mirror, the memory of their kisses deepening the shadows. He plied the comb through her hair, catching the remaining jasmine in its teeth, holding her gaze all the while. When he'd finished, he looped the tails of her hair around his wrist, reaching with his hand for the censers on the table.

He sniffed the first. It was rose. The second smelt of orange blossom—he replaced it. The third was jasmine. He removed its stopper and raised his other wrist, spooling out the tresses of her hair. Then he wove the censer in a circle, scenting her hair from above and below. He set the censer back on the table and buried his face in her hair, feeling a quick, hot rush of desire.

"You should always wear jasmine. It's how I will imagine you now."

Her startled eyes flew to his.

He offered no apology. "If Sinnia hadn't knocked, I would have forgotten the banquet." He gave her a moment to take in his meaning, his gaze hard and steady on hers.

He reached for the sapphire tiara and placed it upon her hair, then fingered the curtain of stones. "I must confess I don't know how to dress you in this."

Marveling at the tenderness of his attentions, Arian showed him how to fasten the band. The sapphire ropes tangled in her hair, glittering through its waves. She came to her feet, savoring the intimacy between them.

"You don't mind this?" she asked. "Waiting upon me like a handmaiden at Hira?"

His silver eyes darkened. "Only grant me this privilege each day."

With great care, he raised her arms and fastened her circlets, tying the ribbons of her sleeves. He took a step back, holding her by the arms to look at her in silence. He hadn't seen her dressed like this since their days at the Library of Candour. He discounted the manner in which she'd been displayed at the Authoritan's court—

the transparent silk of her robes had been intended as a humiliation. This was more subtle and therefore lovelier to his eyes.

The lustrous satin of her sapphire dress was molded to the lines of her body, the skirt draped in folds at her hips. The neck of the gown was wide, its satin collar embroidered with thread in the Black Khan's motif, a trail of silver rooks. The sleeves were similarly patterned and fell away from her arms to reveal delicate wrists, deceptive in their strength. If she wished to reveal her circlets, she had only to reach for the ribbons and her sleeves would come apart. The dress must have been designed with a Companion of Hira in mind.

Arian? Or Ilea? It didn't matter. His attention was transfixed by Arian, aglow in the Khan's sapphires. Daniyar shook his head at himself. *He* should have been the one to gift Arian with these treasures. He thought of the ring of the Silver Mage, the gift she'd once refused. It was all he'd had to offer her, his inheritance looted by the Talisman. He knew none of this mattered to Arian, yet still he felt the weight of his regret. Then he thought of the Damson Vale, the gift he would one day give her.

"I don't know if I find you more beautiful like this or dressed only in your skin, rising from the water."

A warm, bright color stole into Arian's face. He brushed his fingers against her cheek, feeling the heat that pulsed beneath it— the singing clamor of her blood.

"I forget myself," he said. "I shouldn't speak to the First Oralist in this manner—it's enough that I think these thoughts."

Arian reached up and pressed kisses along his jaw. He folded her closer with care, though she was instantly aware of his strength. He bent and took her mouth in a sweet and fiery exchange.

"I'm not the First Oralist with you. And you haven't let me look at you in turn, or tend you as you've tended me."

"Your turn will come," he promised.

But she wasn't content to wait. She stepped back a little to view him. He was dressed in a black tunic that outlined his powerful shoulders, a stroke of green at his throat, a patterned cape flowing down his back. His tunic was threaded with diamond shapes, silver stitched upon silk by the skillful hands of a master. His leather boots gleamed with polish, and he wore a ceremonial sword, inscribed in the dialect of Ashfall. Each verse was the ode of a lover to his beloved, a few so explicit as to cause Arian to blush.

His beard was trimmed, and his indigo-black hair had been restored to order under a crown spiked with pearls. Arian looked at it closely—it was an approximation of the crown of the Silver Mage, reworked by a Khorasani silversmith. The leaves of trees native to Candour were appended to its pointed tines. It was the gift of a prince to a prince, its glittering shine picked up by the glint of Daniyar's eyes, as extravagantly luminous as diamonds.

Arian didn't know she was holding her breath until Daniyar raised an eyebrow in polite query. She exhaled in a rush, stumbling over the words. "My lord puts the stars to shame."

She didn't realize what she'd said until she saw the look of startled pleasure on his face.

Had she truly offered him so little of her love, so measured in her approval? Didn't he see what he was to her after the way she'd kissed him? She felt a slashing pain at his beauty and resolved to be more generous, repeating the words again, this time in a stronger voice.

His features relaxed into tenderness. Arian caught her breath, drenched by an intolerable sweetness. To step away from the war into his arms was a thing she'd begun to believe in.

"It's you who puts the stars to shame, Arian. The stars, the moon, the night."

"You've been reading the poet's verse." She glanced teasingly at his sword, and he smiled, a swift flash of light across his face.

"If I had," he said wickedly, "that would not be how I praised you."

He surprised a laugh from her. "Daniyar—"

He shrugged one shoulder. "I'm still a man," he reminded her, bending to kiss her cheek. He caught the look of yearning in her eyes, and the kiss transformed into a fierce necessity. He held her against the screen, devouring her mouth with his own. When he raised his head again, she was trembling in his arms with need, her hair disarranged by his hands. He combed it through with his fingers, then led her by the hand to the banquet.

At his side, Arian answered, "As if I could forget."

47

WHEN THE SILVER MAGE PRESENTED ARIAN ON HIS ARM, THE COURT seemed to take a collective breath. The nobles of the court were dressed with a grandeur that pretended the war drums beating beyond the capital were merely accompanying the musicians, but even their resplendence faltered before the presentation of the Black Khan's guests.

The First Oralist of Hira exuded a shining authority. The masculine beauty of the Silver Mage quieted the gossip of the court, as a murmur of appreciation took its place. The Begum of the court, Rukh's eldest aunt, welcomed the Silver Mage with grave decorum, reminding him of their earlier meeting. The young women jostled one another to make his acquaintance, the cousins and nieces of the Khan rustling around Daniyar until he was borne away to his seat. But not before he'd taken note of the Khan's ceremonial attire.

Rukh had traded his customary black for a deep blue tunic over silk trousers and a sapphire-studded sword that matched his crown. He wore the onyx rook mounted in its collar, but the ropes of pearls that descended from it had been replaced by strands of sapphires. Over all this, he wore the Sacred Cloak. And in his calculated splendor, he held his courtiers in thrall.

Daniyar glanced from Rukh to Arian, noting the similarity of their costumes: Rukh had dressed the First Oralist as his queen. If Arian noticed, she disregarded it, giving her attention to the court. Arsalan was the first to greet her, then the royal physician, the royal architect, the geographer, the astronomer, the clockmaker, before finally she was greeted by the artisan who had fashioned her stunning jewels. Other dignitaries included poets, storytellers, and historians. Lastly, she was presented to the Begum and the Nizam al-Mulk.

Each greeting incorporated a full spectrum of courtesies, with compliments paid to Hira, the Companions, and the lineage of the First Oralist. Nor were courtesies to Sinnia neglected. Mention was made of the justice of the Negus and of the graceful strength of the women of the Sea of Reeds.

Arsalan took Sinnia by the arm and placed her by his side. His seat was at the Khan's right hand. The Nizam al-Mulk was at the foot of the table, with the Begum seated to his right. The table could seat two dozen courtiers, each with a place that had been schemed over and was jealously guarded from encroachment.

Darya was lost somewhere in the midst, though she seemed cheered to find herself across from the Silver Mage. Arian's place was at Rukh's left hand, Alisher farther along the table, Wafa out of her reach. The boy seemed overwhelmed by the splendor of the table, hardly daring to breathe and too afraid to speak. He'd never seen such wealth or food in such abundance.

The Black Khan proceeded to his high-backed seat, a chair of gold raised on carved lion's feet, higher than the rest. To either side of his seat were the royal spear carrier, who hoisted the Black Khan's heraldic standard, and the archer who acted as his personal guard, both with remote, black-masked faces. The Khan raised his hand and held up his silver chalice.

The members of the court raised their cups.

"A toast," the Khan said, in his richly provocative voice. "In honor of our guests."

He didn't immediately speak, standing at rest with the sinuous ease of a man unfettered by constraints, wholly in control of his dominion and sharply aware of his allure.

"Never has the table of this court been so graced. First Oralist, Companion." His finely shaped head dipped at the Companions of Hira, his gaze lingering at Arian's neck, where the border of her dress was threaded with his emblem. When his gaze dipped lower still, Daniyar's hand tightened on his glass.

Darya's impetuous voice broke in. Holding her own cup high, she smiled a shy smile at Daniyar. "To the Silver Mage," she said. "You honor us, my lord."

"Darya!" The Begum's voice snapped a reprimand across the length of the table. Darya flushed, her cup trembling in her hand. Daniyar intervened, smiling at the Princess and taking some of the sting from the rebuke.

"I was coming to that, Darya." The Black Khan tipped his chalice at his rival. "My lord, the court at Ashfall welcomes your return."

"Excellency." The steel edge to Daniyar's voice promised an accounting for the Khan's betrayal at the Ark. Their eyes met and clashed—a silent and fierce reckoning of will. The courtiers waited in a state of exquisite expectancy. There had never been a man to rival their Khan's magnificence until the introduction of the Silver Mage. The flawless beauty of his face accentuated the clarity of his eyes, adamantine and bold. And decidedly averse to the Khan.

The Black Khan resumed his toast with a studied indifference to the Silver Mage's impact on his court, asserting his dark self-sufficiency.

"Visitors comes with ten blessings. They taste only one and leave behind nine. To the immeasurable treasure of your gifts. May your blessings be Ashfall's."

The assembly echoed the words and drank.

When Arian held up her cup of water, for the Companions of Hira were forbidden wine, the table went quiet, eager to hear the First Oralist's voice.

"*When the One is with you, who then can stand against you? In the One then, let the people of Ashfall place their trust.*"

"May your lips speak only truth," Rukh said with a bold, erotic glance that struck Arian as profane. His eyes traced the newly bruised fullness of her lips. He interpreted the cause for himself; for a moment his eyes were dark and deadly.

Then with a breach of etiquette that stunned the court, he set his silver chalice on the table without drinking from it—a negation of the toast he'd just made. He drew out Arian's chair, his sleeve catching on a sapphire strand woven through her hair. With a shimmer of dangerous promise in his eyes and the brush of his hand against the bare skin of her neck, he untangled the threads that bound them. His hair swept forward on his forehead like the fall of a raven's wing—a polished and glossy black with iridescent tints.

Before the others could take their seats, Arsalan raised his cup to the Khan and proclaimed, "Beautiful to behold is the Khan. Bounteous is his table."

The words completed the rituals of the banquet. Rukh dipped his dark head at Arsalan, a curious response in his eyes.

This time the courtiers' echo rang with pride. Wafa shrank into his seat, overcome by the sound of so much splendor. He looked at Arian forlornly, his blue eyes wide and unblinking. Arian smiled at him, trying to reassure him without speaking. Rukh bent close enough to her that his lips brushed the rim of her ear.

"Tell me what preoccupies you, Arian. Did my gifts fail to please you? For I can offer others more suited to your radiance."

Startled by his trespass after their discord in the scriptorium, Arian murmured her thanks in the fulsome language of the court. Shifting away slightly, she added, "I wonder if Wafa might be moved next to me or Sinnia."

For answer, the Black Khan snapped his fingers at a page. The cousin seated beside Sinnia was displaced, Wafa ushered into her place. He gripped Sinnia's hand, ducking his head before the court. For a long moment Rukh's eyes stayed on Sinnia's radiance, caught by something new in her expression; then they returned to Arian.

"If all your wishes were as easy to gratify." He laced the words with soft innuendo. Arian kept her gaze on Wafa, and he asked, "What is this Hazara to you?"

The table paused to hear her answer. Arian gestured at the Sacred Cloak on the Black Khan's shoulders. "He is an orphan, my lord. As such, he is my trust."

Wafa found his voice, repeating a familiar formula. "I am Wafa, and I will be loyal."

Rukh smiled his insinuating smile at Arian. "You've named him in a word of our language. You honor me."

Arian didn't protest that the honor was intended not for the Khan, but rather for the boy. She nodded politely, bearing the full weight of his renewed attention. He was trying to suggest an intimacy between them, but whether it was purely to torment her or whether he sought to provoke the Silver Mage, she couldn't be entirely certain.

She sought to deflect the conversation. "Your city is beautiful, my lord. Your labors have transformed it since my last visit."

"Every jewel requires an appropriate setting."

Perhaps she felt Daniyar's tension across the table because she was so closely attuned his thoughts; he gave no sign of his displeasure to the members of the Black Khan's court. But when their eyes met, she knew he was angered by the Khan's insinuations. She shook her head. They knew what they needed to achieve. Arian bowed her head and Sinnia followed her lead. The Khan asked for a blessing over his table. Quietly Arian gave it.

Now the conversation moved apace, and Arian took in her surroundings in more detail.

A long wooden table with a ceramic inlay glistened beneath a light fixture composed of crystals. The crystals were reflected in a surface of white porcelain decorated with scenes of the hunt in turquoise, vermilion, and green. The central motif was of a river that flowed from one panel to the next, monarchs reposing at leisure upon its banks, while servants brought news of the chase.

Around the table, place settings were marked by gold plate and silver, the light from the chandelier's crystals dancing upon the plates. Of greatest interest to Arian were the slip-painted serving bowls, inscribed with Nastaliq script beneath a transparent glaze. She cast a glance at Sinnia, dressed like a queen of the Negus in shimmering bronze silk, her close-cropped curls beaded with pearls, a gold diadem the perfect complement to her circlets. She radiated the power and pride of a dignified Companion of Hira.

Though the table was laid with the trappings of a feast and illuminated by the treasures of the court, the sight of the plain earthenware bowls exhilarated both Companions. The vessels were piled high with sugared pilafs dotted with raisins and cherries. They were formed like any other platter, except for the lines of script along the rim, the written word taken as a common-place.

The Black Khan dipped his sleek head at her, noticing her fascination. "In your honor, First Oralist."

"Were these bowls excavated from the ruins of Nightshaper?"

The Nizam interrupted. "And how did you guess that, First Oralist?"

Alisher cleared his throat. He read the verses on the outer rims aloud, delivering them with the cadences of a poet. The table fell silent to listen.

"'Some long for the glories of this world, others for a paradise to come. Lovers take their treasures in this life . . . to earthly delights they succumb.'"

"*Afaarin.*" Rukh murmured the word of praise. "I didn't know you had a poet in your train."

The seated courtiers echoed his praise. Alisher gazed around the table in surprise. Like Wafa, he'd been cleaned up and dressed in a suit of new clothes, grateful for his change in circumstance.

"I was trained at Nightshaper," he said. "It was there I first read the verse."

"Who was your teacher?" Rukh asked. Like all the members of this refined and civilized court, he recognized the name.

"The lady Zebunissa."

The table chattered with excitement. Even the Nizam looked impressed.

"You amaze me," Rukh said. He clapped his hands for wine. It was served from copper basins that were cast, tinned, and inlaid with black compound. "We honor poets in this land. Consider me your patron at Ashfall."

Alisher bowed from his seat. He didn't dare raise the issue of the city's imminent demise.

Darya watched as her brother indicated the single earthenware bowl in black: it was poised before his place setting, its transparent glaze cracked. The large black bowl was empty. The inside rim featured Nastaliq script picked out in white against an ebony glaze. "Can you tell me what this says?"

The poet didn't ponder why he was being questioned in place of one of the Companions. "It's a benediction," he said. "'Generosity is the attribute of the occupants of the afterworld.' But why is the bowl empty, Excellency?"

Darya answered in Rukh's place, eager to contribute to the conversation. "This bowl is always kept empty at my brother's table. It symbolizes that though we feast at Ashfall, others go hungry in the south. No meal is served at the Black Khan's table without an equivalent gift to those suffering the famine."

She looked around the table and saw her interjection wasn't welcome. Though she had only meant to share her knowledge, perhaps she had sounded boastful. Another misstep in a series of missteps. Trying to cover her mistake, she turned her attention to the Silver Mage. "You must be very tired, my lord. Your journey here was a perilous one. It is said you were injured at Black Aura."

"I regret it wasn't I who suffered." Unable to help himself, his glance sought out Arian, remembering the urgent press of his lips against the shadow of her bruises. Darya followed his gaze, struck by a new discovery.

"It was the First Oralist, you mean."

"Yes." Daniyar didn't elaborate.

Darya hesitated. "Does the First Oralist always have this effect?" She waved a hand, her cuff nearly knocking over her cup. She set it back on its stem, hoping the Silver Mage hadn't noticed. He was still staring at the First Oralist, his eyes like pale stars

in a beautiful, dark face. There was something in his glance—
something fierce and possessive and almost cruel.

"Oh," Darya said. "You're— She's your—"

She fell silent under the impact of those eyes.

"My what, Princess?" His tone warned her to be careful.

But Darya failed to heed the warning. "You love her."

"How does that concern you?" The hard edge to his voice made
Arsalan's head whip around. Darya began to stammer.

"I mean—I meant—she's a Companion of Hira. She's *First
Oralist* of Hira. You *cannot* love her. And *she* cannot love you.
Have either of you—"

Darya's judgment caught up to her chattering tongue, and her
young face blanched at what she'd foolishly spoken aloud. She
caught the jeering glances of her cousins, and her hands began
to shake. The pearl at the center of her forehead bobbed with her
inner trembling.

The restraint the Silver Mage imposed on himself now became
evident to her. Without raising his voice, he delivered a warning
to Darya. "You may say what you like to me, Princess, but it isn't
wise to insult the First Oralist to my face."

The insult lay not in the implication that Arian and Daniyar
were lovers: it was the public suggestion that Arian had renounced
the vows of Hira.

Darya braced her hands on the table. If she hadn't, she might
have fallen from her seat at this rebuke. Her sense of humiliation
was amplified by the fact she had brought it on herself: the Silver Mage could have been crueler and far more to the point. "My
lord, forgive my impertinence—"

The Begum cut across her words.

"You must forgive the Princess of Ashfall, my lord. She is barely
out of the schoolroom and still thinks like a child."

347

Worse and worse. Waves of shame washed over Darya; she was drenched by a scalding heat. A red tide rose in her cheeks, a tight knob of pain forming in her throat. Tears burned behind her eyes; she willed them not to fall, her gaze fixed on her plate.

Those seated at the head of the table turned at the Begum's words. Arian and Sinnia looked curiously at the Princess's down-bent head, Arian signaling a silent question to Daniyar. But it was Arsalan who intervened, his scowl formidable.

"Have a care, Begum. You speak to my future bride, and *I* do not view her as a child." His voice softening, he addressed the Silver Mage. "Darya is of a romantic disposition, my lord. She meant no offense to the Black Khan's guests, least of all the First Oralist, whom she so admires."

"Of course." Daniyar focused on Arsalan's news. "May I be the first to wish you good fortune, though the time for joy is brief."

His words brought a hush to the table.

This was the first time either Arsalan or Darya had made public reference to a betrothal; the table should have erupted in blessings and salutations. But in the deep quiet of the hall, lit by lanterns that gleamed through traceries of steel and the heavy musk of flowers, the uppermost sound was the thudding of Talisman drums, sounding ever louder, ever closer. Darya couldn't help but think it covered the pounding of her heart.

The Black Khan reclaimed the table's attention with a sardonic rebuke.

"A feast before dying?" An elegant hand called for new dishes to be brought. "Nothing so cavalier, Lord Daniyar. No enemy has ever taken Ashfall. And with the Bloodprint, the Cloak, the Companions, and yourself—the city has never been mightier."

Arian's eyes flickered to Daniyar's. The time had come.

"It's not enough," Daniyar said. "We must confer at once. I would seek the assistance of your brother."

Darya's head came up with a gasp. She looked hopefully from the Silver Mage to Rukh. Again she broke in when she should have remained silent.

"Darius? You've come for Darius? Do you think he can save the city? Please listen to the Silver Mage, Rukh. Please free Darius from Qaysarieh."

There was nothing Arsalan could say now to save the Princess. To speak of the half-brother imprisoned at Qaysarieh was to publicly announce her treason. Darius had poisoned the Black Khan's chalice with a distillation of aconite from the plant commonly known as monkshood.

The Black Khan studied his sister with hooded eyes, his thoughts shuttered. "You would aid Darius despite everything he stands accused of?"

Darya nodded, oblivious to the danger. The nobles waited, their shining eyes expectant, anticipating Darya's downfall.

"It was a mistake," Darya said. "Darius knows that now. He's said as much many times."

"Hmm. Did he also tell you *this*, Darya?"

"Rukh, don't."

The Black Khan ignored Arsalan's sharp interruption.

"I don't understand . . ." Darya answered.

"Of course you don't—why should that surprise me? It should be obvious to you that Darius views you as a trifle. You remember his inner circle—what did he call them, Arsalan?—the Darian Guard?"

"There's no need to tell her. Let it go, Rukh."

It said something of Arsalan's state of mind that he didn't use the Black Khan's title in the presence of the court. Rukh's black gaze switched to Arsalan. Whatever secret conviction he saw in Arsalan's face, he decided to discount it. His fingers tapped his silver chalice.

"You shelter her too much, Arsalan. It's why she refuses to take on her responsibilities. It's why I continue to rely on the Begum in her stead. I tire of it." He bowed to Arian. "Forgive me that I air this unpleasantness before you, but treason cannot go unanswered."

Darya's eyes widened, the implication of her brother's words finally becoming clear. "I would *never* betray you, Rukh—you know that."

"Do I?" He played with his chalice idly. "But then, I didn't think Darius would offer his own sister to his guard as a prize in a game of darts—they came to your rooms to besiege you."

"No—" Her voice dropping, Darya repeated it. "No, that isn't true."

"I am tired of your foolishness, Darya. Tell her," he snapped at Arsalan. "As she challenges the word of a prince."

He was very much on his dignity, no lenience to be glimpsed from the arrogant set of his head or from his vivid, dark face.

Arsalan spoke in quick, clipped sentences, his gaze scanning Darya's innocent face. "It is true, Princess. Let us speak of it no further."

"But how did I not hear them in my room?"

Rukh slammed his chalice down on the table, causing the courtiers to jump. "Because Arsalan anticipated their malice. He slit their throats with his own quick blade. Ten men dead for your sake, Darya." He shook his head in disgust. "Just one of the trials you force upon the Commander of the Zhayedan." His lips tightened in distaste. "As if Arsalan has nothing more pressing on his mind."

Darya risked a glance at Arsalan. She read the truth in his eyes with a growing sense of horror. Her skin felt sickly and pale; her eyes became huge and haunted.

Rukh snapped his fingers. Two of his guards materialized at Darya's chair.

"Take her where she most longs to be. Take her to Qaysarieh."

"My lord, please."

Yet Arsalan's intervention went unheeded. Sounding tired, the Black Khan said, "With enemies at the gate, I've no need of enemies within." He looked at his sister, small and trembling in the grip of his men. A wave of his hand indicated another command. Carefully, one of the guards raised a hand to Darya's headdress.

"No." The sharp countermand came from Arsalan. With a speaking glance at Rukh, he strode to Darya's side, observing the malicious glances exchanged around the table. Darya had never been a favorite of the court, and there were many who resented Arsalan's influence over the Khan. They waited to see how the Black Khan would respond.

Brushing the guards aside, Arsalan removed Darya's headdress and her cuffs, his hands gentle on her arms. Darya closed her eyes. It was her only defense against his pity.

"Do not cry, Princess," he murmured for her ears alone. "They imagine he does it to debase you; I know it for a kindness. If he didn't punish you for your careless words, the court would think him weak. Some would seek to exploit that weakness at a time when he must demonstrate strength." His hands reached for the fastening of her pearl diadem. "This never suited you," he told her. "And now at last you are free of it."

To the astonishment of the court, he knelt at her feet, reaching for the bells at her ankles.

Humbled beyond bearing, Darya's hand moved to caress the

dark waves of his hair. He looked up at her with a curious mixture of sympathy and regret.

"Darya! How you dare!"

But this time Darya didn't listen to the Begum, standing breathless and grateful under Arsalan's ministrations, her eyes open to what her recklessness had cost her. Sighing a little, she raised her chin, taking the measure of the court—taking the measure of herself.

Ashfall was on the brink of disaster. In the span of a few short minutes, she had insulted its likeliest allies: the Silver Mage and the First Oralist. She had offended the sensibilities of her aunt. And she'd shown her brother defiance at a time when he most needed obedience, interfering where she had no place to speak. She had placed the Commander of the Zhayedan in an untenable position, compelled to rescue her pride by kneeling at her feet.

Her childish daydreams fell away, collapsing into dust. Apprenticeship at Hira entailed the selection of novices whose judgment was measured and wise. The court required a princess whose wayward, chattering tongue didn't dishonor its prince. And Arsalan needed a woman who was worthy of standing at his side.

There is nothing about Darya that attracts me.

And still he knelt at her feet.

She urged him up with a gentle pressure on his shoulders.

"Leave the bells," she said for the courtiers to hear. "My brother likes to know where I am." And then to Arsalan alone, "I won't forget your kindness to me, Commander."

"Darya," her aunt snapped, "you are not being sent to Qaysarieh to die, but to answer for your disobedience. There is no need for these dramatics."

Darya gave her aunt a crooked smile, straightening her shoulders, her neck blissfully free of the weight of the ponderous headdress. "Perhaps *you* will assume my duties now. It's what you have always wanted."

And then she let herself be led away.

Arsalan passed her regalia to one of the Begum's attendants. He caught the flicker of a smile on the Begum's lips. He took his seat beside Rukh with carefully controlled anger, offering an apology to the Companions of Hira for the disruption of their dinner. Sinnia's black eyes were wide and intrigued. Beside her, Wafa balled his hands into impotent fists. He shot the Black Khan a look of loathing, knowing he wasn't brave enough to challenge the Khan on Darya's behalf, as she'd done for his sake during his questioning in the throne room.

Rukh leaned forward in his seat to murmur into Arsalan's ear. An unexpected tension appeared in the strong lines of Arsalan's jaw. He moved a little away from the Khan, as if discomfited by the close contact.

"Don't let her anywhere near Darius," Rukh said.

"I had no intention of doing so."

"Or the prison quarters."

"What do you take me for?"

"I want her to be guarded by women."

In a dry voice, Arsalan said, "I wonder you sent her to Qaysarieh at all."

Arian listened to this exchange, surprised by the lack of deference in Arsalan's tone, expecting Rukh to take offense.

Instead, he shot Arsalan a level look from beneath the fringe of his lashes. Arsalan faced him, unperturbed. He drank from his cup, the first chance he'd had to do so all night. Watching him, a smile of some charm lightened the Black Khan's face. "I trust you'll sort out this mess."

Arsalan frowned into the depths of his cup, swearing beneath his breath. "I'd rather you didn't create these impossible situations to begin with."

"What need would I have of you, then?"

Arsalan raised his head, as if he'd thought of an answer he'd chosen to withhold. He held Rukh's gaze for a long and weighted moment. Rukh was the first to look away.

Arian considered them in silence. The two men were intimate friends. It was the Nizam who should have been at the Khan's right hand, as governor of his empire, but Rukh had chosen to seat Arsalan beside him. It spoke to the bond between the two men.

Just as Rukh would have returned his attention to Arian, he was disturbed by the approach of a man in a black cloak. Immediately Arsalan was on his feet, his sword in his hand, preventing the man from reaching the Khan.

The strangely lithe figure held up his arms in a gesture of peace, disclosing the sight of an unusual pair of elbow-length gloves threaded through with laces fashioned of a silken silver thread. He was tall and slim, with leanly powerful shoulders. When he removed his hood, his face was concealed behind a steel mask patterned with an arcane script. His eyes glowed through a pair of elongated slits. He was accompanied by a page dressed in black, a long, narrow box in his hands.

"How did you achieve access to this chamber?"

Arsalan's eyes sought out members of the Khorasan Guard. No one appeared in the shadows. The stranger ignored Arsalan. He spoke in a voice that sounded oddly hollow, as if he distorted it by some means. Arian felt a chill move over her skin. Why did he disguise his voice? Why did he disguise his *face*? She nodded to Sinnia, warning her to ready the Claim, seeing the solemn strength in Sinnia's proud face. Daniyar was alert as well, distrusting the intruder's proximity to Arian. He came to his feet, the stranger's appearance striking a chord of memory. The stranger dipped his head at Daniyar, then returned his attention to the Khan.

"I have come, Shahenshah." He tapped the narrow box. "I've brought you something of value, something the Silver Mage can use."

Recognizing the box, the Black Khan grasped its relevance at once. The Assassin had brought him an unlooked-for gift, an unexpected advantage. His eyes found Daniyar farther along the table. He made a quick bow to the Companions.

"Forgive me, Arian," he said. "I have need of the Silver Mage. Nizam al-Mulk, will you take my seat?"

"I should be at your side."

"Not this time. Nor you, Arsalan." He dismissed his commander's objections. "Go to the walls where you are needed."

He made his apologies to the Begum and asked her to entertain his guests.

Before he swept from the room, Arian detained him by touching his hand. "My lord Rukh," she said. "Might I advise you as well? Whatever gifts I have, I place at your disposal."

Rukh looked at her without that edge of seduction. His refusal was courteous but firm. "Forgive me, First Oralist. What I would ask of the Silver Mage requires him to think of Ashfall. To that end, your presence will not help."

So he'd seen through to the heart of it. Whatever he had hoped for from Arian wasn't hers to give. He knew that she and Daniyar were inevitably bound.

"Do not endanger him," she said.

For a moment, his face was drawn. Then with a frown he repeated, "I must think of the fate of Ashfall."

48

THE BLACK KHAN AND THE SILVER MAGE FACED EACH OTHER DOWN the length of the cartographer's table, hostility rippling between them like a wave. They were evenly matched in presence, tall and hardened to an edge, with a dark vitality pulsing through the room as each man took the measure of the other. The Silver Mage transmitted a grimly heightened power that was reflected in the sharply honed bones of his skull and the latent fury of his eyes. He had the air of a man whose self-discipline would welcome the chance to break. The Black Khan was more restrained in his animus, though no less prepared to take up the Silver Mage's challenge. He appraised his rival, seeking a means to gain the upper hand.

"Why would you endanger Arian's safety by bringing her through Talisman lines?"

A muscle worked beside Daniyar's mouth at this insolent use of Arian's name. And at the accusation. "She faced far greater danger in Black Aura."

The warning in his voice was unmistakable. There was a debt to be collected from the Black Khan, and he had resolved to collect it. The entirety of Arian's suffering at the Ark could be attributed to the Black Khan's treachery—the humiliation of the slave collar, the tortures of the Authoritan . . . the vicious transgressions of Nevus. The memory of Arian's agony caused rage to rise behind his eyes. But indifferent to his anger, the Khan ignored the warning, spinning the armillary sphere between his elegant hands.

Sounding bored, he said, "The First Oralist has a mastery none can overcome—what harm could she possibly have suffered?"

"What *harm*? She was collared." Daniyar bit out each word. "She was stripped of dignity. Then she was given as a gift to a captain of the Ahdath." He brushed his own cheek. "Nevus, his chief torturer. He assaulted her. He stabbed her with a treacherous blade; her injuries have yet to heal. She is just beginning to recover the instrument of her voice."

"And what of you?" There was a hard recklessness upon Rukh that tested Daniyar's self-restraint. "As Arian suffered these indignities, were you not preoccupied with the attentions of the Khanum?" The Assassin crept closer from the shadows as Rukh's fingers traced a desultory path over the sphere.

Lines of tension bracketed Daniyar's firm mouth. A freezing contempt in his voice, he replied, "I was bled in the bloodrites and whipped for the court's entertainment, if those are the attentions you mean."

The armillary sphere went still. The Khan's unnervingly black eyes cut to his. "Yet you survived."

Daniyar shrugged this off, a masculine impatience on his face. Until this war was won, he could not spare a moment to think of the toll wrested from him in blood. Or of the many men he had sent to their deaths for sport. He knew their faces would haunt him, but there was nothing in what he'd done that would serve to absolve the Khan.

Rukh repeated himself with greater emphasis. "*You survived. No one* survives the bloodrites."

Daniyar's head came up. It was his turn to smile. "No one else is the Silver Mage."

Rukh dipped his head in a momentary acknowledgment of this—his gaze fastened to Daniyar's, mesmerized by two flashing points of light. He felt that strange quickening of his blood again. And welcomed the flare of raw power. The Silver Mage was perhaps physically stronger than he, but Rukh had depths of cunning that no one else could equal.

"It would seem that my plan served you ill, though I cannot regret your trials at the Ark. They brought the Bloodprint to Ashfall."

Daniyar's response was offered with a dangerous and explosive certainty. "I would suffer the bloodrites again to prevent Arian from enduring an instant's pain."

Stepping closer to the outer balcony, the Black Khan considered this vow. A sliver of moonlight outlined the elegant cast of his features. In the wintry light that sheened his skin, he had the dispassionate perfection of a statue. With a sleek and supple grace, he turned to the map on the table, his movements echoed by the Assassin.

"Then she *is* your consort," he said. "If you would venture the bloodrites for her. So I ask you again: Why did you risk Arian's safety by bringing her here to Ashfall?"

Daniyar flashed him a look of scorn. "If you suppose any man bends the First Oralist to his will, you do not know her at all. I offer her my allegiance, but I do not command her course." He offered the words without embarrassment, ceding nothing of his authority or of the undisclosed power he had no need to proclaim.

Rukh's lip curled. "You are hardly *any* man. As you said, you are the Silver Mage, and possibly her lover, as well."

"*You* are the Dark Mage now," Daniyar returned, his anger now unleashed. He rocked back on his heels, his hand resting on his sword, lethal power etched in the tense lines of his body. "How can you not know the vows the Companions of Hira swear?"

The Assassin stirred at Rukh's side, his hand moving to the hilt of his own sword. Rukh quelled the movement with a sidelong glance. "I regret what transpired with the First Oralist, but I would make the same bargain again to ensure the safety of my city."

Daniyar scoffed at this. "You left your outer walls undefended. The Talisman are nearly at your gates."

"The Khan need not account for his decisions to you." The Assassin's voice was shivery with menace. He stepped forward and placed the long, narrow box on the table between the two men.

"Stand down, Hasbah." Rukh nodded at Daniyar. "Your reproaches serve no purpose. I must focus on what can be achieved to deliver my city now."

"What of the outlying villages?"

"Messages have been sent. You reinforced them yourself."

Daniyar turned to the window. By his assessment, the full strength of the Talisman's forces was still a day and night from the city walls. Preparations for the city's defense were half-complete. It was possible the Zhayedan would be able to open the city gates to allow for an influx of refugees, but he didn't think it was likely.

He suspected treachery at the court of Ashfall. He wondered if it came from this stranger who appeared to have the Black Khan's ear. He wondered also why something about the man in the mask seemed familiar to him.

"I presume you called me here to discuss the Conference of the Mages."

"How could I have? The Golden Mage is on her way to Hira. The Mage of the Blue Eye is a recluse. What conference could we hold on our own?"

Daniyar edged the map on the table closer to his chair. He pointed to a spot on the map between Ashfall and the Citadel of Hira. "Captain Cassandane shared word of the Golden Mage. Ilea could be brought back to Ashfall, perhaps in time to aid us. Your brother was Dark Mage before you—did he teach you nothing of our rites?"

Perhaps this was the reason the Black Khan had grown careless— he might have become confident of victory if he knew the extent of his power.

Members of the Khorasan Guard came to the door, seeking permission to interrupt.

"Report," the Black Khan commanded.

"Excellency, scouts approach the western gate. They do not wear Talisman insignia." He indicated the crest at the Silver Mage's throat with a doubtful jerk of his head. "Commander Arsalan sent us to report."

"The Nineteen," Daniyar said. "You face the Nineteen on your western flank."

The Black Khan nodded at his guards. "Find out. Report back to me."

When they'd gone, Daniyar returned to his theme. "I've been in conference with the Mage of the Blue Eye. He wields more power alone than the other Mages together. If he could be persuaded to act as an ally, he could bring his army to the west."

Rukh considered the map. "He wouldn't reach Ashfall in time.

He'd have to cross the Empty Quarter, the stronghold of the Nineteen."

"Then seeing your need is dire, why do you detain your brother at Qaysarieh?"

Rukh's tapping fingers froze on a corner of the map. "What concern is that of yours?"

"When Darius was Dark Mage, he amplified the use of my abilities. Even without Ilea, your brother and I could defend the eastern gate from the Talisman assault."

But Rukh was already shaking his head. "You know nothing of what transpired here, nothing of what this court was like under my brother's rule. Without the Nizam to steer its course, Ashfall would have been lost."

"I attended a Conference of the Mages at Ashfall when *you* were the one imprisoned at Qaysarieh."

"So your loyalty is to the would-be prince."

"*No.*" Daniyar's hand came down on the table, giving vent to his rage. "It is to the people of your city. To all the free people of Khorasan."

"No wonder Arian chose you as her consort," Rukh said, unable to hide his envy. "You think like her; you even speak like her. But I cannot consider a course that would permit my brother his freedom. It would precipitate catastrophe when Ashfall can least afford it."

Daniyar stood up. The Talisman drumbeat was echoed by the sound of infantry on the march. The Black Khan's hawks sped through the skies, their urgent messages arcing back and forth. On the western horizon, he spied a figure he thought was Arsalan striding to the gate.

"If my counsel is of no value to you, why did you summon me

here? Are you able to make use of your gifts? There is a rite I know that would serve the eastern gate."

"You mean the dawn rite, the rite of daybreak." The sensual line of Rukh's lips firmed. "I haven't fathomed my abilities. My sole thought has been for the Bloodprint."

Daniyar swallowed his disappointment at this news, a savage edge to his voice. "Then I do not know how to help you. Except by taking my sword to stand at Arsalan's side."

A canny look came into Rukh's eyes. He knew what the Assassin had brought him, just as he knew how to use it. "You would serve me better at the Emissary Gate." He glanced pointedly at the crest at Daniyar's throat. "The Shin War would take you for one of their own if you meet with their commanders. You could persuade them to abandon their attack."

"They would not heed me without my ring or my sword. With no proof that I still hold the Candour."

Rukh nodded at the Assassin to open the narrow box. A dazzling light spilled from it, glinting off the lacquered throne. Drawn by a strange compulsion, Daniyar moved to the box. He withdrew its contents with a muffled oath: the box contained the ring of the Silver Mage and the sword of the Guardian of Candour. He balanced the fine length of the blade in hands that were sure and strong, causing the Black Khan to shield his eyes from its glare.

Both sides of the sword were inscribed with the Guardian of Candour's motto: *Defend the truth in the face of all dishonor.*

Gripping the sword in his roughened palm, Daniyar faced the Assassin with a dangerous glint in his eyes. "How do you come to have this when it was hidden away?"

Something cold and menacing moved in the other man's eyes. Rukh answered for him.

"Nothing is hidden from the Assassin. He found your tokens

and kept them safe. His followers tracked you here; he brought your sword and ring to Ashfall where he guessed they might serve a purpose."

He watched in silence as the Silver Mage sheathed the sword and placed the ring on his finger. An arrow of light cut through the room, issuing from the ring's translucent stone.

"These may not be enough to hold sway."

Rukh had already thought of an answer. His hand stroked the Sacred Cloak, then moved carefully to unlatch it. "The Talisman would trust a man who wore the Cloak. They would know him for the Guardian of Candour, a man of their own tribe, a man who speaks their dialect. How could they deny your legitimacy?"

He folded the Cloak in his hands, passing it to Daniyar, who now took a step back. "What are you doing?"

"I'm giving you the Sacred Cloak to wear to the Emissary Gate."

Daniyar didn't touch it. His eyes took the measure of the Khan. Yielding the Cloak spoke of the Black Khan's desperation. *He would rather yield the Cloak than trust to his brother's abilities.*

"Take it," Rukh insisted. "I will rely on the Bloodprint in its stead."

Daniyar smiled to himself. It wouldn't take the Black Khan long to learn that the magic of the Bloodprint could be unlocked only by the Oralists of Hira. With the Talisman army at his gates, every choice he made was the wrong one.

Daniyar's hands closed on the Cloak. He held it up and let its soft brown folds fall to the floor. He drew it over his armor, closing its clasp at his neck. It fit him as though it had been woven for him.

"I'll go to the Emissary Gate, but I ask you to think on your brother. There *will* come a time when Ashfall will need the abilities of its Mage."

Rukh's lips tightened. He knew he'd been remiss in learning his skills as Dark Mage. He didn't need the other man's reminder, but Daniyar wasn't finished.

"Nor should you underestimate the First Oralist. For the strongest defense of Ashfall, do not separate Arian from the Bloodprint. Trust to your city in her hands."

When he'd gone from the room in a rush of controlled power, Rukh turned to the Assassin. "You've spared no thought on behalf of Ashfall. You were wise to bring his tokens here."

The Assassin gave a modest bow. "And now, Excellency? What would you have me do?"

"Follow him," Rukh said. "See what he does in their camp. I do not trust him at all."

The Assassin melted away. There was no need to remind the Khan that he was the one who'd proven to be unworthy of trust.

Daniyar returned to his chamber for his weapons and found Wafa curled up at the foot of his bed. He'd expected Alisher to offer his aid, but Alisher had deserted them for the wonders of the scriptorium. It was just as well; they'd asked too much of the poet's resources already.

Wafa recognized the Sacred Cloak at once. He swallowed twice without speaking; then he pointed to it with a finger stained with pomegranate juice.

"Did you kill him?" he asked, his dark eyes hopeful.

"No," Daniyar said, this talk of killing from a child of Candour disturbing to his ears. He began to fasten his weapons to his belt, taking care with the Sacred Cloak.

"Why not? You know what he did to Lady Arian. You *should* have killed him." Daniyar studied his reflection in the tall glass. The Cloak now covered the armor and his weapons. The Shin War crest flashed green at his throat—a symbol he'd once worn with pride, assured of his standing within his tribe. The way he'd once defined himself meant nothing to him now. His city had been transformed into something he didn't recognize, something he no longer valued, reduced again and again by the Talisman's creeping dread.

The Cloak was beauty amid desolation, sacredness against outrage, peace measured in its absence. The Black Khan had touched it with pride of ownership, with satisfaction at a weapon in his arsenal. Daniyar felt its power shimmering through his bones. He understood the Cloak for what it was: a holy mantle of love.

"I've killed too many men," he said. "Today and tomorrow, more will die at my hands. It doesn't help, Wafa. It injures me."

Wafa stared at him, wide-eyed. He sucked pomegranate juice from his fingers. "But the bad man hurt the lady Arian. It's good that he fell dead."

Daniyar nodded, sweeping the Cloak aside to sit next to the boy on the bed.

"The Authoritan was destroyed by the power of the Claim, the power that resides in all of us. There are men I have killed in Arian's defense, and I will do so again. That doesn't mean I enjoy it. What would you think if I did?"

"*He's* like them," Wafa said. He sketched a rook in the air to indicate whom he meant.

"I'm not sure of that yet. He's desperate, I think. Frantic to save his city, though he won't show the depths of his fear. It may not seem like it, Wafa, but he's thinking of all these people, the ones who live within these walls. The Princess who was kind to you. She's his sister and she loves him. Do you think she would if he were as bad as you say?"

Wafa looked confused. "The Princess cries," he said. "At night, alone in her room."

"If the city falls, the Princess will have other reasons to cry." Daniyar made for the door, where he paused to look back at the boy. "It's not always easy to decide why people act as they do. We cannot know what we will do until we are put to the test." He held up a corner of the Sacred Cloak. "I hope to be worthy of this Cloak. I hope to find a way other than raising my sword. Think about that, Wafa. Think of what it means to be a citizen."

But Wafa couldn't understand when he thought of himself as a slave.

49

"THAT WAS TERRIBLE," SINNIA SAID. SHE WAS SWEATING UNDER HER circlets, feeling Darya's humiliation as if it was her own. "Why would he banish his sister like that?"

She was seated on a swing whose chains were twined with honeysuckle vines, ablaze in flaming pink. Hummingbirds hovered above their heads, darting their beaks into the small, soft trumpets of the petals. The beating of their wings and the perfume of the vines engulfed her, drowning out the tang of Talisman fires. She was waiting for Arian to finish changing into her armor. They were due back at the scriptorium, every moment with the Bloodprint precious.

"There is a great deal under the surface of this court. Schemes, machinations, power struggles." Arian yanked her armor into place.

Sinnia snorted. "Darya is scarcely more than a child. What could she have plotted?"

"Daniyar could tell us whether the Princess is guilty of conspiring to unseat her brother, though in this case the Princess seems to be governed by a generous heart."

"It was cruel what the Black Khan told her about her brother."

"Yes, he can be cruel."

The Black Khan disturbed her tranquility. She remembered the urgency of Daniyar's kisses, the glowing excitement that had pierced her. If Daniyar believed his gifts could be called on, he would sacrifice himself without question, a repayment she had earned for her stubborn allegiance to Hira. She said nothing of this to her friend, though, for despite Sinnia's habitual humor, she knew that Sinnia still suffered from the effects of the experiments at Jaslyk.

Sinnia stretched out her limbs. She was well fed and cared for, and had been treated with the honor due a Companion of Hira. Several of the nobles of the court had visited the lands of the Negus, speaking warmly of its regent. The news of home was reassuring, and she'd learned one of the Prince's many cousins had married a man of her country.

She knew the Talisman were advancing across the plains, yet for the span of a night she had enjoyed luxury and peace, seduced by the comforts of Ashfall. On the balcony, the golden glimmer of the lamps offered solace; the twilight shadows and rich, soft air caressed the bare skin of her arms. The city of Ashfall rose on three sides around a giant square, its domes gently curving, its balconies and towers sculpted against the night, peacocks adrift in the gardens, their gemlike tails fanning behind the plumes of their small imperial heads.

It was a city of golden, glowing walls and emerald-green gardens, where flowered crimson trusses framed the arbors and sheets of wisteria flared violet against the crushed gold of stone. Hawks as dark as midnight raced against the sky, carrying messages between the walls. Sinnia was brought out of her reverie at the sight. Salikh had taught her the Claim; he'd opened her senses and spirit to it and urged her to make use of her powers.

Fight, he'd told her. *Fight.*

And now, profoundly strengthened by those moments with the Bloodprint, Sinnia knew she would. She would stand at Arian's side, and Arian would stand at hers, never to be divided again.

"Where do you see us as most useful, Arian? What role can we play in the defense of Ashfall? I could lend my aim to Captain Cassandane. I liked her very much."

"I could see that she respected you." Arian fastened her weapons to her belt. "But there are many archers behind these walls, and only two Companions of Hira."

Sinnia's dark eyes flashed at her, the whites a sharp and bold contrast. "Has the Black Khan agreed to gift you the Bloodprint? Does he know that you were trained to read it?"

Arian pressed her fingers to her temples. The Black Khan's attentions were more than just insistent, they were disturbing. She wondered if he used the powers of the Dark Mage in some secret way to coerce her. She and Daniyar had talked about the Authoritan's compulsive grip, the violence he'd enacted in their minds. Rukh was too subtle for violence, unless his relentless pressure against her senses was a similar intrusion.

"I have asked him," she told Sinnia. "And I read from the Bloodprint what I could under the eyes of the Zareen-Qalam. But it wasn't enough. I need time, and I need you there with me, to catch nuances I might miss."

Read, Sinnia, Salikh had urged. *Read and blaze, sahabiya.*

"I'm not as fluent as I'd like to be," she told Arian, a hitch of hesitation in the words. "There was nothing to study from in the capital of the Negus, and my training at Hira was brief."

"The Claim itself will teach you. It knows your heart; it knows you as the lioness of the Negus."

"I think you may be right." Sinnia's voice was full of wonder. "I have spent some time with the Bloodprint. I've learned to trust myself. I know now what I fight for."

In her voice was a silent recognition of the suffering behind the Wall. Sinnia had had a taste of it: the women they'd left behind and the leaders of the Basmachi—they knew a darkness too monstrous to describe. A darkness at odds with the beauty and elegance of Ashfall.

A hummingbird settled on her wrist for the space of a heartbeat. "The women of Ashfall are treated with grace, as they are in my homeland. But these are things you've never known."

"No," Arian said. "Not for a long time."

"Could the Khan entreat you with his city? Or his scriptorium? Or . . . his person? He wants you for his queen." She gestured with a hand. "Look at the dress he gave you. He couldn't have made it more obvious."

Arian sighed. She knew what Rukh wanted. He would take her sweetness as a matter of course, but what he truly coveted was magic. He believed he would conquer and hold through the use of her gifts. How poorly he understood the Claim.

How poorly he understood *her*.

She watched the Talisman advance from the safety of the balcony. They came for her and Sinnia, for every woman behind these walls. They came for the scriptorium, for each delicately preserved manuscript. Like the raiders of the steppes centuries ago, they would burn the city to the ground.

"When I complete my Audacy, I'll be able to think of myself. This isn't that time. Even my hope to pledge myself to Daniyar means nothing as long as I observe the duties of a Companion. And I cannot think of leaving if another is not trained in my place. How can I forecast a future I do not know? Unlike Lania, I must take my fate as it comes. Until then, if the Bloodprint is to remain here, so be it. I will use it to train the Warraqeen. That is the only future I am able to see."

"But if the Bloodprint were to remain in Ashfall, neither Ash nor Half-Seen would have access to it. Surely their gifts would aid you more than mine would."

"You asked me if I could be tempted. That's what would tempt me, Sinnia."

"And the Black Khan?"

She shook her head, refusing to consider her earlier weakness. "There is only Daniyar for me."

Their conversation was interrupted by the screeching of hawks diving down to the western gate, summoned by a whistle.

Arian and Sinnia rose to follow their progress. There was movement to the west, and they caught the gallant figure of Captain Cassandane at the head of her company of archers. As she strode forth with bold assurance, her attention was directed at the Commander of the Zhayedan, who walked beside her. Daniyar wasn't with them.

Arian's hands tightened on the marble railing. She tested the muscles of her throat—the time for the Claim was at hand.

The Black Khan appeared on their balcony. He was dressed in battle armor, two of the Khorasan Guard at his heels. "Come with me," he said. "I have urgent need of you now."

Rukh took his signet ring from his hand and slid it onto Arian's finger, locking her hand in his own as she tried to pull away.

"Please, Arian." His voice was darkly entreating. "My ring will give you the authority to visit the scriptorium at will."

"Where is Daniyar?" Arian spoke through stiff lips, her heart pounding a drumbeat.

Wordlessly, Rukh shook his head. "He's with the Assassin."

The Assassin.

Now Arian knew why she'd felt that frisson of fear at the sight of the black-gloved intruder. The Assassin's name was a whisper, his deeds a daunting legend.

"Where did you send them?"

"To the eastern gate."

"The Talisman advance from the east."

"I know that. I've had to close the gates to my own people. Many were left behind. The Talisman are using them as shields."

His black eyes glittered feverishly. He brought Arian's hand to his mouth and kissed it, pressing his ring against her fingers.

Arian snatched her hand away. "Tell me the rest."

He looked away from her for a moment. "For the sake of those who were captured, the Silver Mage has gone to treat with the Talisman. He's asked to meet with the leaders of the Shin War."

"No!" Arian's cry rang out against the night. "You must permit me to go after him!"

A strange inflection in his voice, Rukh said, "He's safe enough at the gate. Your presence by his side would put him at risk, for *you* are the Talisman's enemy. Let him trust to his own strengths now."

Fury surged through Arian's blood, clawing at her temples, striking sparks against her thoughts. She welcomed it. It held her deepest fears at bay. If she could have struck the Black Khan down, she would have.

Recognizing this, he covered her mouth with his hand. "Yes," he said with savage satisfaction. "*That* is what I need. Come to the scriptorium now, without delay. I relinquish the Bloodprint to your hands. Study it until you master it. When you're ready, come to the gate."

50

Darya hadn't been taken to the dismal quarters where Darius awaited his fate. Once past the ominous pishtaq that framed the Qaysarieh Portal, she'd found herself in a room with a balcony that overlooked the plains. The ramparts bustled with activity, companies of archers divided between the three approaches to the city, for none would come down from the north.

None, she thought, save the Companions of Hira, and the Silver Mage, whose masculine beauty had held the court of Ashfall in thrall. Each of Darya's cousins had thrust herself forward for his notice; Darya herself had felt a thrill at the burning lance of his strangely magnetic eyes.

For a moment, she lost herself in a daydream. She wondered how the First Oralist responded to the power of those eyes. Did she retain her magnificent composure, or did she flow like mercury in the arms of the Silver Mage, enslaved by the ravishment of his kisses? They had to be lovers; no man could look at a woman with such unrestrained hunger and consent to be kept at a distance, no matter the First Oralist's vows.

She checked herself at once, ashamed of the way her imagination had run wild. She shouldn't be speculating. She need think only of herself and Arsalan. She followed him around the palace like a shadow, but he didn't share her passion, and he'd never been her lover. Why did she assume the First Oralist requited the passion of her consort? Perhaps because Darya herself had found him so starkly beautiful. The silver eyes, the fine-grained skin, the hair sleek and dark like a raven's wing . . .

He hadn't denied loving the First Oralist; he'd simply challenged her right to speak of it.

Sick of her own stupidity, Darya sank down on the cot in her cell. It was night-dark outside the windows, and though her balcony was draped with the sleeves of lemon blossoms, she felt frightened and oppressed by Qaysarieh. She knew there were dungeons where the conditions were unspeakable, where the wails of prisoners haunted the murky halls, but she also knew her brother was not in the habit of inflicting torment. The beating of Wafa had been driven by necessity. But as she'd always told Rukh, cruelty would yield him nothing. It was kindness that had won her Wafa's secrets.

She started at the sound of pebbles skittering across her balcony. She waited a beat and the sound came again, a light clatter that broke through the noise of Talisman drums. She leapt to her feet, unencumbered by her headdress or cuffs. Her bells chimed sweetly at her ankles as she moved out onto the balcony.

Far below in the square, the Cataphracts, commanded by Maysam, were engrossed with preparations to meet the coming assault. The Zhayedan's shock troops were capable of inflicting heavy casualties. They were busy assembling catapults, and the muzzles and projectiles that would be launched en masse over the walls. Maysam moved with relentless focus, scanning the western gate for orders from his commander. Of Rukh, there was no sign, though he should have been at the wall.

Her heart skipped a beat. The morning would bring great danger to the two men who shaped her world: Arsalan and Rukh. What else it might bring to the women of her city, she didn't dare to think. Even as Arsalan had removed her jewels, he'd pressed a powder wrapped in parchment in her hands. "If I cannot defend you," he'd said, "you will be able to choose."

A shadow darted out from among the noise and bustle. Darya ducked.

"Who *is* that?" she whispered. "What do you want?"

She peered over the balcony again. It was the blue-eyed Hazara boy.

"I've come to rescue you," he said, sounding unconvinced.

Darya couldn't repress a smile. "How exactly? And how did you know I was here?"

"I followed the guards. Can I climb up?"

He tested the flourishing vines that trailed down the city walls, ferns and mosses entangled in cane flowers.

"These walls are fifty feet. The vines will never hold you."

Wafa didn't listen. Lithe and surefooted, he scrambled up the vines. When one came loose in his hands, he jumped to another. Darya watched in horror. Surely one of the Zhayedan would see him and an arrow would bring an end to his climb. She drew back into the shadows of her cell to avoid drawing attention to him.

Several minutes later, he hauled himself over the balustrade and landed at her feet. "Come on," he said. "I'll show you the way down."

"What?" she said, aghast. "There are thousands of soldiers in the courtyard—we stand no chance of escape!"

"But they don't know," Wafa said. He motioned at the place where her headdress should have been. "They don't know you're not the Princess anymore."

His words struck Darya painfully. Was she no longer Princess of Ashfall? Had her actions tainted her, stripping of her rank? She wasn't taken by the privileges of court—she had meant it when she said the Begum was welcome to her place. No, what she thought of was Arsalan, slipping beyond her grasp. Why would he pledge himself to her if she was no longer the Princess? She could think of no reason why he would.

She'd let her hair fall loose around her shoulders now that it was no longer supporting the weight of the imperial headdress. She felt young and free again, yet also strangely bereft.

Wafa's sharp blue eyes followed her every gesture. "Come on," he said again. "I don't want to stay here."

Something in the drooping lines of the boy's mouth showed her he'd known a kind of suffering she'd never had to consider. There had been no distinguished guardian to offer the boy a choice.

The door was locked and a grate was on its window, which meant the only route out of the cell was to risk the climb down the vines. But Darya knew she was clumsy and didn't trust herself to try. Besides, if she and the boy managed to reach the ground, one of the guards would find her, and this time she wouldn't be sent to a cell reserved for members of the court. She would find herself in the tunnels.

She heard footsteps outside her door. "Hide!"

Startled, Wafa cast a frantic glance around the cell. Seeing no other option, he rolled his small, wiry body under Darya's cot, pulling the coverlet down. Darya sat down on the bed. A knock sounded on the door.

"Princess, are you asleep?"

The man spoke in the cultured, faintly disdainful tones of the Nizam. Darya darted to the door. "Nizam al-Mulk! Has my brother had a change of heart?"

His scornful eyes dismissed her question. The key turned in the lock and the Nizam let himself into her cell. She scanned the empty space behind him. He had come without his personal guard. With his sleekly sculpted eyebrows lowered into a scowl, he seemed more forbidding than usual.

"Have you come to set me free? Perhaps there is something I could do to assist in the city's defense, if only to be a comfort to my aunt."

The Nizam's reply was cruel. "You must know by now, Princess, that your aunt finds no comfort in you."

Darya's sensitive mouth betrayed the pain this caused her. "Then why?" she asked. "I would be happy to serve the Companions of Hira or the Silver Mage."

The Nizam sniffed at that. "As would every woman at this court, but I think not, Princess. We do not send royal blood scurrying about like servants."

Darya bent her head. "Yet I would like to serve. I just do not know how."

"Yes, your uses have always been limited. Still, you've managed to bring Arsalan to heel."

"I *love* Arsalan," she protested. "I would not coerce him against his will. Or do anything to cause him grief."

"He's accepted the betrothal," the Nizam snapped back. "If you persist in your foolishness, you will lose him to the First Oralist, who was able to entrance him without effort. Did you not see his gallantry at the banquet?"

Tears sprang to Darya's eyes. The Nizam could always make her doubt whether she had any value to the court or any attraction as a woman. "I saw his courtesy to me and that is all."

"Yes, he is ever willing to stand as your champion."

"Because he loves me," Darya said heatedly.

"No," the Nizam said thoughtfully. "I do not believe he does. But he is a man of unswerving loyalty, and he does as his Khan commands for the greater good, as I'm afraid must you."

"What do you mean?" Curiously childlike, Darya looked up at the Nizam, bright tears drowning her eyes. She could feel the power of his presence in her room, feel herself compelled by the weight of his exceptional stature.

"There is no doubt of it," he said. "The city will fall by morning. I cannot allow that to happen."

"But the Silver Mage . . . the Companions—"

"You said you wanted to serve, Princess, so serve you shall."

"How?" Darya asked again. "What do you think I can do? Tell me and I'll gladly do it."

His face seemed to relax. "You must see your brother."

"Rukh doesn't *want* to see me. I'm the last person he wants near him now. He relies on you and on Arsalan."

"Your other brother, Darius."

Darya's mouth hung open. "But why? *How?*"

"Don't you want to?" There was a peculiar twist in the Nizam's voice.

"Of course I want to—I miss him. You know how much I've missed him. I can't bear to think of him suffering in the dungeons. But if I go to him, it will be treason. You *know* this."

"What I know is this: we need every weapon at our disposal. Darius is the Dark Mage."

"I—I thought Rukh was—"

"Don't interrupt me, girl! Your brother's pursuit of the Bloodprint left him no leisure to learn the secrets of the Mage, whereas Darius is skilled in those arts."

"But what could Darius do? Could he save the city alone?"

"No, not alone. But the Silver Mage is among us, and a Conference of the Mages would strengthen us in ways the Talisman could not withstand. Combined with the power of the Companions—"

"But the Talisman's army vastly outnumbers ours."

"That is why you must do this. You must go to your brother and release him. Persuade him to use his gifts as Dark Mage. The Silver Mage awaits him. He sees the wisdom of this course as well as I do."

"All right," Darya said uncertainly. "But why isn't the Silver Mage with you, then?"

The Nizam grabbed her by the wrist and led her to the door, impatient now for action. "He sees to another matter for your brother. He will come, you can trust my word."

"Of course." It had never occurred to Darya to doubt him. "And Darius? If his help is so vital, should you not speak to him yourself?"

She cast a hurried glance behind her as the Nizam locked the door to her cell. Wafa was trapped in her room, unless he scampered down the vines as nimbly as he'd climbed them. She couldn't worry about that now, lest the boy be discovered. Instead, she let the Nizam jostle her along the dark, dank corridors of Qaysarieh. They reached the majestic pishtaq, painted and patterned with tiles, two giant archers poised on either side of the gate. The archers had the torsos of gleaming golden lions and the scarlet tails of dragons. Each archer held an enormous bow in his arms, but the faience that supported the archers had chipped away over time, the legend of the archers incomplete.

Qaysarieh hadn't always been a prison. Before the wars of the Far Range, the gates had led to a magnificent bazaar thronged by hundreds of merchants. An ancestor of the Khan had transferred the bazaar to the square. The sloping arches and narrow tunnels of Qaysarieh had been converted into a prison.

The night was cold around them, the torchlight showing up like mellow gold on the walls, which seemed to curve with the land, the ceilings dropping ever lower. A pair of soldiers was stationed wherever the tunnels intersected. No one challenged the Princess, tugged along by the hand of the Nizam. Certainly, none challenged the Nizam al-Mulk himself, the guards standing at attention, their arms crossed over spears they had sunk into the ground.

Cries of lamentation wound up through the tunnels, echoed by the rush of an underground river. Some cried for water, others for food. Others sobbed the names of loved ones lost to them. The most common plea was for the mercy of the Nizam. The cells were cramped and recessed against the walls, the torchlight occasional and dim. Darya couldn't make out the faces of the prisoners. Their wails pressed upon her soft heart, but she knew these men had found their way to Qaysarieh for crimes against the Black Khan or for treachery against the realm.

When they had reached a final crossroad, the Nizam came to halt. He pointed Darya to the narrow alley that ran to the right, pressing a single key on a giant ring into her trembling hands. "Darius is held in this section. Tell him what is happening outside the city walls. Tell him he must do this service for his brother, and tell him about the Silver Mage."

Darya stared at the Nizam, wide-eyed. She was terrified by the gloom of the tunnels, certain she spied the movement of small and shuddersome creatures in the dark.

The Nizam grabbed her wrists and jerked her around to face him. "You've never been the slightest use to your brother or this city. Can you be trusted with this mission?"

The harsh words acted as a spur to Darya's wounded pride. "Yes!" With an obstinate lift to her chin, she grasped the key in her hand.

"Then do not fail me."

He spun around, his black robes swirling around his booted feet.

"Wait!" Darya called. "Where am I to send him? If Darius agrees, where should he meet the Silver Mage? Where will he find my brother?"

"Leave the Khan to me. Send your brother to the eastern gate."

51

DARYA CREPT ALONG THE LANE. IT WAS BLACK AS PITCH, AND SHE SHIV-
ered as she felt something small scuttle across her slippers. She
moved closer to the wall, losing the sound of running water. In the
abandoned alley, all was quiet and remote. Like the afterworld,
she thought with a shudder, conjuring up images of demons in
her mind.

She felt the dampness of the walls, a stickiness she seemed to
breathe. Then her fingers brushed iron bars, rusting in the damp.
There was no light, no sound, just the fetid stench of centuries of
decay.

"Darius," she whispered, the darkness smothering her voice.
"Darius, are you there?"

He didn't answer, and still the tunnel sloped down.

If only she was as brave as Captain Cassandane or as fiercely
powerful as the First Oralist. But she wasn't, and she shrank from
doing her duty. Several times, she thought of turning back. What if
she encountered a prisoner? Or a guard who didn't recognize her?
Only two thoughts compelled her to keep going: the first being

that at last Rukh had need of her, and the second that she would finally be reunited with Darius again.

She clutched the key on its chain, forcing her feet to move.

Her bells chimed softly in the darkness, and she had the idea that if she lost her way, she could separate the bells and leave a sparking trail to follow back to safety. But where *was* safety? Up in her cell on the ramparts? Under her brother's wing? At Arsalan's side at the gate? Or cowering in the royal quarters with the other women of the court?

A sudden revelation darted through her mind. None of these, she realized. She belonged to none of these. The only place for her now was the place she'd been forbidden. The place she'd witnessed in her vision.

"Darya?" A ragged voice speaking from the darkness shattered her nerve. She let out a small shriek.

"Darya, it's me—Darius."

"Darius?"

Darya found him by pressing her hands against the iron bars.

"Help me." His voice was ragged with despair. "Free me. I've been in the dark so long."

Darya clutched the key ring in her hand, fumbling for the lock with the other. She had just fit the key into the lock when she realized she hadn't passed on the Nizam's message. She pulled the key away.

Darius groaned. "Darya, please—"

"Listen to me. Do you still have your powers as Mage of this city?"

A sudden silence. Then "Why?"

"Don't you hear the drums? The city is under attack."

"What?" His voice cracked.

"You know it's been coming all these years. Rukh went in pursuit of the Bloodprint."

Darius lurched against the iron bars, reaching for Darya's hands. "And? Isn't it enough?"

Darya held his hands, the key pressed between them.

"It doesn't seem like anything will be enough. The Nizam asks you for your help. Please, Darius. You're needed at the eastern gate. The Silver Mage will meet you there."

She could almost hear her brother's frantic thoughts in the silence.

"He's there now? Does the Nizam plan—"

"Yes. He calls a Conference of the Mages."

"But we two alone—"

"The High Companion may return in time to aid us."

"And the Mage of the Blue Eye?"

Darya shook her head. Darius squeezed her fingers. A moment later the key was in his hand, grating in the lock.

"Wait!" Darya cried. "You won't . . . you won't . . . the monkshood, the aconite . . . You won't think of harming Rukh again?"

She caught the black glitter of his eyes as he freed himself from the cell. He grasped her delicate wrist and pulled her along behind him.

"I need you to show me the way." A rare smile flashed back at her, caught in the gleam of a solitary torch. "Rukh can keep his titles and his court—I have no need of either. *I* am the Dark Mage of Ashfall. The city belongs to me."

52

Signal fires burned on the eastern plains, ravaging the villages that lay between the outer ramparts and the city walls. Some had pressed ahead, gaining the safety of the city walls before the eastern gate was sealed. But most had been unable to flee, the warning coming too late. Those had been left to die or had been taken by the Talisman as hostages.

The Talisman army was divided in two, a force of a thousand men near the gates, additional battalions behind the ridge. Save cavalry, the Talisman had everything: infantry, archers, fire-lancers, catapults, and mangonels. The men who'd been sent ahead were further divided into three groups: sappers, who scouted the weakest parts of the wall; engineers, who operated the stone and wood-hewn catapults; and infantry, who led the charge, prodding villagers before them as shields. A red-bearded Immolan with a Shin War crest rode a chestnut horse to the gate, accompanied by men in black capes bearing the Talisman's standards. A fourth man carried a flag on a lance; this he rammed into the gate as a forewarning of conquest.

From the field behind, an ominous chant arose.

"There is no one but the One. There is no one but the One."

Rather than an invocation of the Claim, the words were twisted like the coils of a serpent, a writhing, rampaging force that swathed the city in darkness.

Before the gates, the Immolan blew a small white horn that echoed with astonishing force. He spoke through the horn, his polished voice riding the walls and whispering along the parapets.

"Khan of Khorasan," he called, "open these gates. Submit to the One-Eyed Preacher, and your city will be spared."

For answer, Cassandane's archers sent down a rain of arrows that were blocked by Talisman shields.

The Immolan paused, brushing an arrow from his shoulder. He raised the white horn again. "Is that your answer then?"

"No."

A man gazed down from the ramparts, taking the Immolan's taunts in stride. He made his hand into a fist and raised it high over the wall, so the Immolan could see.

A blinding silver light flashed from the center of his hand. It lanced over the vanguard, halting the army's progress. The man stood straight and tall, a dark brown cloak on his shoulders, his sable hair loose, his quicksilver eyes focused on the party below. The Immolan shaded his eyes. His fingers strayed to the green crest at his throat, seeing its mirror image on the man who commanded the gate.

"Who *are* you?" His blunt demand rang across the plain.

The man on the ramparts had chosen his spot well. Out of the shadow of the Maiden Tower, there was no man in the vanguard who couldn't see him in the Sacred Cloak.

"My name is Daniyar. I am of the Shin War." A flash of light from his ring arrowed through the night. He held up his hand again. "I am the Silver Mage, the Keeper of the Candour."

The Immolan checked himself on his steed. He barked a command to one of his men. A spyglass was placed in his hand. He spied the ring and the silver sword at the stranger's hip. A closer assessment of his face showed he was speaking the truth.

Then the Immolan took note of the Cloak. "Where did you come across that garment?" His voice was hoarse with rage.

With effortless authority, the man on the ramparts moved the Cloak to one side with a broad sweep of his arm. "I wear the Sacred Cloak," he called down. "I am Commander of the Faithful."

The vanguard assumed a deathly stillness. Work on the catapults fell quiet. The sappers who were on their knees along the wall slowly rose to their feet. They had last seen the Cloak on the shoulders of a woman; they had been told that her act of wearing it was an insult beyond description. But this man was Shin War, one of their own—he was the Guardian of Candour. If any man had a right to the authority of the Cloak, surely it was him. A murmur of dissent rose from the ranks, the men casting uneasy glances at the Immolan.

The Immolan was not as easily persuaded. "If you are one of *us*, why do you stand on the other side of the gate?"

"May we confer?" Daniyar returned, so the vanguard could hear. "I call for a loya jirga. Call your chieftains in for consultation."

As much as he distrusted Daniyar's motives, there was no way for the Immolan to refuse. It was the Shin War's strictest code that a course of war could not be determined in the absence of a loya jirga. And whatever the consultations in Candour had been, they had not included the Guardian of Candour.

The Immolan nodded at his men. "Come down. We'll meet outside the gates."

"Have I your word that a truce will hold until the loya jirga concludes?"

Against his will, the Immolan of the Shin War nodded. "The code is sacred to Shin War. And you, Silver Mage of Candour? Do you give your word that you make no use of magic to sway the loya jirga?"

Daniyar nodded, a silver glint to his eyes. "The code is sacred to Shin War."

With a flourish of the Sacred Cloak, he moved to the staircase that spiraled down the Maiden Tower. To Cassandane at his side, he warned, "If I do not return within the hour, do not open the gates again."

"Understood, my lord."

"Fortune fare you well, Cassandane."

"And you, my lord Daniyar."

Wafa watched him go, a thorny prickling in his stomach. Didn't the Silver Mage know? How could he trust the Talisman? How had he gone through the gate without fear, entirely on his own? Tears trickled down Wafa's frightened face. He'd climbed down from the balcony of the Princess's cell, evaded numerous parties of Cataphracts, and found his way to the eastern gate in time to meet the Silver Mage.

"What are you doing?" he asked uncertainly.

And the Silver Mage answered, "Whatever I must to stop this war."

Wafa had protested on Arian's behalf. "But the lady Arian! You haven't seen her. You didn't say goodbye."

The face he found so stern now softened with sympathy. The Silver Mage rested a gentle hand on Wafa's shoulder. "If I saw her again, I wouldn't be able to do this. Keep her safe for me, Wafa. I'm counting on you to protect her."

Though he was terrified by the sight of the Talisman, Wafa felt a quick surge of pride. Like the child he still was, he clasped the Silver Mage's hand, seeking some of his strength. Echoing Daniyar's tone of unwavering resolution, he promised to defend the lady Arian with his life. He couldn't meet the piercing clarity of the Silver Mage's eyes.

"It may come to that, Wafa. You need to be prepared." The Silver Mage glanced around the ramparts, picking out Arsalan at the gate and Maysam in the square below. Of Arian and Sinnia, there was no sign. "Where is she, Wafa?"

"She's in the room of books with *him*." The loathing in his voice made it clear whom he meant.

"Go to her and stay there. The walls are the most dangerous place to be. And it will only get worse."

Wafa stared at the Silver Mage with a peculiar look in his eyes. Then he darted forth and gave him a quick hug, so quick that Daniyar didn't have time to ruffle his hair. He darted away, throwing a few last words over his shoulder.

"Come back," he pleaded. "Come back or she'll be sad."

DARYA TUGGED AT HER ARM. HER BROTHER'S GRIP WAS BRUISING HER
delicate bones. He had led her through the tunnels of Qaysarieh,
and now they traversed a secret route through the gardens to the
eastern gate, dodging Cataphract patrols. The enormous square
was filled with the noise and fury of activity. Darya had always
thought of Ashfall as a city of golden walls and opulent green
gardens, with the drifting branches of plane trees catching against
the wall like the willowy tails of peacocks. To Darya, the city of
Ashfall betokened a fragrant peace. Not this cacophony of ash,
smoke, burnished steel, and the movement of machinery. Grim
faces masked in black, silver-tipped spears, blazing standards; everywhere the urgency of booted, angry feet. As a patrol passed
them by, Darius dragged her into an alcove. The light from a filigreed lantern flickered over his dishevelment. He'd been as handsome as Rukh once, but now his frame was whittled away, his
posture hunched, his fine skin marked with lines of dissipation,
his bleary eyes set in pouches of flesh. His beard and hair were

wildly overgrown, his smile too dim to remember. He retained an air of authority, nonetheless.

"You were always a good child," he said to her. "You know the meaning of loyalty." He nodded to the left. "There. The stairs."

To her surprise, he let go of her wrist. "You don't need to come any farther. Get to the women's apartments and take shelter."

"What will you do?"

She drew back into the shadows as a lumbering mangonel was wheeled past their hiding place by two of the Zhayedan.

"I'll find the Silver Mage. We'll hold the eastern gate."

There was a sudden stilling of noise. Darya heard a fluted horn, followed by a strange metallic voice. She couldn't make out the words, but the activity on the ramparts had ceased. An arrow of silver darted across the sky, piercing through columns of smoke. The light came from the hand of the Silver Mage. He stood tall and resolute at the eastern gate, and for a moment, Darya believed her city would not fall. She reached up and gave Darius a kiss and made for the gates to the palace. She didn't think anyone would trouble to detain a wayward princess at this moment. She had to get to Rukh to tell him what she'd done. He might be angry at first, but he would thank her in time. The Silver Mage and the Dark Mage would unite their magic to hold the enemy at bay, to hold the city a little longer. The Nizam had promised her as much.

She cast a quick look back to determine Darius's progress. She couldn't find him at the foot of the stairs or along the eastern ramparts. She frowned. Then from the corner of her eye, she caught a stealthy moment. A shadow darting this way and that through the humming square where the Cataphracts assembled and prepared for the coming assault.

The shadow chanced across the path of a flaring torch, and Darya recognized her brother.

Perplexed, she realized that Darius wasn't searching for the Silver Mage. He was headed across the square on a path to the Messenger Gate.

Darius was headed *west*.

54

Darya raced through the palace to find the Nizam, terrified of what she'd done.

Rukh can keep his princely titles. The city belongs to me.

What could Darius have meant?

A thunderous noise sounded through the palace, shaking it to its foundations. It sounded as though the sky had cracked open, and Darya's bones were jarred. The Divan-e Shah was empty, as was her brother's war room.

She moved on flying feet. Where would the Nizam be now? She hadn't seen his black-robed figure on the walls. Perhaps he conferred with Rukh in the scriptorium. She changed direction, her bells a plaintive echo as she ran.

At the threshold to the scriptorium, a hard hand caught hold of her arm. She paused, catching her breath. It was the Nizam; in his eyes was a furious anger. "Where is Darius?" he demanded.

"Please, Nizam al-Mulk!" Darya tried to free herself from his grip. He was holding the Shahi scepter in one hand, and he struck it hard against the ground. Darya went still. "I did as you asked," she said. "But Darius didn't listen. He makes for the western gate—I don't know what he's planning. I don't think he plans for a Conference of the Mages. I have to tell Rukh what I've done."

For the second time that night, Darya found herself dragged along by the powerful grip of the Nizam. She found herself in his chambers before a giant enameled wardrobe. They were alone in his rooms. With a speed and agility she wouldn't have guessed him capable of, he bound her hands and her feet with a pair of silken cords.

She tried to twist away and failed. "Nizam al-Mulk! What on earth are you doing?" A gag was thrust into her mouth.

"Your brother doesn't need to be distracted from his councils by you."

A heavy fist pounded the outer door, but Darya couldn't scream. She was bundled without ceremony into the Nizam's wardrobe, the doors sealed shut behind her. She heard the Nizam stride to the door of his chambers. There was no space for her to maneuver. She was so tightly hemmed in by the Nizam's costumes that she couldn't even thump her feet in the hope that her bells might sound. The most she could do was turn her head. She had no idea why she'd been imprisoned, but she struggled to overhear, her ear pressed to the door. She recognized her brother's voice.

"The Silver Mage has called for a loya jirga. The Companions are in the scriptorium. I prepare to ride out with the Zhayedan. The city is in your hands. If the eastern gate is taken, you must hold the palace."

"My lord, one more man at the head of the army makes no difference to our fortunes."

"I must be with my men. What would you have me do?"

"Trust Arsalan. They are as loyal to him as to you. We *need* the magic of the Bloodprint. We need the First Oralist to unlock its secrets—we cannot delay any longer."

"She does the best she can. The Companion, Sinnia, also. Indeed, she seems just as capable as the First Oralist—an advantage I did not expect."

"It won't be enough, Excellency. I have spoken to you of this. The time to act is *now*. Go to her. Ask her to awaken your abilities."

"The First Oralist is not a Mage of Khorasan. How could she undertake this task?"

"Her vocation as First Oralist does not mean she is unschooled in the arts practiced by the Authoritan."

A brief silence fell. Darya wondered what was happening. What did the Nizam mean? She didn't have long to wait for the answer.

"You speak of the arcane arts. Is this your counsel, Nizam? You believe me to be blackhearted?"

Darya's heartbeat thundered in her ears. She wanted to offer her support to her brother, but she couldn't muster a grunt.

"To serve as Dark Mage is not tantamount to villainy." Rukh's refusal was pained; Darya could have wept for it.

Another crack of thunder shook the foundations of the palace.

"What was that?" Rukh asked.

He was frightened, Darya realized. And if the Khan of Khorasan was afraid, she should be terrified out of her wits.

"It's something we cannot fight if you do not do this."

"What of the risk? What if I am suborned or overtaken by the occult? What if Ashfall loses its prince at the moment it needs him most?"

The Nizam's response was gentle. "You have answered your own question. I know you would give your life to win Ashfall another hour. There is no villainy in that."

The silence deepened, and no more was said. Both men left the room. Darya worked at freeing herself, terrified by what she'd heard. The cord bit into her wrists. She could feel the throbbing of her blood. She drew back her head, prepared to slam it against the wardrobe, though it was too late for Rukh to hear. But one of the Nizam's attendants might.

She felt suffocated in the wardrobe, the heavy fabrics pressing against her, cutting off her air. She tried to stamp her feet and fell. Now she couldn't move at all. It was impossible to climb to her feet. Her hands felt along the floor for anything she could use, something sharp-edged and deadly, but she grasped only cloth.

The thunder cracked through the palace a third time, then a fourth. Now she could feel it in her heartbeat, her teeth jarred, her bones rattled. Clothing fell onto her head. She was sweating, suffocating, completely submerged. The wardrobe began to shake. She had a fleeting thought for the city walls. The gates were all that stood between the Zhayedan and the Talisman.

Another crack and the wardrobe was jolted from its moorings. It swayed twice, then tumbled to its side, its heavy doors cracking open. As it shifted again, Darya tumbled from the wardrobe, her head badly knocked and her bruised wrists bleeding. She looked up to find she wasn't alone in the room.

Wafa reached for her, making short work of her bonds with a sheepish air of satisfaction.

"How—"

"The Silver Mage sent me to find my lady. But I saw the bad man take you, and this time I was brave."

Darya hugged him to her. "Wafa, you're always brave!"

"Come with me to the books." He fidgeted at her praise.

But Darya had made sense of the Nizam's counsel to Rukh. She shook her head, determined on a new course. "Wafa, will you do something for me? Will you keep the First Oralist far away from my brother? I need to find Commander Arsalan."

The boy's blue eyes looked a question at her.

"He's the only one my brother will listen to. He might hurt himself—he might hurt the First Oralist."

Wafa didn't need to hear anything else. He parted ways with Darya outside the Nizam's apartments. Though he was growing fond of the Princess, his heart belonged to the Companions. He wouldn't let the lady Arian come to any harm.

The Silver Mage trusted him to keep her safe.

With the thunder threatening to sunder the palace, he hoped that he wasn't too late.

55

Arian left Sinnia with the Bloodprint, stumbling as a rumble of thunder jolted the ground at her feet. She knew in her bones that the thunder wasn't something the Zhayedan could fight. Perhaps that was why Rukh had summoned her—to consult on a plan of battle. But his guards didn't lead her to the war room. Instead, she was taken to a set of rooms not far from the Khas Mahal. The guards left her at the door, then stood to either side of it, an action that made her frown.

The Black Khan was waiting inside, a somber expression on his face as he watched her examine the room. His private chambers were far less opulent than she'd expected; in fact the marbled room was nearly empty. A pair of enameled tables held a selection of scrolls, one of which was unfurled on its surface as if the Khan had been reading. A giant canopied bed on one side of the room was hung with black silk panels embroidered with silver rooks. The panels were reflected in the mirrored doors of a wardrobe placed across the bed. Close to it, a marble arch opened onto an antechamber, where a fresh breeze wafted inside from a gallery of cantilevered windows.

In the center of the room was a paneled wooden table with a pair of stools set before it. A meticulously crafted bowl rested on its surface, a jug of water beside it.

The Black Khan beckoned her closer. Arian stayed by the door.

"Why do you call me to your private chambers? What is it you would have from me here?"

She thought uneasily of his reference to her vow of chastity. Did he know the verse that bound the Companions to their duties? Did he seek to undo it to hasten her construal of the Bloodprint? Or had he misinterpreted her confession in the scriptorium or her acceptance of his gifts?

His eyes flicked briefly to the bed. He shook his head. "If my empire was not at stake, perhaps I would attempt to persuade you to choose me in place of the Silver Mage." He held up a hand before she could react, ushering her to a stool. "But *I* have greater need of his talents than you, so in his absence, I turn to you."

Not entirely convinced, Arian took the seat he held for her, her long hair falling forward in a curtain. He brushed it back over her shoulder, inhaling its subtle fragrance.

"You will need to see," he explained. He clasped his hands together in a gesture that was almost prayerful before he took the stool by her side.

"I'm needed in the scriptorium. Every moment with the Bloodprint is precious."

"This won't take you long." His voice held a note of bitterness at odds with the expression on his face, a fatalism she hadn't expected.

"What is it you want me to do?"

"Look at the bowl, Arian. Please read its inscriptions to me."

Arian bent closer to the table. "May I?"

He nodded as she placed her hands on the boat-shaped bowl.

"It's a kashkul, an alms vessel. It's beautifully engraved." She traced the bowl's markings with her fingers. The body of the bowl featured a series of diamond-flora medallions crowned by a miniature rook. A brass lip ran along both sides, separating the design from the delicate script above it.

Arian frowned to herself. It was Nastaliq script, a script of Khorasan; a man as well schooled as the Khan would know how to read it for himself. And there was another peculiarity she had never seen in an alms vessel: both ends of the bowl were raised up to form two dragon-headed extremities, their mouths gaping outward, their eyes obsidian black.

She was struck by a chill and dropped her hands, tilting her head up at Rukh. For a moment, she glimpsed a probing assessment in his eyes. Then seeing her watch him, he masked it.

"What does it say?" he asked.

"You must be able to read it for yourself."

"Read it to me. You have nothing to fear from the words."

He was telling her the truth: she'd read the four couplets above the rim. They were verses that enhanced the legitimacy of the Messenger of the Claim. Even in the quiet of the room, they hung like grace notes on the air.

Not quite certain of her ground, Arian recited the words to Rukh, her voice sweetening the verses to a slow and rhythmic cadence.

"Again."

Arian offered the words again, growing more disturbed by the minute. Rukh's shoulders and back were tight with tension, his head held at an autocratic angle.

"Once more." There was a pulsing urgency in his voice, a throb of something like magic. Arian was struck by the feverish glitter of his eyes. She did as he asked, hoping the words would soothe the strain he seemed to be under.

When the words had died away, his shoulders slumped a little. They were close enough to each other that he could touch her hair again or take her hand, or hold her under the spell of his darkly languorous gaze. He did none of these things, his attention fixed on the bowl. Then he straightened his shoulders and turned the bowl so that its mirror-script faced Arian.

"And these. Please, Arian. Three times."

Arian read the couplets to herself, strangely tense. What did he hope to gain from this? These verses were as innocuous as the others, descriptions of the mission of the Messenger of the Claim. Was Rukh a man of deeper faith than she'd imagined? Did he seek to anoint himself before riding into battle?

She gave him the verses as asked, and when the echo of her voice had died away at the end of her third recitation, he came to a moment of decision. With a curt note of demand, he asked her to give him her hand.

Compelled by that pulsing throb in his voice, Arian placed her hand in his. He turned her hand palm up, the gesture measured and careful, absent of seduction.

Their eyes met and held for a moment. Arian wished she could read his thoughts.

"Forgive me," he said bleakly. And before she could react, his dagger flashed up and sliced at the center of her palm. She cried out, trying to snatch back her hand. He held it firm above the kash-kul, letting her blood drip into the bowl until its base was covered.

"Wait," he said. "Don't use the Claim against me—it would be dangerous at this moment."

She believed him. An oppressive aura of augury, the foretelling of a dark descent, rose like a mist in the room. Her blood oozed slowly from her palm. When he let her go, she sprang away, drawing her hand to her chest.

"*Why?* Why do you never allow me to trust you?"

He ignored her. Her bleeding palm, her pale face—he made no attempt to soothe her or to explain his actions. Instead, he read the verses on the bowl himself, repeating them three times—a repetition she now recognized as a formula. He turned the bowl away and did the same with the other side. Then he inhaled deeply, almost as if he were steeling himself to a course.

A shout sounded outside the door—Wafa's voice, Wafa seeking entry before his cries were muffled. Booted feet thudded across the floor, echoed by the ring of steel. The Black Khan's men were defending the door to his chambers. Arian ran to the door, but before she could throw it open, Rukh's sudden movement arrested her flight.

He rose to his feet and raised the kashkul to his lips.

Horrified by his action, Arian flew back to his side to wrest the bowl from his hands. "Stop!" she cried, oblivious to her bleeding palm. "What on earth are you doing? This is—this is . . ."

"Necromancy," he supplied. His lips were stained by her blood. "Dark sorcery, dark power, for *I* am the Dark Mage."

Arian backed away, her hands falling to her sides. His black eyes were lit by a flame, the pupils outlined by fire, a sorcerous dark corona.

"In Ashfall's name, I rise." This time he didn't hesitate. He tipped the bowl forward and drank again.

Arian let out a cry—he was linked to her, twisting her by claiming her blood. Her circlets tightened on her arms. A pulsing resistance to the Claim rose inside her throat.

"Stop it!" she demanded. "You don't know what you're doing.

To drink my blood from the kashkul—these are the Authoritan's rites. *You are occulting the Claim!*"

Someone was pounding on the door. There were sounds of a skirmish outside the Black Khan's chamber. Rukh set the bowl on the table.

Arian's blood dribbled from the corners of his mouth. A terrible dark tide rose behind his skin, covering him with deadly animus.

"Come here." Even his voice was different—colder, sharper, a projection of itself.

Arian called up the Claim to meet it, fighting against herself.

"Do not barter the messages of the One for this small and trifling gain!"

The words stopped him. He raised his hands to his throat. A wild trembling took hold of his limbs. She watched him master it, dipping his hand inside the bowl. He smeared his fingers with Arian's blood; then he brought his hand to his lips and licked his fingers. A cruel smile shaped the edges of his mouth.

"Your necromancy will overtake you," Arian cried. "You don't know what you're doing. You do not know the bloodrites; your powers are untapped. This *is not* how to awaken your gifts. Call Daniyar back," she said in a frantic voice. "The Silver Mage will guide you."

Terrible words fell from Rukh's lips. Esoteric curses, threats of annihilation, a litany of destruction.

Death to the Silver Mage. Death to Darius. Death to the Council of Hira.

The words spilled like a tide of blood, and with each one, he moved closer to Arian, his arms reaching for her, overcome by what he'd unleashed.

"Give me your hand. I would drink your blood from its source."

Flames danced at the centers of his eyes, expanding outward

like a nimbus. Arian had seen it before: it gave his eyes a crimson tint. She stared at him in horror, twisting her palm behind her back, calling out verses of the Claim.

Her desperate words didn't matter. He'd called up a sorcerous inversion of the Claim: untrammeled and unloosed, his powers were staggering. He grabbed her by the wrist, raising her palm to his lips, drinking from the open wound.

"Don't!" Arian raged at him. Even the Authoritan had not bled her. "This will not save Ashfall. It will only damage and darken us both. The blood-madness will destroy you!"

His sleek tongue lapped at her palm, sending spears of fire through her veins. She tried to bend him with the Claim, but what it was doing to either of them, she couldn't begin to guess.

The noise outside the door ceased. A hard hand forced the door open—Arsalan, breathing as if he'd run a great distance, his hair disheveled, his face taut with apprehension. He took in the scene at a glance, then barred the door behind him. He ripped Rukh away from Arian, the violence of the act upending the bowl on the table. It crashed against the floor, the remnants of Arian's blood leaking into the stone.

Rukh raised his arm, pointing at them both. Arsalan moved swiftly, so that Arian was sheltered behind him. In turn, she was murmuring the Claim, harboring Arsalan in the refuge of her words. He wasn't conscious of it; his first instinct was to shield Arian from the Black Khan's assault.

Rukh held up his dagger. He traced its crimson edge with the tip of a finger, then brought the finger to his lips. Shocked, Arsalan watched him savor the taste of the First Oralist's blood.

"You are not wanted here, Commander." Rukh spoke in the silky accents of a prince, dismissing Arsalan with a cold disdain. "You should be at the ramparts."

Arsalan faced the Black Khan like an enemy, keeping his hand on his sword. The loyalty he'd offered Rukh was stripped in an instant from his voice. "How *dare* you harm the First Oralist?"

As sharp-eyed and unerring as a hawk, Rukh flicked the dagger at Arsalan. Arsalan leapt aside in time, keeping Arian behind him.

"My prince—" His face was rigid with disbelief. "You have never raised a hand against me."

Triumph blazed from the Black Khan's crimson eyes. "But I am *not* your prince. I am the Black Khan."

No sooner had he said it than his throat convulsed and he began to choke. Arian tugged at Arsalan's arm, her palm slippery with blood. She whispered to him to take hold of the Khan and restrain him. Arsalan eased Rukh to his knees, a fine tremor in the hands that held him by the shoulders.

Arian reached for the brass ewer. As Arsalan restrained the Khan, she tipped back his head and poured water down his throat. He coughed and spat it back up. Arsalan moved one hand to his jaw. Careful to keep her bleeding palm away from his face, Arian poured the water again, a second time and a third, until her blood was rinsed from his mouth. Then she made him drink the rest of the water.

When it was done, she knelt at his side next to Arsalan. Rukh drew several gasping breaths, bent double over his knees.

"*'Do not barter away My messages for a trifling gain,'*" she repeated softly. "*'The One is much forgiving, the sole dispenser of grace.'*"

This time the words seemed to reach him. He sank back on his heels, the red tide receding from his eyes. He brushed a hand across his face. It was stained with Arian's blood. He stared at his hand as if it was foreign to him. He could see himself in the wardrobe's mirrored door. He looked like a demon at a blood-feast, a monstrous, misshapen shadow of himself.

He wasn't the Prince of Khorasan. Nor was he the Black Khan. He was no longer sure *who* he was.

The magic drained from his body in a staggering, blood-quenching rush.

He shook himself free of Arsalan's grip, blundering to his feet. Arsalan turned to Arian; she stood with her hand clasped awkwardly to her chest. He strode across the room to the bed, where he stripped away one of the panels. He tore it into pieces and used a single strip to bind her palm. Something in his manner of tending her showed her his great reverence for Hira.

"What brought you here, Commander?"

A grave distress shadowed his eyes—yet it wasn't on her behalf. "Darya begged me to come. She said the Nizam had urged the Prince to a course of self-destruction. I didn't know what she meant, but she insisted I had to find him."

He had left the walls at the moment of attack at the merest hint of danger to his prince. She was stunned by the depth of his loyalty. If in his darkest hour the Prince of Khorasan had a man like Arsalan at his side, there was reason to hope that his recklessness would not bring the city to ruin. Arsalan was akin to Daniyar—a man to be relied on.

He was already looking for Rukh, who had wandered into an antechamber: when they followed him, they found him at the windows, brooding over the sight of the Talisman's formidable army. His hands gripped the stone wall, his face austere in his despair.

Arian tried to soothe him with soft incantations of the Claim, freed of the abhorrent sense of dueling her own abilities.

But Rukh tossed his head like a mettlesome horse, his restless gaze lighting on her injury. "I'm not worth it, First Oralist. I cannot be redeemed by the Claim." He turned on Arsalan with sudden fury. "You overstepped your bounds. You acted to aid the First Oralist, when your first allegiance is to *me*."

Arsalan sounded bewildered by the charge. "This is how I demonstrate allegiance. By stopping you from doing damage to yourself." He paused for a moment. "What were you doing? Why did you taste the First Oralist's blood?"

When Rukh remained silent, Arian answered for him. "He had some idea of unleashing a power like the Authoritan's. He thought he would be able to use it to make his stand against the Talisman."

"He used the kashkul as a *bloodbasin*?" There was a gray tinge beneath Arsalan's healthy color. "Sahabiya . . ." Whether he was more alarmed on her behalf or on Rukh's, Arian couldn't tell. Then she realized the truth. Arsalan was a man of faith; he viewed the occulting of the Claim as a sacrilege.

"It is a perilous magic," she told him. "It cannot be awakened in an instant. He could have destroyed himself."

"Did you know this?" Arsalan seized Rukh's shoulder. "Did you have so little faith in my ability to defend you that you were willing to sacrifice yourself? Don't you know what that would have cost us—what it would have cost *me*?" A powerful current of emotion ran beneath the words.

Rukh turned his bloodstained face to Arsalan. He tried to shake off the grip on his arm, seething with rage at the contact.

Arsalan dropped his hand but didn't cede an inch of his ground. "Answer me, Rukh. You risked the First Oralist as well."

Rukh didn't look at Arian. He made a careless gesture that pointed to the Talisman advance. Drained of the power that had infused him, he spoke with a sense of defeat. "You were at the walls; so was the Silver Mage. The Companions were with the Bloodprint. Every last soldier of the Zhayedan was prepared to defend this city. How could I do any less? I am the prince of this empire, and the Nizam warned me—"

Arsalan cut him off. "I should have known the Nizam was behind this."

Rukh scowled at his general. He reached past Arsalan for Arian's injured hand, perhaps thinking to make amends. But Arsalan stood toe-to-toe with Rukh, keeping Arian out of his grasp. She'd had no notion of Arsalan as a protector, and no thought at all that she needed one. She was that thing unknown to Hira before her coming: linguist, visionary, conqueror of the Word. But her battle with Rukh had shown her there was no part of the Claim's vast mystery that she could take for granted.

Impeded by Arsalan's actions, Rukh snapped, "Get out, Arsalan. Go back to the walls. You don't want me as your enemy."

"You could *never* be my enemy, nor I yours." His brows raised in disbelief, Arsalan gestured at Arian's injured hand. "Is this how you take your measure as a man? By wreaking violence upon a woman?"

And when the Black Khan didn't answer, he gripped Rukh by the shoulders again, forcing him to meet his gaze.

A bitter fury broke through Rukh's control. "I know how *you* would take my measure," he snarled. "I am not blind to your lust. Get your hands off me, Arsalan. Don't *ever* assume I share your corruption or that I ache for your touch."

Arsalan staggered back, the shock of betrayal in his face. He looked at Rukh as if he'd never known him—as if he hadn't sacrificed everything he had . . . everything he *was* for Rukh. It was a sundering even the bloodrites had not been able to achieve.

In an agonized voice, he said, "*You* touched *me*. You are the one who trespasses, the one who always encroaches. You gave me leave to think—"

Rukh cut him off, the color high in his face. His rejoinder was relentless and cruel. "You saw what you wanted to see. You chose to ignore my desire to make the First Oralist my queen. Next to her, what are you? Debased, debauched, unworthy." He spat the words in Arsalan's face.

Arian gasped at the insult, at all that had been revealed.

Rukh's fury subsided in a rush. He pressed his hands to his eyes, weakness swamping his limbs. Arsalan made no move to help him, and Rukh was left with a hollow sickness at the damage he knew he'd done. At the wound he'd inflicted in Arian's presence, dishonoring Arsalan in her eyes.

Slowly Arsalan said, "I did not think myself unworthy of serving you, my prince. Of loving you, perhaps." He shook his head.

That even for a moment he'd allowed himself to believe . . .

"Though I witnessed your treatment of Darya, I did not know you thought of me simply as a means to an end." Humiliation darkened his face. "You had no need to deceive me. I would have done anything you asked."

"Arsalan—" The pain in Rukh's voice spoke to the depths of his remorse.

Too little, far too late.

"Excellency." Arsalan bent his head. "You have defamed me before the First Oralist. I thought better of you." Though his voice was even, its resonance was colored by grief.

Hesitantly Rukh touched Arsalan's arm. Arsalan shook off his hand, his face pale beneath the blotches on his cheeks. Arian watched the two men and wondered. She had admired their closeness, but this was something she hadn't guessed. This was deeper and more intimate—more painful to them both.

Arsalan attemped an explanation, speaking to Arian stiffly.

"You must think me errant, sahabiya. I should be outcast from the army. Instead the Prince of Khorasan has raised me to this rank, just as he has protected me from the time that we were boys. I know how deeply he harmed you, but you must believe he acts as he does on behalf of the city he loves."

"Arsalan." Rukh murmured his name again, a note of entreaty in his voice. That Arsalan would still defend him . . . But Arsalan had nothing more to say.

Arian fought back a blush. She had never spoken of these matters with a man. She had seen the Talisman execute men who sought their pleasure in each other, but she had known their conduct for hypocrisy: there was nothing they had outlawed for themselves.

Now she tried to reconcile this hidden truth with her notions of the Black Khan's general, a man who was relentlessly forthright. After a moment she said, "I do not think you errant, Commander. Love is a gift to be given, wherever it arises."

He turned to her, a frown of surprise sketched on his brow. "I thought Hira held that those of my kind are errant from the path."

"Yet you honor Hira and its teachings," she said gently.

"Without question," he answered. "My mother was a member of the Council, though she died many years ago."

Sympathy swelled in Arian's breast at this point of connection between them. "I am sorry for your bereavement, Commander. It is a loss I share."

He bent his head in a courteous bow. "Your story is known to me, sahabiya. But I think there must be mercy in her passing. *She* would have thought me errant, and it would have grieved her."

Though she hesitated over what to say, Arian made herself speak. She was a Companion of Hira; it was her duty to offer the promise of renewal and the hope, one day, of love. Especially as she had witnessed the reason for Arsalan's pain. She touched her circlet with her undamaged hand and pressed it softly to his heart.

"Those *are* the teachings of the old world, Commander, I do not deny it. But when I have thought of this, I have thought of it differently. It is for the One to know our hearts' desires, and the One speaks only of love. Your path was laid before you, just as mine was for me."

Arsalan bowed his head, the silver tracks of his tears disappearing into his collar. "Your kindness has long been rumored," he said, "but that you would touch me with a gentle hand or offer me your understanding when the Talisman—and others—promise only hate . . . The stories do not do you justice."

His eyes met Rukh's over Arian's head, a haunting desolation in his own. Rukh's words echoed in his head.

Don't ever *assume I share your corruption or that I ache for your touch.*

Yet his agony was reflected in Rukh's eyes.

He didn't know what it meant. He didn't want to know if it would only cause him greater pain. Better to go on as he had, accepting what he was granted without pushing for more. Because he couldn't bear the thought that Rukh would send him away.

Not here . . . not now. Not ever.

The history of their long association passed between them in a glance—love, friendship, loyalty, respect, but also competition, discord, anger. Never, though, envy or distrust. Had Rukh's bitter insult altered their perception of each other? And if it had, was it the kind of loss that could never be redeemed?

He realized that Rukh was speaking to him, uncertainty weighing down his voice. "Forgive me, Arsalan," he said. "I should never have said such a thing."

But the truth was now open between them, and Arsalan's sense of honor would not allow him to renounce it. "If this was how you thought of me, you should have said it sooner."

Rukh made a sound of protest. "I couldn't . . . I don't."

Tears glittered on his lashes, and Arsalan was vanquished by the sight. "You were always a danger to yourself, Rukh." He couldn't bring himself to smile, but his voice was immeasurably soft.

Rukh drew a ragged breath. He had played with Arsalan's feelings, just as he would have used anyone who could serve his ruthless ambition. Yet to have done the same thing to Arsalan and now to witness its effect made him shudder with self-disgust. Nor could he blame his actions on the bloodrites' taint of corruption—he went still as he realized that he'd used the same word to slander his closest friend.

He wasn't worthy of Arsalan's forgiveness, yet he couldn't let his selfishness destroy the one thing he valued most. If only honesty would serve him, why not confess the truth?

He'd never been as lost.

He didn't know what to do.

He turned back to his view of the Talisman, unable to conceal his dread. Quietly, he wondered, "And now that I am bereft of any claim to magic, what do you say I should do?"

Arsalan moved to his side, observing the army at the gates. Tentatively he touched Rukh's shoulder. For a moment the Black Khan tensed. Then he accepted the touch, leaning into it . . . drawing strength from it. Arsalan's hand tightened on his shoulder.

Arsalan raised his chin, his voice low and firm with conviction. "Now we fight, my prince. Now we fight and we win."

They looked at each other again. Then they moved as one. They locked their forearms together, pulling each other close. Just as swiftly, they broke apart.

Arian observed this in silence, sole witness to the truth. However Rukh had hurt him, Arsalan loved him still.

And from the anguish in Rukh's dark eyes, it was plain he loved Arsalan as deeply. Yet Arian couldn't have spoken to the nature of that love.

56

Behind the Wall at Black Aura, Larisa Salikh darted through passageways under the Ark. She was searching for a prisoner named Uktam. She needed his report on the Khanum's plans to defend the Wall, now that the Khanum ruled in the Authoritan's stead.

And there was more she needed to learn.

An Ahdath patrol swept by. She hid in the shadows, a pair of daggers braced in her agile hands. She was murmuring the Claim to herself, no longer doubting its power to guide her. The alleyways slanted down, darker, deeper, steeped in the stench of decay, except for the occasional hint of peach blossom carried down to the cells by a teasing, evocative breeze.

She moved from cell to cell, her eyes scanning the faces of prisoners. This time she did more for her confederates than she'd been able to risk at Jaslyk. She unlocked each door with the same set of instructions. They had to wait until she'd found Uktam. After that, they were free to wreak whatever havoc they could.

At the farthest end of the deep decline, a skeletal figure was hunched in one corner of a cell. He held up a finger to his lips. A pair of yellow snakes were coiled before him, predators who watched him with narrow, fearless eyes. Larisa pried the lock loose from the door. With swift and sure movements, she used her daggers to fling the snakes out along the passageway.

"Uktam." She passed him a roll of bread she'd stuffed into her pocket. He fell on it with a ravening, insatiable hunger. She waited until he'd finished to offer him her canteen. When she thought he was ready to speak, she made quick work of her questions.

"Who does the Khanum send to take charge of the Wall in Marakand? Who commands the forces of the Registan? How many men, and how soon will they arrive?"

Uktam tried to squeeze more water from the canteen. "Is it time to escape, Larisa?"

"Yes." She cast a brisk glance up the incline, searching for signs of ambush. "You've been here long enough. You've done all that we asked for and more."

"Then you'll take me with you?" The prisoner's eyes were haunted by pain. A whisper of hope trembled in his voice.

"I'll carry you myself, if I have to. First, answer my questions. Who does the Khanum send to Marakand?"

"Temurbek. When Nevus and the Authoritan were killed, Temurbek seized his chance."

Larisa nodded. She helped Uktam out of the cell, pained at the sight of what he'd been forced to endure as a Basmachi spy. His clothes were reduced to rags, and through the tears on his cotton shirt, she could see the marks of the six-tailed whip.

He spilled his secrets into her ear, secrets she had waited to hear, struggling closer to the Ark. Her purpose hardened inside herself as she listened to him speak.

There was still a chance, then. A chance to take down Temur-bek before he reached the Wall. A chance that she and Zerafshan would take Marakand for themselves.

Dragging Uktam along, she hurried back the way she'd come, sowing chaos in her wake.

57

FLUSHED WITH FEAR AND WORRY, DARYA CLUTCHED AT THE THIN FAB-
ric of her dress. The Silver Mage wasn't at the eastern gate, nor
could she find Darius. She'd confessed her actions to Arsalan, and
though he'd told her to retreat to the safety of the women's quarters, she refused to do so. She had to know what kind of calamity
her careless actions had wrought. Perhaps she could do something
to help. She blamed herself for not guessing at the Nizam's treachery. He'd tricked Rukh into attempting some form of dark magic,
just as he'd arranged for her to set Darius free—who knew what
he planned for the Silver Mage?

Where *was* he?

Despite the crackling thunder, the Talisman were quiet, a
pitched tent at the center of the vanguard guarded by Talisman infantry. What transpired inside the tent at this hour? Darya wished
she knew. She wished she knew anything at all.

Moments later, Arsalan and Rukh strode past her to the head
of the gate, Arian with them. Of the three, it was the First Oralist who seemed most in control, certain of the outcome of battle.
Arsalan split from them to make for Captain Cassandane at the

Maiden Tower. She followed him back with a group of her best archers. Rukh pointed to the tent under guard.

"There," he said. "Light your arrows, burn it down. As soon as the loya jirga scatters, the Zhayedan will rain down fire from the mangonels."

Darya crept closer. She could now see the outrage on the face of the First Oralist. "You *cannot* fire on the loya jirga. Daniyar convened it at your request. Any break of faith will seal his fate."

Rukh shrugged. "What choice do you imagine I have? The Silver Mage wasn't thinking of you before he left these walls."

"He went to them *because* he thought of me. There's nothing you can say to make me doubt him."

A tongue of white fire licked the sky above the tent.

Rukh nodded at Captain Cassandane. "Fire."

Arian grabbed Cassandane's arm. Confused, the captain waited. She turned to Arsalan for guidance.

"Do *not* fire," Arian said with impotent fury. She turned on Rukh. "What kind of man are you? Can you *never* be trusted to keep your word—even after what you suffered in your chambers? Give Daniyar a chance to see his mission through." She thrust his signet ring back at him. "I would never have worn your token if I'd known that this was what you'd planned."

Rukh jerked Arian around to face the walls, his hands biting into her shoulders, his jet-black eyes ablaze.

"Do you see their army? We're outnumbered a thousand to one. Their commanders are gathered in a single place, and you ask me to hold my fire?" He glanced back at the golden walls of his palace, cracks running through their foundation like a tracery of opened veins.

"You think of *one* man. I think of every single soul I've promised to defend." He grabbed her wrists and drew her close. "You wouldn't aid me with the dark rites that might have saved my city, so think of a way to help me now! Use the Claim. Use the Bloodprint—I gifted it to you."

Arian fought him off. "I won't utter a single word if you fire on the loya jirga."

Darya held her breath. A strange, fierce tension arced between the First Oralist and her brother, their eyes caught in a merciless duel—a duel they had clearly fought before. For a moment, Darya thought she saw her brother's face soften as he glanced at Arian's hand. Then he thrust her aside.

"Captain."

Cassandane and her archers fired.

The arrows swooped through the dark fall of sky, their progress silent and sure, silver tips aflame, a trail of ruin configuring the night.

Arian's cry rent the silence; Darya caught a glimpse of her brother's wretchedness before he steeled himself again.

"Wait," he said. "And see."

But the arrows had been timed with precision. The tent was alight; the Talisman commanders tore it down themselves.

"Arsalan."

A quick chop of Arsalan's hand and the mangonel pounded forth destruction. A boulder landed in the loya jirga's midst. A second mangonel was loaded and fired.

Arian's scream was terrible to hear. She wheeled from the wall, pushing past Cassandane and Arsalan, making for the Maiden Tower.

"Arian!" Now Rukh begged her. "Everything else is lost to us. I need you at my side."

But in a moment she was gone, flying down the stairs to the

courtyard below, desperate to find a horse that would take her through the gates.

Darya stole to Rukh's side. "Brother, I must speak."

"Darya, I've no time. Surely you can see—"

She cut him off, no longer afraid. "The Nizam told me to set Darius free and I did. He told me he was wanted for conference with the Silver Mage, but he was lying. Darius has disappeared. I don't know where he went; I don't know what he's planning."

Rukh's hand swept up, a furious, instinctive reaction. Before it could fall, Arsalan blocked it, the blow bouncing off his armor.

Rukh staggered back, his face suddenly haggard. "The Nizam—my teacher? My *father*? That's not *possible*."

There was a very real despair behind the words as he considered now what the Nizam had intended by asking him to try the bloodrites. He had shielded himself from the machinations of the court, but with his Nizam he'd been as vulnerable as a boy. He felt the pain of it bite deep, a wound he could not reveal.

He didn't love you, he told himself harshly. *You were a means to an end.*

Then there was no more time to talk. The Talisman assault had begun, with mortars launched by their catapults. They pounded through the square, deafening the company on the wall, showering destruction upon the gardens, though the Cataphracts were just beyond their reach.

A horse and rider were at the Emissary Gate demanding exit.

Arsalan gave the order to bar the gate. Zhayedan leapt to block the rider's path. She wheeled back around and brought her horse to the steps of the tower. Cornered by Zhayedan and unwilling to use the Claim against them, Arian raced back up the steps to Rukh.

"Where is he? Do you see him?"

They searched the smoke for a sign of the Silver Mage. Thick clouds of smoke rose up over the walls, bringing the scent of burning flesh.

"We *must* press our advantage—it's all that we have left. Think of your trust, First Oralist."

She speared him with a glance. "To think I pitied you once."

"Hate me until I draw my last breath, but defend the people of this city."

Her green eyes burned with rage, her earlier vows forgotten. Though she had never intended to do otherwise, she acted now to give cover to Daniyar. She'd had little time with the Bloodprint, interrupted by Rukh's summons to his chambers, so she used the Verse of the Throne. She rained it down on the Talisman, letting it burn through their ranks, scattering men and materiel in columns of blood and smoke.

Their ears bled, their progress faltered, but there were too many to be overcome. As she drew men away from the loya jirga, the sky overhead cracked in two, a bolt of fury aimed down at her head. She was thrown to her knees by a furious tackle, a scrap of a boy who threw her out of the way.

Wafa grabbed her hand and dragged her into the shadows. "Don't use it!" he cried, motioning to his throat. "Don't use it—he'll find you!" The boy's face was grimy with smoke, his hands as dirty as she'd ever seen them, his new clothes torn and stained with blood.

"Wafa, where have you been?"

"Everywhere," he said with feeling. "But the Silver Mage told me to keep you safe. He *trusted* me with you."

Tears formed in Arian's eyes at this proof of how much she was loved. "They have him, Wafa. I must do what I can to save him."

"Please," Wafa begged. "The Silver Mage will find a way out. You need to watch for *him*." He pointed at the sky.

"Who, Wafa? Who is it you fear?"

Wafa couldn't say the name.

"Arian!"

They were interrupted by a voice from below. Arian rolled across the parapet and scrambled to her knees. Sinnia was crossing the square, too far away to be heard, a terrible urgency in her stride. The thunder moved west, rippling across the wall. Arian grabbed a spyglass from one of Cassandane's archers. She squinted down at the square, losing sight of Sinnia through the movement of the Cataphracts. She used the Claim to find her and heard its response from Sinnia. Urgently, she centered the glass, expecting to see the Bloodprint wrapped in Sinnia's hands. But Sinnia's hands were empty: there was a bloody lump on her forehead. She was shaking her head, desperate for Arian to understand. She spread her hands wide and bent her head to imitate the gesture of reading. Slashing one hand through the air, she mimicked the closing of a book.

Arian's heart dropped, the blood stilling in her veins before leaping forth again in a glittering presentiment not of danger, but of total devastation.

She seized Wafa in her arms. "*Who* do you fear, Wafa? Why do you tell me not to use the Claim?"

A sobbing breath broke from the boy. He tipped his sweating forehead against Arian's, tears of fright leaking from his eyes. He was huddled in on himself, trying to appear small. "*He* speaks it, too. He knows how to find you with it."

Arian shook the boy lightly. "Tell me, Wafa, please."

"*Him*." Wafa's voice cracked. "The One-Eyed Preacher has come."

Thunder cracked to the west of the Maiden Tower. A disembodied voice filled the air. "Come!" it commanded.

Come and nothing else.

A chill set in Arian's bones. She thought of Darya's tearful confession. Her head swept around. Arsalan at the Maiden Tower, Rukh at the opposite end, shouting orders to his men.

And the Messenger Gate to the west, as yet undefended.

She sought out Sinnia in the courtyard. Sinnia was headed west. Suddenly it was clear. She had to reach the gate before Sinnia. Sinnia couldn't stand against the One-Eyed Preacher on her own.

"Look!" Darya gasped. She was moving slowly, a step at a time, to trace Arsalan's footsteps to the Maiden Tower. Halfway along the wall, she had an unhindered view of the Messenger Gate.

"Arsalan!" she shouted.

The assault continuing all around them, Arsalan didn't hear. But closer to Darya, Arian did. She followed the direction of the girl's arm, pointing like an arrow to the Messenger Gate. There was movement along the ramparts. A man in a black cloak was hunched over something he held in his arms. Another man was at the gates, dressed in the clothes of a beggar, a wild mane of hair straggling down his back.

Arian lowered her spyglass. She swallowed over a constriction in her throat.

A bell sounded from the Maiden Tower, clanging a terrifying warning. Frozen in place, she saw Arsalan move from his position to stride along the wall. Shouts sounded in the square below, and by a series of signals that passed from the ramparts to the square, units of Cataphracts moved west, weakening their forces to the east.

Daniyar was to the east.

And if she'd understood Sinnia's warning, the Bloodprint was headed west.

But Arsalan hadn't rung the bell of the Maiden Tower to defend the Bloodprint. At his orders, cavalry, archers, and infantry rearranged themselves, dividing their forces between east and west, a massive upheaval of men and horses that filled the air with strident clamor.

The man in the black cloak and the man with the wild hair outpaced them all, distant from the Maiden Tower, distant from Sinnia, distant from Arian and the Black Khan.

She looked at Darya, horror-struck beside her. Then the Princess was running fleet-footed after Arsalan, bells chiming madly in her wake. Wafa stared up at Arian for a moment. "Don't come," he said.

He took a moment more to decide, then went haring after Darya.

Arian's gaze swept the eastern plains, searching for something to break through the smoke, a sign of Daniyar, the light from his ring.

All was chaos and smoke.

Halfway to the Tower of the Mirage, Arian caught the Black Khan's eye. She pointed west. He followed her gaze and halted midstride. He could now see what Arian had seen moments before. The vanguard of the Rising Nineteen, a long black line snaking across the west, at a pace to reach the Messenger Gate by dawn.

From the moment's indecision in his glittering dark eyes, she could see the Black Khan wasn't persuaded of his course. She decided it for him. If Ashfall fell to the One-Eyed Preacher, nothing she did for Daniyar would matter. The empire would burn, and all of them with it.

Rukh had forced her hand. And in a brief moment of empathy, she realized he'd had no choice. Nothing else had served him, not even the arcane magic he'd so ill-advisedly tried. To stand against the Preacher, all that was left was her knowledge of the Claim. She would have to trust Daniyar's safety to a man who'd now betrayed her three times. And she knew she would.

As First Oralist of Hira, this was her unswerving course.

"Hold the eastern gate," she said firmly. "Sinnia and I will take the west."

58

THE CLAIM WAS AN ANCHOR. THE CLAIM WAS A GUIDE OF GUIDES. THE Claim was a devastation, and Arian and Sinnia wielded it along the western wall. It stopped the escaped prisoner in his tracks, and the Nizam along with him. It built a second wall before the first, an illusion that appeared as strong as a stone buttress to the vanguard that had crossed the Empty Quarter.

Sinnia was sweating with the demands of the Claim upon her skills. Words thundered through her skull, exacting every last vestige of heart and soul.

So *this* was what it meant to be an Oralist of Hira. *This* was what it meant to belong to a sisterhood as powerful as hope.

A line of Talisman archers had taken them by surprise, sneaking across the south to prepare the way for the Nineteen. They fired with a purposeful discipline, volley after volley, the Teerandaz not yet in place to counter their rapid-fire bursts.

Arsalan was farther ahead of the Companions along the rampart; they invoked the Claim to shelter his body from the archers. Step by step, he advanced on the Nizam, Darya at his heels like a shadow.

"Get away, Darya," he called. "Get to safety. Your presence is a distraction."

She didn't listen, shooting past him to throw herself at her half-brother's feet. "Darius," she cried. "Darius, what are you doing?"

Darius flashed a half-mad smile at the Princess.

"It's mine! It's mine and it will restore me as Dark Mage. It will restore this empire to my hand." A trace of spittle edged his lips. "So Nizam al-Mulk has promised me."

The Nizam winced. From the power of the Claim or the preposterousness of the suggestion, Sinnia couldn't tell.

"Yes, my Prince," he said. "As I promised, so it will be. For I have won you an ally."

Arsalan lunged forward, sword in hand. The Nizam al-Mulk moved swiftly, unhampered by the Claim. He grabbed Darya's hand and jerked her into the circle of his arms, one powerful hand at her neck. "Move another step and I'll snap her neck like a twig."

The Zhayedan commander halted his advance, a cool, assessing look in his eyes. "So you'd betray the Khan of Khorasan."

From his tone, Sinnia knew there was no greater crime, not even setting hands on the Princess.

The Nizam jerked his head at the prisoner who held the Bloodprint. "*This* is the Khan of Khorasan—he's always had my loyalty."

A chuckle escaped Arsalan's throat. "This poor devil—driven mad by his addictions and thoroughly under your sway. Under his rule, Ashfall was brought to ruin, a dissolute place unworthy of the name of the jewel of the empire." He nodded to himself. "But you preferred it that way because then it was *you* who ruled Khorasan, not Darius or Rukh. Rukh could never see through you, as I could."

"What of *you*?" the Nizam jeered. "I know of your twisted

proclivities—I know what transpires between Arsalan and his Khan. Look to your own debauchery."

Arsalan's eyes narrowed. Each word he uttered was sharpened to steel. "Do not insult the Black Khan. Especially after what you've just done. You hoped the blood-magic would undo him, but the First Oralist defeated your plan."

A canny look came into the Nizam's eyes. He knew exactly what he stood accused of, just as he now knew that his plan had failed.

Each man held still and no one else spoke. Darya groaned under the pressure of the Nizam's grip. She raised her hands to tug away his arm, and Arsalan spotted the red welts along her wrists. He started forward.

Darya held him back with a word. "Darius," she moaned. "Won't you help me? I'm your sister—I love you. You must remember that, just as I remember you before you were lost to yourself."

Darius clutched the Bloodprint like a shield to his chest. Confusion appeared in his clouded eyes.

"This was never you," she whispered. "This was what the Nizam made you."

He seemed to struggle toward an acceptance of this. "Let her go, Nizam," he said at last.

"Not just yet, my Prince. Look—he comes."

A clap of thunder above their heads broke the impasse.

Sinnia and the others glanced up at the sky, cowering before the sound. The cracking noise was inside her head, boldly, blindly shattering. The Claim faltered in her throat. She looked back to Arian, now advancing along the parapet. Arian's head was cast up, her long hair thrown back, her circlets afire on her uncovered arms. Sinnia tipped back her head to follow Arian's gaze. The roiling clouds of smoke were assembling into a shape—the outline of a skull beneath a smoke-singed hood. The skull was insubstantial—feather-traces of cloud and dust—but its single eye burned like the sun.

A voice boomed out overhead.

"Which of the One's favors will you deny?"

The Companions screamed at the impact of the words.

"Which of the One's favors will you deny?"

Their hands pressed to their ears, the Companions fell to their knees, the others forgotten.

The voice was everywhere. It *owned* them.

Blood spurted from the Companions' eyes and ears, resinous and hot, leaving ghastly tracks on their skin.

The voice became amplified. *"Which of the One's favors will you deny?"*

Blood now foamed from their mouths. They wiped it back with sticky hands.

"Arian—" Sinnia managed. "Arian—say it with me."

Sinnia let out a moan, beating her hands against the ground. When she'd gathered herself again, she reached for Arian's hand. "Arian, help me! *Whatever good befalls us is from the One, whatever evil from ourselves.* Say it with me."

With a strength she didn't know she possessed, Sinnia arrowed an arm straight up at the sky. She chanted the words at the image of the skull. For a moment she was able to breathe.

The voice echoed back again. *"Which of the One's favors will you deny?"*

Bolstered by Sinnia's support, Arian fought her way to her feet. She flung her head up at the sky. "Whatever it is that you are, you do not speak for the One. You are *nothing* like the One. You are nothing save lies and illusion."

A peal of thunder threw her from her feet, so loud that it cracked the wall fifty feet down to the ground. She found herself at Sinnia's side—the place where she was strongest—and managed to summon the words.

"Whatever good befalls us is from the One, whatever evil is from ourselves."

She grasped Sinnia's hands, drawing strength from her presence, from the fire that raged in her brilliant dark eyes and that altered the timbre of her voice. In the smoke of twilight, their circlets began to glow a translucent, cleansing gold. The flow of blood from their eyes abated, then eased altogether. They wiped their faces clear, staining their leather gloves.

Emboldened by their common purpose, they chanted the words again.

Clouds gathered over their heads, a column of clusters whose midnight mass was edged in hues of violet. The pressure in the atmosphere built and built until it was intolerable, snatching the air from their lungs and the strength from their recitation.

"Whatever good befalls us is from the One, whatever evil is from ourselves."

A riveting shaft of lightning exploded along the wall directly across from Arsalan. His hair and beard were singed, the tips of his fingers smoking. Then the clouds receded and the skull vanished into mist and into the growing quiet came the sound of Talisman drums, steady and throbbing like a heartbeat, pulsing behind their ribs.

Arian stumbled to her feet. She made her way to Arsalan, bent double on his knees. Her voice raw, she whispered the same verse directly into his ear. He sat back upon his heels. Together they looked for the Nizam. A cry escaped Arsalan's lips. Heedless of Arian, he blundered forward to the shapeless mass near the gate. With his boot he kicked the Nizam to one side.

The Nizam lay lifeless against the stone, his eyes burned from their sockets. Beside him, the would-be Prince of Khorasan lay with his limbs spangled out, his hair and beard seared from his skull, leaving him curiously young.

Arsalan pushed their bodies aside, searching for the Princess. She had fallen under her brother's arm—he gave a great gasp of hope as he found her. Then he saw her still white face.

A white streak arrowed down the masses of her untamed hair. She didn't speak, she didn't move. The Princess of Ashfall was dead.

With a broken cry, he took her in his arms and heard the last sweet chiming of her bells.

The Black Khan looked across the courtyard to the wall that had cracked from the parapets to the ground. If it crumbled, the Talisman advance wouldn't matter—they'd be overrun by morning from the west. He searched for evidence of irrecoverable damage. A company of Cataphracts had gathered to brace the wall. He frowned when he saw that Arsalan was not at the head of their group. Maysam was more than capable, but it was Arsalan's judgment he relied on. He shifted his spyglass up along the wall until he spied the Companions close on Arsalan's heels. Arsalan was on the ground, bent over a bundle he had gathered in his lap.

Rukh's heart thundered in his chest. Terror limned the edges of his vision; a seismic shock rocked his heart. The spyglass went black before his eyes. He let it fall, his chest racked with agony, his throat raw with regret at the sight of his only sister lifeless in Arsalan's arms.

What else would he lose this night?

He shoved one fist into his mouth. Then no longer able to contain himself, he threw back his head and roared his rage at the sky, the cry of a wounded lion. The power of his grief silenced the movement below. Men called up to the gate, but through the pounding in his skull, he was able to fathom only the peaceable murmur of the Claim—the First Oralist was trying to soothe him with the same gifts that had failed to save Darya.

Blinking, he dragged a hand from the hollows at his temples to the tightly clenched muscles of his jaw. He needed to think of Darya; he needed to hold her in his arms and prove to himself that her life force had dimmed to a state of permanent darkness.

But he knew there would be other griefs before this night was through.

He hardened his heart and turned to the gate.

His sister would have to wait.

59

WITH THE FINAL CRACK OF THE ONE-EYED PREACHER'S THUNDEROUS assault, the Bloodprint vanished into smoke. And those who were gathered in the war room knew the end would come soon, though no one dared to speak it aloud.

The Black Khan sat on his lacquered throne, his hands balled into fists over its arms. He held two despairing thoughts in his mind. His Nizam had never loved him. And his sister, Darya, was dead. Neither was a grief he could take the time to indulge.

"Report," he snapped. One after the other, the commanders of the Zhayedan reported their progress against the enemy. There had been a momentary disruption of the Shin War's lines, a confusion that had been caused by small but powerful explosions in their midst. The vanguard had fallen back until the morning.

Within the walls, the Zhayedan were prepared, regiments arranged to meet the threat from both flanks, men working through the night to repair the damage to the walls, given cover by the work of the Companions. The violet-hued thunder that had seemed to doom the capital had not recurred, and far to the west, the Nineteen held their lines, not yet seeking to advance.

He heard their report, and when the war room went quiet, he turned at last to Arsalan, who knelt at the foot of the long table where the bier of the Princess had been placed. The Companions of Hira and Wafa waited to one side, none speaking, listening to the council of war.

"Arsalan."

The Zhayedan commander rose to his feet, his skin gray, his face set in lines of despair, an expression he banished as he met the eyes of his Khan. He realized the Zhayedan were waiting for his orders. He relayed these with a clarity of mind that promised his listeners the capital could still be held.

"Someone out there is helping us, perhaps the Silver Mage. We must press our advantage while their forces are in retreat. If the Companions hold the western gate, we can attack from the east."

"Then I should ride out with my men."

"No, Excellency. Stand at the gate with the Shahi scepter, as a symbol to the people of Ashfall. I'll ride at the head of the Cataphracts, covered by Cassandane's archers."

"It won't be enough."

"Then perhaps the lady Sinnia would lend us her support, if the First Oralist can hold the Messenger Gate alone."

Distraught, Arian said, "I cannot access the Bloodprint, but I'll use whatever I can."

She didn't reprove the Black Khan with his sister lying dead before him, but he heard the reproof all the same. It was a blow neither of them had anticipated, relying entirely on the Bloodprint. She hadn't come to terms with its loss; she didn't know if anything she did would make a difference now. He heard the devastation in her voice . . . witnessed its impact on his men.

It was *his* job to hearten his commanders; he had taken enough from her. "Strength to the commanders of the Zhayedan," he said firmly. "This night we hold."

They came to attention, answering in one voice. "Strength to the empire of the Black Khan. This night we hold."

Arsalan dismissed them. He conferred with Cassandane, then returned to his prince, summoning two of the Khorasan Guard. "These will be your personal guard as I ride out to meet the Immolans."

A bitter smile twisted Rukh's lips. "And you trust them? As I trusted my Nizam, who would have seen me overtaken and destroyed?" He shrugged his desolation aside, pretending to himself that the Nizam had never been of significance in his life. "No matter. Your judgment is keener than mine. But how could I have guessed that such an alliance had been made?"

"This was ever a court of intrigues. While you were imprisoned in Qaysarieh, the Nizam was laying his plots. Darius was easy for him to mold, lost in his voluptuary pleasures."

Rukh rose stiffly from his throne, moving at last to the bier, where he came face-to-face with Darya, preserved in her state of innocence and lost to him forever. He took her cold hand in his own and looked at Arian, bereft of his usual arrogance. A curious twist in his voice, he said, "Is there nothing you can do for her, First Oralist, with all your knowledge of the Claim?"

Arian gave her response with as much compassion as she could. "You would need dark magic to counter dark magic, arts forbidden to the Companions. You know what happened in your chambers. If Darya *could* be resurrected, you wouldn't recognize your sister."

"Wouldn't I?" He brushed a hand over the white streak in Darya's hair, his fingers holding a loose curl. "The only thing she asked for was love." He flicked a glance at Arsalan, his words unwittingly cruel. "Each of us failed her in that."

The blow landed. Arsalan straightened his shoulders and gathered up his shield. "Grieve later," he told Rukh. "You have an empire to defend."

He paused for a moment beside Darya's body, his hand slipping to her ankles. The chime of Darya's bells sounded in the quiet of the room. He freed Darya's anklets and tucked them under his breastplate. Without explaining himself, he bowed and left the room.

Rukh turned to Arian. "What hope can you offer me without the Bloodprint?"

And he found himself waiting as trustingly for her answer as any of the Warraqeen.

"We'll do what we can to hold the city. Your army is legendary, my lord. With the Talisman's ignorance of tactics, the Zhayedan will hold your walls for many a night after this."

A look passed between Arian and Sinnia, a quick question and a tightening of lips in response. Rukh caught it, his brief flare of hope quashed. "Tell me all of it. I would know what Ashfall faces."

"Did you see what transpired at the western gate? Did you witness the One-Eyed Preacher?"

Rukh nodded. "I'd seen something similar at a Talisman trap upon the road to Ashfall. But does that mean the Preacher is a creature of dark magic? Formless yet all-powerful?"

"I cannot be sure what he is. An apparition? An enlargement of himself, perhaps achieved by his knowledge of the Claim. If so, he creates this form of himself from a knowledge of necromancy that none of us possess."

Rukh prodded Wafa. "But you, boy. You saw a man?"

Of them all, only Wafa grieved Darya openly, his pointed face streaked with tears, his blue eyes wide with suffering. He struggled to find his voice. "Yes, a man. A man with a tall turban and a black patch over his eye. His voice was like a storm."

"So he is mortal."

A burning desire for vengeance raged inside Rukh's thoughts. He needed it and he would use it, no matter what else he lost. The One-Eyed Preacher would be forced to answer for the murder of the Princess. For Darya, who had never found her place at her brother's serpentine court. And in a sudden fit of jealousy, he wondered why Arsalan had sought Darya's anklets for himself. And why there was no one he could speak to of the things that damaged him most.

Unless the First Oralist had softened toward him now . . .

He felt the harsh sting of self-contempt. Even in death, he sought to use his sister as a pawn.

But Arian was at the window, watching the Talisman retreat, seeing the small explosions that dotted their camp, a frown etched between the winged line of her brows.

"He wanted the Bloodprint. All this"—she gestured at the Talisman vanguard and the main army appearing around the fringes of the salt lake—"all this was for the Bloodprint. Now that he has it, his legitimacy is assured. He will wield it like a hammer, bringing Khorasan under his rule."

For a moment her despair matched the Black Khan's. Wafa looked at them, feeling lost. He'd picked up Darya's hand, and cold though it was, he clasped it in his own for comfort, sensing whatever temporary safety he'd found would soon crash down around his ears.

The Khan's words echoed his bleak thoughts. "Then Ashfall is doomed, no matter what the Zhayedan accomplish on the field."

Sinnia broke into their conversation with a cough. "I don't know who the Preacher is or where he came from." She gave an elaborate shrug of her shoulders. "So he knows a few tricks with the Claim." She nodded at Arian. "So did the Authoritan, if you recall, and in the end, he collapsed into dust. *Lania* did that," she stressed. "If Lania could do it with such scant knowledge of the Claim, think of what *we* can do, Arian. Our power is barely tapped." A throbbing self-assurance filled her voice.

"We do not have the Bloodprint—it is now in the hands of the Preacher." Yet Arian's protest was token, a faint possibility taking root in her thoughts.

As if hearing Arian's lack of conviction, Sinnia pressed on. "The Preacher will need time for study. The Bloodprint will not relinquish the secrets of the Claim all at once. It will require patience. We learned that for ourselves." Sinnia approached the Black Khan, placing his sword in his hand. "Do you concede before the battle? That is *not* our way in the lands of the Negus." A graceful gesture of her arm dismissed the Talisman's forces. "There is only an army to fight, my lord. Surely, you do not quail before it?"

Another explosion sounded in the Talisman camp. Sinnia's great dark eyes narrowed. "We would seem to have an ally."

"Indeed you do." A new voice spoke, cool and strangely distorted.

Sinnia looked to the door. A stranger in black approached, his hair covered, his features hidden by his mask. He strode down the length of the room to Darya's body. He made a brief bow before the Companions.

"First Oralist. Lady Sinnia." A cold smile glinted through the mask. "Yes, and you, the useful boy."

Arian examined his mask, astonished that she couldn't read its script—yet struck by something all the same: a mercurial familiarity, as if they'd both been tested by the raging fires of the Claim. "Do I know you, messenger of the Khan?"

The mask turned toward her. "Our paths have crossed many times, First Oralist, but we have never met. Unless you have had need for the services of an assassin?"

Rukh interrupted before Arian could puzzle this through. "You return just in time, Hasbah. Are the fires in the Talisman camp evidence of your work?"

"My men do what they can to purchase grace for a night."

"What do you foresee for us?"

"Not the defeat you expect."

The Black Khan laid back his ears like a cat. "Why is that? Are you not aware that the Preacher has taken the Bloodprint?"

The man known as the Assassin bowed low. He placed both of his gloved hands on Darya's bier, spreading his fingers apart as if he rested his weight upon them.

"The Preacher will need time for study, especially as he has murdered so many of those who read."

Sinnia looked gratified by the Assassin's reinforcement of her conclusions. "You *can* win the field, my lord. But the Talisman will return."

"Then how do I defeat them? My powers were of no use to me. Will *you* pursue the Preacher to win back the Bloodprint for me? Anything you ask for would be yours."

For a moment the Assassin's eyes slipped to the unmoving form on the bier. "I have searched," he admitted. "But I cannot discover the Preacher's origins or the place he considers his nest. I fear you must abandon any further pursuit of the Bloodprint."

The Black Khan looked the Assassin over from head to toe. He didn't have the look of a man who was bringing his Khan dangerously hopeless news. All his senses alert, Rukh leaned forward over the bier to within a hairsbreadth of the Assassin's mask.

The Assassin's silver laces were missing from his elbow-length gloves. "When I left the walls, I did not see the red-bearded Immolan at the gate." The Assassin flexed his fingers. "Because he is dead," he said modestly.

Arian caught her breath, the sound audible in the quiet room. "And the Silver Mage?" she asked.

The Assassin directed his answer at Rukh. "It is the Silver Mage I come to you about. I told you of the Conference of the Mages."

Rukh rocked back on his heels. "I'm unskilled as Dark Mage, as you well know. I've had that proved to me again. And even if there was a possibility of it, the Silver Mage is lost and the High Companion is at Hira."

"Not so." The Assassin dropped the words into the silence. "My men bring her to you as we speak. The Golden Mage shall be here soon, and the Silver Mage is alive. My assassins are searching for him. They will see him restored to your walls."

Desperate to believe, Arian moved to Rukh's side, facing the Assassin. "How do you know this to be true?"

A peculiar twist to his lips, the Assassin reached into a pocket under his hood. He opened his palms, displaying a small object that played a brilliant light over his gloves.

Wafa gasped aloud. It was the ring of the Silver Mage. He reached out to touch it and the Assassin closed his fist with uncanny speed.

Wafa ran to Sinnia. She gathered him to her side, slicing a look of disdain at the Assassin to hide how his swiftness had stunned her. "You seem to know a great deal about the Silver Mage," she said warily.

"We've met." He made an unwarranted bow to Arian. "In another guise, I sold him a manuscript in the stalls of Maze Aura."

That fleeting chord of recognition moved through Arian again. "Were you sent to Black Aura by His Excellency?"

Impenetrable eyes gleamed at her through the mask. "I was."

"Did I see you in the audience at the Ark?"

"Perhaps."

"No, I would have remembered. It was at Hira that I saw you."

"Perhaps I told the High Companion there was something of merit at the Sorrowsong."

Mystified, Arian fell silent. The Assassin was showing her a nexus—the points of connection on her Audacy, connections he couldn't know anything about.

She heard Daniyar's voice telling her about a manuscript, one he had purchased in Maze Aura. It described the attributes of the One as found in the Verse of the Throne.

A chill settled in her bones. Who *was* this man?

Rukh's voice cut across her thoughts. "Three Mages at Ashfall—what then, my friend? Without the most experienced of our kind, the Mage of the Blue Eye, what is it you claim we can achieve?"

The answer came in a single word. "Mastery."

Rukh glowered at him. "This is no time for your riddles. Speak plainly, Hasbah."

The Assassin stared down at the ring he held in his palm, shifting it this way and that, until for a moment its silver light arrowed through his mask, illuminating his face.

Sinnia sucked in a breath. His face was the face of a monster. Yet something about it was familiar. The light winked away, and the brief illusion disappeared.

"You will have mastery over everything. These walls. Their army. And of course—" Here he bowed again to the Companions. Then his gaze dwelt once more on Darya's still face. "I would think you'd be pleased to rout the Talisman without asking for anything more."

"And if the Preacher returns once he has mastered the Bloodprint? I know of no magic to withstand him." The Black Khan's attempt at sorcery weighted his voice with gloom. He had failed at everything he'd tried.

The Assassin moved to the Black Throne, withdrawing a scroll from his satchel. He laid it on the seat of the throne, holding it down with Daniyar's ring. "But *I* do, Excellency, and *as* I do, you have nothing to fear."

A black-gloved hand beckoned Arian. "Do you recognize this scroll, First Oralist?"

Arian peered at the scroll but kept her distance from the Assassin. A gruesome aura of death emanated from his armor.

Her eyes widened at the sight of the parchment delicately inscribed with ink.

It was the green mirror—the Verse of the Throne*—a page from the missing Bloodprint.*

She had last held it in her hands in the safehold of the Bloodless, a mausoleum in Black Aura. When she'd returned it to the Bloodless, she'd unlocked the secret of the Bloodprint.

Concealing her shock, she asked him, "How did this fall into your hands? How is it you found this page of the Bloodprint?"

The Assassin ran a finger over its graceful green script. He was reading it. Easily. Fluently. And Arian realized something she hadn't known: this deadly assassin was *literate*.

"Sahabiya," he said, "this folio is not from the Bloodprint."

"Explain yourself," the Black Khan interrupted. "It cannot be other than the Bloodprint. And all we have is this page, while the Preacher has the manuscript entire."

Gloating a little, the Assassin dipped his head at Arian. "Think, sahabiya. Think of what you know." His glance enfolded Sinnia. "Think of what you both know, what you witnessed in the scriptorium."

Sinnia edged closer. Her time in the scriptorium had been brief; if he referred to the verses that preceded the Verse of the Throne, she wouldn't have been able to distinguish them. Her brow puckered, she stared at the scroll, her knuckles white against her skin.

Arian was examining it as well, her heart thudding an anxious beat. Bewildered, she shook her head. She didn't understand.

Life, knowledge, power, dominion, will, and Oneness. It was there in the Verse of the Throne, the most powerful verse of the Claim. Could it stand against the Bloodprint on its own?

Appearing to read her thoughts, the Assassin shook his head.

Startling them all, Sinnia let out a cry. "By the fertile lands of the Negus—Arian, don't you see? *This is the green mirror.*"

The Verse of the Throne was inked in green—a color that had outlasted the wars of the Far Range, the destruction of the holy cities, and the Talisman's ascent. The long lines of its script formed a perfect chiastic structure inked in green.

The Bloodprint she'd studied twice was written in rusted *gold*. Its strong, square script was marked in gold, the ink losing its color over time, its original luster lost, the manuscript penned in the same burnt shade.

"Where is this from?" she said breathlessly. "A suhuf found in a cave?"

"It's too beautiful for that, too well preserved."

"Then where?"

The sound of another explosion came to them from behind the walls. It rippled through the square and drifted up to the windows of the war room.

"There is a reason the Mage of the Blue Eye has forsaken the Conference of the Mages. Tell me, sahabiya—what do you know the Bloodprint to be?"

Arian answered him with a hint of suspicion: "The oldest-known record of the Claim."

"Transcribed in the ninth century before the wars of the Far Range? Perhaps the tenth?" the Assassin mused. "Yet what if I told you there is another, even older? Unmarked by holy blood—as clear as the day it was written by a well-schooled, devoted hand."

"Nothing of the old world survives." Sinnia's words rang out like a bell in the sudden silence of the war room. She spoke with the sure knowledge afforded a Companion of Hira.

But even as Sinnia made the claim, stars flickered behind Arian's eyes. A wild, improbable hope flared up in her thoughts. The words meant nothing to Sinnia and Rukh, but she had been trained at Hira. She knew its histories by heart.

"What can you mean, Assassin?"

The Assassin dared to touch her, brushing one of his gloves against her shoulder. "You *know* what I mean, First Oralist. Will you tell them, or shall I?"

For a moment, Arian was lost in contemplation of the parchment on the seat of the throne. The Verse of the Throne she'd thought of as a green mirror. A sudden strength in her voice, she said, "There was an older manuscript written by a woman's hand, the woman who *first* collected the scattered verses of the Claim. She was a Companion of Hira—she was known to us as Hafsah."

"Hafsah?" Sinnia echoed, the name unfamiliar.

"Half-Seen," Arian said with certainty. "Half-Seen, the Collector."

The Assassin picked up his tale, oblivious to the fading sounds of battle beyond the city walls.

"You know the manuscript's name," he said to Arian. "And I believe I know its origin." He nodded at the Verse of the Throne.

"Do you speak of the Sana Codex?" Arian demanded, outraged that the Assassin would attempt to perpetrate this hoax. Her voice cold, she warned him against the lie. "The Codex was burned in the wars of the Far Range when the holy cities were destroyed."

The Assassin was shaking his head. "You were misinformed, First Oralist. It was spirited away to a kingdom of the desert, to the city of Timeback, and there it has remained safe."

Indescribable joy warmed Sinnia's eyes. "Timeback? Timeback is on the border of the lands of the Negus. I have been there in my youth; it's a wondrous city of the sands." Her words slowed, a sense of understanding flowing through them. She looked at the Assassin with an air of momentous discovery.

"The Mage of the Blue Eye," she said. "Timeback is his city."

The Assassin made her a bow. "Just as the Sana Codex is his trust."

60

A FIRE WAS LIT IN A GREAT ROOM EMPTIED OF ITS COURTIERS, TWO BRA-
ziers burning on either side of the Peacock Throne, where Rukh
looked down on them with an air of avid attention. The Assassin
had never failed him, nor had he ever lied. If he spoke of the Sana
Codex as a fact, then its existence would prove to be real.

He studied the weary faces of the Companions. The Cataphracts were making fresh incursions into the enemy. Arsalan was
at the wall with Cassandane's archers. They had taken losses, but
not as many as they would have without the Assassin's men dotted
about the Talisman encampment. He didn't know how the Assassins carried out their legendary tactics; he was only grateful that
they did.

There was still no sign of the Silver Mage, but messenger
hawks relayed news of the High Companion. Soon he would call
the Conference of the Mages; his dark powers would be awakened. Then he would send out his forces to cut the Talisman down.

For the first time since his bedevilment in his chambers, he felt
a small spark of hope. If the Preacher returned to his walls, the
Companions would stand against him with the Sana Codex in

hand. If they would journey to Timeback and retrieve the Codex for themselves—a journey full of dangers with no promise of success at the end.

Watching Arian's face, he asked, "What have you decided to do?"

"Whatever I must."

She spoke in a voice whose clarity still beguiled his senses, and though he would hate to lose her, she had never been his to lose. As the Silver Mage had warned him, Arian belonged to herself.

His hungry eyes searched her face, wanting to keep her by his side. "You have your conditions, I imagine."

She gave him a frank glance from between her lashes and he felt his heart seize up. How could he have thought to harm her?

"Tell me," he said, his voice rough.

"I must speak to the High Companion. If I am to leave for Timeback, I must be discharged from my quest to seek after the Bloodprint." A grimace twisted her lips. "Otherwise, I must set out after the One-Eyed Preacher."

"A pointless quest. Trust me to convince the High Companion the time has come to yield."

He believed the word of the Assassin, whom he'd sent to assist in the search for the Silver Mage. He also knew nothing would please Ilea more than to send Arian beyond the Empty Quarter. "What else?"

"I cannot leave without speaking to the Silver Mage. He hasn't been captured or killed." She spoke more to herself than to him, a trace of fear in the words. "I would not leave him without a word."

"He left *you* without a thought," Rukh reminded her.

"Because he trusted you to wait upon his consultations with the Shin War."

"More fool he," Rukh said, jealous of her loyalty to his rival.

"Yet I know I cannot dissuade you from your course. What hope do you offer *me*, then?"

"I think you know well enough. Just as you knew what I would do in that moment up on the walls."

So she hadn't forgotten. Or forgiven him his transgressions. Even with Darya's sacrifice between them. Suddenly weary to his bones, he turned away, speaking with feigned courtesy. "Once you have resolved upon your journey, I will assign you a Zhayedan escort."

His eyes ranged over Sinnia and Wafa. Both looked instantly at Arian, both reached for her hands.

"Where you ride, I ride," Sinnia said, the pulse of unwavering loyalty beneath her words. They were sisters bound by the Claim . . . by all they had risked together. Neither she nor Arian would ever need to stand alone.

"And me," Wafa added shyly.

Arian felt a resurgence of hope, even without the Bloodprint, and though she may have been strengthened by the Claim, she knew it was just as much the certainty that she was neither helpless nor alone.

She had driven the One-Eyed Preacher back with the unchallenged power of her voice. Now the courage and commitment of her friends served to cleanse her of self-doubt. "I hadn't thought otherwise," she promised.

A horn sounded in the outer hall, a single clarion note. Sinnia shot a sharp glance at the Khan.

"We'll need to cut across the western plains through the lines of the Rising Nineteen. How do we escape being seen? Do you send the Assassin in our train?"

"No." Rukh moderated his tone. "I need Hasbah at Ashfall. The battle has just begun."

He thought of his sister's bier and of the terrible final task she had carried out, believing that her actions would aid him. He should have given her reason to come to him. He should have listened to her dreams—he should have been worthy of her trust. The smallest fissure in his self-possession appeared.

"You will leave through the Qaysarieh Portal. The prisons tunnel under the city. You will head south before you head west; thus you will bypass the Nineteen. Though I admit I do not know why the assault from the west doesn't come."

Arian hoped she did. She held up the scroll that contained the Verse of the Throne. As long as her gifts were buttressed by its power, the One-Eyed Preacher would not recklessly spend the Nineteen. He would utilize the Bloodprint first.

She reached for Sinnia's hand and smiled. "The Verse of the Throne held him back. He will need time to regroup."

A thrill of anticipation surged through Arian's bones. If the scroll had come from the Sana Codex, it would serve to gain her admission to the presence of the Mage of the Blue Eye. She had never visited the lands of the Negus or seen the capital at Timeback. How joyous it would be to travel through lands that were free, leaving her struggles behind.

The clarion call sounded again. The great doors of the Divan-e Shah were unerringly pushed aside. In the dim corridor beyond, two figures could be spied. They moved into the light and Arian gave a cry from the heart, her eye falling on Daniyar, bloodied but upright, his silver sword blazing in his hand, his dark hair disordered by the wind, his face slick with sweat and grime under the shadow of his beard. He had never looked more beautiful to her, more a part of herself than she'd had the courage to admit. His eyes burned like silver stars, sweeping the room with a glance, his face tight with fury, as he sought and found the Black Khan.

At his side was a woman whose armor had been tested by battle, whose gold hair flowed down her back, and whose features were all too familiar. Either Rukh's men or the Silver Mage himself had persuaded the High Companion of the need to return to Ashfall, delaying her return to the Citadel.

With a shock, Arian realized Daniyar was holding Ilea's hand. He *knew* her, something Arian hadn't thought to consider. He'd mentioned the Conference of the Mages; she'd never thought to question him about a connection to the Golden Mage. Now it hurt her to see them so close. But as soon as Daniyar found Arian, he released Ilea's hand, crossing the room to take her in his arms. He buried his face in her hair, speaking into her ear. "I never would have left you by choice. But there was a chance that the Shin War would hear me and put an end to this madness."

She marveled at the entreaty in his beautiful dark voice—was he asking for forgiveness for committing himself to the same course of honor that she had always been bound by? Did he think she'd felt abandoned, when all she'd seen was the danger he faced in the heart of the Talisman camp? Oblivious to their audience, she clasped him fiercely to her heart; she pressed her lips to his throat, inhaling his familiar scent. Then she pulled back to look at him properly, running her hands over his chest and arms, searching for hidden wounds.

"I saw you trapped at the loya jirga—I saw the fire. I thought . . ."

The horror of all she'd faced rose up in a powerful surge, choking off the words in her throat. Her tears spilled over. With great care, he brushed them aside. Then shielding her from the view of the others, he kissed her with breathtaking tenderness . . . a kiss that gave her everything she had ever yearned to have from him.

Her arms wound up around his neck, her need as urgent as his.

"First Oralist!" The scathing lash of Ilea's voice wrenched her from Daniyar's grasp. She pressed a hand to her throbbing lips; her eyes found the High Companion.

"Exalted . . ."

The Claim hung over Arian's head like a punishment etched onto stone. "Is this how you fulfill your oath? By dishonoring the vows you swore to uphold? If this is the path you have chosen, consider yourself dismissed."

Arian stared at Ilea in shock, as did the others in the room. Save for the Black Khan, who was watching the High Companion with a cynical twist to his lips.

But Arian shivered at the enmity behind Ilea's words. Her voice was darkened by a bitterness that had now corroded into hate.

Yet what defense could Arian offer when she couldn't deny the charge? She loved Daniyar—no, she *longed* for him with an ache that anchored her heart. Even now she wanted him to take her in his arms and make her forget who she was and what she had sworn to do.

And clearly he felt the same. He held her firmly at his side, his strong arm circling her waist. His silver eyes scorched Ilea like two furious bolts of fire. His voice was deadly soft. "Though Arian is bound to me, she has not forsaken *any* of her vows."

It was a reminder to the High Companion that *she* was the one who had plotted to send Arian to the Authoritan, under the guise of an Audacy that had resulted in Arian's torture.

Ilea glared back at him. She lowered her voice to a murmur and offered a pitiless response: "How bravely you stand as her champion. But you've erred before in believing the First Oralist would choose you over Hira. Do you not recall? You came to me to ask for dispensation on your beloved's behalf. When I refused to grant it, did Arian run back to you?" Ilea shook her head, her golden eyes filled with rancor. "She preferred the hunt to the safety of your arms. And watch her now, my lord, as she chooses Hira once more." She dismissed them both with a turn of her head, facing the throne of the Khan. "She has already made the decision to set you aside again."

Daniyar's gaze flashed to Arian, who stood motionless at his side. "That isn't true." His voice was rough with denial, but he read that the High Companion was certain of her words. He cupped a hand under Arian's jaw, tilting her face up to his. "Arian, tell her."

Arian stared into his beautiful face, searching for words that would soothe him.

The Black Khan's guards were waiting to take her to Qay-sarieh. And she *would* seek out the Sana Codex if Ilea approved her Audacy. She had witnessed the rise of five armies—armies who would not scruple to destroy the world she knew: the Talisman, the Ahdath, the warriors of the Cloud Door, the Zhayedan . . . and the Rising Nineteen to the west, who would be strengthened by the magic of the Bloodprint and the power of the One-Eyed Preacher. The only weapon she could wield in return was the secret of the Sana Codex.

But despite the call to the Conference of the Mages, she had cherished the hope that Daniyar would ride at her side. She had planned to tell him . . . urge him . . . *beseech* him . . . in their first moment alone. In truth, she had believed he would need no urging at all.

Arian, you are everything. You have always been everything.

He read her decision in her eyes, yet he couldn't have known what she hoped for. His gaze flicked to Wafa and Sinnia, dressed for travel on the road. And then he caught sight of their escort, and his warm hand dropped from her waist.

His eyes closed briefly, his lashes lying like two dark crescents on his cheeks. A muscle ticked in his jaw. When he opened his eyes, he looked at her with the courteous indifference of a stranger. "Go then, if you wish."

The weariness in his voice struck to the core of her heart. He chose to ask no questions and pressed her for no explanation. And the worst of it was, she knew why. She'd left him in Candour after promising him her love, promising to stay at his side; she knew she'd betrayed his trust at the deepest level she could. And in all her years of chasing the slave-chains, she'd never returned to Candour to ask him to reconsider—to ask if he would take as much as she was able to give. She'd never tried to convince him that the love that burned so fiercely between them would see them through the struggle ahead.

Now she was stunned to learn he'd come for her instead, humbling himself before Hira.

You asked me for dispensation on your beloved's behalf.

Why had he never told her? But she realized it didn't matter. The Silver Mage of Candour had bent his knee before the Council, showing her how greatly she was loved. A love she had always returned. And she'd thought he would know in his heart that whatever her purpose now, her path would be at his side.

"Don't listen to her, Daniyar."

His gaze shifted back to hers. For a moment his silver eyes burned with his buried anguish. But his voice was expressionless when he said, "Ten years, and you didn't suffer the same agony of separation—I shouldn't have forgotten how easily you let me go." A grim smile touched his lips; the sight of it shattered her heart. "But I will remember it now."

"Daniyar, *please* . . ."

Without looking at her again, he strode to the High Companion's side. He raised his regal head to face the prince of the realm.

For a moment, Arian felt paralyzed . . . helpless to make him understand.

Then memory of the Ark returned to her—the place she had *truly* been helpless, and Lania's dire premonition resounded in her mind.

What waits for you beyond the Wall will cause you a suffering unlike anything you have known.

But Arian was tired of suffering. And she was anything but helpless.

She turned from the throne to face the room. Raising her hands before her, she configured an abstract incantation. She gestured at Sinnia to take Wafa to her room and compelled the Khorasan Guard to wait for her outside the doors.

Her actions happened too quickly for any of the others to protest. And then she was alone in the room with three of the Mages of Khorasan.

She looked over at Daniyar and considered his studied indifference. Then at the High Companion, so duplicitous in her decrees. Then finally at the Black Khan, readying himself on his throne. She faced them all and said, "Do you disbelieve in the Day of Resurrection?"

Daniyar's silver eyes narrowed. They tracked her like a cat on a leash.

But the leash was in Arian's hand.

And she wasn't asking the question to offer an opening to answer.

She conjured the Claim in the room, choosing the verse with care.

"On that day, you will not proclaim a single remorse; you will suffer many regrets."

She raised one hand in the air. The Claim lashed the Black Khan's face. Once, twice, a third time—each stroke of the lash more severe. "For your betrayal at the Ark. For how you deceived me on the ramparts. But most of all, I punish you for daring to taste my blood."

The Black Khan's head whipped back. He pressed a hand to his cheek. It came away without blood. Stunned, he dipped his head, acknowledging her unfettered power.

Next, she turned on Ilea. She summoned another verse.

"Whoever commits injustice among you will taste severe retribution."

Ilea tried to deflect her with an incantation of her own. Arian closed her fist, rendering Ilea immobile. Arian's cold gaze lanced over the Golden Mage.

"I was a child of Hira long before you arrived. You speak of my vows as a commonplace, not knowing the nature of my sacrifice. What right do you have to command me when your own legitimacy is forfeit?" She flicked a glance at Rukh, freeing him from her grip. "You renounced your vows on a whim when you took the Black Khan as your lover." Her smile was as grim as Daniyar's had been. "Did you think I didn't know? I simply bided my time."

The High Companion struggled against Arian's irrefutable hold. Arian watched without sympathy, flooded with the justice of the Claim.

"What did you think I was doing that decade I spent in the south?" Ilea's hands scrabbled blindly at the air, for Arian used only her voice. She waited for Ilea's surrender. Though the golden eyes raged at Arian, in the end she bowed her head. Arian nodded to herself.

"I was training. I was *reading*. I was making myself strong. How else did you think I was able to vanquish so many men?"

Ilea began to cough. Daniyar moved as if to aid her, and Arian turned to him, releasing the Golden Mage.

"And then I come to you, my lord. The only man I have loved."

"Arian—"

She waited for him to speak, but he didn't say anything more.

She held the Claim in abeyance. She could never use it against him. He was free to oppose her if he wished. But he stood there watching her in silence, a grudging admiration in his eyes. She didn't want it. What she wanted was his acknowledgment of the truth.

"What do you know of my suffering? What do you know of how it felt to cut out my heart from my body? How little you think of my love—I would have *begged* you to ride at my side." Her furious gaze encompassed the Black Khan. "Instead, you would hold me here captive. And isn't that what every man expects? For me to give up who I am? And all that I've sworn to do?"

She grabbed hold of Daniyar fiercely, shaking him in her rage. "*He* rules this empire, and *you* watch over Candour, but I—who have inherited the legacy of the Claim, I, who am the *First Oralist*— I am to yield to your needs. Or to his, if he wills."

Her nails dug into his shoulders as she raised her eyes to his. "Love me for who I am, or your love means nothing at all."

Stunned, he let her rail against him until the tempest of her fury was spent. He didn't try to restrain her or to shield himself from her blows. Then when her body was trembling with the aftershock of emotion, he gathered her in his arms. His glance sought out the other Mages. Neither had moved, even to strengthen the other. They waited for him to act. To cast the First Oralist aside. Instead, he pulled Arian closer.

She had scratched his throat and the bare skin of his chest in the openings beneath his armor, and now her tears stung his flesh.

He bore the little stings as if these were gifts she had given him, gifts of her deepest self. He knew what it said of her love that she hadn't invoked the Claim. That he was the only one she hadn't been able to harm.

His breath whispered over her hair. "You cut out my heart, too."

One fist beat against his chest. He captured it in his hand and brought it to his lips. It was the same hand the Black Khan had sliced with his blade. When he saw the wound, he muttered a violent oath. "He bled you?" Rage stirred in his voice.

Arian freed herself from his arms. She moved away from the Mages, stumbling toward the great doors.

"*Each* of you has bled me, yet you cannot defeat my aims." She dismissed Ilea's dominion with a savage twist of her voice. "I need no command of yours to seek out the Sana Codex." She glared at Rukh, who had come to attention at the words. "I do not act for you. Nor will I bring the Codex to you—it will serve the women of these lands. That is my only charge."

She confronted the Silver Mage. "I make no apology for it."

And witnessing her conviction, he loved her as he never had before. In that same annihilating moment he was struck by a surge of raw terror—and by a piercing sense of loss. Too late to accept how reckless his actions had been.

He tried to call Arian back. "My love, I *beg* you to hear me. You *cannot* leave me like this."

Her hand was on the door, but she turned back at his words. "Why?" she demanded, the rage still fresh in her eyes. "When *you* left me long ago."

She strode back to him, ignoring the others. She jerked him close and kissed him as fiercely as she could, letting him taste what he'd lost.

Then she left him without a word.

The Black Khan came to his feet, astounded by Arian's power. At how effortlessly she had wielded it against the Golden Mage. And truthfully, against them all. And yet it excited him too, fueling his desire for Arian. If the Silver Mage was foolish enough to allow the First Oralist to leave him, he would claim her power for himself. The alchemy of the Dark Mage leapt within him like a flame, even as the presence of the other Mages fired his thoughts like a call to arms.

No matter what he'd lost—his young and innocent sister, the Grand Vizier of his empire, even the mad half-brother who had died unredeemed on the wall—his city had something to hope for in the First Oralist's return. In Hasbah, his deadly Assassin. In Arsalan's fearless command of his army of Zhayedan. In the presence of the others still waiting for him in this room.

And distinctly in his awakening as Khorasan's Dark Mage.

He braced his arms on the Peacock Throne and drew himself to his feet. "It's time," he said with purpose, summoning the others with his words. "I call you to the Conference of the Mages."

HERE ENDS BOOK TWO OF THE KHORASAN ARCHIVES

Acknowledgments

THANK YOU TO EVERYONE AT HARPER VOYAGER FOR YOUR SUPPORT OF this series, but especially to David Pomerico and Vicky Leech, for your amazing insights on *The Black Khan*. I keep rereading your letter and thinking of how much I learned. Thank you also to Natasha and Jaime for that great conversation in London and for our time together. To Priyanka and Shailyn, thank you for your unwavering efforts on behalf of these books and for keeping track of what I'm up to. And thank you to Steve, Micaela, Paula, and Ashley for your incredible work.

Thank you to everyone at the Nelson Literary Agency for your support—and especially to Kristin Nelson, for taking charge the night of *The Bloodprint*. And where would I be without the amazing multitalented Danielle, who wears so many hats, of which my favorite is undoubtedly First Reader. Thank you for the time and effort you put into *The Black Khan*, and for how our discussions add so much to my books.

To all the women who form my Council of Hira, my gratitude and love: Ayesha, my brave and beautiful Sinnia; Uzmi, like Arian leading her world into the light; my flourishing garden of Farahs, the Khanum's entrancing doves, except that none of you can dance; my worthy rival, Irmy, an omnipotent Lania; my sweetly loyal Haseeba, a Darya enchanted by the word; Fereshteh and Firoozeh, unerring Teerandaz archers; Nozzie, the formidable general of our Citadel; and Yasmin and Semina, my Elena and Larisa, travelers and warriors both. As for you, Hema Nagar, you are all things in one—warrior, assassin, princess, best friend . . . irreplaceable lifelong companion. Mostly you remind me of Wafa.

And to the Council's inheritors who must remedy the ills of this world, I send my love: my princess-warriors, Summer, Maysa, Zayna, Noor, Naseem, Negean, Zahra, Hanna, Maariya. And to my clever, courageous Citadel Guard: Casim, Layth, Ameer, and Amin.

To my brothers, who uplift me with everything they do: Irfi, a Zerafshan whose generous heart rules a brilliant kingdom; and Kashie, an Arsalan, who proves his love and loyalty each and every day. (I have no doubt Arsalan would have been admitted to the Buddies' Republic.)

To my dear friend Uzma, thank you for so wondrously and patiently reading so many versions of this book, and for loving the characters I love in exactly the same way. What a difference your insights made. Thank you to the doe-eyed Sajidah, whose integrity I rely on for my books. I was so alone in my work before I found the two of you, and now you've become my inner Council.

Thank you to the lovely Shannon Chakraborty for your beautiful words on *The Bloodprint* and for sharing the language of our books—it's been such a joy to meet a Zareen-Qalam. Thank you to the exceptionally generous and frankly amazing Saladin Ahmed, who would make a fantastic Mage of Khorasan. Or possibly an Assassin.

Thank you to the wondrous Amalie Howard, who in between

Acknowledgments

spinning her own enchanting tales devoured *The Black Khan* and kept me going with her praise. Somewhere in Colorado, there's a scrying chamber, isn't there? Thank you to Viniyanka and Sasha of The Word, two lovely diviners of the Usul Jade, for encouraging writers like me.

And thank you to my Warraqeen for your devotion to Ashfall's scriptorium. Michael D'Souza, your kindness and charm know no bounds. And I am deeply grateful to this incredible group: Rim-Sarah Alouane, Nafiza Azad, Émilie Gascon-Léger, Irene Lau, Ali Lawati, Melati Lum, Ardo Omer, Rachel Purtteman, Hussein Rashid, and London Shah. Thank you to all the writers and readers who have taken the time to talk to me about this series and to fill me with hope.

Finally, thank you to Nader for a love like Daniyar's.

Cast of Characters

THE COUNCIL OF HIRA

Ilea: the High Companion
    Other titles: The Golden Mage, the Exalted, the Qari, Ilea the
    Friend, Ilea the Seal of the Companions
Arian: First Oralist, a Companion of Hira
Sinnia: a Companion from the lands of the Negus
Ash: the Jurist
Psalm: the General of the Citadel
Other Companions of Hira, the Affluent: Half-Seen, Mask,
    Moon, Rain, Saw, Ware, Zeb; and in the old world, Hafsah
The Citadel Guard: Captain Azmaray, others

CANDOUR

Daniyar: the Guardian of Candour
    Other titles: The Silver Mage, the Authenticate, the Keeper of
    the Candour
The Akhundzada: the Guardian of the Sacred Cloak
Wafa: a Hazara boy of Candour

Cast of Characters

THE TALISMAN

The One-Eyed Preacher
The Immolans
The Talisman Tribes: the Shin War, the Zai Guild
Captain Turan

THE EAGLE'S NEST

The Assassin/Hasbah: the founder and leader of the Assassins

ASHFALL

The Black Khan: Rukhzad, Rukh
  Other titles: Commander of the Faithful, Prince of West
  Khorasan, Khan of Khorasan, Sovereign of the House of
  Ashfall, the Black Rook, the Dark Mage
Darya: the Princess of Ashfall, sister to the Black Khan
Darius: the half-brother of Rukh and Darya, formerly the Dark
  Mage
The Begum: the eldest aunt of the Black Khan
Nizam al-Mulk: the Grand Vizier of Ashfall
The Zhayedan: the Army of the Black Khan at Ashfall
Arsalan: Commander of the Zhayedan
The Cataphracts: shock troops of the Zhayedan
Maysam: Captain of the Cataphracts
The Teerandaz: the Zhayedan's all-female company of archers
Cassandane: Captain of the Teerandaz
Dilaram: an archer of the Teerandaz
The Khorasan Guard: the Black Khan's personal guard, the home
  guard of Ashfall
Khashayar: a Zhayedan soldier of the Khorasan Guard
The Zareen-Qalam: the curator of the scriptorium of Ashfall

THE WANDERING CLOUD DOOR

Zerafshan: Aybek of the Wandering Cloud Door
   Other titles: Lord of the Wandering Cloud Door, Lord of the
   Buzkashi, Aybek of the Army of the Left

THE WALL

The Authoritan
   Other titles: Khagan, Khan of Khans
The Khanum: Lania, sister to Arian, the First Oralist of Hira
   Other titles: Consort of the Authoritan, the Augur
Alisher: a poet of Black Aura
Donyanaz: Alisher's betrothed
Pari: Alisher's sister
Gul: one of the Khanum's doves transferred from the Gold House
   to Black Aura
Uktam: a prisoner of the Ark at Black Aura
The Ahdath: Suicide Warriors, Guardians of the Wall
Araxcin: Commander of the Wall
Captain Illarion: second in command at the Wall
Semyon, Alik: soldiers at the Wall in Marakand
Captain Nevus: Commander in Black Aura Scaresafe
Spartak: a soldier of the Ahdath
Temurbek: newly assigned Commander of the Wall

JASLYK PRISON

The Warden: administrator of Jaslyk
The Technologist: chief torturer, responsible for the Plague
   experiments
The Crimson Watch: the elite company of the Ahdath who guard
   Jaslyk prison

Marat: a soldier of the Crimson Watch
Lilia: a prisoner of the Plague Wing at Jaslyk, Illarion's sister
Mudjadid Salikh: a prisoner at Jaslyk, founder of the Usul Jade

THE BASMACHI RESISTANCE

Larisa Salikh: leader of the Basmachi Resistance
Elena Salikh/Anya: second in command
Ruslan: Basmachi captain

THE BLOODLESS

Guardians of the Bloodprint
First Blood

Glossary of the Khorasan Archives

ab-e-rawan. A type of silk known as running water.

Adhraa. The most highly venerated woman mentioned by name in the Claim.

Afaarin. A word of praise and appreciation.

Affluent. Those who are fluent in the Claim.

Ahdath. Suicide warriors who guard the Wall.

Akhundzada. A member of the family of the Ancient Dead, guardians of the Sacred Cloak.

Al Qasr. Literally "the Castle," but in this case referring to the women's fortified quarters inside the royal palace at Ashfall.

alam. A flag.

Alamdar. A title of utmost respect given to an elder of the Hazara.

All Ways. The fountains of the Citadel of Hira, imbued with special powers, and a foundation of the rites of the Council of Hira.

Amdar. A river of North Khorasan that flows on both sides of the Wall.

andas. Blood brother.

Ark. The stronghold of the Authoritan in Black Aura Scaresafe.

Aryaward. A territory of South Khorasan.

Ashfall. The capital of West Khorasan, seat of the Black Khan.

asmaan. Sky.

asmani. Sky-blue lapis lazuli.

Assimilate. The proclaimed law of the Talisman.

Audacy. A mission assigned to any of the Companions of Hira; a sacred trust.

Augur. One who foretells the future, a rank in the Authoritan's court.

Authenticate. A title given to one who can verify the truth. *See also* Silver Mage.

Authoritan. The ruler of North Khorasan, the land beyond the Wall.

Avalaunche. A Talisman warning horn used to defend the Sorrowsong.

Aybek. Commander of the Buzkashi, leader of the people of the Wandering Cloud Door.

aylaq. Summer camp of the Buzkashi.

Basmachi. A resistance force north of the Wall who follow the teachings of the Usul Jade.

Begum. The highest-ranking woman at the Black Khan's court, in this case the Khan's eldest aunt.

Black Aura Scaresafe. The Authoritan's capital beyond the Wall.

Black Khan. The Prince of West Khorasan, the Khan of Khorasan.

Bloodless. The guardians of the Bloodprint.

Bloodprint, The. The oldest known written compilation of the Claim.

Buzkashi. The name of the people of the Wandering Cloud Door.

buzkashi. A game of sport involving the carcass of a goat chased by horsemen.

Candour. A city in the south of Khorasan captured by the Talisman, home of the Silver Mage.

Candour, The. The book of the Silver Mage, instructing him in the history, traditions, and powers of the Claim, as well as his responsibilities as Silver Mage and Guardian of Candour.

Cataphracts. The shock troops of the Zhayedan, the Black Khan's army.

chador. Shawl.

Citadel. The stronghold of the Council of Hira.

Citadel Guard. Warriors who guard the Citadel of Hira, assigned to the protection of the Companions.

Claim, The. The sacred scripture of Khorasan; also a powerful magic.

Clay Minar. A tower in the city of Black Aura Scaresafe.

Common Tongue. A language common to all parts of Khorasan and beyond.

Companions of Hira. Also Council of Hira, Oralists, the Affluent, sahabiya in the feminine singular, sahabah in the plural; a group of women charged with the guardianship of Khorasan and the sacred heritage of the Claim.

Council of Hira. See Companions of Hira.

Crimson Watch. An elite company of the Ahdath who guard Jaslyk prison.

dakhu. Bandit, disreputable person.

Damson Vale. A valley north of the Wall and east of Marakand.

Death Run. A chain of mountains that forms one of the boundaries of the Wandering Cloud Door, east of the Valley of Five Lions.

Divan-e Shah. The throne room at Ashfall where emissaries are received.

Eagle's Nest. The fortress of the Assassin, north of the city of Ashfall.

East Wind. A people of a sister-scripture to the Claim, also known as the Esayin.

Empty Quarter. The lands of southwestern Khorasan, destroyed by the wars of the Far Range.

Everword. A people of a sister-scripture to the Claim.

Far Range. The uninhabitable country beyond Khorasan.

Fire Mirrors. A mountain chain that forms the northern boundary of the Wandering Cloud Door, just south of the Wall.

First Oralist. A rank of highest distinction among the Companions of Hira, reserved for the Companion with the greatest knowledge of and fluency in the Claim.

Firuzkoh. The Turquoise City, lost to time.

Five Lakes. A territory of Khorasan, north of Hazarajat.

ger. Home, tent, yurt.

geshlaq. Winter camp of the Buzkashi.

Gold House. A palace in the Registan where women are trained in the arts. *See also* Tilla Kari.

Golden Finger. A minaret at the meeting place of two rivers.

Graveyard of the Ships. A desert near Jaslyk where the lake bed has dried up.

Gur-e-Amir/the Green Mirror. A tomb complex in Marakand.

Hafsah. A Companion of Hira, the Collector of the Claim.

Half-Seen. A descendant of Hafsah.

Hallow. A hall in the valley of Firuzkoh.

haq. Truth, right, justice.

haramzadah. An epithet that means "bastard."

Hazara. A people of central and east Khorasan, persecuted by the Talisman.

Hazarajat. A territory of central and east Khorasan, home of the Hazara people.

Hazing. A district of Marakand that is home to the Basmachi resistance. *See also* Tomb of the Living King.

High Companion. Leader of the Council of Hira.

High Tongue. The language of the Claim.

High Road. A river of central Khorasan; also called the Arius, the Tarius, the Horaya, and the Tejen.

hijra. Migration.

Hira. The sanctuary of the Companions.

Ice Kill. A valley at the entrance to the Wandering Cloud Door, home to the Buzkashi.

Illustrious Portal. The entrance to the Black Khan's palace at Ashfall.

Immolans. Deputies of the One-Eyed Preacher, tasked with book-burning.

Inklings. Scribes from the Lands of the Shin Jang.

iqra. Read.

Irb. The language spoken by the people of the Wandering Cloud Door.

Jahiliya. The Age of Ignorance.

Jaslyk. A prison of the Authoritan's, northwest of the Wall.

jorgo. Fast mountain horses.

kaghez. Paper manufactured from mulberry trees.

Kalaam. Word, one of the names of the Claim.

kamish. A type of calligraphy pen.

karakash. Black jade.

Khagan. Khan of Khans or King of Kings.

Khamsa. One of five mythical mares.

khamsin. A desert wind.

Khanum. A consort of the Khan, the Authoritan's consort.

Khost-e-Imom. A protective cover or place for the Bloodprint.

Khorasan. The lands of the people of the Claim, north, south, east, and west.

khubi. Bounty, spoils of war, an endearment meaning "enough/ everything."

khuriltai. Council.

kohl. Black eyeliner.

Kufa. A style of calligraphy taken from a city of the same name.

kuluk. Load-bearing horses with stamina.

Kyzylkum. The Red Desert. A desert in northern Khorasan.

lajward. Lapis lazuli.

lajwardina. A lapis lazuli glaze.

likka. Raw silk fibers used in the practice of calligraphy.

loya jirga. A consultation of Talisman chieftains; also a council of war.

Mangudah. A death squad of the Buzkashi, a regiment of the Army of the One.

Marakand. A city of North Khorasan beyond the Wall.

Mausoleum of the Princess. A tomb complex in the Hazing, an area of Marakand.

Maze Aura. A city of central Khorasan.

Mir. Any leader of the Hazara people.

mllaya moya. My sweet, my love.

morin khuur. Horsehead fiddle.

Mudassir. Respected teacher, a form of address.

Mudjadid. A teacher of great knowledge, a form of address.

Nastaliq. A type of calligraphy.

neeli. Dark blue lapis lazuli.

Negus. Ruler of the lands south of the Empty Quarter, also the name given to these lands; the leader of Sinnia's people.

Nightshaper. Site of the Poet's Graveyard, an abandoned city of Khorasan.

nurm. Soft.

One-Eyed Preacher. A tyrant from the Empty Quarter whose teachings have engulfed all of Khorasan.

Oralist. A Companion of Hira who recites the Claim.

Otchigen. The Prince of the Hearth, a title given to the youngest male member of the family of the Lord of the Buzkashi.

pagri. A thick wool cap worn by the Talisman.

Pit, The. The dungeons of the Ark.

Plague Lands. A northern territory of Khorasan destroyed by the wars of the Far Range.

Plague Wing. A section of Jaslyk prison where prisoners are held for experimentation with the effects of the Plague.

Plaintive. A warning horn sounded by the Buzkashi.

qarajai. A dangerous form of the sport buzkashi.

Qari. One who recites the Claim.

Qaysarieh Portal. The prisons underneath Ashfall.

qiyamah. Resurrection, rising.

rasti, rusti. Originally, "safety is in right"; the Authoritan's motto, "Strength is justice."

Registan. A public square in the heart of the city of Marakand, literally translated as "sandy place."

Rising Nineteen. A cult that has come to power in the Empty Quarter.

Russe. A name given to the people of the northern Transcasp.

sabz. Green lapis lazuli.

Sacred Cloak. A holy relic worn by the Messenger of the Claim.

Safanad. One of the five mares of the Khamsa, Arian's horse.

Sahabah. A title given to the Companions of Hira in the plural; sahabiyah, feminine singular.

Sailing Pass. A mountain pass en route to the Sorrowsong Mountain.

Sar-e-Sang/Sorrowsong. The Blue Mountain, location of the oldest continuously worked lapis lazuli mines in Khorasan.

Sea of Reeds. A sea that divides the Empty Quarter from the Lands of the Negus.

Sea of the Transcasp. A body of water that divides West Khorasan from the Transcasp.

Shadow Mausoleum. A crypt used for storing the bones of the Authoritan's enemies. *See also* Shir Dar.

shahadah. The bearing of witness.

shah-mat. Checkmate.

shahtaranj. A chessboard.

Shin Jang. A northeastern territory of Khorasan.

Shin War. One of the tribes of Khorasan, allegiant to the Talisman.

Shir Dar. A former House of Wisdom in the Registan. *See also* Shadow Mausoleum.

Shrine of the Sacred Cloak. A holy shrine where the Cloak has been stored for centuries and guarded by the Ancient Dead.

shura. A council or consultation.

Sihraat. The scrying room where

the Khanum conducts her Augury.

Silver Mage. The Guardian of Candour, Keeper of the Candour.

Sorrowsong. See Sar-e-Sang.

suhuf. A sheaf of paper or parchment.

Sulde. The spirit banner of the Buzkashi.

tahweez. A gold circlet or circlets worn on the upper arms by the Companions of Hira, inscribed with the names of the One and the opening words of the Claim.

taihe. A princess of Shin Jang.

Talisman. Followers of the One-Eyed Preacher, militias that rule most of the tribes of Khorasan.

Task End. A city of North Khorasan beyond the Wall, the original home of the Bloodprint.

Technologist. The chief torturer at Jaslyk prison.

Teerandaz. A division of archers in the Black Khan's army.

Tilla Kari. A former site of worship in the Registan. *See also* Gold House.

Tirazis. A city of West Khorasan.

Tomb of the Living King. A lost tomb in a district of Marakand known as the Hazing.

Tradition. The accompanying rites and beliefs of the Claim.

The Transcasp. Lands of northwest Khorasan.

Usul Jade. The teachings of the New Method of studying the Claim, by Mudjadid Salikh.

Valley of Five Lions. A territory in central Khorasan, fought over by the Shin War and the Zai Guild.

Valley of the Awakened Prince. A territory in central Khorasan.

Wall. A fortification built by the ancestors of the Authoritan to ward off the Plague, dividing North Khorasan from South.

Wandering Cloud Door. The lands of the Buzkashi in northeast Khorasan.

Warden. The administrator of Jaslyk prison.

Warraqeen. Male students of the teachings of the Claim at the scriptorium in Ashfall.

Yassa. The law of the people of the Wandering Cloud Door.

Yeke Khatun. Great Empress of the people of the Wandering Cloud Door.

yurungkash. White jade.

Zai Guild. One of the tribes of Khorasan, allegiant to the Talisman.

Zareen-Qalam. Title of the curator of the Black's Khan scriptorium, literally "Golden Pen."

Zebunnisa. A revered poet in the history of Khorasan.

Zerafshan. A river of North Khorasan, beyond the Wall.

Zhayedan. The army of the Black Khan, headquartered at Ashfall.

ziyara. A religious pilgrimage.

zud. Animal famine.

About the Author

AUSMA ZEHANAT KHAN holds a PhD in international human rights law with a specialization in military intervention and war crimes in the Balkans. She is the author of the award-winning debut novel *The Unquiet Dead*, the first book in the Khattak/Getty mystery series. Her subsequent novels include *The Language of Secrets*, *Among the Ruins*, *A Dangerous Crossing*, and *The Bloodprint: Book One of the Khorasan Archives*. Originally from Canada, she now lives in Colorado with her husband.

www.ausmazehanatkhan.com

Facebook: /ausmazehanatkhan

Twitter: @ausmazehanat